Susan Krinard

Prince of Dreams

BANTAM BOOKS

New York   Toronto   London   Sydney   Auckland

PRINCE OF DREAMS

A Bantam Fanfare Book / February 1995

Grateful acknowledgment for the permission to use the following:

Homer *The Odyssey* Translated by Robert Fitzgerald
Book XIX, 1. 560
Vintage Classics, Random House, Inc. NY

W.H. Auden *Collected Poems* ed. by Edward Mendelson
"As I Walked Out One Morning," stanza seven
Vintage International, Random House, Inc. NY

ISBN 0-553-56776-4

Published simultaneously in the United States and Canada

Bantam Books are published by Bantam Books, a division of Bantam Doubleday
Dell Publishing Group, Inc. Its trademark, consisting of the words "Bantam
Books" and the portrayal of a rooster, is Registered in U.S. Patent and Trademark
Office and in other countries. Marca Registrada. Bantam Books, 1540 Broadway,
New York, New York 10036.

PRINTED IN THE UNITED STATES OF AMERICA
RAD   0 9 8 7 6 5 4 3 2 1

"I learned long ago how deadly the act of love could be between one of my kind and one of yours."

He forced his voice to a still, emotionless calm. "A mortal's life force is at its peak at two times: during dreaming and during mating. But we are no more capable of perfect control during lovemaking than human beings." Memories slashed through him. "In joining with a mortal woman, we can take too much—drain every last vestige of life force that keeps your kind alive."

In spite of all his resolve, the last words dropped into a trembling whisper.

"Is that what Adrian did to Clare?" Diana asked quietly.

Nicholas closed his eyes. "I don't know. I pray I never find out. But he was capable of it, Diana. As I am."

Unable to form the words, he railed at her in his mind —drove her from him with threats, commanded her to leave him in peace. But she was the first to act. His body went rigid as she approached, paused, pressed her hand lightly to his back. She might as well have struck a fatal blow.

"No," she murmured. "I may never fully understand what you are, Nicholas. But you aren't Adrian. And you would never do to me what he did to Clare."

His intended roar came out as a whisper. "I am not mortal," he said. *"I am not human."*

"But you are a man," she said, spreading her fingers against his spine. "And you weren't meant to be alone."

Bantam Books by Susan Krinard

Prince of Wolves
Prince of Dreams

Thanks to Wendy McCurdy,
who has shown me the value of a sharp editor;

to Rosemary and Jennara,
for their patient advice;

and, as always, to Serge.

PROLOGUE

For some must watch, while some must sleep:
So runs the world away.
> —William Shakespeare, *Hamlet*

Nevada County, California, 1891

Nicholas had learned as a child, over a century ago, that immortals did not cry.

There were no tears now, though his throat was tight and aching. He knelt beside the new grave in the moon-cast shadow of a crude wooden cross, set in a gentle valley fresh with spring grass. But the promise of new life was empty, a cruel joke on the young woman who slept under the freshly turned earth.

There were no flowers here; he would not mock her by decorating her grave with blossoms that would shrivel and die, like everything in this world. Except himself. And Adrian.

His hopes of becoming mortal—human—had died with Sarah. Once he had believed she was the one woman strong enough to fulfill the ancient legend of his kind—to carry him over the threshold that separated him forever from humanity.

But his dreams were gone. They had been murdered as surely as she had been.

By his brother. His pitiless, immortal twin.

Nicholas spread his hand on the rich earth and dug his fingers into it. He lifted the fistful of dirt and let it fall. *Forgive me, Sarah, for forgetting what I was. What Adrian is . . .*

He wouldn't forget again. He would follow his brother wherever he had fled.

His gelding nickered behind him. He rose to his feet, leaning against the animal's broad barrel and stroking its questing muzzle as he stared blindly into the night.

There would be no one to weep for Sarah. Her father was dead, and her infant daughter would never know what she had lost. Nicholas had already seen to it that the child had a good home. With her own kind, a responsible couple returning to San Francisco.

Nothing bound Nicholas to this place now.

Sweeping his hair from his eyes, he gathered the reins and swung up into the saddle. One last time he looked down at Sarah's quiet grave, burying his heart beside her. Clicking softly, he urged the horse into a trot. They left the pleasant valley behind, left Sarah to her long sleep. Nicholas let his mind go blank, filling his senses with only one purpose.

To find his brother, and make certain he could never hurt anyone again.

He and Adrian were two of a kind—in appearance, in

immortal nature, in the need that drove them to steal life force from ordinary mortals in order to survive. Two beings who lacked the élan vital that every other earthly creature possessed. Like the legendary vampire, they lived on that invisible, intangible energy that flowed through mortals like blood. And like the vampire of ancient folklore, they could all too easily kill in taking what they must have.

Nicholas had learned long ago to take no more than he required from his female dreamers, skimming life force as they slept and leaving them unharmed. He'd always rejected the temptation to enter their bodies as he did their minds—that method, so much more effective, could be deadly to humans. Nicholas survived, but his strength was hardly more than that of an ordinary mortal.

But Adrian had always taken what he wanted with no regard to the consequences. Sarah was the terrible proof. He had stolen nearly all her life force in a single act of sexual possession, leaving her too little to sustain her own body.

She had died in Nicholas's arms.

Now it was only a few hours before dawn, and Nicholas could not ride by day, in sunlight that would sap the stolen life force that nourished him. Adrian, still flush with Sarah's dying energy, would be able to travel in daylight—inhumanly powerful and ruthless in his desperation.

Nicholas bent his head over his mount's neck. Adrian had to be stopped at any cost. *My doing,* he thought bitterly. *I am no better. I wanted too much. I didn't love Sarah enough. . . .*

Because his kind could no more truly love than weep.

Nicholas rode through the dying hours of night, following his instincts and his knowledge of the man he pursued. He could have tracked Adrian for many nights, deep into the mountains. But when he found Adrian's trail, the track of shod hoofprints led Nicholas into a ravine close to home, where abandoned mine tunnels gaped like accusing mouths to either side of the overgrown path. It was almost as if Adrian wished to be found.

Nicholas dismounted slowly, listening to the tentative sounds of approaching dawn. The gelding raised his head and whickered.

"I've been expecting you, brother," Adrian said softly, emerging from a tunnel like a creature from some ancient myth. Green eyes, a paler shade of Nicholas's own, glittered like a predator's. Golden hair framed his head like a fallen angel's halo. His black cloak swept out behind him.

"You know why I'm here," Nicholas whispered.

Adrian walked closer, arrogantly unafraid. "Must it come to this, Nicholas? We are the last of our kind. . . ."

The last. Nicholas refused to close his eyes, to submit to the pain that could only weaken him. "You've gone too far, Adrian," he said tonelessly.

Adrian's lip curled. "You always cared too much for these humans, brother. They are only the means to keep us alive. Your quest for mortality is futile." He extended his pale, elegant hand. "We are brothers. She was *nothing*—"

"Why?" Nicholas's anguish escaped him in that single word. "Why did you kill her?"

No flicker of regret passed behind Adrian's crystalline eyes. "Did you truly believe she could have made you human, that she was the perfect mate to give you what you lack? That her life force was so powerful that the simple act of sex could transfer her mortal nature to you without harming her at all? No, Nicholas. That legend was no more than an old man's pathetic fantasy. I have proven it most effectively."

Adrian's sonorous voice roughened. "*She* could not have taken you from me. I exposed her weakness." He gestured at himself. "Am I mortal now, Nicholas? Do you think she would have survived *your* demands?"

"It was different with Sarah," Nicholas whispered hoarsely. "I would have—"

"Loved her?" Adrian shook his head in a parody of sadness. "What is human love to us? Your dream is doomed to fail just as our mother's did. You will remain as I am, brother—blessed, immortal, a god among these humans. As you were born to be." His eyes grew hard. "It appears I will have to teach you the error of your delusions."

Stalking toward Nicholas, Adrian drew something from the folds of his cloak. Metal clanked in the silence. Manacles—forged of heavy steel—and chains the thickness of a man's wrist.

"It seems," Adrian said regretfully, "that I must show you what you truly are."

Nicholas understood the threat clearly. His gaze jumped to the mouth of the cave, and Adrian nodded.

"I've prepared a little place for you, brother, a place where you'll have time to . . . contemplate reality. A year should be enough. When I return you will be more than happy to discard these foolish mortal longings."

Lifting his head and bracing his legs, Nicholas shook his head. "No, Adrian. You can't win—"

"Because *justice* is on your side?" Adrian laughed. "Human justice. Not ours." He sighed. "Your strength can never match mine—another lesson you must be forced to learn. I promise you, when this is over you'll thank me—"

But Nicholas never heard his brother's mocking appeal. With a roar he sprang at Adrian, losing himself in the primitive rage that grew out of sorrow he could not express.

He never knew, afterward, how he managed to defeat his brother. Something cold and grim drove him beyond exhaustion, beyond the ordinary limits of his strength and Adrian's superhuman power.

When it was over Adrian lay unconscious, his classically handsome face strangely at peace while Nicholas stood over him, loathing what they both were. Loathing himself most of all. Longing for tears that would never come.

He could not kill Adrian. It was an ironic fact that their inhuman instincts, the same that drove them to take mortal life force, would not permit them to murder one of their own. And even had that not been the case, those of their blood were almost impossible to kill in any way except the total severing of the spine.

Nicholas had no choice but to stop Adrian in the only way left to him.

The same way Adrian had intended to punish Nicholas for his dreams of mortality.

He found the prison his brother had prepared deep in the abandoned mine, within a small cavern off the main tunnel. Inside the cavern entrance Adrian had built a high wall of heavy brick with only a small opening and a stack of loose bricks beside it. Nicholas dragged Adrian into the makeshift cell and spent the long daylight hours in the lightless cave, putting the manacles on his brother and driving deep spikes into the rock to hold the chains in place.

When he was nearly finished, Adrian groaned and opened his eyes. As Nicholas began to fill in the single opening in the wall, Adrian was cursing him.

Nicholas made himself deaf and dumb and lost to emotion, driving his body to complete the prison. His strength began to fail him as he lifted the final brick, the seal that would lock his brother away from the world forever.

"You fool," Adrian snarled.

Nicholas pressed his cheek to the rough, cold brick and curled his fingers into claws, leaving bloody streaks in the drying mortar.

"Do you think this changes anything—that imprisoning me will free you from what you are?"

Any hope of reply locked in Nicholas's throat. *Forgive me,* he begged silently, *for all the failures that have led us to this moment.* Prayers gathered in his throat, unspoken, as the tears remained forever unshed.

"You'll go on as you've always done—creeping in the shadows, hiding from the light because you're afraid to take what you must to live as you were meant to live. Denying what you are." Adrian laughed weakly. "*Mortal.* You'll never have mortality, Nicholas. Or love, or any of these mortal conceits. If you find another like Sarah— what then? Will you take her as I took Sarah, and find you're no better than I am?"

Nicholas's breath seared his lungs. "*No.* But I can't set you free, Adrian. You'll go on as you have, destroying lives—"

The tortured scrape of metal shrieked in the silence. "You've always been so sure you're right, brother mine. Yet you know so little." Chains rattled. "You hate yourself, and I pay the price. But you'll never face your own blindness—"

Closing his ears to the sound of Adrian's relentless voice, Nicholas wedged the last few bricks in place.

"I'm all you have, all you'll ever have," Adrian cried, the sound muffled to a whisper. "You'll be alone, brother, for all eternity. Alone—"

Nicholas staggered back from his handiwork, turning

blindly for the cavern entrance. He slammed into stone, reeled sideways, and plunged through the passageway into the mine tunnel, feeling for the vast boulder that Adrian had left to block the cavern entrance. Nausea spiraled through his gut as he worked the slab into place. He staggered down the lightless adit and into the night; with the last of his strength he scrambled up the hillside above the timbers bracing the mine entrance and sent rock and earth tumbling down to block the tunnel's dark mouth.

Nicholas!

In his mind he thought he heard his brother's cry. It pursued him as he left the sealed mine behind and stumbled to his horse. He let the gelding carry him out of the ravine, past the abandoned mine shafts and tunnels that Bill Danvers, Sarah's father, had closed a decade ago.

No one would come here again. Tomorrow he would have the property sealed off with barbed wire fencing, and hire a man to watch it.

A few years should be sufficient. In a few years . . .

He could think no further. Where there should have been terrible grief was only emptiness—the emptiness of the long years that stretched ahead.

Alone. They were all gone now: his mother, Adrian—and the mortals who had briefly shared their lives.

He tried to straighten as he turned his mount onto the muddy, rutted road among the pines. His battle with Adrian had nearly depleted the last of his strength; it had been days too long since he had fed. The need for sustaining life force drove him inevitably back toward the haunts of men.

There was a woman in Grass Valley who could provide what he required. She was no threat to his heart, nor was he a threat to her survival. She would give him what he needed, and no more.

With a single soft word he urged the gelding into a

rocking canter that ate up the miles to town. He welcomed the punishing agony of weakness that jarred his bones and made every breath a torment. By the time he reached Widow Brecht's small, neat house on Main Street, his hunger was devouring him like a fire consuming itself. He tied the horse to a convenient post in a side alley and eased his way into Mrs. Brecht's silent bedchamber.

She looked nothing at all like Sarah. Nicholas let his need drive emotion to a place where it could no longer reach him. He knelt beside the young widow's narrow bed and touched her grief-lined face. Her aura glowed softly in sleep, a halo of light visible only to his unique senses. The contact of flesh on flesh provided the gateway to her innermost being; slipping into her sleeping mind, he felt for the source of life itself, that mystic energy that infused her mortal body.

And he entered her dreams, weaving them like the craftsman he was, becoming part of them. Dreams of pleasure in her lost husband's arms, of wholeness and the happiness she had almost forgotten. And while she dreamed, he skimmed the life force that her mind set free, the part she would never miss, taking it into himself until it filled him to satiation, until he knew he would survive another day.

She would remember nothing of his visit but the fading images of the dreams they had shared.

As he released her mind he willed her contentment, peace to come with the morning, and the courage to live on in the face of her loss.

He had no such hopes for himself.

Drawing a handmade quilt gently around her shoulders, he left her, knowing he would not visit her again. Within the week he would be gone from this town and the mortal life he had once hoped to make.

His weakness, his hope—his false immortal dreams—would be left behind with Sarah. And Adrian.

He slipped from the house as silently as he had come, mounted the gelding, and rode for his cabin in the hills. He raced the coming of day, and yet he risked the first touch of sunlight to visit Sarah's valley one last time.

"It's over, Sarah," he whispered. "Sleep now. Sleep as I cannot. And dream of your mortal paradise."

Nicholas turned his mount and rode away from the false hope of dawn.

ONE

—

Two gates for ghostly dreams there are: one
    gateway
of honest horn, and one of ivory.
Issuing by the ivory gates are dreams
of glimmering illusion, fantasies,
but those that come through solid polished
    horn
may be borne out, if mortals only knew them.
                                    —Homer, *The Odyssey*

San Francisco, present day

She couldn't remember his face.

Diana Ransom blinked the sleep from her eyes and stared up at the ceiling of her bedroom, snatching at the last vivid images of the dream.

The rest of it was still clear. She closed her eyes again; the scarlet light behind her eyelids suffused her memories. It was always red in the nightmare, drenched in the color of passion or rage. The figure who turned away from her sister was tall, ominous, a dark shadow washed in bloody light.

The man's breath was harsh and grating as he rose from Clare's bedside, his dark cape swirling about him. In the morbid atmosphere his hair was the single point of radiance; it was gold, like an angel's. But the creature who had killed Clare was no angel.

She could see his teeth, sharp incisors revealed by the lift of eloquent lips. Fangs, like a vampire's, awash with blood. Nothing else. Only her sister's lifeblood spilling from the mouth of a fiend out of hell itself . . .

The rhythmic beep of her alarm clock jerked Diana free of the nightmare's spell. She let her breath out carefully, running her hand through her tangled curls.

"Damn," she whispered. "I almost had it that time—"

With clumsy fingers she found the alarm's off switch. Everything in the dream was exactly the same as it had been when she was a child. Fifteen years ago, when Clare had died.

Swinging her legs over the side of the bed, Diana set her jaw and marched into the bathroom. She stared at her own face in the mirror: a pale, sleep-smudged, delicate oval framed with short, curly dark hair—and tilted blue eyes that didn't see deeply enough when she tried to look into her own heart. Twenty-nine years old, serious and practical. Maybe— Diana's lips thinned. Maybe a little too driven, as Keely had told her more than once. A face that didn't resemble Clare's at all.

But the face she wanted most to see was the one in the nightmare. The one that continued to elude her.

The face of Clare's murderer.

She'd thought it was behind her. She'd come to terms with the sorrow long ago. Her private practice had finally begun to thrive this past year; her cousin Keely was doing well, and Diana had long since learned to live with the absence of those vivid dreams she'd had before Clare's death. Reality could be just as satisfying as the old childhood fantasies, and helping others overcome the problems that had destroyed Clare had filled the emptiness left when the remarkable, soaring, sometimes prophetic dreams of her youth had stopped.

But now the nightmare was back. The first dream she could clearly remember in fifteen years. A dream she didn't want and could not escape.

Diana Ransom, psychologist, one-time lucid dreamer, couldn't manage what she asked her clients to do when they worked with dreams to heal the mind.

She pushed her mouth into a defiant smile. "Even the shrink needs shrinking."

The words smacked a little too much of self-pity. Diana turned on the faucet and splashed her face. *I'm a damned good psychologist,* she told herself, knowing it for the truth. She had a knack for understanding others' problems, and her treatment record spoke for itself. Her clients almost always left therapy far better off than they'd come into it. That was all she could ask, all she had a right to expect.

But her mind refused to let this little problem go, even as she set about getting ready for the day's first therapy session. Selecting a neatly pressed pair of tailored slacks and a blouse from her closet, she went over the nightmare again for the hundredth time.

She knew all the theories. She'd kept up with all the latest dream research because dream therapy was part of her practice. That was what she always told herself.

Diana methodically worked her hair into its neat, simple style and frowned at her reflection, the brush still caught in her curls. It would have been simple if the nightmare was the ordinary sort, a construct of her subconscious, a tangle of symbols meant to alert her waking mind to issues she had to face. Unresolved issues left from that time when she'd been an adolescent trying to cope with tragedy and loneliness.

The problem with that theory was that she knew the man in the nightmare was real.

Something's happening to you, Diana, a small voice mocked her.

Setting down the brush with a controlled, deliberate movement, Diana turned away from the mirror. Walking to the window, she tilted up the blinds. The early autumn sunlight filtering between the slats seemed to hold a reddish tinge, reminding her of the dream. And of the past.

She was honest enough with herself to know she couldn't dismiss the nightmare because it was painful. There had to be a logical reason that she was remembering a dream—*this* dream in particular—after so many years.

Letting the blinds fall, Diana made the bed with a few neat, efficient motions, taking satisfaction in the simple act. Yes, it was only a matter of working with the nightmare until the meaning came clear. She knew the key to it all lay in the face of the man she could never quite remember.

And if you finally do remember?

Diana froze, listening to that small, distant voice that wouldn't be silenced.

It was a little too late to track down the man responsible for Clare's death, especially on the evidence of a dream. *Is that the way to let it all go once and for all?* she thought. *Bring that hidden memory to the surface and act on it somehow?*

Shaking her head, Diana left the bedroom and took in the comforting familiarity of her living room. The quiet, neutral colors, clean-lined modern furniture, pastel abstract paintings, and uncluttered simplicity of the place had a lot in common with the office on the ground floor of her small Victorian, and that suited her very well. There was no great transition from work to home and back again, no disruption to her orderly existence.

A haze of red glazed the pleasant view like an omen of destruction. Diana blinked and walked into the kitchen, plugging in the coffee maker with suddenly unsteady hands. *What are you afraid of? It's only a dream.*

But there had been a time in her life when her dreams had been more than merely dreams. A time when she had ridden her dreams like wild horses into realms of wonder, and created her own worlds—when she had believed unicorns and elves and creatures of childhood fancy were real. A time, too, when her dreams had sometimes seen far more clearly than waking sight.

As when Clare had died . . .

No. Clare was gone, and the vampire in the nightmare long gone as well.

Diana poured the hot coffee into a plain white mug and sucked in her breath sharply as a few drops of the liquid sloshed onto her hand. She plunged her hand under the tap and let the cold water soothe the burns.

Damn, she thought grimly. *Get yourself under control.*

Control. Once she'd been able to control her dreams, mold them into whatever she wanted them to be. Now she focused on the real world. And in the real world she had appointments, people to see and talk with. People with real problems.

She had plenty to think about between the new relaxation techniques she planned to try with Mrs. Zeleny and the exciting progress José Sanchez was making in overcoming his depression. Much more rewarding than dwelling on her own past.

And then there was Keely. . . .

Diana smiled, her grim mood forgotten. She'd never seen her young cousin happier than she was now. Not since she and Diana and Clare had been kids together, secure in their belief that nothing could ever shatter their safe little world.

Clare had been lost, but Keely, so much like Clare in many ways, lived on to fulfill the promise of their childhood dreams.

The doorbell rang just as Diana finished her coffee. She glanced at her watch; too early for her first client, unless there'd been an unexpected crisis . . . Setting down the mug, she left her second-floor flat and hurried down the stairs. Bypassing the ground-floor office, she opened the front door to the back of her next-door neighbor.

Tim Reynolds turned, a lopsided grin settling on his pleasant face. "Sorry. I hope I didn't wake you up, Diana."

She looked up the length of his tall, gangly frame and smiled, grasping at the distraction with relief. "Not at all. In fact, I was just having coffee. Care to come in?"

"No. It's just that they delivered your paper to my door again this morning." Tim shifted, flipping straight black hair out of his eyes. "I was just on my way to the school." The paper in question was clutched so tightly under his arm that it appeared he had no intention of giving it up. Diana widened her smile, urging the young man to relax. Something else was obviously on his mind.

"Thanks for bringing it over," she said softly. Her glance flickered to the paper. "Is there something else—"

"Oh." Tim released his hold on the paper and passed it to her, nearly dropping it in the process. "Well . . . I was just wondering . . . do you think you'll be seeing Keely today?"

Ah. That was the heart of the matter. She hadn't been the only one thinking about her cousin. "I'm meeting her for lunch." She thought quickly and took a gamble. "If you'd care to join us—"

"No. No. I was just wondering . . . if maybe this weekend—" He broke off, his ears reddening. Diana looked over his shoulder at the slender figure coming up the walk.

"Keely," she said. "I didn't expect her this morning."

Tim pulled nervously on his crooked tie. "I'll let you get to whatever it is you have to do, Diana. I'll—be in touch." With a tilt of his chin that suggested a man about to face an executioner, Tim turned and marched down the steps to meet the young woman.

Diana shook her head and closed the door. Tim was the proverbial "nice guy"—the kind women said they wanted but claimed never to be able to find. Unlocking her office door, Diana crossed to the window and watched Keely and Tim talking—Tim's telltale gestures of self-consciousness, Keely's offhand courtesy that stopped just short of encouragement.

Keely was never drawn to "nice guys." That was the one problem she had yet to overcome, an expression of the defiant recklessness she hadn't learned to let go. In that way, too, she was like Clare.

Clare, Keely, and Diana. Once they'd been inseparable.

Diana sighed and focused her eyes on the scene outside the window again. With a flip of her long brown hair, Keely gave Tim some casual send-off that had him retreating with his dignity intact, if not triumphantly. Keely pursed her lips and rolled her eyes as she continued up the sidewalk and opened the front door. Diana walked into the hallway to meet her.

"You had to leave me alone with him," Keely complained, embracing Diana.

Diana drew back, tugging gently at a loose lock of Keely's hair. "Give the man a break, Keely. He has a crush on you."

"Which I don't need," Keely retorted. "He's a nice guy, but—"

"You don't go in for nice guys. I know."

Keely's smile thinned. "I didn't come here for a lecture, Di—"

"Sorry." Diana pushed stray curls back from her forehead and gestured to one of the comfortable armchairs in the office.

Keely grimaced. "I always get the feeling I'm going to be analyzed when you sit me down in here."

"Want to go upstairs?"

"No. I just came to bring you something." Keely's eyes narrowed, focusing on Diana's face. "You've been thinking about Clare, haven't you?"

Her cousin's insight always came as something of a surprise to Diana, even after the past two years. Keely was adept at never taking anything too seriously, throwing herself into everything she did with a kind of heedless abandon. It was her way of dealing with old pain. She'd never been good at hiding her emotions.

But there were times when Keely's apparent cheerful lack of concern was deceptive. . . .

"I miss her too," Keely said softly. "I still remember when me and Mom came to live with you right after Dad left us. It was like getting a whole new family."

Diana nodded, letting herself drift on a tide of memory. When Keely and her mother, Diana's recently divorced aunt, had come to live with Diana and Clare's parents, the cousins had taken to each other instantly. The differences in their ages—five years apart, with Keely the youngest at six and Clare eldest at sixteen—hadn't mattered at all.

Clare and Keely had been the artists. Already brilliantly talented, Clare had taken Keely under her wing, and the two had spent endless hours drawing and painting together. Diana had turned her creativity in a different direction: reading and daydreaming—and, by night, losing herself in fantastic worlds where she could create and mold her dreams as she wished.

But the three of them had sworn a pact to stay together forever. The death of Jane and Eric Ransom and Aunt Eileen in a terrible car accident had changed everything.

The three girls' secure, happy world had been torn apart. Their separation, when Keely's father had come to take her away, had been hardest of all on Clare and Keely. Only eight years old, Keely had returned to New York kicking and screaming. Clare, just having reached her majority, was left with the care of her younger sister and a future of fading dreams. In the end the struggle had cost her her life.

After Clare had died, Diana had tried to find Keely again. But John Ames had been a wanderer, never living anywhere for long. Not until the night a bedraggled, twenty-two year old Keely had turned up on Diana's doorstep had the cousins been reunited at last.

Now, as Keely began to rummage in her oversized patchwork purse, Diana studied her with an analyst's trained eye. She couldn't help but compare this morning with that day two years ago.

It hadn't taken much expertise to realize that Keely had had a rough life, and that she wanted nothing more to do with her father. But Diana had never been able to learn much about those years. She would have done anything to help Keely then—given her a home, found her a job, gotten her a good therapist—but Keely had vanished again after a few days. Frantic with worry, Diana's subsequent search had turned up no leads at all.

I made her run away, Diana thought sadly. *I was overprotective, afraid of losing Keely as I lost Clare.*

Diana had thrown herself into her newly established practice, telling herself that Keely would be all right—and that *she* could go on as she always had.

Alone.

And then one day Keely had shown up again—changed, better, confident, ready to start over. She had a job in San Francisco, was back in school, had a place to live and a studio to paint in—all achieved without Diana's help. But she'd been as uncommunicative on those recent developments as she'd been about her earlier life.

But Diana had learned. She didn't push. She took the gift she'd been granted, giving Keely what love, help, and support she could—and tried to remember that Keely was not Clare.

At times it was painfully difficult.

As if she sensed Diana's intense regard, Keely glanced up. The vintage seventies clothing she wore—hip-hugging jeans, ruffled blouse, long vest, and black beret—made her seem very young, gave her a look of vulnerability that wasn't entirely deceptive. She was a tough young woman, but there was still a needy little girl inside she wasn't always successful in hiding.

Diana knew all about that kind of protective camouflage.

"Here it is," Keely proclaimed, waving a slightly wrinkled envelope in her hand. "I knew you'd have a few minutes before your first client showed up, and I wanted to give you your invitation to the opening. I kept forgetting." She grinned, passing Diana a hand-addressed envelope of fine linen stationery.

Diana opened the envelope and felt a burst of almost personal pride. Keely's first solo art show was opening at Gallery Newbold in three weeks. She was achieving what Clare had never had the chance to do.

The elegantly printed words on the invitation blurred and faded from Diana's sight, and she looked up to study Keely once again. They didn't really look much alike; Clare's hair had been darker, and her eyes hazel rather than brown. Sometimes Diana saw a reflection of Clare in Keely's gestures and voice, the quicksilver changes in mood that were so much a part of the artist in her.

And they had both suffered. Clare had been forced to give up so many of her artistic dreams, only to find false solace in the arms of a man who had taken what remained of her spirit and driven her to suicide. . . .

"You will be able to make it?" Keely asked, breaking into Diana's thoughts.

"Of course. I wouldn't miss it for the world."

And that was no less than the truth. *You'll have every thing Clare never did,* Diana told Keely silently. *Success, happiness, independence. A full life.*

Diana sighed. After so many years, the old pain was finally healing. If it weren't for the nightmare, she could have consigned the past to oblivion.

As if to mock her, the sinister figure in the swirling black cape rose again in her memory. *I know what you are,* she told him, *even if I can't remember your face. I control my own mind. I'm going to get rid of you once and for all. . . .*

"I won't be able to make it for lunch this afternoon, Diana."

Diana started, her eyes focusing on Keely's face. "Why not? I'd been looking forward to—"

"I know." Keely shifted, her body language shouting guilty secrets. "It's just that—something else has come up."

Something else. Intuition and experience came to Diana's aid, and before she could stop herself she blurted out the first thing in her mind.

"You mean—*someone* else," she said, more sharply than she'd intended.

Keely rose to the defensive, her ordinarily candid face taking on a guarded look. "Yes." Her chin tilted up. "A guy I met last week at the gallery."

Diana kept her neck rigid to keep from shaking her head. "Keely—"

"You don't know anything about him, Di," Keely said. "He's—not like any man I've met before—"

Diana shuddered. Clare had said those very words fifteen years ago. "And not, I suppose, anything like Tim," she said calmly.

Keely's lip curled and then eased into a stiff smile. "No more matchmaking, Di. Do you want to put your seal of approval on all my boyfriends?"

Yes, Diana cried inwardly, but she knew Keely too well. Her heedless pursuit of dangerous men was a kind of rebellion against her brutally strict, unloving father. She was still rebelling, even now, after she'd left her father far behind.

But Diana had hoped it was ending, that Keely was overcoming her propensity for falling in love with the wrong kind of men—that she wouldn't need the deceptive intimacy and false romance such men provided.

Diana swallowed. "If you'll just use common sense—"

Keely stood up. "You don't trust me, do you? I'm not

Clare, Diana. *I'm not Clare.*" Keely tossed hair from her eyes and set her jaw. "Maybe your problem is that you're scared of any relationship with men that doesn't take place in a fifty-minute session in this office."

Reeling inwardly from Keely's words, Diana averted her eyes. Keely could cut right to the heart of matters, things even Diana consciously denied.

Physician, heal thyself. . . .

"God. I'm sorry, Di." Hurling herself at Diana, Keely gave her a strong, exuberant hug. "That was nasty of me. I didn't mean it." She drew back, smiling crookedly. "Forgive me?"

Composure restored, Diana clasped her cousin's hand. "Sure thing." She checked her watch. "Ten to nine. My first client's due here soon—"

Somewhere out on the street a horn honked, and Keely's face lit up like an incandescent bulb. "I got to go anyway." She sobered. "Don't worry, Di. I'm a big girl now. I'll be in touch." With another sudden grin, she dashed out of the office and out the door, pelting down the steps to the sidewalk.

Moving stiffly to the window, Diana peered through the half-closed blinds. A red Porsche idled at the curb. Keely was laughing as she slid into the passenger seat, leaning over to kiss the driver. A man with golden hair that caught the morning sunlight—a flash of classic profile, mirror shades, and a reckless grin that would melt most feminine hearts. Diana saw no more of him before he pulled away from the curb with a screech of tires, Keely still laughing at his side.

"Dr. Ransom?"

When she turned to greet José Sanchez at the office door, her professional façade was completely intact. Her client would never see the irrational fear that she'd buried in the deepest part of her heart.

"Please come in, José," she said with a smile. "How have things been this week?"

As she gestured him to the armchair near the window, Diana gave herself to her work once again and consigned the face in the nightmare to oblivion.

The man who called himself Nicholas Gale sat at a table in an isolated corner of the coffeehouse, thinking of another woman he had lost.

Keely wasn't here tonight. She hadn't shown up in the two weeks since he'd been forced to reject her declaration of love—since she'd marched away with tears in her eyes and the rags of a sensitive young woman's pride drawn around herself like armor.

But he'd wanted to see her again. Even though he couldn't explain why he could not love her, he had been haunted by the memory of her pain.

And so he'd hoped she'd resume her usual habit of showing up in the late evenings. Mama Soma's was one of the few coffeehouses south of Market that stayed open after midnight; Keely had always had trouble sleeping. That was how they'd officially met the first time, a pair of lonely insomniacs in search of companionship. And Mama Soma's was known as a hangout for artists and slackers and neobeatniks, outsiders in a city of stubborn noncomformists.

Nicholas was the ultimate outsider.

He nursed his strong coffee, gazing into the dark liquid. One of his few vices, this—along with fine brandy. His body required little food such as mortals consumed, and a minimal amount of liquid; too much of either was a mild poison to his inhuman system. But now—he took a deep swallow of the coffee. Now he didn't give a damn.

He wondered if Keely knew that Gale meant

"stranger" in an ancient language. She would appreciate that; she was a romantic, a girl who had found his reticence hopelessly attractive, a child who felt deeply and could not understand why he could never return her love.

Nicholas stared into the smoky darkness as he listened to the irregular beat of the avant-garde music blasting from the wall speakers. He should have seen the warning signs, known what was coming when Keely had approached him that night. Judith would have known if he'd bothered to ask her. That was the danger of keeping himself separate, aloof from the society of those he needed to survive.

He thought back to the night he'd found Keely on the street in the Tenderloin, painting vivid murals on the side of an abandoned building with pastels she'd found in a Dumpster. She hadn't seen him then; he'd briefly regarded her as a source of life force, a woman whose dreams he could skim while she slept. The creative ones, the artists and musicians and writers, were always the most vivid dreamers.

But he'd sensed her pain even then, the trouble that shrouded her. He would not use such a one. And so he'd passed her by, gone to Judith, and set events in motion to pull another lost, talented kid off the street.

Keely had never known who paid for the treatment to clear the drugs out of her system, found her a place to live, and got her back into school and therapy. Judith had seen to that. Judith had also convinced the girl to renew contact with relatives in the city, and Keely was well on her way to being the success she deserved to be.

She wouldn't learn the name of her benefactor, the anonymous founder of the Dreamseekers Foundation who had provided the grants. She knew Nicholas as someone she'd met by chance, seeing in him what she wished to see.

"You're a worthless parasite, all right," Judith had told Nicholas once in a rare burst of temper. *"Pulling kids up out of the gutter and giving them a new start. I wish we had more parasites like you in this world."*

Nicholas closed his eyes. Judith could never be truly objective about what he was. Of all the mortals on earth she knew the most about him, and even she didn't know the whole truth.

Keely would never know the half of it.

The old guilt rose in him, pain he felt even through the frigid veil around his heart. Nicholas flattened his hands palm down on the table top and examined the tracery of blood vessels and tendons that crisscrossed under the skin. How fragile human beings were, how easily hurt. *You did what you had to do,* he told himself. But a hidden part of him was still able to mourn, reminding him of his own deadly vulnerability.

Keely was strong enough to get over her imagined love for him. She'd go on to find someone else, one of her own kind. And he'd go on as he had for so long, taking what he needed to survive. Surviving because it was in his nature, and he had no other choice.

"You look like you could use a drink."

He looked up slowly. Barb, the late-night waitress and barkeep, regarded him with a sympathetic grin. Barb had hardly a trace of an aura; her life force was so faint to his senses that it affected Nicholas hardly at all. His hunger lay safely dormant. Ordinarily he could relax in her presence—feel almost human. She was no threat at all.

He fingered his empty glass ruefully. "I don't think so, Barb. I'm about ready to call it a night."

Idly tugging the nose ring that pierced one nostril, Barb shook her head. "Haven't seen Keely lately. Know what's up with her?"

Nicholas looked carefully away from her eyes. "No."

He rose from the table slowly, feeling the onset of weakness that meant he must take sustenance soon. He'd put off visiting his dreamers too long, affected far too much by the confrontation with Keely.

Somehow he had to regain his detachment. Perhaps the key was getting away for a few weeks, even if it meant missing Keely's opening. There was business he could take care of on the East Coast, interests he hadn't personally looked into in some time. There'd be a different set of dreamers there as well—at a time like this he'd do better to distance himself from his regulars in San Francisco.

Distance. He could never afford to forget how essential it was.

He handed Barb a neat stack of bills and smiled. "I may be away for a few weeks, Barb. Don't let them close Mama Soma's while I'm gone."

"Fat chance of that," Barb joked. She punched Nicholas in the shoulder. "See yah around." She left the table with a toss of narrow leather clad hips just as a young man with a cigarette dangling from his mouth dropped into the chair Nicholas had vacated. Warm air from a space heater swirled around Nicholas as he headed up the narrow stairs for the door, buttoning his coat against the chill of an unexpectedly cool September night.

"Leaving so early? The night's still young."

Judith stood in the doorway, looking down from the top step. He saw her aura first—steady, unremarkable, familiar. The faint halo around her body faded as he adjusted his vision.

"Young for me, but not for you," he said, offering his arm. "This is hardly your usual haunt, Judith. You should be in bed."

Judith Fortier—his oldest surviving friend and confidante, the only mortal who knew what he was—made an eloquent face. Her frizzy gray-shot hair refused to hold any real style, and there were deep creases engraved around her mouth and between her heavy brows. She had never been a beauty—not even forty years ago as a young woman in Europe—but there was a solid strength about her that Nicholas had learned to trust. It was that very strength that had allowed him to risk their friendship at all.

He knew the source of every line, every angle and curve that time had molded over her sixty years of life, just as he understood the perpetual sadness in her deep brown eyes.

"I had a notion you might want company tonight," Judith said. She waved her hand in front of her face and reached for his arm. "Let's get into the fresh air. You know what smoke does to ex-nicotine fiends like me."

Nicholas obligingly led her out onto the sidewalk, leaving the noise of Mama Soma's behind.

"You were waiting for Keely," Judith said softly.

He avoided her gaze. "I haven't seen her."

"Nor have I. She's been spending most of her time away from home, it seems." Judith sighed. "Don't blame yourself, Nicholas."

Pausing to tuck several bills under the ragged blankets of a homeless man sprawled on the sidewalk, Nicholas turned to face her. "I couldn't give her what she wanted, Judith," he said evenly.

For a moment her eyes revealed everything, all the unrequited love she'd tried to hide from him since she'd come to womanhood. She would understand exactly how Keely felt.

Ah, Judith. . . .

"I know," she said, her thin lips curving into a sad smile. Nicholas stared at her aged fingers curled over his arm and covered her hand with his own.

They walked side by side in silence, united by memory and affection and things that could not be spoken. The few transients and late-night club-goers who chanced to meet them moved quietly out of their way. Perhaps they sensed some part of what Nicholas was.

But even the most destitute among them would find some sheltered corner in which to close his eyes and sleep. Judith would be free to escape into her own dreams. Nicholas could only borrow and weave the dreams of those he touched for sustenance; for his kind—for him—there was only endless wakefulness. He had never known the benediction of sleep.

He would have traded everything he had for those simple gifts.

He would have given anything to be human.

"I'll take you home, Judith," he said.

Keely should have been at the center of it all—this night of nights, the grand opening of her first solo show. The crowd was mixed: young artists with black vintage clothing and slightly blasé airs, society women dressed in Chanel suits, a few high-profile investors to lend a cachet of excitement to the affair.

As she threaded her way through the clumps of people, Diana thought about Keely's reclusive patron. The anonymous individual behind the Dreamseekers Foundation was more than merely wealthy enough to provide generous grants to disadvantaged young artists; he or she had considerable influence to pull in a crowd like this.

Diana's thoughts scattered like the light flashing from the diamond bracelet on the arm of a woman reaching for a glass of Chardonnay on a passing caterer's tray. She turned down an offered glass and stretched in an effort to look over the nearest heads. Keely was nowhere to be seen.

A familiar sense of irrational dread coiled in Diana's belly. She knew full well the cause of her unease: not only the persistence of her own nightmares, but also Keely's obsessive behavior in the weeks since they'd last spoken in Diana's office.

The fact that Diana was having the nightmares just as Keely had gotten involved with a mysterious man she refused to discuss—it was surely only coincidence, not an omen. Irrational. Clare and Keely had overlapped far too often in Diana's mind after Keely had come back into her life.

Feeling suddenly oppressed by the bright chatter around her, Diana withdrew to the far side of the gallery, away from the main display. She closed her eyes.

Keely hadn't even told Diana her new lover's name. *Because she didn't want another lecture about her love life,* Diana thought grimly.

But that wasn't all of it. Not when Keely had twice broken lunch dates with Diana, hadn't returned Diana's calls—and when Diana had at last managed to reach her, Keely had shown no interest at all in the opening that she'd been preparing for so diligently over the past year.

Clare had acted the same way when she'd begun to see Adrian, fifteen years ago. Distracted, dreamy, distancing herself from her beloved sister. Searching for wholeness in the arms of the wrong kind of man. Sacrificing everything on the altar of what she'd believed was love . . .

God. Diana scraped her hand through her hair, heedless of the disarray. Whatever the risk of offending Keely, Diana knew she had to talk to her again. Face to face. She'd force herself to be utterly detached, play the logical therapist rather than the overprotective relative.

Making her way back out among the knots of people, Diana resumed her search. Each time she found a likely place for Keely to be basking in the praise of her new admirers, she came up empty. The bright, expressionistic paintings that lined the walls collected the glowing comments that Keely should have been receiving herself.

Diana reached the far end of the gallery and turned around, clenching her fists. A tall, middle-aged woman brushed by, and Diana reached for her arm to stop her.

"Judith!"

The older woman turned and smiled warmly. Judith Fortier was Keely's landlady; she owned two row houses near Potrero Hill and rented out rooms to young men and women of an artistic bent. Diana had met her a few times and liked what she knew of her.

"Diana. I haven't seen you in a while." Judith gestured at the displays. "Quite impressive. Keely is uniquely talented—"

"Have you by any chance seen her lately?" Diana said.

Judith arched a dark, wiry brow. "Not recently. I've been looking for her myself. Not that she's behind in the rent, mind you, but—"

"There she is." Diana caught sight of Keely at the far end of the gallery, in the act of opening a side door. Giggling, the young woman glanced around as if bent on eluding any possible pursuit, and slipped out into the alley behind the building.

Diana smoothed the tense frown creasing her forehead. "If you'll excuse me, Judith—"

"Of course. I'd appreciate it if you'd send her over to me when you can—"

Muttering agreement, Diana strode purposefully toward the door through which Keely had disappeared. She flung open the door, wincing at a blast of cold air.

A laughing couple stood in the alley between graffiti-marked walls. There was no mistaking the woman, with her light brown hair coming loose from its coil atop her head and the willowy figure poured into a black ribbed dress. Keely was utterly unaware of Diana's presence, her fingers clutched on the sleeve of the man at her side.

Swallowing hard, Diana looked at Keely's escort. She could not quite make out his face. He was tall, elegantly if somewhat unconventionally dressed, and moved with the grace of a man who knows his own worth. Brilliant blond hair caught the faint glow of a distant streetlight.

Keely's voice rose in a laugh—a strange, forced sound, almost too bright, like a shout of defiance. The man's hands laced in her hair, pulling Keely intimately close.

There was nothing even remotely rational about Diana's feelings then. She remembered Keely's accusation: *"Maybe your problem is that you're scared of any relationship with men that doesn't take place in a fifty-minute session in this office."*

For a moment Diana felt herself in Keely's place, in the man's arms, with his mouth covering hers. Burning heat gathered in her cheeks. Anger surged through her, anger such as she hadn't felt in fifteen years. Passionate, envious, protective rage.

Overwhelmed by her reaction, Diana was already backing away when the kiss ended and the man looked up. Pale eyes met hers; Diana saw a classically handsome face, eyes narrowed with amusement or satisfaction, a mouth curved in a smile of challenge.

Challenge. The impression stunned her, but Diana had no chance to analyze it. Within a moment the man had swung back to Keely, kissed her again, and turned on one elegantly shod foot to disappear into the darkness of the alley.

Struggling to find the sense of purpose that had deserted her, Diana stared after the man until Keely came up beside her. Her cousin smiled with perfect, impersonal gaiety. "So glad you could come, Diana," she purred. "Shall we go inside?"

The moment they stepped back into the gallery Keely was engulfed by her thwarted admirers, and all the questions Diana had meant to ask died in her throat. Keely never so much as glanced at her again.

Diana left then, troubled and haunted by that brief glimpse of Keely's lover and her own bizarre reaction. She went to bed early, too disoriented to worry about the usual nightmare.

But it came. And this time the faceless vampire rose, grinning, from Keely's lifeless body.

TWO

I know how men in exile feed on dreams of hope.

—Aeschylus, *Agamemnon*

Nicholas came back to Mama Soma's the night he returned to San Francisco.

He'd made the decision on the long flight back from New York: If Keely didn't turn up tonight, he'd break his rules and visit her at her apartment. Six weeks should be long enough; he'd waited a full week after her opening before returning to San Francisco.

In all the time he'd known her, he'd always confined their friendship to neutral ground, here at Mama Soma's or similar places. That was his usual safeguard against dangerous intimacy with human beings, with those who thought they knew something of him.

His dreamers—those from whom he fed—never knew him at all except in their dreams.

Nicholas paused on the steps that led down into the basement, standing on the threshold between cool, fresh night air and the smoke and heat of Mama Soma's.

The fanciful part of himself—the part he had almost suppressed, along with uncontrolled need and emotion—sometimes imagined that this descent was like a mortal's plunge into the subconscious at the onset of dreaming. Or perhaps, given the atmosphere of the place, a downfall into the netherworld that some said awaited humans after death.

Death and dreams were both beyond him. Nicholas shrugged off his useless fantasies and moved down the narrow stairs.

His usual table, the one set farthest back in the shadows away from the small stage and the bar, was empty this evening. He settled on the patched vinyl seat with a strange sense of homecoming and looked around the room. For once there was no blare of music to drown out the voices of the regulars. Nicholas listened idly to a poet at a nearby table reciting for a rapt audience of friends. Something very profound, no doubt. Love, or death.

His eyes wandered to the bar where Barb was serving beer and espresso, noting that she'd shaved her head since the last time he'd been here. She was leaning over the scratched countertop, locked in conversation with another young woman. Someone Nicholas didn't remember seeing before. Someone who . . .

Nicholas froze. There was nothing outwardly remarkable about the woman; she dressed more conservatively than most of Mama Soma's regulars, but that was a minor distinction. Her short brown hair was neatly styled, her body slim and petite under the tailored trousers and blazer.

Nothing remarkable at all, until he looked with his inner senses, those that enabled him to hunt what he must have to survive.

In the dim light her aura was almost blinding. For a moment he saw nothing of her except a silhouette, ringed by bands of brilliant color. His heart labored in his chest. Unexpected pain and longing gripped him, and he struggled to push it away.

He hadn't sensed an aura like that in over a century. The colors pulsed about the woman, violets and reds and golds, banded by white and blue. Barb literally paled by comparison; even Keely was nothing to this one.

Nicholas forced his eyes away from the woman and stared at his clenched fists. He could never forget the last time he had seen an aura so powerful, so desperately compelling.

Sarah.

His first instinct was to get up and walk away. If he stayed— Deliberately Nicholas dulled his inner senses, until he could see only the surfaces that mortals perceived with their limited sight. He dared to look up then, just as Barb pointed in his direction and the woman turned around.

He knew then it was too late to rise and walk away. Clear blue eyes fixed on him unerringly, with the conviction of recognition. As if she knew. As if she were Sarah reborn.

He composed himself as she walked toward him, dispassionately noting her determined walk and the way her fists clenched at her sides. His gaze rose to her face. Not like Sarah's, not at all. This woman had a fierce set to her jaw that belied the delicacy of her oval face. Full lips were taut with emotion, and dark brows were drawn down over those direct, fearless eyes.

"You're Nicholas Gale?"

He hardly heard her. It was all he could do, in that moment when she drew so close, to lower his racing heartbeat and control the surge of hunger that overwhelmed him. He no longer needed to see her aura; he felt it, could touch the pulse of her psychic energy without trying.

The life force on which he fed was like a subtle fire, coursing through the human body to be drawn forth by his kind. In most mortals it was a quiet burning. In a very few it was something more. As it had been in Sarah. As it was in this woman. . . .

She leaned over the table, bracing her hands flat on the scarred surface. Nicholas stared at the soft hollow of her throat where her silk blouse opened in a vee, mesmerized by the pulse that fluttered under her translucent skin.

The sound she made was blunt and effective. Nicholas snapped his gaze back to hers. Her eyes flashed defiance, but her ivory skin was flushed under the light makeup. Her lips parted slightly, and he could hear the soft sigh of her breath.

She was afraid. He knew nothing about this woman, but he knew she was afraid, and her fear vibrated through him as if it were his own.

"Nicholas Gale," she repeated, the barest hint of a tremor in her voice. "Is that your name?"

Nicholas felt his inner balance slip back into place as the old disciplines took hold of his body. The tension drained out of him; he leaned back in his chair and stretched his legs under the table. He let his eyes rake over her, drawing on his nearly perfect memory to find some record of her face.

"Should I know you?" he countered softly.

The woman jerked, almost as if she hadn't expected him to answer. The frown deepened between her brows. Without a word she dropped into the opposite chair.

"I'll get right to the point," she said. Her voice was

low and well modulated; musical, Nicholas thought dispassionately, if it hadn't been for the way she tried to strip it of emotion.

"I'm looking for Keely Ames."

He sat up a little straighter in his chair, and for the first time Diana saw a flicker of emotion cross that impassively handsome face. She breathed in very deeply and released the breath as silently as she could. After a week of searching, she'd finally found the man she was looking for. She'd recognized him in an instant.

"Keely?" he echoed. He blinked, the first time she had noticed him do so; deep gold lashes swept down over eyes the color of dark jade. They had looked paler in the gallery, and his hair, in this dim light, was a more prosaic blond. But his remarkable, aristocratic good looks were rather overwhelming at this proximity.

Oh, yes, he was quite beautiful. Not so beautiful as to have lost his masculine edge; he had that in plenty, radiating outward from his seemingly relaxed body. A dancer's body, she thought, remembering the way he had moved with Keely on his arm. Lithe but strong, in a way his casual denim and leather couldn't conceal. The kind of man who would attract attention and expect it as his due.

She let herself meet his eyes, looking for the challenge she had seen in the alley outside the gallery. Surely that had been her imagination; there was no mockery in his gaze now. In fact, the abandon with which he'd conducted himself in Keely's company was entirely absent.

The twitchy unease she'd felt when she'd seen him here in the coffeehouse was fading, leaving more confusing emotions in its wake. She could tell herself a million times that her interest in this man was limited to his connection to Keely, but somehow the explanation seemed dishonest. She remembered the way she had felt in the gallery, transported for an instant to an alternate reality where she was the woman in his arms, laughing and wild. . . .

Her eyes fell unwillingly to his lips. Strong, mobile lips, last seen kissing Keely with unbridled passion. Was it any wonder Keely had fallen—

Diana snapped herself out of her treacherous thoughts. She leaned forward, clasping her hands on the table top.

"Where is she?" she asked, schooling her voice to calm.

The man's eyes narrowed as he settled back into his seat. A fine network of tiny creases radiated outward from the corners of his eyes, and Diana wondered how old he was. Thirty? Surely not much older. Her own age.

"I don't know," he answered. His voice was deep and even and laced with vibrations like the purr of some great tawny cat. His simplest words held a note of refinement, the barest trace of an accent Diana couldn't place. He looked away, gestured to someone over Diana's shoulder. "Would you care for a cup of espresso, Miss—"

"Dr. Ransom," she supplied, watching him carefully.

He lifted one straight, golden brow. "The name sounds familiar." He paused with maddening nonchalance to order two cups of espresso from the leather-clad waitress and slowly turned his attention back to Diana. "Are you a friend of Keely's, Dr. Ransom?"

Diana struggled with the hostility and anger that suddenly threatened to overwhelm her necessary detachment. *Detachment?* a small voice mocked her. *You never had that where Keely was concerned.*

She forced her mouth into a cool smile. "Yes, Mr. Gale. I am Keely's friend. And right now I'm very concerned about her. I'd very much like to speak with her."

A trace of bemusement—feigned or otherwise—crossed Nicholas Gale's face. "I'd like to speak with her myself, Dr. Ransom. I haven't seen her in over a month."

The waitress appeared with the espressos, and Nicholas looked up with a smile that warmed his sculpted features like sunlight striking marble. He exchanged a soft word with the woman, and there was still a trace of the smile on his lips when he turned to Diana again.

"If you have come here looking for Keely, Dr. Ransom," he said, pushing one of the espressos toward her, "I can't tell you anything. I've been out of town for several weeks." He took a sip of his drink and glanced inquiringly at Diana's. "I don't believe we've met before, though Keely may have mentioned your name. . . ." He shook his head, and a wave of golden hair tumbled over his forehead. "Is there a particular reason why you came to me?"

Reaching for her espresso, Diana concentrated on the slow and steady movement of her hand. What kind of game was he playing? Their eyes had met at the gallery a week ago, and it wasn't an overabundance of ego that made her believe he wouldn't have forgotten her so quickly. He claimed that he hadn't seen Keely in a month. . . .

"Mr. Gale," she said, feeling her control slip away. "Let me refresh your memory. I was at Keely's opening at Newbold's a week ago Sunday night. I saw you with her there, and I've been trying to locate her ever since. You weren't easy to find either, Mr. Gale. No one seemed to know your name or who you were. I came to this place because Keely mentioned it once or twice, and I—"

He did no more than lift his hand, but that single gesture stopped her words as if he had shouted. "I'm afraid you must have me confused with someone else, Dr. Ransom. I was in New York during Keely's opening."

She knew she was staring at him, dumbfounded at his barefaced lie. Confused with someone else? Not in a million years. And if she wasn't able to trust her own eyes and memory . . .

She wanted to lean forward over the table and stare him down, take him by his leather lapels and shake him. Irrational, irrational. Just like the feeling she'd had when she'd seen him take Keely in his arms and kiss her with passionate abandon.

"That's very interesting, Mr. Gale," she said at last. "Quite a number of people seem to remember seeing you with Keely recently."

Gale looked at her through half-lowered lids. "Not more recently than six weeks ago," he said. Diana thought she detected the trace of an edge to his voice. Abruptly he sat up again. Energy seemed to course through him, an almost visible thing. "Why are you looking for Keely, Dr. Ransom? Has something happened to her?"

Diana stood up so suddenly that she almost knocked over her chair. "If anyone knows, it's you. I don't know why you're playing this game, but I only want to talk to her. Or are you so insecure in your relationship that you have to keep her to yourself?"

She knew she had gone overboard, and she almost didn't care. The past weeks of growing worry and up-welling memory had done their work. All her attempts at objectivity were going right down the tubes, and the old emotions were coming back like furious, hungry ghosts.

Gale looked up at her. His face was expressionless, but she knew she had struck a nerve. "Ransom," he muttered. He looked away for a moment, and then back again. His green eyes were hard as crystal. "Ransom. Keely has a relative, a psychologist of some sort—"

"Yes. Keely is my cousin. I've been looking for her

ever since that day in the gallery, when she seemed to drop off the face of the earth—"

Easy, Diana, she told herself. *Antagonism will get you nowhere.* Just because the same thing had happened to Clare before Adrian had abandoned her, just before she'd taken her own life . . .

It wasn't difficult to pretend earnestness as she leaned over the table, using her position above him to reinforce her authority. She stared into Gale's eyes, searching for signs of recognition or guilt. "I only want to talk to her. She hasn't even been to her apartment, and I need to know where she is. Family business." She breathed in slowly. "I know your relationship with her is between the two of you, but I see no reason why you've had to hide her away from her family and friends—"

"I didn't, Dr. Ransom." He was on his feet before she realized it, his face inches from her own. She caught her breath, leaning more heavily on the table, unable to look away from him.

"I didn't," he repeated quietly. "Keely and I are friends, but not in the way you're implying. I left town several weeks ago because she wanted our relationship to change." He looked directly into her eyes. "She wanted us to be lovers, and I—declined."

His gaze held hers for another long moment and then snapped away. As if at a silent command, the shaven-headed barkeep wandered over to the table, looking curiously from Nicholas to Diana.

"You rang?" she said to Nicholas, flicking one of several earrings with a black-painted fingernail.

Nicholas sat down slowly, ignoring Diana. "Barb, when was the last time you saw me in Mama Soma's?"

The young woman rolled her eyes thoughtfully. "A few weeks ago, I guess."

"And have you seen me anywhere else recently?"

"Well, as I told this lady here, once or twice as I was going home I saw you on the street with Keely. Haven't seen her here in a while, either."

Diana watched Gale's face. He was frowning now, a look of open puzzlement. "Are you certain it was me you saw her with, Barb?"

The woman wrinkled her nose and ran a hand over the smooth dome of her skull. "I don't know too many people who look like you, Nick," she said with a grin. "But it was kinda dark. . . ." She shrugged. "If it wasn't you, it had to be your twin." Someone called out behind her, and she winked at Nicholas. "Gotta run."

Nicholas muttered something and stared blankly at Diana. It was as if he looked right through her.

Diana gritted her teeth. She'd always considered herself a reasonably good judge of people—a very handy trait in her profession—but Nicholas Gale was an enigma. His bemusement seemed genuine. What possible reason could he have to deny his relationship with Keely, construct such an act to refute it, unless—

She had no chance to follow the wisp of thought. Nicholas leaned forward, and she found herself meeting his gaze, held fast by crystal green eyes.

"Did Keely ever mention the name of the man she was seeing?"

His voice was low and even, but his words held all the intensity of a roar. She shook her head. "No. That was why it was so hard to find you, Mr. Gale. No one at the gallery had been introduced to you either—"

"Because it wasn't me," he said. "I've already told you, Dr. Ransom. I wasn't here."

Cold, sourceless fear raced up Diana's spine. She fought it with anger. "*Do* you have a twin, then, Mr. Gale?" she snapped.

Her words echoed in Nicholas's ears, rebounding and gaining power with each mocking repetition, carrying him away. *A twin, a twin, a twin* . . .

The woman faded from his sight as he withdrew into memory. Back to another time and place.

He had stopped counting the years long ago, accepting the burden of guilt he would always carry. But he could never forget the day he had last seen that fallen angel's face.

Adrian.

Nicholas let the name settle into his mind. He hadn't spoken it, even inwardly, in all the time since he had condemned Adrian to eternal damnation.

A living death. He'd realized what it meant the day he left Adrian imprisoned deep in the earth, sealed away from the only thing that could keep him sane and whole. Mortal life force, forever denied him. . . .

There was no afterlife for their kind. So their mother had told them over two centuries ago. Elizabeth had met only a handful of their blood in her long life. She had never known what became of the rest, those who had vanished without a trace.

But she had learned, in the end, the hell that awaited their kind if they attempted to defy their inborn natures. If they were driven or forced to stop taking life essence from mortal men and women.

It was the hell to which Nicholas had sent his treacherous brother. A hell with no hope of redemption. Adrian could not have returned from his terrible exile.

"I don't know too many people who look like you, Nick—"

Impossible. Nicholas felt a chill in his heart that worked its way through his body, draining his strength like a long fast. His instincts responded, bringing him back to himself and to the source of warmth and life so close at hand.

For a moment the woman across the table was no more than a jumble of colors and heat and flaring life force. Nicholas struggled to focus on her face, on her stubborn, intelligent eyes.

He said the first thing that came into his head. "Do you have a first name, Dr. Ransom?"

She blinked at him, caught off guard and resentful of it. "I don't see what that has to do with Keely or where she is, Mr. Gale. That's all I'm interested in at the moment. If you—"

"Then we're back to where we started, Dr. Ransom. As it happens, I share your concern for Keely." He lost his train of thought for a moment, looking at the woman with her brittle control and overwhelming aura. He could almost hear the singing of her life force in the three feet of space between them.

He nearly reached out to touch her. Just to see what she would feel like, if that psychic energy would flow into him with so simple a joining. It had happened like that with Sarah sometimes.

He stopped his hand halfway across the table and clenched it carefully. She had never seen him move. "Since you seem to require proof that I'm not hiding Keely in a closet somewhere, I'll give it to you." Withdrawing his hand, he reached into his inner jacket pocket. He set the card on the table between them.

She stared down at it. "Proof?" she echoed.

"This is the name of the friend I was staying with in New York over the past several weeks. He can vouch for me, and direct you to others I did business with during that time."

The delicate skin of her neck shivered as she swallowed. Abruptly she snapped up the card and tucked it into the breast pocket of her blazer.

"What *is* your business, Mr. Gale?" she asked. The antagonism in her voice had grown muted, and there was a flicker of uncertainty in her eyes.

"I have many varied—interests," he said honestly. He smiled, and for a moment he loosed a tiny part of his hunter's power. "But my business and your first name don't have anything to do with Keely, do they?"

She stared at him and lifted a small hand to run her fingers through her short brown hair, effectively disordering the loose curls. That simple act affected Nicholas with unexpected power. He felt his groin tighten, a physical response he had learned to control and ignore long ago.

When was the last time? he asked himself. The last time he had lain with a woman, joined with her physically, taken some part of what he needed in the act of love?

Before he could blunt the thought his imagination slipped its bonds, conjuring up an image of this woman, her aura ablaze, naked and willing and fully conscious beneath him. Knowing what he was, giving and receiving without fear, as Sarah might have done before Adrian destroyed her . . .

"Diana."

"What?" Reality ripped through Nicholas, dispelling the erotic, impossible vision.

"My first name is Diana," she murmured.

Her face was flushed, as if she had seen the lust in his eyes. She was an attractive woman. Mortal men would pursue her, even blind to her aura as they must be. Did she look at him and observe only another predictable male response to be dissected with an analyst's detachment?

His hungers were not so simple. He would have given the world to make them so.

"Diana," he repeated softly. "Huntress, and goddess of the moon."

She wet her lips. "It's getting late, Mr. Gale—"

"*My* first name is Nicholas."

"Nicholas," she echoed, as if by rote. "I'll be making a few more inquiries about Keely. If you were serious about being concerned for her—"

"I was."

Diana twisted around in her chair and lifted a small, neat purse. "Here," she said, slipping a card from a silver case. "This is where you can reach me if you should hear from her."

Nicholas took the card and examined the utilitarian printing. *Diana Ransom, Ph.D. Licensed Psychologist. Individual psychotherapy. Treatment of depression, anxiety, phobias and related sleep disorders.*

Sleep disorders. Nicholas almost smiled at the irony of it. She could never cure his particular disorder. He looked up at her. "If you need to talk to me again, I'm here most nights. Or you may leave a message with Barb or one of the regulars. They'll make sure it gets to me."

"Then you don't plan to leave town in the next few days?" she asked with a touch of her former hostility.

His gaze was steady. "No, Diana. I'll make a few inquiries of my own."

They stared at each other. *Diana.* Was she a child of the night, as her name implied? Did she dream vivid dreams that he could enter as he could never enter her body? Or was she part of the sane and solid world of daylight, oblivious to the untapped power that sang in her aura like a beacon in darkness?

She was the first to look away. Hitching the strap of her purse higher on her shoulder, she rose. "Then I'll be going." She hesitated, slanting a look back at him with narrowed blue eyes. "Perhaps we'll see each other again—Nicholas."

He watched her walk away and up the stairs. Her words had held a warning. No promise, no hint of flirtation. With even a little effort he could have won her over. He could have learned more about her, perhaps enough to determine if she would be a suitable candidate to serve his needs. One glimpse of her aura was enough to tempt him almost beyond reason.

But she had affected him too deeply. He could not afford even the slightest loss of control with his dreamers. Emotional detachment was a matter of survival—his, and that of the women he touched by night.

Diana Ransom was something almost beyond his experience—except for Sarah. Remembering Sarah was enough to stop his futile fancies cold.

He would never sample the promise behind Diana Ransom's unremarkable façade, would never slip into her dreams and skim the abundance of energy that burned beneath her skin. Far less would he ever revive the old hope that had cost Sarah her life. . . .

As he had done a thousand times before, Nicholas schooled himself to detachment and consigned hope and memory to their familiar prisons. If he arranged matters correctly, he need never see Diana Ransom again.

And there was still Keely. Something was wrong, and though reason told him it could not be what the slight evidence suggested, he knew he couldn't let it go. If Keely had found someone to give her the human comfort he'd denied her, he wished her happiness. But if her cousin believed she was in trouble, if there was any chance at all that the impossible had happened . . .

Nicholas stood, pushing the chair against the wall behind him. He glanced at his watch. The sun would rise in a few hours. Too late to make the drive into the mountains

—he couldn't risk the massive drain on his energy that full sunlight would take from him. He'd have Judith look into the matter tomorrow, and plan the trip for sunset.

Insanity, he told himself. His heartbeat accelerated and he leaned heavily against the wall. He would go back as he hadn't done in a century, as he had always feared to do. The thought of what he might find turned his stomach and filled his body with a wasteful surge of adrenaline.

His weakness reminded him that he must feed—feed well this night, to replace what emotion had cost him. His regular dreamers would be safe, giving him just as much as he required and never upsetting the careful stability of his life with unwanted desire.

Not like Diana Ransom.

Nicholas pushed away from the wall and tossed a handful of bills onto the counter as he passed the bar. There were enough hours left in the night to do what he must, and in the morning—in the dim silence of his house —he would have all the time he needed to recover his discipline and prepare.

He remembered what a wise man had said to him once, a hundred and fifty years ago: *"There is no calamity greater than lavish desires. There is no greater guilt than discontentment. And there is no greater disaster than greed."*

He thought he had learned that lesson long ago.

Diana told herself that she had every reason to keep an eye on Nicholas Gale.

His references had checked out, as she had known they would. The "colleague" in New York had been more than happy to refer her to people Nicholas met with on the East Coast.

Who are you, Nicholas? she'd asked herself, remembering the way he'd avoided discussing what business kept him flying between coasts and hanging out at a place like Mama Soma's.

She shouldn't care who he was. In every way that counted, he'd convinced her—in practical terms, at least —that he wasn't the man she'd seen with Keely at the gallery. Even if it *was* strange that there could be two men in San Francisco who had the same looks, the same charisma. Two men who knew Keely.

But if she could trust her intuition and her newly resurrected dreams, Nicholas Gale was not entirely the uninvolved party he pretended to be.

She sat in her car on Folsom Street, staring at the nondescript, graffiti-marked doorway to Mama Soma's, her damp hands clutching the wheel. When her last client had left at six, she'd come directly here in search of Nicholas. And promptly lost her nerve.

She gave a short, dry laugh. What was she afraid of? Falling under Nicholas Gale's spell? She didn't even know the man.

If it hadn't been for the new dream, the one she'd had last night, she might have put Nicholas Gale out of her mind. Nicholas, with his crystalline eyes, his impassive, handsome features, had dominated the dream. And Keely had been in it as well, her face pale and drawn, mouth working in a soundless cry. The rest was a blur, except for an image of a rope that stretched between Keely and Nicholas, pulled taut and fraying. Someone else was there —an ominous masculine figure, someone she couldn't see —and she'd known that when the rope snapped it would hurl all four of them into the abyss.

The dream had a perfectly rational explanation. It could be analyzed in layers, from a statement of simple surface anxieties to deeper levels of the psyche. But Diana had been left with one overwhelming conviction.

Whatever he might claim, Nicholas had something to do with Keely's disappearance. Keely seemed to have vanished off the face of the earth—and she was in trouble. Diana was more certain of that than she'd ever been.

Could she dare to trust her dreams after so many years? Could she believe they were, once again, sending a warning she couldn't ignore?

Do I have any choice? she thought, leaning her head back against the seat with a sigh. And so here she was, watching the entrance to Mama Soma's and observing with a deliberately clinical eye the eclectic assortment of people wandering up and down the street in search of a Friday night's diversion.

She almost didn't see Nicholas come out. He stopped at the top of the stairs, a silhouette against the light pouring from the doorway, and vanished around the corner before she could start the car. She followed—slowly, carefully, hoping he wouldn't notice—as he hailed a taxi.

Somehow she wasn't surprised when Nicholas ended up on Seacliff Avenue, in one of San Francisco's most exclusive neighborhoods. He paid off the cabbie and disappeared into the house. Mansion would be an accurate description. In an area of substantial Spanish Colonial Revival houses with stucco walls and red tile roofs, and a smattering of more eclectic styles, his Neoclassical mansion drew the eye. The white, columned façade rose magestically above a neatly manicured lawn and sculpted shrubs; it was separated from the adjoining properties by a high wall punctuated with a wrought iron gate.

Diana cradled her chin in her hand, listening to the faint crash of surf at the bottom of the cliff that gave the area its name. So, along with a god's looks and charisma and enough fundamental sex appeal for any ten men, he was wealthy enough to afford a place like this.

She frowned and tossed her notepad to the car seat.

Sex appeal. She snorted. Simple attraction; no more, no less. Nicholas was an attractive man, just as his supposed look-alike had been. *It's human nature to feel attracted to the opposite sex.* She'd have to be dead not to react to a man like that, no matter how uninterested she was in any kind of romantic entanglement.

And she wasn't interested. Categorically. Her life was fine as it was, or it would be once things got back to normal. It *wasn't* that Clare's tragic experience had soured her on men. She had male friends and colleagues and clients, men she liked and respected. She just didn't *need* a man to be whole.

She forced her attention back to the object of her surveillance. Not one light had come on behind the high rectangular windows since Nicholas had gone through the porticoed front door. Did he spend his Friday nights alone in that big house? She didn't know what she was waiting for.

She shook her head. She was behaving childishly. Meeting Nicholas Gale had only aggravated a situation that had begun with the return of her old nightmare. One encounter with him had disposed of her normal composure with ridiculous ease. And she was no closer to resolving the meaning of the nightmare.

Biting her lip, Diana rolled down the window and looked up at the stars to the west above the ocean. The Indian summer warmth of the day had been replaced by an autumn chill. In less than an hour it would be midnight, and she would have spent the entire evening getting exactly nowhere.

With a sharp movement Diana grabbed her keys from the dashboard and jammed them into the ignition. Time to go home and face reality. Maybe, she thought grimly, she'd have another dream that would tell her what to do next. . . .

Her fingers froze on the key ring before she could turn on the engine. A dark silhouette moved behind the nearly invisible wrought iron of the closed gate in front of the house. The silent figure opened the gate and passed through, and the light from a street lamp skimmed across golden hair.

Diana shrank down and watched Nicholas walk to a dark van with tinted windows parked in the long driveway. He never looked in her direction.

When he pulled onto the street she was on his tail. There was something sinister about the van, its unrelieved black gliding almost silently through the darkness.

A few weeks ago Diana would have scoffed at the whim that made her track Nicholas Gale through the night, guided by intuition, dreams—and not a shred of evidence. But sometimes she needed intuition in her profession, as little as she liked to rely on it. Sometimes she had no choice but to accept the part of herself she'd hidden away so long ago.

It was that part of herself—the dreamer, the child of imagination—who followed the van as it moved out of the Richmond District and across the city, taking the freeway out of San Francisco. The bay was a vast, ebony pool edged by light; the upper deck of the Bay Bridge seemed to press down on Diana with the all the weight of dark foreboding.

Or a nightmare.

Diana knew, as the van merged on to Interstate 80 headed northeast, that she would not sleep at all that night.

THREE

—

The fire which seems extinguished often slumbers beneath the ashes.
　　　　　　　　　—Pierre Corneille, *Rodogune*

A thousand things had changed in the century since Nicholas had been in the Sierra foothills of Nevada County.

There were paved freeways in place of the old dirt roads, cars in place of horse-drawn vehicles, retirees and land developers in place of miners, ghost towns—the remnants of once-booming gold towns—eclipsed by new cities sprawling along the highway.

But much remained the same. Nicholas's more-than-human night vision took in the changeless rolling hills sweeping up from valleys studded with blue oak and chaparral. By day the trees would still be gold and brown with turning leaves, falling to scatter over dry grass and red earth. The sky would be a blue more brilliant than that of the city. In the old days his work at the mine had forced him into the sunlight on occasion, and he had carried those memories with him for over a century.

Nicholas turned the van away from the main highway and on to the narrow, winding road that would take him deeper into the foothills. Douglas fir and ponderosa pine replaced oak and chaparral; steeper cliffs rose up to cradle the road, and signs of habitation became sparse. Even after so long, this was still untamed country. When most of the easily accessible ore had been played out, men in search of fast wealth and glory had passed on, leaving the wilderness behind.

But some had stayed, like Sarah—tragic Sarah, who had died because of an immortal's jealousy and greed.

Adrian.

Lost in memory, Nicholas almost missed the dirt road that turned off into the forest. The sign that had stood at the crossroads had long since vanished.

But Nicholas remembered the way. He'd never fenced off this part of the land; better to leave it open for those whose curiosity led them down deserted pathways.

He parked the van and got out, drawing in a deep breath of mountain air. The stars were incredibly vivid here; if his nature had permitted he might have spent all his time in places like this, where even immortality seemed inconsequential in the vast face of heaven.

Nicholas laughed softly at himself. *Poetry was always Adrian's province.* The thought sobered him instantly.

It was only fitting that he was forced to confront the thing he most dreaded. For a century he'd avoided this place, unable to face the memories and the guilt.

Now he had no choice.

The high barbed wire fence was still intact, and the locks were relatively new. He'd seen to that much. The gate squealed on rusty hinges as he pushed it open.

Nicholas moved easily over the rough terrain, silent as the predator he was. He needed no source of light other than the stars. Small night creatures went still as he passed; it was the profound quiet that made the single sharp sound of a snapping twig echo like a gun blast through the forest.

He froze, staring back the way he had come.

"Damn."

The muttered oath came from the top of the ridge. A beam of light sliced the air. Nicholas reached out with his senses and felt her presence just before she appeared at the edge of the sharp drop. She caught sight of him, opened her mouth for a second oath, and lost her balance.

Diana rolled to a stop at the foot of the hill and knew immediately that she hadn't come through unscathed.

A noose of pain tightened around her ankle, provoking a gasp as she tried to get her feet under her. She looked up at the towering silhouette of Nicholas Gale.

"Damn," she repeated under her breath.

Nicholas came toward her, no more than a shadow against the stars. Diana's heart leaped into her throat. Her unwelcome imagination had been working double time since she'd followed Nicholas to this deserted place. Now he stood over her with clenched fists, his expression masked in darkness. Everything in the set of his body shouted threat.

The flashlight lay just out of reach where it had fallen from her hand, ineffectually aimed at dirt and grass. Her imagination sparked images of night-stalking phantoms. Only Nicholas's eyes were visible: glittering like a wild animal's, a glow she'd never seen in the eyes of a human being.

He bent down to reach for her, and her panic-stricken blows slid off the leather of his jacket without drawing a sound from him. He caught her wrists with bewildering ease as he dropped into a crouch before her.

"Are you hurt?" he demanded. His voice was a rough growl, nothing like the cultured purr she had heard before.

Diana looked away from his eyes and down to the hands that trapped hers. She had thought them elegant hands in Mama Soma's, warm ivory skin dusted with silky golden hair, but now she felt their strength. She felt *him*. Sensation stabbed through her, dispelling everything else in its wake.

His hands were not merely warm. They were made of fire molded to human shape, licking at her skin and nerves and burning into the bone. Heat swept through her body like a fever. A weakness came over her, a drowsiness that dulled the pain in her ankle and made her long for sleep. . . .

She snapped to attention when he jerked his hands away, rocking back on his heels just out of reach.

"Are you hurt?" he repeated.

Bracing her hands behind her, she pushed up. Her ankle sagged under her weight as she stood and tested it gingerly. "I'm fine," she said shortly. *An absurd answer,* she reflected, any hint of humor driven from her thoughts by the look on Nicholas Gale's face and his imposing height as he got to his feet.

"Why did you follow me?" he asked in an edged whisper.

She had no ready answer. She'd never meant for him to see her at all. Until she'd been stupid enough to fall down a hillside and land right at his feet.

He smiled unpleasantly at her silence. "May I offer a guess as to what was going through your mind, Dr. Ransom? My efforts to convince you that I haven't seen Keely weren't successful. It's apparently my misfortune to resemble someone you feel has less than honorable designs on Keely, even though she's a young woman well able to take care of herself. For some reason you decided that I was lying, and felt it necessary to—observe me." He shook his head. "Your devotion to your cousin is admirable, Doctor."

His eyes glittered with a strange, mocking light. Diana balled her fists, struggling to find a response.

"Having decided that I was the prime suspect in Keely's supposed disappearance," he continued relentlessly, "you followed me here. And a thousand lurid possibilities ran through your mind. Could I, perhaps, have spirited Keely away, to be held captive in this wilderness? Or would I lead you to her body?"

The blunt statement of Diana's craziest suspicions gave them a ring of such absurdity that she almost dropped her eyes. She tilted her chin up instead, but he wasn't finished.

"A pity you didn't have any proof but supposition," he continued softly, folding his hands behind his back. "The police wouldn't have anything to go on. . . ."

"That's enough." Diana took a step forward and nearly lost her balance as her ankle cramped with pain. Nicholas reached for her and she flinched away. "You're right, Gale. Your references checked out, but I—" She swallowed. How could she tell this stranger that she'd dreamed he was involved in ways he wasn't admitting? When she had no solid reason to trust her own dreams, after so many years without their guidance? "I had reason to believe that you weren't telling the whole truth."

"Ah." Nicholas tilted his head and looked her up and

down. "Reason." His gaze grew distant. " 'The sleep of reason produces monsters. . . .' "

A drawing she'd seen once flashed into her mind: a man in the costume of the previous century, his head in his arms, bent asleep over a table while fantastic creatures —monstrous bats and owls—floated above his head.

"Goya," she murmured. Nicholas glanced at her sharply.

"You recognize the title?" he said, lifting one eyebrow. "But that shouldn't come as a surprise. The drawing does have interesting psychological significance."

Diana wanted to laugh. She shivered instead. This conversation was more than crazy—standing here in a dark forest with a twisted ankle, talking to a man who fascinated her for no good reason, who might be the very kind of predatory male she most despised, or worse. . . .

She sucked in a deep breath. "You know why I followed you," she said at last. "Why did you come here tonight—Nicholas?"

The smile left his face, and the sculpted planes and hollows of finely molded flesh and bone seemed eerily inhuman in the faint starlight. "This is my property, Dr. Ransom. If I choose to come here in the middle of the night, it's my privilege. My business is private."

He lifted his head as if scenting the cool predawn wind. Abruptly he shrugged out of his expensive leather jacket and draped it over his arm.

"It's fortunate that I'm not what your overactive imagination has suggested." The corner of his mouth lifted. "If I should ever need the services of a psychologist, I will let you know."

Turning on his heel, he started away, booted feet almost soundless among the fallen pine needles. Diana found her voice before he'd gone more than a few yards.

"Wait a minute. Where are you—"

Nicholas turned back in time to see her attempt a step and wince in pain. He almost felt sympathy for her, and hardened his heart against it. She'd brought this on herself with her interference. She hadn't had the sense to leave him alone, keep far away from him. . . .

His anger faded as he studied her. The tailored trousers and blazer were crumpled and smudged from her tumble down the hillside, and her hair was tangled with twigs and dead leaves, but she had managed to keep her dignity.

At least she had sense enough to be afraid. Her aura betrayed her, flickering and flaring around her like an uncertain flame. He hoped he wouldn't find it necessary to use more effective means of driving her away. The one time he had touched her had nearly been his undoing.

"Are you going to leave me alone out here?" she asked evenly.

He glanced at the jacket over his arm. "Only temporarily, Doctor. The weather is mild for this time of year." He walked back to her and tossed her the jacket. She caught it awkwardly and hugged it in her arms. "Make yourself a nest of leaves and try to sleep. I'll be back before dawn."

He left her then, ignoring her choked protest. His mind was already moving ahead, to what he would find when he reached the abandoned mine.

He stopped when he caught sight of it. There were still twisted bits of track and half-buried ties along the bottom of the ravine. The portal of the tunnel was buried under fallen rock and intertwined foliage; small trees that clung to the side of the steep, rocky hill concealed the wooden support timbers.

Nicholas breathed deeply. To all appearances the mine hadn't been touched. He crouched in front of the entrance and began to pull away the loose stones and brush, making an opening big enough for him to enter. The ground around the portal looked stable enough to hold during the brief time he'd be in the tunnel. He wouldn't be staying long.

He would know the truth in an instant.

The air in the tunnel was rank with the scent of small animals and bitter memories. Nicholas plunged into utter blackness. Only his inhuman night vision enabled him to find the way.

Adrian's prison was some distance down the gently sloping adit. At last his searching eyes found the heavy slab he had placed over the cavern entrance in the tunnel wall so long ago. It was no longer in place, but pushed to the side and half-fallen. The fine hairs rose along his arms and the nape of his neck. He fought off a wave of nausea and took the final steps.

The heavy brick wall built across the narrowest portion of the cavern seemed intact until his meticulous inspection revealed the breach.

His heart stopped beating. His legs were weighted with lead, as if he hadn't fed for a fortnight. The stale air grew thin and harsh in his lungs.

He moved forward and stopped in midstep as his foot struck something that rolled away with a hollow rattle.

It was a human skull. Picked clean, almost perfectly preserved.

"Fool," he whispered. "You fool."

"My God."

He spun, and the beam of Diana's flashlight caught him full in the face. Her eyes were wide, her lips parted, and even here Nicholas could see that her skin was drained of color. She angled the flashlight down to wash the skull in an eerie nimbus.

"My God," she repeated. She stumbled back, and Nicholas went for her without thinking. He was not gentle when he took her arm and yanked her against him, dragging her away from the cavern entrance.

Her fear leaped through him, almost overpowering his awareness of her incredible vitality. He drove her from his senses and ignored her gasp of pain as he pulled her down with him into a crouch and took the flashlight from her hand, sweeping the beam of light across the opening in the brick wall.

The heavy manacles lay on the ground within the chamber, broken and empty.

Adrian was gone.

Diana's icy flesh was no colder than his own soul at that moment, as he understood the magnitude of what had happened. What he had *allowed* to happen.

Adrian had escaped. There had been one witness—one mortal witness—to that escape, and he hadn't lived to tell what he had found.

"Fool," he repeated savagely. Diana jerked in his grasp, and he almost released her. He wanted to hurl her away, curse all her kind for the vulnerability they were born with. The mortal fragility that could not withstand the unleashed hunger of his kind.

But he held her close, deliberately cruel. "I underestimated you, Diana," he said, his lips moving against her soft hair. "Your curiosity overcame both pain and common sense. What do you think you've found?" He closed his eyes and breathed in her scent. "The lair of a killer? Do you think there might be other bodies here, hidden away until the flesh falls from the bones?"

Her shudder vibrated through him. "Keely—" she gasped.

"No, Diana. Keely isn't here, and never has been. There are no other bodies, none but that poor devil who chose the wrong place to do his exploring."

He stood and kept her with him, sweeping the walls

of the cavern a final time. "What is this place?" she whispered.

She couldn't see his bitter smile in the darkness. "A place that no human being should ever have discovered. A place where the past was buried and should have been left in peace."

If he had been less numb he might have considered now what he would do about Diana. She had seen just enough; a woman like her wouldn't be content to let a mystery lie. But Diana was only a part of the problem he faced. How long had Adrian been free? What had he become after what Nicholas had done to him, after such a terrible imprisonment?

Diana had seen Keely with a man who looked exactly like Nicholas.

So easily was his carefully balanced life thrown into chaos. This was the price he paid for risking involvement with mortals beyond what he must have to survive.

Sarah. Keely. And now Diana, whose very presence was exquisite torture.

If Diana spoke he was deaf to her words. He took her with him from the cavern and hesitated in the tunnel, staring bleakly at the rock slab that had failed to make any difference at all. After a moment he let Diana go and pushed it back into place. He could hear her ragged breathing behind him. Her feet scuffled on fallen rock, and he turned.

"Wait," he said sharply as she backed away. The flashlight in his hand captured an expression of primitive terror on her face. He advanced on her slowly, meaning to reassure, but she continued to retreat.

The tunnel was narrow, and Diana was utterly blind. Nicholas heard her sharp expulsion of breath as she hit the timber-braced wall.

"Diana," he breathed. "Stop where you are. This is

an old mine, and the timbers are half-rotten. They could give way with the slightest jolt."

"Stay back," she said in a flat, low voice.

With a soft curse, Nicholas flicked off the flashlight and adjusted his sight to its most acute. "I won't hurt you, Diana." He raised his hand in entreaty, as if she could see the gesture. She shifted again, jerking against the timbers at her back, and then there was no more time to think.

The timbers were already falling as he reached her, swung her up in his arms, and hurled her away. His head and shoulders felt the shattering pain as a weight of wood and earth rained down from above.

As the last echoes of the collapse faded in the tunnel he found himself on his side, one arm trapped beneath him and one leg twisted at an impossible angle. For a long moment he could see or hear nothing at all.

He spat dirt from his mouth and tasted blood. "Diana," he croaked. A scrape of movement rang in his ears. He repeated her name in a whisper, imagining her fragile, mortal body broken like a porcelain doll.

"Nicholas?"

Her voice was small as a child's, but free of pain. Nicholas closed his eyes and hissed as broken ribs protested his efforts to breathe.

"I'm here, Diana. Are you hurt?"

The scraping came again, and after a moment he could sense her near him, feel her warmth like a fire on his cooling body.

"I can't see you," she said. She sounded calm, unafraid—now, in the face of disaster. "I'm following the sound of your voice." Stones rattled; her breath caught. "Say something, anything—"

In a haze of shock, Nicholas laughed. "Shouldn't you be—going the other way?" he rasped.

There was no reply, but a moment later he knew Diana was beside him, close enough to touch if he'd been able to move.

"Are you—" He felt dirt shift around him as her hands reached blindly, found the beams that pinned him to the ground. "Dear God," she whispered. Her fingers brushed his exposed arm, touching flesh where the shirt had torn away. "You're bleeding—"

"A—minor consideration," he said. "What about you?"

The sound she made could only just be called a laugh. "Unscathed, except for the ankle—"

"Which I thought would prevent you from following me."

She was silent. Nicholas could clearly imagine the thoughts running through her head. He was almost grateful for the beams that kept him from touching her.

But *she* was still free. Her fingers, warm and pulsing with life, were suddenly on his face. Brushing across his cheek, his eyelids, his forehead, stroking back his damp hair. It could have been no more than blind groping, but it felt achingly like a caress.

Nicholas closed his eyes. To feel a woman's touch— he had not allowed himself that pleasure in over a century. Now he was helpless to prevent it. And Diana's touch was unlike any he had experienced in all his life. Except Sarah's.

Sarah. Adrian escaped . . . He tried to concentrate on the current danger, but Diana's nearness made that impossible. Her heartbeat was piercingly audible to his augmented senses. Her pulse accelerated as her hands left his face and began to move searchingly back down the length of his body.

Burning pain seared through his leg at her gently probing touch, driving every coherent thought from his mind. Diana jerked her hand away.

"You're trapped," she said hoarsely. "Your leg—" He saw the vague silhouette of her shape move over him. He braced himself for more pain, but her touch was meticulously gentle. "I can't see anything. Can you move at all?"

"Not at the moment." The damage to his leg and his right arm was very clearly delineated in his mind. He wasn't going to be able to free himself, or get them both out of this predicament, without exhausting his minimal store of life force.

And if he should become desperate enough . . .

"How bad is it?"

Diana's soft question was not that of a woman who feared for her life. He remembered his last glimpse of her face, frozen in terror. He had nothing to go on now but her voice.

He made no effort to dissemble. "My right leg is broken, and one of my arms. My spine seems to be intact. Blood loss is minimal, but—" he coughed, and his cracked ribs felt like white-hot bands around his lungs. "It may be somewhat difficult to get out from under all of this."

"Damn." Nicholas heard Diana shift, settling down beside him. She swallowed. "I'm sorry."

Nicholas angled his head carefully toward her. Gravel bit into his cheek. "Sorry?"

"This is my fault," she said heavily. "If I hadn't panicked and brought the tunnel down on our heads, this wouldn't have happened."

Choking on a laugh, Nicholas caught his breath. "A justifiable response, given what you thought—think—I was up to."

Silence hung between them, as profound as the darkness. No denials from Diana, for all her words of regret.

Bitter anger rose in Nicholas, fueled by pain and helplessness.

"Whatever you may think of me, Diana, you haven't anything to fear now. I dropped your flashlight just before the timbers collapsed. Try to find it. Even in full daylight this tunnel will be pitch dark. With the flashlight you may be able to see if there's a way out."

Her breathing quickened. "I may bring the rest of the mine down on our heads."

"There's always that possibility," he conceded, "but the alternative is even less pleasant."

He didn't need to elaborate. It didn't matter that she would never guess his true meaning. Without a word she began to move away, scattering stones as she felt her way across the tunnel floor.

In the moments that followed, Nicholas withdrew deeply into himself. Diana's warmth was there, just beyond his reach, just distant enough to push aside. If he could gather his energy, use every means he had ever learned to channel and control it, mend his body just enough to work free and find them a way out—

"I found it!"

A brilliant shaft of light cut triumphantly through the darkness. Nicholas altered his sight as the beam splashed over his body and moved to his face.

Instantly the light flicked away, painting a path across the tunnel floor for Diana to follow. He could see her now: oval face smudged and bruised, hair coated with dust, once-immaculate trousers and blazer stained beyond salvation.

He had never wanted a woman more than he wanted Diana in that moment. Even the anticipation of touching her, drawing from her, was enough to make the pain recede.

She crawled to her knees beside him, raking his body

with the light. Her soft oath was heartfelt. Careful to aim the beam away from his eyes, she studied his face.

Her hand came out as if to touch him again and withdrew. Nicholas could see the glitter of her eyes, hidden once and again as she blinked. "I'm not a medical doctor," she said, "but I may be able to make you more comfortable. If I'm strong enough to get some of this junk off you . . ." She gathered her legs under her and started to rise.

Nicholas stopped her with a harsh laugh. "That makes very little sense, Diana," he said. "You won't be able to help me unless you get out of here. Take the flashlight and search for an opening in the rubble, anything you can widen. Use your energy on something useful."

She stood over him, hands on her hips, like the goddess whose name she bore. "And leave you here alone, in pain?"

"You were running before, Diana. From me, if you recall. Find a way out and you'll be safe. You can send someone back for me—and go to the police." He smiled unpleasantly. "Remember Keely. Remember what you saw in the cave—"

"You saved my life."

The words were said in a whisper, but they were unequivocal. She folded her arms across her chest and stared down at him.

Nicholas tried to move, to twist his head in order to see her face, and endured a fiery lance of pain. "Is that sufficient proof that I'm not involved in Keely's disappearance, that I'm not—whatever you thought I was?"

"You said I had an overactive imagination, and you were right," she said. "I thought I had that under control a long time ago."

"You seem reasonably intelligent," he said hoarsely, "Find a way out of here and go for help. Otherwise—"

She dropped her hands from her hips. Lifting her chin, she tossed her bangs free of her eyes. "You're right, of course." And then she smiled—tremulously but warmly, transforming her weary, serious expression. Nicholas closed his eyes against the brilliance of it.

He listened to her walk away. Her footsteps echoed back to him, telling him exactly how far she went—first toward the entrance, and then, minutes later, past him to the rear of the tunnel.

When she returned she crouched beside him, her movements slow and stiff. The flashlight dangled from her fingers.

"It's no use. The tunnel is completely blocked." She rubbed the palm of her hand over her forehead. "There's no way out."

Clenching his free hand into a fist, Nicholas focused on her face. Her dark lashes swept down to brush the curve of her cheek; she trembled, and Nicholas trembled with her. Her weariness, her discouragement reached into him like a spectral hand to clutch at his heart.

"I'm going to have to try to free you," she said at last. The briskness of her voice hid any trace of doubt or fear. "I think I can do it if I'm careful. I'll have to work slowly." The flashlight beam skimmed over Nicholas. "Let me know if anything I do hurts you. Once I have you free, I'll see about setting your arm and leg."

Rigging the flashlight against a rock so that the beam illuminated the area where Nicholas lay, Diana bent over the pile of rubble and wood.

Nicholas let his head drop back to the ground. As Diana began to scrape away the top layer of dirt and rock, Nicholas felt resolve slip away as surely as his ebbing life force. At this moment he was no match for a small mortal woman and her suicidal determination.

He let her work in silence, hoarding his strength. One

by one she removed the smaller stones and splinters of wood, working free the larger pieces and tossing them into the darkness. By the time she had reached the broken timbers closest to his body she was breathing heavily. Her hands gripped the topmost timber and Nicholas heard her soft gasp of pain as she lost her balance under its weight.

"Diana," he said hoarsely. "You can't—"

"Almost there," she breathed. She managed to push the beam away and struggled with the next. Nicholas felt a shift in the rubble pinning his legs, and the weight suddenly grew heavier, grinding his bones together. He made no sound, but Diana stopped suddenly. A rattle of small stones cascaded down around Nicholas's head.

"Damn," she whispered. "This beam is stuck, and when I pull on it—"

A second wave of pebbles followed the first, and this time there was no mistaking the ominous movement in the timbers that trapped Nicholas and those that remained precariously upright along the tunnel wall.

"I can't," Diana said. She backed away and stood staring at the wall, limned in eerie light. "If I try to move anything else, it may all come down." She dropped to the ground beside Nicholas, drawing her legs against her chest. Dark hair obscured her face as she pressed it to her knees.

Nicholas tested the weight on his arms and legs. With a slight effort he was able to free his uninjured arm. "Diana," he said.

She looked up. "I'm sorry, Nicholas." The despair in her voice was thready with exhaustion.

He had moved his hand within touching distance of her foot before he stopped himself. One touch was all it would take to taste her life force, to begin to draw. . . . His fingers dug into the dirt.

"You did what you could, Diana."

He felt—far too much of what she felt. He felt her as if a bond had been established between them, as if he had already skimmed her life force. A moment ago he'd cursed his sensitivity to Diana, the vitality within her that drew him like a moth to a flame. But now that vitality might make it possible to do what he must to save them both.

It would be the greatest test he had faced since his time with Sarah. Then he had been seeking mortality through the abundance and power of Sarah's life force; now he sought only a means of survival.

When he drew from his dreamers in sleep he was never near starvation as he was now—never in pain and desperate need of healing. He took only what he needed to sustain life from day to day. But now he must take enough life force from Diana to enable him to heal himself, augment his normal strength to work free.

Adrian had done that as a matter of course, reveling in his superhuman power. He had seldom bothered to take life force only when his victims slept; he stole it from them waking, when the danger to mortals was far greater, drawing it out rather than skimming the excess. Sometimes he had taken what he wanted in the most direct and deadly way—through the act of sex.

As he had done with Sarah.

Nicholas closed his eyes. That, at least, was beyond his power, a temptation he could resist. He could make Diana sleep, hurry the onset of her dreams.

She hadn't been strong enough to free him, but she *must* be strong enough to give him what he needed. If, in his hunger, he drew too much, too quickly—

His fists clenched, stretching tendons to the point of pain. He felt his life force flicker dangerously low, like a guttering candle. Years of discipline could be undone in an instant of miscalculation. He could still destroy her, driven by instinct, by the need that made him akin to the vampires of legend. Diana would as surely die without her life force as she would drained of blood. Or she would be left with just enough to go on a few days or weeks, only half-alive, unable to sleep until her body surren-dered. . . .

But he had no choice. In time the madness would come on him, as it had once claimed his mother, and he would have no rational mind left to control the act at all.

No choice? He mocked himself. *You want her, and now you must take her.* . . .

"Diana," he said softly. "You're too tired to do any-thing more now. You need rest—"

"How can I rest knowing you're in pain, perhaps badly hurt?"

"Because you won't be any good to either one of us if you're dead on your feet." He stretched his fingers flat on the ground, reaching as far as he could. She seemed not to notice. "I'm hardly dying, Diana. A few hours of sleep—"

She looked up at him suddenly, her eyes gone very wide. "Sleep?" she whispered. She tossed back her head. "In this place?"

The words quivered with wry humor, but Nicholas understood there was more behind them. She had hidden her fear well since the accident, but now, as she looked at him, he could see it cold and silent within her.

"Are you afraid of the dark, Diana?" he asked softly.

Her jaw went taut. "Afraid of the dark? Don't you think we both have more important things to be con-cerned about?"

"That isn't what I asked."

She blinked rapidly, as if to clear her eyes of dust. "Do I seem afraid to you, Nicholas?" she asked with forced calm. "Do I seem like a fearful child looking for monsters in the closet?"

Nicholas felt his heart clench. "Perhaps, sometimes, there *are* monsters in the closet."

She laughed hoarsely. "The monsters in the subconscious mind? Oh, yes. I should know all about those." Raising the flashlight, she scanned the tunnel walls and floor from one end to the other, as far as the light could reach. "What would you think of a psychologist who's afraid of what lies in the shadows?"

"I'd think she was—human."

Human, as he was not. Diana couldn't guess the things that went through his mind as she spoke. Monsters, darkness and shadows—they were not mere symbols to him.

But Diana didn't know his thoughts. She turned the flashlight so that the edge of the beam brushed his face.

"Most people expect their therapists to be above all that," she said with a weary smile. "Closer to perfect, somehow. Maybe most of us try to be flawless—in control, detached, rational—but it doesn't quite work."

Perfection. Perfect control, perfect detachment, freedom from illness and death. Mortals sought the latter, which he had been given at birth without asking. And he had spent his life striving for control and detachment, the same qualities that Diana most prized.

"I am—afraid of the dark."

Diana's soft statement pulled Nicholas back from his thoughts. She shifted, squirming like a child caught in a lie, but her gaze was direct on his.

"It's ridiculous, really," she said. "When I was a very young child, I was afraid of those monsters in the shadows. The experts told my parents that my imagination was unusually vivid. I outgrew it as I got older—" She stopped, as if she'd touched on a subject she could not bear to examine. "Most children do. I learned how to dismiss those monsters. But one day something happened—" Again she broke off, shaking her head almost violently. "One day the fear came back."

Nicholas closed his eyes. *The fear came back.* His fears, like hers, were being resurrected one by one.

"We're all afraid of something, Diana," he said.

"Even you, Nicholas?" She moved closer, resting her weight on her hand. Her fingers nearly touched his. "What are you afraid of?"

He was silent a long while. He understood what she needed—reassurance that he was as human as she was. That they were the same, trapped together in the dark.

"We aren't so different, Diana," he said at last. "Isn't the fear of darkness akin to the fear of being alone?"

She moved her fingers on the ground, and they brushed his. The contact was like a jolt of lightning that passed directly to his heart. Under the rubble his loins hardened as they had done the first time he'd met Diana, responding to his instinctive hunger.

Diana's fingers quivered. He closed his fist to trap her hand in his, basking in the sudden absence of pain, the pulse of her psychic essence that lay just beyond his reach.

He could not wait much longer.

"Diana," he murmured. He looked up at her, stroking the softness of her palm with his thumb. "You must sleep."

She stared at the movement of his thumb as if mesmerized. Her tongue darted out to wet her lips. "I— can't . . ."

It would have been better if he could let her take the time she needed to find sleep on her own. Exhaustion would overcome her fear eventually. But the longer he waited, the more he would need to take from her. He couldn't afford the risk.

He tuned his voice like a fine instrument, making it as soft and persuasive as a lullaby.

"You must sleep. You won't be alone in the dark, Diana. I'll be here with you."

Dark lashes dropped over her eyes. "I can't sleep," she protested thickly.

"You can, Diana. Sleep will bring answers. Sleep will make the world new again."

"Answers . . ." Diana dropped her chin to her chest. "So many questions . . ."

"Come here, Diana. Come to me."

She resisted. She blinked, tried to focus on his face, but her body wanted what he offered. It needed little of his influence. And her heart wanted the comfort he could give.

"Come," he coaxed, and she came, stretching out on the cold tunnel floor beside him. He bent his arm to gather her small, warm body against his chest. She was everything beautiful and human, soothing his pain like a healing goddess. He stroked her hair and watched her eyes flutter closed.

"Sleep," he whispered.

And she slept.

At first it was dark, and cold. Diana shivered—alone, isolated, knowing she was the last of her kind on the earth.

The cave was her only sanctuary. Outside were predators, circling in silent vigilance. She knew they were waiting—waiting for her to venture from the cave, to expose her small naked body to their claws and fangs.

She had never been so afraid. Here she was safe, but there was no light. No future, no hope. To win free she must leave her sanctuary. She would have to walk out into the night, with nothing but her own determination to shield her.

I can't, she thought, hugging her arms tight against

her body. *I can't.* But even as she heard the howl of some long-fanged beast beyond the cave's entrance, she knew she had no choice.

Her legs nearly gave way as she rose, levering herself up with her hands. The hard rocky floor was frigid on the soles of her feet. The small hairs rose along her neck. Icy wind whipped about her like a cloak of sorrow.

The mouth of the cave was darkness on darkness, but she knew exactly where it was. She walked out to the edge and looked down.

The beasts that lay in wait were invisible, but the ominous whisper of their paws came unceasingly to her straining ears.

"I know you're there," she said. Her voice echoed, and the beasts fell silent. "I know you're waiting, but you won't find me easy prey. Do you hear me? I'm strong. I can beat you—"

There was no answer but the bitter soughing of the wind. Diana lifted her chin and stepped off the lip of the cave.

She fell. Her body spun helplessly into an abyss, blacker even than the cave. A scream caught in her throat. Her arms and legs flailed for something, anything to hold on to.

A strange calmness came over her then. *I don't have to fall,* she thought. The thoughts took shape in her mind, became the one solid thing in her universe. *I don't have to fall, when I can fly. . . .*

And she flew. Her arms arced to hold the air, her legs moved to control her spin. Her plunge began to slow. The air, that had been so cold, began to warm. It slid across her naked skin, soft puffs of breeze that coiled about her body. Warmer, and warmer still. She looked down, and there was light below, a bottom to the abyss—red light, formless and intense.

Red. Red as blood, red as fire, red as passion. The heat grew, and Diana spread her arms wide to stop her flight.

She had been cold in the cave, but she could no longer imagine an absence of warmth. Below her the red light seethed, calling her and repelling her, tempting her to dive into the flames like a sacrifice to an ancient, hungry god.

Afraid. She was still afraid. There was something in that fire that wanted her, wanted everything she was and could be. The flames would consume her utterly. She might be reborn in the ashes, or she might be lost forever.

"Diana. Come to me."

The voice rose from the blazing pool, deep and seductive. She knew it for the voice of the god—a god of primeval forces, barbaric and untamed. A god of fire. She could not see him, but like the beasts outside the cave she knew he was there.

Her body throbbed in answer to his words, a deep ache that began at the core of her womanhood and spread like liquid gold to the farthest reaches.

"Come."

He would be her lover. Before he consumed her, he would love her as she had never been loved. She would know ecstasy in his fiery arms, such ecstasy as would make her sacrifice worthwhile.

What use have you for ecstasy, Diana? she asked herself, staring down until the whole world was fire. *You will be destroyed.* And she remembered someone she had loved who had flung herself into that fire and never returned.

There is only pain in that warmth, she told herself. But the voice rose again, molten with desire.

"Come to me, Diana. Give me what I must have."

She shivered, as if the god had already begun to caress her willing body. Oh yes, she wanted that. She wanted his hands to stroke her, his mouth to burn hers, his tongue to invade her most intimate places.

But that is forbidden. It is death. . . .

She still had a choice. It came to her that she could choose, now, whether to fly back up to the cold and lonely heights or fling herself into the crucible of fire. Once she had made that choice, there would be no going back.

As she hovered on the brink, the fire beneath her coalesced. It took shape, tongues of flame molding themselves into human form. The being that rose toward her was beautiful as fire is beautiful, hot and untamed, a force of nature come to life.

"Do you want the fire, Diana?" he asked. She knew his voice, but his face remained a blur in her sight, too bright to look upon. She could see his body clearly—powerful, long legs and arms, perfectly sculpted muscle and tendon. And his hunger for her—unmistakable to her eyes—was as potent as the rest of him.

He would enter her body. He would take her, lancing deep and hard and hot. She wanted to be taken. Oh, she wanted to let go.

He rose to hover before her, not quite touching. His hands lifted, extended toward her, and she felt her skin contract from his heat.

"Give yourself to me, Diana," he said.

She closed her eyes and stepped into his arms.

Pleasure surged through her, more intense than any she had ever known. There was no pain, no searing agony. Jolts of sensual energy set her nerves alight. Erotic fire licked her body on every side, stroking her hardened nipples and the softness between her thighs. She shuddered again and again, gasping and crying aloud, as the god took possession of her.

Completion came as a flare of light so brilliant that it

obliterated the darkness. She felt herself flying up, borne on wings of passion. Her body was wrapped in the brilliant feathers of the phoenix, a creature of limitless beauty and power, born anew from the ashes. She burst, whole and free, from the abyss. Her lover's voice rose soft and sated from behind her.

"It is enough."

But she paid no heed and flew higher and higher, until a new fire lay before her: the sun, source of life itself. The heat seared her feathers, but she felt no fear. Not until her wings caught fire and she knew she had flown too far.

She fell like a stone, and the darkness that swallowed her up was absolute.

FOUR

—

Sometimes a thousand twangling instruments
Will hum about mine ears; and sometimes
   voices,
That, if I then had wak'd after long sleep,
Will make me sleep again.
        —William Shakespeare, *The Tempest*

Diana woke with a start, a silent cry of half-remembered fear locked in her throat.

She sat up in bed, pushing her hair away from her face. Tendrils of it, damp with perspiration, clung stubbornly to her forehead.

What an amazing dream.

Diana shoved the tangled covers away from her legs and lay very still, trying to hold on to the images in her mind.

Sunlight splashed across Diana's face through the window blinds, but its brilliance felt strangely out of place. She remembered darkness. That had been the last thing in the dream. And before that—she squeezed her eyes shut.

It came back slowly. There had been darkness, and fear. Suddenly she sat up, arrested by the details she was only beginning to recall.

Nicholas Gale.

For a few moments the line between the dream and reality blurred. The dream had been that convincing. If she hadn't known better, she would have believed that she'd driven out into the Sierras in pursuit of Nicholas Gale and spent a number of hours trapped in a mine with him.

Diana let out her breath slowly, wondering at the emotions that flitted through her mind, too elusive to hold and examine.

In many ways the dream seemed more real than what she'd actually done that weekend. She'd gone home Friday night frustrated after her talk with Nicholas Gale, checked up on his references, and come to the conclusion that he wasn't the man she'd seen with Keely after all. She'd spent the rest of the weekend running errands and following a few leftover leads.

The dream had mimicked the passage of real time, a drifting of hours through a long, imaginary night. Only the end of the dream remained strangely blurred, except for the memory of infinite darkness. And heat . . .

Diana looked slowly around the room and shook her head.

You're really dreaming again. The way you used to.

She turned the realization over in her mind, adjusting to it. She'd thought the return of the old nightmare an aberration. Until this . . .

Sitting up on the bed, Diana pulled open the small drawer in her bed table and found the dream journal under a neat stack of books and magazines. She withdrew the notebook and held it in her lap, her fingers clenched on the spiral-bound cover.

It would be easy to write the dream down, exactly as she had her clients do when she worked on dream analysis in her practice. For the first time since she'd become a psychologist she had the opportunity to study her own dreaming mind.

Diana opened the notebook and stared at the blank, lined page.

And are you ready to analyze this dream? Are you prepared to dig that deep?

With a sharp breath, Diana yanked open the drawer and shoved the notebook back in, upsetting the careful stack of professional journals. She slammed the drawer closed and crossed her arms across her chest.

Coward, an inner voice mocked. Diana set her jaw and stared at the bedroom wall.

"And is it so cowardly," she said between her teeth, "to deal with things one at a time?"

The voice had no answer. Diana pushed herself up from the bed and tested her ankle cautiously. It was still a little tender; her dream had neatly incorporated that, too. Tripping on an uneven section of sidewalk on Market Street was not nearly so dramatic as falling down a wooded hillside in the middle of the night while pursuing a mysterious stranger.

Diana grimaced and walked into the bathroom.

Take things one at a time. That made perfect sense. Her priorities were clear. Before she could devote time to her own quirks she had to find Keely.

She turned on the water in the shower and stepped under the warm spray. The dream refused to leave her mind. She remembered the skull in the cavern and shuddered.

Imagination. She'd always had too much of it. The mind was an amazing thing, but it was ultimately constructed of logical patterns that could be understood. Wild surmise wouldn't help her locate Keely.

And what about Nicholas Gale?

Diana stepped out of the shower and froze, dripping water onto the bathroom rug. Her heart gave a sudden lurch.

Nicholas of the golden hair and green eyes and enigmatic air. Nicholas, whom she'd met only once in a smoke-filled coffeehouse—who had invaded her dreamworld, berating her and comforting her and saving her life.

Nicholas, who could make her heart pound as if she'd known him all her life, in the most intimate way a woman could know a man. . . .

Diana grabbed a towel and began to dry herself briskly, forcing the images from her mind. In reality he'd ultimately convinced her that he hadn't been the man she'd seen with Keely, that his concern for her cousin was genuine. In the dream, Diana's doubts about him had manifested themselves, resolved at last when he had saved her life, when she and Nicholas had become allies in the tunnel.

Allies in the dark reaches of the subconscious mind . . .

Diana grimaced. She hung up the towel and began to work tangles out of her hair with her fingers. It seemed she couldn't get away from analyzing her dream after all.

"All right," she sighed, meeting her own troubled gaze in the mirror. "So the dream may be acknowledging that you saw Nicholas as a threat, but now he's a potential ally."

Her own face gazed back at her impassively. An ally —She bit her lip. He'd seemed to know Keely fairly well. If it came down to it, she could talk to him again. He'd said he'd be making his own inquiries.

Diana frowned. *Her* inquiries certainly weren't getting her anywhere.

And you want to see Nicholas again, her mind whispered. She shivered. Only because of the dream? Or was there something else. . . .

Turning on her heel, Diana marched back into the bedroom and began to search for a clean outfit. *Did I only dream I went to the cleaners?* she asked herself wryly. She settled at last on her navy blue tailored pants and a cream-and-navy cashmere sweater.

"Maybe I *should* look up Mr. Gale again," she said defiantly, pushing her feet into low-heeled navy pumps. "It certainly won't do any harm."

But she had to swallow back an undeniable feeling that no amount of common sense would dispel. Her dream—and Nicholas Gale—had affected her on a level that defied surface understanding. Exactly like the old nightmare.

The vampire in the nightmare had been the man who'd destroyed her sister. Nicholas Gale was a man she found undeniably attractive. One man a symbol of all she had worked to overcome, the other a temptation to a part of herself she had long ago left behind.

She didn't know which she feared more.

"If you'll start working on those relaxation techniques we discussed today, I think you'll begin to see some real improvement in relieving some of the tension that's been building up."

Diana smiled at Mrs. Zeleny, coaxing a hesitant answering smile from the older woman. "Then this isn't—permanent?"

Leaning forward in her chair, Diana shook her head. "Far from it. The nightmares you've been having are a natural reaction to all the changes in your life due to the complications of your divorce. When you feel overwhelmed, those feelings come out in your dreams."

"I—do feel overwhelmed sometimes."

"Everyone does. But next week, if you're feeling comfortable with it, we'll begin working out a plan to record those dreams and start talking about what they mean to you. There are lots of different things we can try, and I think you'll find the process both interesting and valuable."

Standing slowly, Mrs. Zeleny tucked her handbag under her arm. Her smile brightened. "I'd like to try, then. And I will work on those relaxation exercises."

"Great. Please don't hesitate to call if anything comes up in the meantime." Diana rose and followed her client to the office door. "I'll see you in a week."

Diana watched Mrs. Zeleny walk down the steps, rolling her shoulders to release the tension of a long day. *I'll need some of those exercises myself.* Not that any of her clients suspected the nature of her own troubled thoughts. She was a professional; only now, with the workday done, did she turn back to the personal problems waiting to be solved.

Diana sighed and bent down to gather her mail in the box under the mail slot. Her social life had taken a back seat to her career while she'd been working so hard to establish her private practice the past two years; there were colleagues she could talk to, but all too few close friends. Relatives were in even shorter supply. If Keely were here, Diana would have valued her unique and often unconventional perspective. But Keely wasn't here—

A glossy postcard fell from among the envelopes in her hand to lie faceup on the hardwood floor. Diana stared down at the photograph of blue sky and surf.

The handwriting on the back was familiar and arresting.

"They change their clime, not their disposition, who run across the sea."

There was no signature, but Diana needed none. She read the small print in the upper corner of the postcard. *Marina Blanca Motel, Las Playas, California.* The postmark was dated Friday.

Diana released her breath slowly and returned to her office, dropping the rest of the mail on the desk. Keely was—had been—in Las Playas. That was right across the Golden Gate Bridge in Marin County, less than an hour's drive north.

At least Keely was close by, and back in touch. The obscure quotation on the postcard was odd, but not entirely out of character for Keely. She had an artist's flair for the dramatic. Across the sea—did she mean across the bay? What was she trying to convey?

Troubled by disquiet she couldn't shake, Diana tucked the postcard in her blazer pocket and locked up the office. Fresh air was what she needed now, brisk evening air to clear her mind. It wouldn't be much of a drive up to Las Playas. Easy enough to drop by that hotel on the postcard—Marina Blanca—tonight.

Her heart began to beat faster as she walked down Lake Street past the rows of modest Victorians and shingle-style houses, sidestepping cars parked halfway across the sidewalk. She thought about Tim, who'd dropped by twice to ask about Keely with a studied casualness that didn't fool Diana at all. She'd given some vague excuse for Keely's absence, well aware that Tim was smart enough to sense that something wasn't right.

Lost in her thoughts, Diana found herself in front of the small mom-and-pop market near Presidio Boulevard, remembering that she needed a gallon of milk. Mr. Hong nodded to her from behind the cramped counter, and she gave him a distracted smile as she headed for the refrigerated section in the back.

She stopped with her fingers on the handle of the dairy case, thinking of darkness and whispered words and a pair of vivid green eyes.

Grabbing a carton of milk, she closed the door just as her reflection in the glass dissolved into Nicholas Gale's.

She spun on her heel. The vision locked in her mind was suddenly before her, solid and real. Nicholas stood less than two feet away, his eyes intent on her face.

Diana swayed. The dream washed over her with undeniable power, and she examined him from brown suede desert boots to the top of his golden head, searching in alarm for the injuries she was sure must be there.

But he was whole. His legs, long and smoothly muscled in deep brown corduroy trousers, supported him with a dancer's poise. His carriage was erect, his arms crossed casually across his chest. The moss green cable-knit sweater he wore did nothing to hide the breadth of his chest and shoulders. And his face—his face was as it had been the first, the only time they'd met: unconsciously arrogant, aristocratic, cut like a fine gem to masculine perfection.

Only in her dreams had she fled from this man in fear, struggled in despair to free him from near-certain death, lain down and slept in his arms under the velvet chant of his voice.

A fragment of the dream came back in a rush, the ending that she had been unable to remember. A dream within a dream. Wild beasts and flying and fire: a god who made love to her as she'd never been loved before. . . .

Heat flared in Diana's cheeks, and she looked away from Nicholas's viridian eyes.

"Mr. Gale," she managed at last. "I didn't expect . . ." Words failed her, and she felt her jaw tense with instinctive defiance.

He smiled, an expression that tilted the corners of his finely shaped mouth without warming the marble contours of his face.

"I thought we'd agreed to dispense with formalities— Diana," he said softly. The sound of his voice sang in her blood like a drug.

She forced herself to relax. "So we did. What brings you to this neighborhood—Nicholas?"

There was something about the way he looked at her —a heated intensity veiled under a façade of nonchalance —that made her skin prickle. She looked quickly away.

"I'm here to see you," he said.

Her eyes snapped back to his. Across the brief space between them she could feel a strange intimacy, like the whisper of skin on skin or voices in darkness. "About Keely?" she said, grasping at the obvious explanation.

He smiled again, this time with a wry, mocking twist that might have been aimed at her or at himself.

"Yes. About Keely." His eyes raked her from head to foot, and his smile faded. "I was concerned after our discussion, so much so that I made a number of inquiries in an attempt to locate her."

Diana took a step toward him. "And?"

He shook his head. "Nothing. In fact, I hoped you might have heard from her since we spoke last Friday."

Pursing her lips, Diana thought back over the meeting in Mama Soma's. The memory of it seemed blurred, not nearly so vivid as last night's dream. One element remained clear in both dream and reality: her initial distrust of Nicholas Gale and her gradual realization that he was not what she had at first believed.

Only that morning she'd been convincing herself to find him again, talk to him in hopes of learning anything more that could help her locate Keely. And now he'd come to her.

Something impulsive and visceral stirred in her then, an instinct to trust and accept this man as the ally her dream had told her he could be. She reached inside her blazer pocket and pulled out the postcard. As she passed it to him their fingers touched; she almost dropped the postcard before he took it from her.

She had touched him before only in the dream. . . .

"I got this today," she said. "I recognize Keely's handwriting, but—"

She fell silent at the look on his face.

"Keely sent this?" His resonant voice was suddenly harsh with strain, the lines of his face gone taut and grim. His mouth moved, forming the words of the quote on the postcard soundlessly. He turned it over, staring at the photograph of the ocean off Las Playas. "Nothing else?"

Unreasoning alarm pierced her. "What is it?" she whispered. "Does the quote mean something to you?"

As if he'd heard her from a great distance, he turned very slowly to look at her. His eyes had darkened to the color of jade.

"No," he said. "No. Nothing at all." He handed the postcard back to her, bent at the corner where his fingers had crushed it. "She must be—all right if she sent this to you." The tension went out of his body. "I wouldn't worry about Keely, Diana. She is occasionally prone to impulsiveness, but she can take care of herself."

He was lying. Diana didn't know what the lie was, but she knew enough about reading human body language to see through his offhand manner.

Sometimes there are *monsters in the closet. . . .*

His words, words spoken in a dream. *Remember what you saw in the cave.* A pale, grinning skull and empty manacles, as if some horrible thing had escaped. Symbols, dark images that she could not quite interpret . . .

Without thinking she reached out to stop him as he turned to go. Her hand hovered just short of his shoulder. "You obviously know Keely well, Nicholas," she said to his back. "But I'm still concerned about her. If you can give me any information that I can use—"

He turned as if she'd spun him around. "We've had this conversation before," he interrupted. "You don't need to worry about Keely. I give you my word that she'll come to no harm."

Diana set the milk carton down on the nearest shelf and stared up at him, hands on her hips. "I see. You'll personally guarantee it? I thought you didn't know where she was."

"I do now."

"Las Playas?" Blowing out her breath, Diana paced away from him. "I'm heading up there myself. This evening, in fact."

"Then that makes two of us." His voice changed, almost softened. "Keely's well-being is important to me."

Nicholas watched her with narrowed eyes as she turned and regarded him steadily. He remembered that stubborn tilt to her chin, the cool challenge in her blue eyes, the low voice that could ring with authority or quiver like a child's.

Oh, yes, he remembered. He remembered the long wait in the cave, the endless day when he had held her while she slept and skimmed her mind while she dreamed. He remembered the feel of her skin under his fingers, the fire of her hidden passion, the rich pulse of her life force as it poured into him. Abundance unlike any he had known in all his long life.

He remembered the dream they had shared, drawn from her deepest mind. Her fears, and his, intertwined beyond separation. Darkness and fire and completion. Rebirth . . .

She had slept while he healed himself, cleared the fallen rubble away, and carried her to freedom. She had slept, her body recovering from what he had taken, as he drove her home. He'd even hired a couple of Judith's impecunious young tenants to drive up to the mountains, retrieve Diana's car, and deliver it to her curb before she could miss it.

And he had made her forget it all—except as a remarkably vivid dream.

He remembered every moment with painful intensity. He had thought the years of discipline would make it possible to see her again without temptation, because the necessity was past. He had sought her out—so he told himself—only to be certain that the false memories he had given her held true.

And they had. She didn't remember. As far as Diana Ransom was concerned, she had met him only once, in Mama Soma's.

But her eyes, her manner, her flaring aura told him that her body, her deepest instincts were imprinted with what they had shared. And the knowledge flayed what remained of his restraint.

He should never have seen her again.

"I'm heading up there myself."

Nicholas stared at her, weighing the options. Because of Diana's dream-memories—those he had given her—she no longer openly distrusted him; her suspicions about him had been allayed. But he could see a flicker of unease behind her eyes.

What was in her mind? Did she long to touch him as he longed to touch her, without any understanding of her own desires? Was she analyzing herself even now, determined to control and conquer her child's fear of the dark?

Nothing about her had changed since that night in the mine. She was the same stubborn woman bent on walking blindly into trouble.

Stay away from me, Diana, he ordered her silently, meeting eyes as blue as the daylight sky he never saw. She had provided him with a vital clue in finding Keely. And, if his deepest fears were realized, the key to finding his brother as well.

"You needn't trouble yourself, Nicholas," she said, breaking into his thoughts. "I can look after my own cousin."

"I assure you that it's no trouble at all."

Diana raked her hand through her short brown hair, frowning darkly. "Then we might as well go together."

He might have laughed if it weren't for the way her nearness strangled the sound in his throat. God—like Sarah, only a thousand times more potent. "I don't remember inviting you."

She smiled sweetly, though the effect was ruined by the subtle antagonism in her eyes. "Aren't you the one who wanted to dispense with the formalities? We're both concerned about Keely, and we're both going to be driving up to Las Playas. It doesn't make sense to go separately."

Nicholas hovered between retreating from the tangible pulse of her life force and reaching out to touch her.

"I admit to being a little surprised, Diana. We hardly know each other." He made the words deliberately mocking. "Did you plan to share more than just the ride?"

Her fair skin went white. She swallowed visibly, her eyes like mirrors reflecting unwelcome emotions he understood all too well. Did she recall his careful, coaxing dream-possession, deliberately blurred into symbolism for the sake of them both? Did she want him in that hidden part of herself where the fire burned, as he wanted her?

Abruptly she looked up again, jaw set. "I see no reason why we can't be back late tonight. Keely's there or she isn't—"

A discreet cough interrupted them. A young woman in a business suit squeezed past Nicholas with a sideways glance as she retrieved a pint of nonfat yogurt from the dairy case. Diana backed out of the way, color flooding into her cheeks.

"We can continue this discussion outside," she said, snatching up her milk. She brushed by Nicholas and walked purposefully up to the cashier, exchanging pleasant words with the elderly Asian gentleman and ignoring Nicholas entirely.

Sweeping up her change, Diana left the store, her slim, petite legs working like pistons.

Fool, Nicholas thought. No mortal slip of a woman had ever gotten him so completely off balance. He'd never allowed it to happen, not even with Sarah.

The choice was clear. He could end this now, convince Diana—one way or another—to steer clear of him.

He smiled grimly. Diana still didn't understand that there were human passions that couldn't easily be controlled by a mere act of will. What had driven her to bank the flames he had found smoldering behind the cool, professional façade she showed the world? One spark could ignite the ashes again. . . .

And she had burned him deep. Too deep to forget. Her life essence fed him to satiety, like a lord's feast after a pauper's crust. He might indulge himself, take what he needed and no more, as he had done a thousand times.

But his dreamers since Sarah had been ordinary women. If he let himself touch Diana again he might never be satisfied with mere survival. He might lose the control he'd taken several human lifetimes to achieve.

Let her go forever, or take an unconscionable risk.

He caught up to her in a few long strides.

"Can you be ready in two hours?"

Diana stopped in the middle of the sidewalk, clutching the milk carton to her chest. "Don't misunderstand me, Nicholas. I'm interested in finding Keely, and nothing else. If that isn't clear—"

He took her arm and propelled her into motion again, ignoring the current of desire that hummed through his body. "It's clear. I wouldn't have come here in the first place if I didn't want to find Keely as much as you do." He dropped his hand just as Diana pulled free. "I apologize for my earlier—implication."

She looked—beautiful, standing there in the harsh glare of a streetlight. Beautiful and mortal and vulnerable.

"I don't understand you," she said at last. She won her struggle for composure, calming her breathing and smoothing her expression to bland ambiguity.

"Not an easy admission for a psychologist to make," he said, carefully clasping his hands behind his back. "But I've never seen the advantage in being easily understood."

Unexpectedly, she smiled. "Then perhaps I'll have to regard you as a professional challenge."

Nicholas felt a strange elation as he looked down into her eyes. He let himself savor it for the rare thing it was, let his discipline slip like a hunting hound from its leash.

A challenge. Did she sense, even in the smallest degree, what a challenge he was? A challenge to the very limits of her body and soul . . .

"—your car or mine?"

He caught himself quickly. "Mine," he said, "if you have no objections."

She had begun to walk again, a faint frown between her dark, slightly arched brows. He could see her puzzling out something—a fragment of suppressed memory, the recollection of another journey by night.

"A van," she murmured. "Black with tinted windows."

"How did you know?"

Her glance at him was startled. "I—I must have seen it parked outside of Mama Soma's." With an air of distraction she fumbled inside her purse for a set of keys and unlocked the door to her Victorian row house.

A moment of awkwardness settled between them, clearing the look of puzzlement from her eyes. "I'd ask you in, but if you're coming in a couple of hours—"

Nicholas stepped back, watching her body relax as he put space between them. "Some other time," he murmured. He retreated down the short flight of steps to the sidewalk. "In two hours, then, Diana."

Suddenly she looked at him with piercing awareness. "I'll be expecting you, Nicholas."

The words were a kind of challenge, like her prophetic farewell in Mama Soma's the first time they'd met. Nicholas watched her disappear into the house, listening to the rapid drum of his heart against his ribs.

Are you any better than Adrian? This was his kind of game. He would have played it with relish, and not cared whom he destroyed. . . .

But Nicholas would go with Diana only after he'd taken enough sustaining life force from one of his regular dreamers to dispel the sweet temptation of Diana's unique and passionate vitality.

Thrusting his hands in his pockets, he strode down Lake Street and turned onto Tenth where his van was parked. He drove through thinning traffic past Golden Gate Park, through the Haight and south of Market to a certain apartment building in Noe Valley. He parked at the curb and looked up at the flat brick façade, searching out the row of windows on the fourth floor.

It was just past seven, but the windows were dark. The woman worked a shift that usually saw her in bed early in the evening; Nicholas came to her when he could not wait for sleep to claim his other dreamers.

He took the stairs up to her apartment and paused outside the door, listening. The hallway was empty. He drew the correct key from the ring in his back pocket and let himself in.

The woman lay in her king-size, canopied bed, blond hair spread over the pillow in luxurious abandon as if she expected a lover. Perhaps, in a way, she did. He knew what he gave her exceeded anything she could expect from a human partner. And she was willing in her dreams, eager to accept his phantom caresses in exchange for the subtle thing he took from her.

He shrugged out of his jacket and draped it over the delicate chair beside her antique dressing table. The scent of her perfume lingered in the air. Like her, it was romantic and voluptuous. She was neither subtle nor demure, waking or in her dreams.

It took only a moment for Nicholas to know she was ready. He brushed the covers away from her arms and sat beside her on the silken sheets. He was not tempted by the curve of her breast barely covered by the sheer teddy, or by her full, slightly parted lips. She needed no foreplay at all. Gently he curled his fingers over her bare shoulders.

Closing his eyes, he plunged into her dreams. They coalesced around him and he gathered the disparate images, weaving them into a tapestry of erotic fantasy. He sent his dream-shadow to her in the form of a true vampire, seductive and sensually menacing, playing out the drama she preferred above all others. And while he loved her within her mind, he skimmed away the overflow of life force that reached its peak as she dreamed.

The woman sighed, her body relaxing as he released her. A sated smile curved her lips. Nicholas stared at her, feeling nothing. He had what he must have, the bare minimum of what he needed to survive. For a hundred years that had been enough.

Until he had touched Diana Ransom.

He sat on the woman's bed and transformed the energy he had taken from her, feeling the renewal of strength and life flow throughout his body. If he held to his discipline, he would be able to fight off any temptation to touch Diana again.

But he was empty. Utterly empty. The emptiness had always been there, of course; he had only learned to ignore it. Such was the price he paid.

He rose, automatically pulling the covers over the woman's lush body. He left as silently as he had come.

An hour remained to drive home, collect the few items he needed, and return to Lake Street where Diana would be waiting.

He laughed grimly. She would never guess how he came to her tonight—aching with unappeased need because he had thrown away a century of careful indifference.

How Adrian would laugh at him now.

FIVE

Our life is twofold: Sleep hath its own world,
A boundary between the things misnamed
Death and existence: Sleep hath its own world,
And a wide realm of wild reality,
And dreams in their development have breath,
And tears, and tortures, and the touch of
   Joy . . .
        —George Gordon, Lord Byron, *Dreams*

Yes, I remember a girl like that," the bottle-blond, forty-ish night manager told them, sipping at a cup of coffee. She smiled at Nicholas over the rim—a flirtatious smile that she probably considered subtle, Diana thought uncharitably—and nodded. "Dark hair, rather pretty, young —she checked in last Thursday, I believe. But not under that name." She set down her mug and consulted the computer screen. "Alicia Kenner. Yes, here it is. They're still here, in fact."

Nicholas smiled at the manager with practiced charm. "Excellent. We're quite concerned about her—she was upset when she left home. She has a tendency to be impetuous."

"I know what that's like," the woman said, leaning forward against the counter to display an abundance of charms below the plunging neckline of her dress.

Diana refrained from rolling her eyes. "Can you describe the man she was with?" she asked impatiently.

The woman pursed her lips, a pout designed to look provocative. "He never came into the office, so I only saw him from a distance. Blond, I think. Tall. They came in a red Porsche." She fluttered false eyelashes at Nicholas. "Is that any help?"

Nicholas nodded, his smile fixed. "If you can give us the room number, we'll go up and talk to her. I'm certain we can get this straightened out."

The manager hesitated, then shrugged and consulted her computer. "Three-twelve. Lovely room, balcony facing the ocean."

Pushing away from the counter, Nicholas glanced at Diana. "Let's go," he said.

"Please let me know if I can be of any further assistance," the manager called after them, tilting her head fetchingly. Nicholas flashed her a dazzling grin that vanished the moment they left the office.

Diana pushed ahead of him and walked rapidly toward the nearest stairwell. *Do you always have such an effect on women?* she thought, amazed at her own pique.

"It has its uses."

She stumbled, flushing as she realized her thoughts had been spoken aloud. She found herself profoundly grateful for the cool night air that eased the heat in her cheeks. "I'm sure it does," she muttered. Vivid images of Nicholas surrounded by cooing, compliant women filled her with revulsion.

Exactly the sort of man she detested.

She stayed ahead of Nicholas until they reached room three-twelve. Diana noted the "Do Not Disturb" sign hung on the door, balled her fist, and prepared to knock with considerable force.

"No one's there."

Diana glanced back at Nicholas guardedly, her hand still poised in midair. He was staring at the door, head cocked to one side.

"How do you know?"

"Listen."

She hesitated a moment, and pressed her ear to the cool, painted wood. Nothing. She frowned and knocked anyway, waited, and knocked again. Only silence answered.

"The manager said they hadn't checked out," she said, biting her lip. "A red Porsche . . ."

She moved to the railing and looked down into the parking lot. There were only two cars in sight, one of them Nicholas's black van.

"At least we know she's here," Diana said. She gripped the balustrade tightly. "We'll just have to wait."

Wait. Diana stood on the landing and turned her head into the night breeze, breathing in the scent of the ocean. All during the drive into Marin, she'd been altogether too aware of Nicholas—achingly, inexplicably aware.

She was beginning to wonder what had compelled her to drive up with Nicholas when she could so easily have come on her own. It had been an entirely irrational action, the kind of thing she should have been able to take apart and examine, expose to the clear light of dispassionate analysis.

She glanced at Nicholas. *A professional challenge.* That was what she'd called Nicholas Gale, to his face no less. She was losing the battle to convince herself that that was all he was.

The dream about Nicholas and the mine had a certain uncanny resemblance to what was happening now. A drive by night—only this time she wasn't pursuing Nicholas, but accompanying him. *Semantics,* she thought. *Be brutally honest, Diana—aren't you still pursuing him?*

No. They were both looking for Keely, nothing more or less than that. . . .

"The ocean is only a short walk away," Nicholas murmured. "Why don't we take advantage of this fine evening while we wait for the return of the prodigal?"

Diana stiffened, staring at his extended elbow. A walk on a northern California beach after nine P.M. in October didn't ordinarily strike her as an ideal pastime. But something about the vaguely challenging way Nicholas looked at her broke through all her defenses. *A short walk on the beach, nothing more.*

With a tilt of her chin, Diana linked her arm through his. Her skin jumped and trembled beneath the layers of shirt and jacket at the warmth of his body.

How long had it been since she walked by the sea? San Francisco was ridiculously close to the ocean, yet it'd been longer than she could remember since she'd found the time to breathe in the salty air and listen to the lonely cry of gulls.

Maybe that was the reason. Loneliness. The ocean was vast, so wild, and it always made her feel—small. Alone. It reminded her of how she'd felt as a girl, why she'd worked so hard to make herself independent and strong.

But now, on Nicholas's arm, she didn't feel alone. The wariness with which she'd touched him drained out of her as she watched the timeless play of the waves.

The ocean was vast, but it no longer seemed overwhelming. She could almost feel the flow of its primitive power in her veins, the tide like a rush of blood. Like the force of all life itself. The surf whispered and roared a thousand secrets she could almost understand.

Slowly she recognized the unfamiliar awareness for what it was. *Freedom*. Simple joy, like a child's. *Happiness*.

She glanced at Nicholas. His expression was almost rapt, his gaze turned out to sea. What did he feel when he walked by the ocean? Did he, too, know what it was to lose what you loved and walk ever after in lonely isolation, barricaded within your own heart?

Something turned over in Diana's chest. He was still almost uncannily beautiful, like a god just risen from the sea foam, but he was also vulnerable and human. Moonlight softened his features, made the curve of his mouth seem sad and weary.

She stopped and he looked down at her questioningly. Some trace of that vulnerability lingered, for an instant, in his shadowed eyes.

"I want to take my shoes off," she said, averting her face so he wouldn't see her blush. Carefully turning her back to him, she sat down in the sand and began to pry off her sneakers.

"Good idea," he said behind her. A light spray of sand fanned over her bare feet as he crouched beside her and removed his own loafers.

She glanced at him, feeling as strange as if he'd suddenly stripped in front of her. His feet were long and elegant, like his hands. He stood and offered his hand to her.

His strength was effortless as he pulled her up. She

didn't let go of his hand for several feverish seconds, and then he was the one to pull gently free.

They walked in silence along the shore, just out of reach of the gentle pulse of the surf. The water was chill, the sand little warmer, yet Diana savored the feel of it between her toes. The breeze tousled her curls and stirred the shock of wavy hair that fell over Nicholas's forehead.

"When I was a girl—" she began. She faltered, almost losing her nerve. Sheer stubbornness lashed her on. "When I was a child, I used to dream about riding wild horses on a beach like this."

Afraid to see his reaction to the admission, she kept her eyes locked firmly on her toes as they dipped and lifted in the sand. The moment of silence that followed was agonizing.

"And did you ever do it, Diana?" he asked softly.

She didn't realize they'd stopped until she found herself looking up into his eyes. Her heart froze in her chest. She didn't need light to see his face, or to touch him to feel his warmth.

"I—" The words ran out of her like sand in an hourglass. Nicholas stole them away like a thief, with the look on his face and the soft rush of his breath. He held out his hand, and she took it. His fingers caressed her palm, sending helpless shivers through her. Behind him she could see stars gathered about his fair head like a coronet.

Diana jerked her hand free. "There aren't many wild horses in California." Suddenly she started to walk again, leaving him behind. "My parents could never afford a horse."

His feet whispered behind her. "Perhaps it's not too late."

Unexpected tears stung her eyes. Furious with herself —and with him, unfair as it was—she swiped at her face.

Too late, much too late to go back to those adolescent dreams.

"What about you, Nicholas?" she said with feigned heartiness. "What did you dream of as a boy?"

She hadn't expected a detailed answer. All she wanted was to deflect the conversation away from herself. But he was very quiet as he caught up with her, altering his pace to match her shorter strides.

"I never dreamed, Diana," he said at last.

She stumbled over a half-buried stone. "Never?"

Her legs regained their stride automatically even as her mind drifted back to her own past. For years and years—until only a month ago—she had lost the ability to remember her dreams. She hadn't wanted to remember them, not when the first to return was the nightmare. But if she hadn't known better, she might have believed she had stopped dreaming entirely.

"Everyone dreams," she said, catching her breath, "even when they don't remember."

He turned his head just long enough for her to catch a wry smile that was almost a grimace. "Then I didn't remember mine, Diana. Not one."

She wanted to say she was sorry, but the word seemed inadequate. Dreams could be fascinating things. But, uncontrolled, they could also hurt, and mislead, and fill a person with false hopes.

"And now?"

The silence held so long that Diana was sure he'd misunderstood. The breeze grew cooler, and she zipped up her jacket with unsteady fingers.

"Now," he said, his voice muffled, "I am quite accustomed to doing without them."

Taken aback by the undercurrent of pain in his words, Diana grasped at professional zeal. "It doesn't have to be that way, Nicholas. There are so many techniques now for aiding dream recall. You should at least have the chance to remember your dreams if you want to. I might be able to—"

"I don't need a psychologist, Diana." For a moment he looked ferocious—feral, uncivilized—and she remembered the last time she had seen him this way. In a dreamwood, when she had followed and confronted him with half-formed suspicions. . . .

She swallowed, lost in a limbo between memories false and true. "What *do* you need, Nicholas?" she whispered, unable to stop the words even as they left her mouth.

Stark, wordless despair, unlike anything Diana had seen, passed over his features for the span of a heartbeat. He closed his eyes. When he opened them again the Nicholas she recognized was back, smooth and unmoved as marble.

"A good night's sleep," he said, "or a good day's labor."

A flash of intuition caught Diana unaware. "You don't sleep much either, do you?"

His expression flowed into a distantly mocking smile. "I assure you—I'll come to you first if I ever require therapy."

Diana stepped back from the precipice gratefully. She wanted no more confidences, no more intimacies she was unprepared to deal with. And yet . . .

She looked away from his gaze. They should go back now and check on Keely. It would be by far the safest thing to do.

But Diana's sensible mind refused to turn her feet back toward the motel. When she looked down again Nicholas was crouched on the beach, his feet bathed by the surf, weighing something in his hand. Abruptly he stood and tossed the object into the breaking waves.

His eyes caught some faint source of light, glowing eerily from within like gems. "It's not such a terrible handicap," he said. "I've done well enough over the years."

Diana stared down at the pile of small stones he'd gathered at his feet. She bent down and picked one up, caressing the water-smoothed surface.

"How many?" she asked.

He laughed. "Years? How many do you think?"

She remembered the first time she'd seen him in Mama Soma's. She'd judged him about her own age then. Perhaps a little older. But there was something about him that hinted at greater experience than his appearance indicated.

In one smooth, graceful motion he drew back his arm and hurled the stone into the ocean. In the faint moonlight Diana could almost see the play of muscle through the layers of his clothes, the way each part of his body worked in perfect harmony with every other, no effort wasted.

"Thirty," she blurted suddenly. "I'd say you're about thirty."

He straightened and regarded her with a cocked eyebrow. "A flattering estimate," he said softly. "But I'd hazard a guess that you're considerably younger than I am."

Diana tightened her fist about the stone in her hand. "It's something of a cliché that a woman generally doesn't prefer to reveal her age," she said lightly. "But I'm sure you're too much of a gentleman to ask."

"I try to be a gentleman, Diana," he murmured, "even when I'm sorely tempted to give up the effort."

Off balance in more than one sense, Diana wound back her arm to throw her stone and tilted precariously sideways. Nicholas caught her as she stumbled, pulling her against his warm, solid body.

Dizziness made her clutch at him as memories of the dream overwhelmed reality. She remembered the feel of his arms around her, the seductive whisper of his voice in her ear: *"Come to me."* His fingers caressing, the rush of his breath against her skin; darkness, heat and fire. . . .

It was an instant or an eternity before she broke free. He held her hand until she had her feet braced steadily under her and then let her go.

She must have thanked him, muttered something unintelligible before she pushed sandy feet into her shoes and started back for the motel. He followed her until she came to the foot of the low dunes that rose between the beach and the motel.

"I'll be staying out for a while, Diana."

She had not meant to look at him again. Here, just within reach of the glaring motel lights, his features were clearly visible, starkly delineated. Not like the dream at all.

"That's fine," she said, glancing away from his glittering eyes. "I'll check for Keely."

She fled without a trace of shame.

They never knew he was there.

Adrian had watched them arrive at the hotel, search for Keely and walk out to the beach, and not once had they suspected they were not alone.

How blind you are even now, brother, Adrian thought.

But not blind enough. Nicholas was hardly unaware of the woman at his side, the woman Adrian had so briefly confronted in the gallery one week ago.

Clare's younger sister, and Keely's cousin.

Adrian had only suspected the paradoxical truth that first night he'd exchanged stares with Diana Ransom. Suspected that, once again, he'd pursued the wrong woman.

He glanced at Keely, who stood beside him in the shadow of a dune, shivering in her thin sweater. Her eyes were blank, focused not on her cousin as she returned to the hotel but on the faint white line of surf at the ocean's edge. Keely knew nothing but what Adrian willed her to know, felt only what he willed her to feel. But until this moment he hadn't been certain.

Keely, like Clare Ransom, was not the threat.

Watching Nicholas drift away down the beach, Adrian weighed the options. There was little point in holding Keely longer. Her professed love for Nicholas would not be returned, and her part in the game had been played out.

Adrian waited until Nicholas was well out of sight and Diana had disappeared into the motel office. He grasped Keely's slack hand and pulled her in the direction of his car, parked several streets away from the motel.

All these years since he had escaped the mine, since he had begun to track Sarah's descendants, Adrian had been wrong. Nicholas had never bothered to discover what had become of Sarah's only child, or of its offspring. Perhaps he had given up his obsessive desire to become human.

But Adrian hadn't been willing to take that risk—the risk that one day Nicholas might discover one of Sarah's blood and try again for mortality. And so, years after his escape from his prison, when he had overcome the effects of his long fast, Adrian had located Sarah's great-great-granddaughter, Clare Ransom, in San Francisco. He had seduced her and let her go only when he was sure she could not give Nicholas what he'd once coveted above all else.

It had been a wasted effort. Clare had died, and Nicholas had never known her. But he *had* known Keely Ames, oblivious though he was to her ancestry. She'd gotten dangerously close to Nicholas, and after fifteen years Adrian had been compelled to act again.

Seducing Keely had been a simple matter. But the night Adrian had come face to face with Diana, everything had changed. He'd read the strength of her aura—and her will. She had not remembered him, of course. She'd never seen him clearly when he'd been with Clare.

But Adrian had played the hand fate had dealt him.

Fifteen years ago he'd ignored the frightened child left behind when Clare died. He'd not been inclined to repeat his experience with Clare, and had left San Francisco to wander the world. Until his recent return, and his discovery of Keely's friendship with Nicholas, he'd been content to leave matters as they were. And leave Diana Ransom alone.

Now that was impossible.

Ironic how neatly events had worked to Adrian's benefit. He had been able to make certain that Keely was no more dangerous than Clare had been—and flush out the final remaining threat at the same time with a minimum of effort. Out of concern for her cousin, Diana Ransom had tracked down Nicholas and confronted him, mistaking him for Adrian. Inevitable that Nicholas would patch the clues together and discover his brother had escaped. Simple for Adrian to send Diana a message that would bring her to Las Playas.

And Nicholas had taken the bait. He'd gone after Diana like a moth to a flame.

She *might be the one.* . . .

The only one Adrian truly feared.

Adrian herded Keely into the Porsche and paused, leaning against the car. Perhaps it would prove to be a far more interesting game than he'd anticipated. Perhaps Diana Ransom would be a greater challenge than her sister and cousin had been.

But he would defeat her in the end.

You will not have the chance again, brother, Adrian swore silently. *You and I will be together for eternity.*

Smiling to himself, Adrian dropped into the car seat and glanced at Keely. He touched her face, brushing his knuckles along the soft contour of her jaw.

"For eternity, my dear. For eternity."

He started the engine, put the Porsche in gear, and ground the gas pedal to the floor.

By midnight Keely and her mystery lover hadn't returned.

Nicholas secured himself and Diana two rooms overlooking the ocean. "You, at least, need your sleep," he told her, though the look in his eyes made her shiver.

The rooms, as it turned out, were adjoining; an interior door connected them. Diana's was like a thousand other motel rooms, stamped out in a pattern of deliberate blandness. She paced the length of it, glancing at the king-size bed with its three large pillows.

"Why don't you try to get some rest?"

Nicholas stood just inside the outer door, his movements so silent that she hadn't even heard it open.

"What about you?" she blurted without thinking.

"We've discussed my sleeping habits—or lack of them. Did you have something else in mind?"

She felt herself bristling and refused to rise to the bait. His innuendo seemed calculated to get under her skin, and she didn't understand his game.

"Only professional interest," she said coolly. "I have a number of clients who'd be overjoyed to give up the necessity of sleep. There's nothing worse than being unable to sleep when your body desperately needs it." She envisioned Clare's haggard face in the weeks before she'd died.

Nicholas was very still. "Nothing, Diana? Do you speak from personal experience?"

Diana couldn't force a glib response past the tightness in her throat. "I think," she said at last, looking blindly over his shoulder, "that I'll rest for a few hours after all." Striding to the scratched desk where she'd dropped her purse, she pulled a wad of bills from her wallet and thrust them at Nicholas. "Here. This should cover my room."

She waited until he took the money and closed the door behind him before flinging herself down on the bed. Sleep was the farthest thing from her mind, but she'd be damned if she'd let Nicholas Gale turn her into an insomniac.

Diana covered her head with the nearest pillow and squeezed her eyes shut, thinking about counting sheep.

But it was wild horses she saw instead.

The temptation was too great.

Nicholas stood at the door between their rooms, listening. He had known it would come to this, even though he'd walked the beach for hours, telling himself that it could bring nothing but temporary gratification.

And isn't that how it's always been?

He listened, and the sound of her breathing came soft and steady to his ears. He knew the pattern that accompanied the most profound stage of sleep, the one that came before the onset of dreams.

It was time.

He opened the door. Making sure it was left unlocked had been the simplest matter of all.

Diana lay on her side with the bedspread and blankets bunched at her feet, only a thin white sheet drawn up to her chin. Her body looked small in the king-size bed;

Nicholas paused just inside her room, cycling through the arguments one last time.

His eyes were as keen in darkness as a human's were in daylight. From across the room he could see the details of her face, relaxed and unguarded in slumber. Her short hair formed a tangled halo around her head. One hand was curled up beneath her chin, clutching the cheap cotton of the sheet. Her knees were drawn up like a child's.

Did she feel safe with the sheet wound close about her, safe from the darkness she feared? She didn't remember that first admission she'd made to him in the mine. He had done his work well.

But she remembered enough. He had no doubts of that at all. When he slipped into her dreams, he would not come as a total stranger.

Silently he moved to the bed. An image of the last woman he'd visited flashed through his mind; his lips narrowed in a grimace of distaste. Beautiful as she was in the eyes of men, lush and blond and willing, she had been no more than meager sustenance to him.

Not like Diana. He'd had one taste of her, and knew he could never have enough.

He knelt by the bed, not yet daring to touch her. The dark sweep of her lashes against her cheek fluttered gently. Her lips were parted as if on a sigh. He traced the outline of her body through the sheets with his eyes—all soft curves, understated and small, nothing bold or showy about her.

Nicholas felt his mouth lift in a smile. He knew by now how reluctant she was to make use of her subtle loveliness. But her real beauty, the allure that brought him to her bed, she hid deep within herself.

Her fears were still too much a mystery to him, but when he rode her dreams he would begin to understand her. Perhaps better than she understood herself. It was a side effect he had little use for among his other dreamers, except as an aid in weaving their dreams. But with Diana . . .

Slowly he reached out, letting his palm touch her face with feather lightness. He curled his thumb over her jaw, stroked the lobe of her ear with his smallest finger. The untapped tide of her life force hummed against his skin.

With Diana it was already more than he'd ever wanted with the others. He wanted to understand her, foolish as the desire was. He wanted to ease her fear of the dark and see the sunlight through her eyes.

Diana's fingers tightened on the sheet under her chin, and Nicholas stilled his hand. He whispered to her, meaningless singsong phrases like a tuneless lullaby.

Tenderness, Nicholas? he mocked. *Perhaps you need the services of a good therapist after all.*

Withdrawing his hand, he closed his eyes and pulled back into himself, preparing every cell in his body to accept and absorb what Diana would give him. And as he reached for her again, detached and ready, he opened his mind to discover what her hidden heart most desired.

It was a strange twilight through which Diana walked, neither dark nor bright.

She lifted her face to the breeze. Sand was soft as a caress under her feet. The ocean sighed like a thwarted lover.

How fanciful, Diana, she thought. But it was easy to be fanciful, caught between sea and sky and utterly alone.

Looking down at herself, she saw that she had worn neutral colors today, though she didn't remember putting on the gray blazer and trousers and oatmeal turtleneck sweater. The blazer was buttoned up, and the sweater was so high about her neck that she had a sudden thought that she might choke.

An illusion, she scoffed. But the feeling of tightness, of binding, seemed to extend about her entire body beneath her clothes, as if she wore a whalebone corset like some woman of the previous century.

She put the notion out of her mind and stared out to sea. The waves were very quiet. The ocean did not seem so vast, so impossible to compass. She felt almost as if she could reach out and cup it in her hand.

Wet sand squelched between her toes. She watched the surf retreat before her, the chaos of nature fleeing human rationality. It was so easy. She waded still further out, but her trousers remained dry.

I have you, she told the timid waves. *I have you under control.*

Her eyes were drawn to the horizon, where the edge of water almost blended into the colorless sky. Light flashed there, gone in an instant. *It can't touch me,* she thought. But the lightning flashed again, and wind stirred in its wake.

Without thinking she began to walk backward, her feet slipping into the soft impressions they had made before. Air that had been no more than a tender breeze began to buffet her face. Something stirred on the horizon; the sea darkened, and then the sky.

She heard the rumbling then. Faint at first, no more than a tremor in her bones. But it grew, sourceless and terrifying. Diana ran far back onto the beach where the sand was dry, and stared at waves that began to leap under the lash of sound.

Proud. She had been so proud of defeating the vast ocean. Now it meant to teach her how foolish she had been.

She looked wildly around, searching for shelter. Behind her rose a sheer wall of unscalable cliffs. Seabirds shrieked mockingly overhead. There were no openings in the walls of stone, no caves where she might find refuge. And the surf began to race towards her like a voracious predator while the roar grew loud as thunder.

Don't fight it. The voice came into her mind; her own or another's she had no way of knowing. *Let go. . . .*

Diana closed her eyes. The roar swept over her in a torrent, around her on every side. Warm air rushed by, carrying an elusive scent from some distant and half-forgotten past.

Her eyes snapped open.

Horses. There were horses on every side, wild horses with windblown manes and flanks glistening with sea spray. Their hooves made impossible thunder in the sand; they veered around her and left her untouched, nostrils flared and eyes rolling. Diana put out her hand, and rough fur brushed her palm.

And then they were gone, save one. A stallion, gray as mist, blowing breath like a furnace on her hair as it reared and plunged to a halt beside her, casting sand like sparks from its massive hoofs.

On the stallion's back was a man.

He rode the stallion easily without rein or saddle, a masked figure cloaked in the same tones of gray. He looked down at her, and she saw his face below the mask and the pale hair above it that seemed almost colorless in the uncertain light.

His legs were encased in boots of shining black leather that reached to his knees. Breeches that clung to his powerful thighs like a second skin were visible under the sweep of his cape. His shoulders were broad as a hero's, and his gloved hand rested on the stallion's velvet neck as if he needed nothing else to keep the beast in check.

He was masculine perfection, like the magnificent horse he rode. Wild, uncontrollable, terrifying. Masked like a thief to steal her soul.

"Who are you?" she whispered.

He gave her no answer. His mount danced, and he quieted it with a touch. Through the slit in the mask she could see the glitter of his eyes—watching her, staring in ominous silence.

"What do you want?" she cried. But he looked away, his profile carved by the sky. The drum of hooves and the lilt of laughter echoed across the beach.

The horse that appeared behind the gray rider was as bright as the stallion was pale, rich chestnut in color. The woman who rode it wore a dress as red as blood, sleeveless and slitted nearly to the waist. She laughed again, her face turned away from Diana. Her thighs were bare against the horse's flanks.

The gray rider wheeled his horse about to face the woman in red. His body blocked the woman's slight form like a cloud over the sun. Diana knew that he kissed her; she could feel desire beat in the air, heating her skin and tightening her nipples under layers of constricting cloth.

Between one moment and the next it was over. The woman kicked her horse free of the gray rider's entangling cloak and guided the animal around the stallion's bulk. She looked down, laughing, into Diana's eyes.

The woman's face was Diana's own. And not: blue eyes far too vivid, lips too full and lush, hair too streaked with red. But Diana gasped, and the woman's smile vanished. She slid to the sand, flashing white skin, and held out her hand.

The choice was clear, and terrible.

Behind her the gray rider watched in silence, as if the whole world hung on Diana's decision. Diana closed her eyes, swallowed, and took her double's hand.

The transformation was instantaneous. Diana felt the caress of sheer silk against her skin, the utter freedom of nothing at all beneath it. She touched herself slowly, running her hands over her body.

"Diana."

She looked up at the gray rider. Only the two of them waited on this empty beach now. The rider's voice was husky and heated, charged with sensual promise. Diana knew what he wanted, experienced the touch of his mouth on hers within her double's memory.

Freedom. Diana tossed back her head, and laughed. The chestnut horse, riderless, curvetted in the sand. At once the gray rider dismounted and moved with easy grace to her side.

Diana slid away, evading his touch. She laughed again and caught the chestnut's mane in her fist, tangling the thick strands through her fingers.

And then she was astride. The horse exploded into motion beneath her the moment she touched its back. Muscle and sinew bunched and released between her thighs. Joy unlike anything she had known filled her to overflowing.

The gray rider could never catch her. She bent low over her mount's back, red silk snapping behind her like a banner. Water flew from the horse's hooves. Her pulse beat in her ears, mingling with the sounds of pursuit.

Free. Free . . .

An arm like a steel band caught her about the waist, lifting her from the back of her mount. For a moment she hung suspended in air, and then she was in the gray rider's embrace, one leg across his hard thigh.

She tried to fight him. She fisted her hands against his chest, made her body rigid. The soft leather of his breeches rubbed against the delicate, naked skin of her inner thigh. The steady friction of it made her gasp.

The stallion began to slow. The gray rider turned her so that she sat astride his lap with her breasts clamped to his chest, her belly against his. The hardness between her legs was unmistakable.

"Diana," the rider whispered. They were so close now that his warm breath caressed her cheek. His half-concealed face was taut with masculine power and desire.

He caught her face between his gloved hands and kissed her.

It began gently, a slight pressure on her lips that she defeated with a turn of her head. But he was ready. His mouth found her cheek instead, feathering a second kiss there and then down to the corner of her jaw. She shuddered, tried to find words of protest, but the urge to fight drained out of her like sand through spread fingers.

Fire. She remembered fire, and ecstasy.

I want it again, she thought. And within her mind she heard the rider's low cry of triumph.

This time when he kissed her she responded. She let him part her lips and enter her mouth with his tongue, moaning in surprise at the erotic invasion. The rider was all strength and gentleness intermingled. There was hunger in him, hunger she could feel through her hands buried in his cloak and her thighs over his.

Her own hunger answered. She pressed against him as he kissed her eyelids, her brows, the edge of her jaw. His tongue flicked her earlobe, drawing a deep shudder through her body. The supple leather of his gloved fingers slid around her neck, down to the flimsy silk over her shoulder.

Her head arched back as he pressed his mouth into the hollow of her shoulder, running his tongue along the delicate ridge of her collarbone. Masculine scent engulfed her. He licked the base of her throat where the pulse beat;

she felt as if all her being gathered there. Beneath them the stallion had come to a stop, and its wind-roughened mane brushed her bare thighs.

The rider pushed her back, gently and inexorably, against the horse's broad neck. His hands caught her hips and urged her legs to grip his waist. The silk slipped away from her shoulders, down her arms, held in place only by the swell of her breasts.

She could no longer see the sky. The rider was all her world, bent over her in silent adoration. The silver cloth of his mask whispered on her skin. She glimpsed the flash of his eyes just before he arched her back over his arm and took one silk-veiled nipple into his mouth.

The memory of speech was lost to her utterly. She heard the low sounds she made in time to his gentle suckling, aroused beyond control by the stroke of his tongue through wet silk. Then he brushed the last barrier away, cupped her breasts in his hands and caressed each of them in turn until even her moans were silenced.

Diana never wanted it to end. She could not conceive of an ending; existence was ecstasy, and ecstasy itself had become timeless. She would lie here in the arms of the gray rider forever. . . .

When he withdrew his hot mouth from her skin the shock pulled her up with a cry. She reached for him and caught the drifting edge of his cloak. He looked down at her, silent, supporting her with one powerful arm. The crash of the waves cried out her frustration; her body ached with a nameless need.

"Please," she whispered. The word might have been in a foreign tongue. But the gray rider smiled. He lifted her legs to free his own and slid from the stallion's back with easy grace. His hands caught her waist and lifted her down along his body.

His kiss was hard, demanding. Diana clutched at his shoulders, swaying with sudden dizziness. The rider buried his fingers in her hair, holding her captive. He let her go only long enough to pull her with him into the sand.

Soft as down, the sand cradled her back and buttocks as the rider pressed her into it. Hands—hot, strong hands stripped of their gloves—raised her hips and lowered them again onto cloth. Her silent lover knelt over her, sliding the silk of her skirt up her parted thighs.

Diana gasped as his fingers stroked the source of her desire. They moved over her, seeking and finding, drawing paths of pleasure that made her tremble and cry out. A flood gathered within her, a flood that quickened between her thighs and ached for release.

He held her there on the edge. She opened her eyes and looked at him, at the face of a stranger who made love to her in the half-light of a phantom world.

Stranger. A spark of lucid thought flashed through her mind. The gray rider watched her face, and his caresses grew more intent.

Surely he was no stranger. Surely this was no mere fantasy. She knew, if she could only hold the memory. She knew. . . .

And then her mind and body shattered into a thousand shards of light and sensation. Her vision darkened as the rider rose above her, drew his gray cloak up and over them both. Lassitude overcame her; she felt her eyelids grow heavy, vitality melt out of her bones and muscles like the retreating tide.

The rider's warmth settled beside her, and he drew her close. With a last spurt of strength she clutched his flowing shirt and pressed her face to his chest.

"Nicholas," she whispered.

"Nicholas."

She stood at the door in her rumpled blouse and slacks, staring at him through heavy-lidded eyes.

"May I come in?" he asked, drawing the collar of the overcoat higher around his neck. It was nearly dawn; he saw Diana frown in bleary puzzlement at his sunglasses and fedora, knowing how he must look to her. He was strong now—stronger and more replete than he had been in uncounted years—but he would not let the sun steal any part of what he had gained.

Not when Diana stood looking at him so silently, pale and disheveled and lost as a child.

She blinked and stepped back from the door. "Yes. Of course."

He followed her in and shut the door behind him. He watched her walk toward the bed, altering his vision to read her aura. The colors were dimmed; he could have expected no less, after what he had taken. Her deliberate movements were those of a woman awakened from a deep sleep.

Nicholas released his breath. He had never taken so much from a dreamer—not even with Diana in the mine, when he had had no choice.

This time the choice had been entirely his. He had been as intoxicated by their shared dream as by her life force. And if she had taken pleasure from him, he had taken far more from her. It had not been so long since the last time with her, and there was always an element of risk when he drew life force too often from the same dreamer. The risk of leaving her weak, sleepless, apathetic—all the warning signs that meant he could take no more.

She turned and caught his intense regard. There was no trace of apathy in the look she gave him.

"I'm sorry," she said, raking her hand self-consciously through her hair. "I just woke up."

He moved closer, looking deep into her eyes. "Did you sleep well, Diana?" he asked softly.

Color flooded her cheeks. "Very well."

Turning away, Nicholas gave her a moment to collect herself. He hadn't attempted to dull her memory of the dream, only his own identity within it. None of his dreamers, save Sarah, had ever known him in waking life. A small manipulation of Diana's sleeping thoughts insured that she would not recognize him as the gray rider of her erotic fantasy.

But he could not forget a single moment of it.

He heard the whisper of her feet on the carpet as she walked into the bathroom. Water splashed; she emerged from the bathroom with a towel held up to her face and eyes averted.

"Have you already checked on Keely?" she said, her voice muffled.

"That's why I've come, Diana," he said, clasping his hands behind his back to keep from touching her. "I received a call earlier this morning from—a mutual friend of mine and Keely's. She's back home."

Diana blinked. "Home? In San Francisco?"

"Yes. She—left the hotel without checking out a few hours after midnight."

Diana's eyes changed, lost their dazed look all at once and grew sharp as glass.

"You let me fall asleep and didn't watch out for her?"

"Evidently my vigilance was imperfect," he said. He had no intention of explaining the nature of his failure, or why he had been too preoccupied to keep watch during a certain part of the night. Why he had forgotten everything but the woman who stood before him.

"Were you able to find out anything at all?" she said sharply. "Is she all right? Was the man with her?"

"As far as I could learn, Keely was in good health.

She was no longer with her lover when she turned up at her apartment."

"Damn," Diana whispered. The anger seemed to drain out of her in a rush. "Give me five minutes to wash up, and we'll head back."

Nicholas looked after her as she vanished into the bathroom. He leaned against the wall, relieved that his worst fears for Keely had gone unrealized.

Not that the problem was solved. Not yet. And now he'd added yet another complication. Diana Ransom. She —with her powerful life force and her brilliant dreams— was like an addictive drug, tempting him to take a fatal overdose.

Nicholas clenched his fists behind his back, tendons straining under the skin, until Diana reemerged, her face flushed with recent washing and her blazer concealing the creases in her clothes. She looked at him quizzically.

"Is it really that cold—and bright—outside?" she said, gesturing at his overcoat and sunglasses.

Nicholas suppressed a grimace. Until now she'd never seen him during the day; except for Judith he'd let no one close enough to him for his peculiarities to become an inconvenience.

"I have a small problem with the sun," he admitted at last.

"What kind of problem?" she asked, slipping automatically into her therapist's impartial manner.

He smiled tautly. "Not a matter you can help me with in your—professional capacity," he said.

Her frown was quite impersonal. "The tinted windows on the van," she said, watching his face.

"Yes." Nicholas glanced restlessly at the door. "It's a physical condition. There's a name for it—photodermatitis. Prolonged exposure to sunlight creates rather unpleasant symptoms."

"I've heard of it, though I've never met anyone who—" She caught herself, as if suddenly aware of her tone. "Sorry," she murmured.

"It's not something I care to advertise, and I seldom find it—unduly inconvenient."

Diana studied him covertly, noting the unaccustomed stiffness with which he spoke, the careful enunciation of a man dismissing a despised vulnerability. Not inconvenient, to be forced to bundle up in the sun and walk freely only by night? Diana remembered him at Mama Soma's, so much at his ease there. Did he haunt the clubs and coffeehouses and deserted streets, returning at dawn to that elegant mansion in Pacific Heights like a prisoner to his cell?

And her dream. In her dream she had followed him by night into the mountains. He had seemed like a part of the darkness, moving soft and sure like a nocturnal predator. Had her subconscious mind already guessed the truth?

She looked up at him slowly. "I'm sorry. I can't imagine what it must be like."

"Because you're a child of the sun, Diana," he said, "in spite of your name."

Diana, goddess of the moon. She made a face. "You're right," she said. "Only I don't have such a good excuse. Sometimes I'm simply afraid of the dark."

In the silence that followed a flash of memory came back to her, déjà vu so powerful that she shivered with it: crouching in the blackness of an abandoned mine, admitting her childish fears to Nicholas as he lay wounded beside her. And his voice, in the dream: *"Isn't the fear of darkness akin to the fear of being alone?"*

God. "We're even now," she said, forcing a smile. "One dark secret for another."

His eyes were strange in the semidarkness of the

room, the deep green of an ancient forest or the ocean after a storm. "Are we, Diana?" he asked. The tension in his body seemed to leap across the space into hers, causing the hair on the nape of her neck to stand on end.

She knew the tension for what it was. She wanted no part of it, even though her breasts felt suddenly heavy under her blouse and she was overwhelmingly aware of the ache between her thighs.

That quickly. That mindlessly, like any other female animal.

With a sharp breath she broke free of his gaze and the spell he wove around her.

"I'm ready to go now," she said thinly. "It'll be full daylight soon—"

Nicholas bowed half mockingly. "You may have the honor of driving. The tinted windows do have a purpose."

They stared at each other, something intangible pulsing between them, a bolt of pure energy that had no rational source. Nicholas was the first to look away.

"After you, Diana," he said softly. Grabbing her purse, she preceded him into the morning sunlight, wondering why it felt so little like freedom.

Six

———

Did you think the lion was sleeping because he
    didn't roar?
        —Johann Christoph Friedrich von Schiller,
            The Conspiracy of Fiesco

Keely! Thank God you're all right."

Keely pushed up from the worn couch and let herself
be drawn into a fierce hug, vaguely surprised at the unexpected emotion in her cousin's voice.

"Shouldn't I be?" Keely pulled back, focusing with
effort on Diana's pale face. She felt a twinge of nebulous
guilt, realizing she'd probably forgotten another lunch
date, and Diana had come after her. But . . .

Her eyes swept past Diana's shoulder and stopped at
the man standing behind her cousin. Tall, blond, green-
eyed, altogether too perfect to be real.

"Nicholas," she breathed. Suddenly she was too dizzy to stand; she backed toward the couch, and Diana was there to help her down.

Three faces looked down at her: Diana's, set in a frown that hinted of lectures to come; Judith, who'd been with her, brewing English tea and talking about inconsequential matters, ever since Keely had returned to her apartment—oh, hours ago; and Nicholas, his eyes so intent that it seemed they could bore a hole right through her skull.

Until this moment she'd been content to lie on the couch, lost in dreams, letting Judith look after her like a child or an invalid—exactly as if she'd just come down from some colossal high. A wave of nausea washed through her. That was over. Over. But the sense of blind well-being had suddenly turned into something vaguely sinister, like a blot of red paint in a field of stark black. . . .

"What's wrong?" she asked weakly.

Diana's struggle for detachment was a visible thing. "What's wrong? Where have you *been* for the past week and a half?"

Keely almost laughed, but the dizziness trapped the sound in her throat. "Since when did you have to know everywhere I go, Di?" She paused to examine her strange light-headedness and found herself matching Diana's frown. "I was—somewhere. . . ."

Sliding between Judith and Diana, Nicholas crouched beside the couch. "What about the man you were with, Keely?"

The man I was with. A whirl of disconnected images danced through Keely's memory. She looked hard at Nicholas, wondering why it was so difficult to focus on the past.

Strange. The pain of Nicholas's rejection now seemed

like an old wound, long since healed. *I thought I was in love with him,* she thought dazedly. *But it's—gone.*

Looking at him now, she felt nothing but formless confusion and an artist's appreciation for his masculine beauty. She could easily remember leaving Mama Soma's the night he'd turned her down, walking up Folsom in a haze of emotional pain. And then she'd met a man. . . .

A man.

The rest was all a blur.

She should have been terrified. No matter how hard life had been in the past, she'd always accepted the consequences of her own actions. Her judgment hadn't always been good, but now—now she couldn't even seem to remember what decisions she'd made.

Two weeks, Diana said.

"Not the drugs," she blurted aloud, glancing wildly at Diana. "I'm off that stuff."

Nicholas touched her, his face an unreadable mask. "We know that, Keely. Can you remember anything at all?"

Leaning back into the flattened cushions of the couch, Keely tried. It was like attempting to hold water in cupped hands. Memories spilled away, leaving only the aftertaste of excitement, passion—and a touch of fear. . . .

"I can't," she whispered. The fear, like the memories, refused to stay. Detachment walled her away from every emotion. "You're the shrink, Di," she said, looking at her cousin. "What's wrong with me?"

Diana brushed the hair out of Keely's eyes. "Don't worry about that. We'll find out. You're okay now."

Glancing from her cousin to Nicholas, Keely felt the pull of lassitude she couldn't shake. *I haven't been sleeping well,* she thought with sudden clarity. But that was nothing new.

Her gaze drawn to Nicholas, she stared at him in fascination. Something about him was important, but she lost the thread of thought as soon as it rose to her mind. His eyes, locked on her face, had narrowed to slits, opaque as antique glass.

"Do you remember sending Diana the postcard from Las Playas?" he asked.

"Las Playas—" Keely trapped an image as if it were a painting waiting to be born on canvas. "The beach. We walked along the beach."

Even in the midst of her strange lethargy, she noted the way Diana and Nicholas glanced at each other. When had they met? She'd never introduced them. . . .

"But the man," Nicholas continued, taking her hand in his gently. "Can you tell us anything about him? His name, or what he looked like?"

The words were on the tip of Keely's tongue. Nicholas's eyes were the catalyst, the key. The key to it all.

She licked her lips. "The man . . ."

"What was his name?" The grip of Nicholas's fingers grew almost painful. He leaned forward, a subtle madness in his gaze that seemed hauntingly familiar. "Keely—"

"Nicholas," Diana said sharply.

He looked up, releasing Keely from the bonds of his stare. She closed her eyes in relief, feeling a sudden overwhelming need to sleep. The voices of her friends receded into a vague, wordless drone.

"I need to talk to her alone," Nicholas said.

"Don't push her. Please." Diana lowered her voice to a whisper.

"A few minutes, Diana."

Diana bit her lip. If he could learn anything at all that could help them . . .

"All right." She deliberately unclenched her clasped hands and backed away, moving across the small living room of Keely's apartment to stand beside Judith. Nicholas's voice faded to a murmur, his head bent close to Keely's.

"Is she all right?" Judith asked softly, her husky voice touched with the trace of a European accent.

"She seems to be. Temporary memory loss isn't unheard of. But it's something I—" She shook her head. "I'll have a specialist look at her later. We want to make sure this isn't anything serious."

Judith touched her arm, a brief gesture of comfort. "I wouldn't worry too much. She's a survivor."

Diana managed a smile. Judith embodied the kind of competent control that Diana considered a personal and professional ideal; she guessed that very little would faze the older woman. Judith rented out apartments in the row house adjoining her own—Keely's apartment was in the gabled attic—and worked out of a home office as an accountant.

Judith was also the mutual friend who'd called Nicholas in Las Playas when Keely had returned. Considering the connections between Keely, Diana, Nicholas and Judith, it was a wonder Diana hadn't met Nicholas before that night in Mama Soma's.

It seemed almost inevitable . . .

"You've known Nicholas a long time?" she found herself asking.

Judith gnawed her lip, felt in the pocket of her loose raw silk jacket, and sighed heavily. "I keep forgetting I've given up smoking," she muttered. Her eyes focused again on Diana, deep brown and thoughtful in their nest of creases. "Yes, it's been a while." The corner of her lip curled up. "You like him, don't you?"

Taken aback, Diana opened her mouth and shut it

again. "He's been a great help with Keely," she said at last.

"Ah." Judith loaded that one word with a wealth of meaning, and Diana dropped her eyes. Inevitably her gaze slid back to Nicholas, and the impossibly tangled emotions he aroused held her spellbound.

Perhaps it was only the memory of dreams. There had been that vivid one of horses and passion last night, after their long walk on the beach. A dream so much like the old ones, the ones she'd had as a child—but interwoven with erotic imagery she had been too young to conjure up so long ago.

Nicholas had sparked that in her. Had she dreamed of him as well? Had the gray rider symbolized Nicholas, the attraction to him she was afraid to admit to her waking mind, the desire to abandon herself to passion like the red-clad woman on the beach?

Everything she still didn't know about Nicholas Gale eddied in her mind, layer upon layer of mystery and enigma she hadn't come close to fathoming. . . .

She turned her thoughts from herself and focused them on Keely. But even that was no relief; Keely's disappearance remained a troubling puzzle. The deeply shadowed hollows beneath her eyes, the loss of short-term memory were disturbing symptoms.

Keely looked too much like Clare—just before Clare took her own life.

Her grim memories faded as Nicholas rose from the couch and came to join them. His gaze was flat and unreadable.

"She's sleeping now," he said. "I couldn't learn anything more."

"Let the professionals take care of that, Nicholas," Judith said softly. "Diana's suggested it's short-term memory loss—"

"An instant diagnosis, Diana?" Nicholas asked, his mouth forming a faint, cynical smile.

"Something has happened to her, and I don't pretend to know what it is," she said with forced calm. "This isn't like Keely at all." Walking away, she turned her back on Nicholas. "Except the impulsive behavior with men. Maybe I was too disapproving when she needed unconditional support, pushed her into this." She laughed bitterly. "Treated her as if she were a patient—"

"Don't blame yourself, Diana," Nicholas whispered.

His sudden turnabout caught her unaware. She looked over her shoulder. "I don't—"

"You could say it's my fault that this happened," he said, as if he hadn't heard her. "I told you that Keely had wanted—a closer relationship with me. I rejected her, and she turned to someone else for comfort. Someone who clearly wasn't good for her."

The self-recrimination in his voice lashed at her heart. "You're even less responsible for her than I am, Nicholas." Her eyes dropped. "I tend to forget we can't live other people's lives for them."

Silence fell between them, charged with strange tension, as if the weight of things left unsaid hung in the air. Judith cleared her throat.

"I think Keely should rest now," the older woman said, looking from Diana to Nicholas.

"I should take her home with me—" Diana interjected.

Judith shook her head. "No need. I'll stay with her for a while." She gestured them toward the narrow apartment hallway. "Believe me, I don't mind at all, and I think she needs to be in her own place."

And with someone who's a lot more detached than I am. Diana smoothed the frown from her face. "All right. But you'll call me if anything changes?"

"I will." Judith withdrew a key from the pocket of her jacket and locked the apartment door behind her. "You have nothing at all to worry about."

At the front door of the house, Nicholas gave Judith a sideways glance that the older woman returned. The exchange was so swift that Diana almost missed it, but it seemed somehow secretive. Judith nodded to Diana and walked a few brisk steps to the porch of the adjoining house, leaving Nicholas and Diana behind.

Nicholas snagged his light overcoat from the coat tree near the door and put on his sunglasses. Diana wondered how uncomfortable he'd be in the midmorning sunlight. There must be times when he'd have to go out by day. . . .

"You'll need a ride home, Diana," he said.

Now that they were alone again, now that her immediate fears for Keely had been laid to rest, Diana was uncomfortably aware of Nicholas's nearness. "No need. I can catch a taxi back to the office in time for my ten o'clock appointment—"

"I insist," he said softly.

She could have given him a polite and distant refusal, but it was easier, far easier, to surrender to the velvet command of his words. All the will to shield herself from her dangerous, inexplicable attraction to Nicholas Gale seemed to have fled, just as her self-control had deserted her in the dream of the gray rider.

She followed him as he hurried out to the curb and let him hand her into the van. He pulled into morning commute traffic with a deft touch on the wheel and turned the van from Potrero Hill toward the Richmond district.

Diana's mind was still teasing facts and impressions that seemed almost to be part of a puzzle she hadn't known existed. "You know Judith pretty well, don't you?" she asked.

Nicholas was silent for a long, uncomfortable moment before he sighed and leaned back against the headrest. "Yes. Since long before I met Keely."

"But you didn't mention that when I was looking for Keely, the first time we met."

He shrugged. "It hardly seemed important at the time."

Diana could find no arguments for that answer. Keely had never mentioned Nicholas either, though he claimed she'd wanted him for a lover. Keely had found it necessary to hide her personal life from Diana as well. She felt a sting of annoyance that sharpened her voice. "Why do I get the feeling that you're deliberately concealing things from me that have bearing on everything that's happened?"

Turning onto Lake Street, Nicholas gripped the wheel with unnecessary tightness.

"We all have things to hide, Diana," he said. His face showed no expression at all, but there was a touch of regret in his voice. Diana turned to look at him as he parked at the curb beside her house, her heart pounding with something other than anger.

"Like—your sensitivity to sunlight?" she asked.

"Or your fear of the dark."

Heat flooded her cheeks. "There are things you can tell a stranger that you'd never admit to a friend."

"But we aren't strangers—are we, Diana?" he murmured.

She went absolutely still as he lifted his hand, fingers drifting toward her face. "No," she whispered.

"Are we friends?"

The back of his knuckles brushed the edge of her jaw, so lightly that she might not have felt it at all except for the flare of heat and electricity that swept through her body at the contact.

"Yes." She closed her eyes, but he withdrew his hand, offering nothing more. The skin over her cheekbones was scalding hot.

Nicholas sighed. "There's nothing very mysterious about my relationship with Judith, Diana. You asked me once what my business was. The fact of the matter is, I have numerous—investments, business interests both here and on the East Coast. It's always been my preference to keep a very low profile, and hire others to administer my interests for me."

Diana forgot her embarrassment. "And Judith is your —employee?"

He gave a short, wry laugh. "In a manner of speaking. She's far more than an accountant. She acts as my broker, business administrator, investment counselor—she organizes my interests into a cohesive whole."

"Interests. What kinds of interests?"

"All legitimate, I assure you. I make it a point to leave the details in Judith's capable hands." He arched an eyebrow. "Judith can provide you with a complete list, if you like."

"Judith is also Keely's landlady."

Nicholas folded his arms across his chest. "Judith does own both the houses on Arkansas Street. When I first met Keely and learned she was looking for an inexpensive place to live, I contacted Judith. She has a soft spot for struggling young artists."

"Like you do?"

His mouth curved up at one corner. "As I said, I prefer a quiet life and a low profile. I'm not a philanthropist by nature."

The words had a supercilious ring to them, as if Nicholas were trying to hide emotions he wouldn't admit to.

Unconsciously Diana leaned sideways in her seat, closer to him, as if proximity alone could uncover all his secrets.

"But you are, I think, a reasonably wealthy man."

He gave her a look of mocking reproach. "You'll have to talk to Judith about my net worth, Diana, but I think it's safe to say that I'm not about to drown in the River Tick."

Abruptly he uncrossed his arms and extended his left along the back of the seat, letting his hand rest a hairs-breadth from her shoulder. Diana felt the proximity of his skin as if living flame curled from his fingers to her skin and drifted through the hairs at the nape of her neck.

"Wealth, I understand, can be a powerful aphrodisiac."

Diana jerked as if she'd been slapped. Bitter chill replaced the subtle heat running through her veins. "I'm not interested in your money, Nicholas," she said icily. "Or in whatever else you're offering. Now, if you'll excuse me—"

She caught the door handle and flung it open, blinking in the vivid morning sunlight. Nicholas leaned out over the passenger seat, regarding her from behind the shield of his sunglasses.

"I trust I satisfied some part of your curiosity, Diana," he said silkily.

She turned around and braced her feet on the sidewalk. "Satisfied?" she retorted.

"There are many kinds of satisfaction, Diana. Perhaps the kind you're looking for can't be found in mere words."

He withdrew into his van with a smile that was all mocking seduction, and pulled away from the curb without once looking back.

———

"You haven't heard a word I've said."

Judith studied Nicholas's profile as they descended the wide curving stairway in the elegant lobby of Davies Symphony Hall. All during the performance of "Eine Kleine Nachtmusik" he'd seemed far away; he loved Mozart—a devotion he'd carried from youth—and normally the music would have fully absorbed his attention.

But not tonight. Tonight his mind was on something else, and Judith thought she knew what it was.

Who *she* was.

The voices of departing concertgoers rose around them like discordant music. Judith slid her hand along the polished brass railing of the stairway and stared past the tall white columns and high glass walls of the hall, out into the bustle of the night-bound city.

"Have you seen Diana Ransom since last week, Nicholas?"

He might have dissembled; he could deceive almost anyone else. She saw the twitch in the muscles of his jaw, the narrowing of his eyes as he guided her out the green tinted glass doors and onto Van Ness. The evening was chill and clear.

"Am I so transparent, Judith?" Nicholas asked softly.

"Not often, Nicholas. Not often." Judith pulled the edges of her coat more closely across her chest, concentrating on keeping every hint of sadness from her voice. *You knew it would come to this one day.*

He laughed, a rare and unexpected and somewhat brittle sound. "Have you seen her, Judith?"

Oh, yes. She had been right. She read it under the unnatural stillness of his face, in the viridian, inhuman brilliance of his eyes as they caught the glow of a street lamp overhead.

"If you're asking if she came to question me about you, the answer is no."

The set of his shoulders relaxed almost imperceptibly. "But you've spoken to her?"

Judith nodded. "About Keely." *But it was the things Diana didn't say that told me the most.* She clenched her fingers a little more tightly on the sleeve of his suit jacket and wistfully observed a young man lighting up a cigarette. Nicholas had made her quit: "I don't want to lose you before I must, Judith," he'd told her in a rare moment of vulnerability.

The memory could still bring tears to her eyes. She sucked in a breath of bracing air.

"Diana did let you know that Keely was given a clean bill of health?" she said quietly.

His eyes had taken on a distant expression, one she knew well. The look that meant he was sojourning in a past she had no part of. He was a hundred and fifty years older than she was. He had seen things she could scarcely imagine. And yet there were times—times like this—when she thought he was only the young man he appeared to be.

A young man she'd loved nearly all her life.

"I've seen Keely—in Mama Soma's," Nicholas murmured. "She's—back to normal."

Keely. Not Diana. He dodged the subject on both their minds with deliberate remoteness.

They made their way in silence to Meyer's Libretto Café just down the street from the symphony hall, as they did after every concert. This was Judith's time with Nicholas, when she had him all to herself, when there wasn't Foundation business to be taken care of, papers to sign, decisions to be made about Nicholas's considerable wealth.

But he wasn't truly with her at all tonight, even when he seated her at a table and took her coat and made her feel like a young woman again.

A waiter maneuvered among the closely packed tables to take their orders. Judith glanced at the dessert menu, sighed, and ordered herself coffee and a salad. As usual, Nicholas confined himself to coffee. The drone of conversation made it impossible for anyone to eavesdrop.

Clearing her throat softly, Judith stirred cream into her coffee and studied Nicholas. "The day Diana brought Keely home, Diana told me how she found you in Mama Soma's."

That caught his interest. He tilted his head like a cat twitching its ear to capture a drift of sound.

"She said you two got off to a bit of a rocky start." She took a measured swallow of her coffee. "But she told me very little about your trip to Las Playas." *Not much— except with her eyes whenever she mentioned your name.*

"Why should she?" Nicholas muttered. "We went up to look for Keely and didn't find her."

"Yes, I know." She set the mug down carefully. "All very practical and proper, I have no doubt."

His eyes snapped to hers, blazing to vivid intensity, and even after all their time together she almost flinched. "Are you mocking me, Judith?" he asked softly.

"You know better than that."

He jerked his gaze away from hers, the agitation of his movements more eloquent than any words.

"When you called to tell me Diana might come by to ask questions about you," she continued, "I knew she wasn't just a woman who happened to share your concern over Keely."

"Did you?"

She ignored the subtle, warning edge in his tone.

"Tell me about her, Nicholas." *Tell me why I knew something powerful was between you the moment I saw you together. Make me understand. . . .*

He stared out the tinted glass windows of the café.

The battle within him was just visible to her trained eyes. When his gaze swung back to her, the distance in it was gone, and she knew his human side—the vulnerable part of him so seldom revealed—had won.

"She's a dreamer, Judith. A dreamer such as I haven't seen in a century."

Judith looked down at her hands. "Is that all?"

"All?" He laughed almost silently. "She's nothing like the others."

The others. Those women he called "dreamers," who fed his physical need for human life force but not the hunger in his heart.

Judith felt a rush of tenderness—an emotion she couldn't show and he wouldn't accept. "So you've— touched her," she said carefully. "And yet you've had dealings with her in waking life, unlike your other dreamers."

"I've never had any—*need* to know the others."

He didn't have to explain further. She knew his reasons for touching his dreamers only in sleep. Those few mortal friends he kept were never subject to his inhuman hunger. The line was always carefully drawn, as it had been drawn with Judith in postwar Europe when she'd grown old enough to fall in love with him.

"I never sought her out," Nicholas said suddenly. "I never looked for her." He breathed in deeply and let out a long, shuddering sigh. "She knows nothing of what I am. She doesn't recognize me from her dreams." He closed his eyes. "I've touched her twice, the second time in Las Playas. I haven't fed since, Judith."

The significance of that admission did not escape her. She had been aware of Nicholas's needs since her eighth year, when she'd caught him skimming life force from a dreamer in a bombed-out building in Paris. That had been the one and only time she'd seen him do it, but the image was imprinted on her memory: Nicholas leaning over the woman as she slept, his hands cradling her face; the expression on his own as he took what he needed—a raptness, a concentration frightening and alien in its intensity.

It had been the one time she'd ever feared him. Until he'd explained it all to her . . .

"I took more from her than I've ever taken from a single dreamer," he whispered. "I almost lost control, Judith."

Lost control. For a moment those two words rang in her ears, blotting out the others. Nicholas never lost control. He held himself to a rigid discipline designed to prevent harm to his dreamers and keep his own hungers in check. A discipline that held him apart from the rest of the world like a Tibetan monk in a mountain cave.

Had Diana Ransom unwittingly found her way into that cave?

"I don't know Diana well, Nicholas," she said. "But if I understand you correctly, you're saying that Diana has such abundant life force that the usual rules don't apply."

His eyes seemed to darken all at once, the centers black with a corona of green flame. "There are still things you don't know about me, Judith," he said softly.

She threw caution to the winds. "I know you're afraid of getting close to anyone who might threaten that precious 'control' of yours. I know that you loved a woman once who could have given you something you desperately needed, and that you lost her. I know you're afraid of letting that happen again."

Nicholas went very still. "I never told you how I lost her."

"You don't have to. You blame yourself, and because of something that happened a century ago you've cut yourself off from the greatest joys a human being can know."

His smile was chilling. "Human, Judith?"

Without thinking, Judith slapped her palm on the tabletop. "Don't hide behind your supposed inhumanity, Nicholas. You're more human than most people I know." She glared at him. "That's it, isn't it? You want more from Diana than her life force. You want something that's a lot riskier—not for her, but for *you.*"

Suddenly he rose, swift as a leopard, only the table a barrier between them. Faces turned toward them curiously. "Don't presume to speak of something you can't understand," he hissed in a biting undertone.

She raised her hands. "Forgive me, Your Lordship. Did it ever occur to you that you might possibly underestimate humankind? That there might be a few other people out there who can accept what you are?"

His jaw worked, and slowly, slowly he sat back down. The diners around them returned to their meals and their private conversations. All at once the tension drained out of Nicholas's body; his lips curved into a pleasantly neutral smile, and Judith knew she'd lost him again.

With practiced ease he changed the subject, asking her about the forthcoming Dreamseekers Foundation Halloween Ball. She found herself surrendering, giving him the report he asked for without resistance.

But when they got up to leave and Nicholas paid the bill, Judith knew the other matter was far from resolved. *You can't run away forever, Nicholas,* she thought sadly.

As he drove her home, she was already wondering how to make Nicholas face what he feared. He never saw the slight smile that curved her lips in the darkened van.

She had no doubt that Diana would wish to support an excellent cause like the Dreamseekers Grant for Young

Artists—especially considering how it had helped Keely. The annual fundraising Halloween Ball was a masquerade affair; Nicholas would be there incognito.

And, with an invitation and a little luck, so would Diana Ransom.

Bravo, Nicholas.

He let himself in the house and stood in the foyer, listening to the silence. The grandfather clock in the hall beat out its eternal rhythm, the only welcome he ever received.

He'd managed to upset Judith on a night that should have been enjoyable for both of them. He'd been poor company, had revealed too much—and Judith had naturally gone right to the heart of the matter.

Diana.

Jerking at the knot of his tie, he played over the last time he'd been with Diana. He'd sent her off in high dudgeon, exactly as if it had been his plan to get rid of her. The problem was that it hadn't really been a plan at all. He'd driven her away because of his instinctive need for self-protection.

Judith had known. It seemed she always did.

But Diana knew almost nothing at all. She would hardly be able to penetrate his deepest secrets, even with all her psychological skills. But he realized that his desire to know more of her was becoming as much a hunger as his need for her body's life force. That life force still beat through him, made him stronger than he'd ever been. Stronger, more whole, more alive . . .

He couldn't risk seeing her again. He'd made that mistake by going with her to Las Playas. He would not play these games with Diana and his own dangerous desire.

Games.

Adrian had loved to play games.

Nicholas closed his eyes. He remembered Keely's expression when she had first returned, blank and bruised with weariness. And her supposed loss of memory—so much like Diana's when Nicholas had made her believe their time in the mine was all a dream.

Keely had been unable to describe her lover's face.

Coincidence. It could *still* be nothing more than coincidence. . . .

Nicholas was turning toward the hallway and the library when the finely polished toe of his shoe brushed something just inside the door. It was an envelope—white, plain, indistinguishable from any other.

A nameless dread sliced through him. He bent to pick it up.

Mon Frère, the handwritten letters spelled out across the front of it. His blood turned thick as sludge and bile rose acid in his throat.

The note was written in an elegant hand. Nicholas drove the tremors from his fingers as he began to read.

My Dearest Brother,

This letter may come as a Surprise to you, but I think perhaps not an unexpected one.

I had the Pleasure of meeting your dear Friend Keely Ames a few weeks ago. Such a charming girl. I would have thought her a little unpolished for your tastes—as I remember them—but much may Change in a century, as I have had reason to learn.

It seems that Miss Ames was Bereft because you would not be her cher amant. She was quite pleased to accept a reasonable Substitute. She was truly Delightful, and so very cooperative. Her Dreams were quite out of the ordinary way. She might easily have provided me with everything I needed for a Year or more before she Faded.

But thoughts of you, Dearest Brother, intruded upon my pleasures. You see, I have Changed. A hundred years of Solitude gives one a great deal of Time to think. I should not have liked to begin my new Life with such an Iniquitous Act.

By now you will have seen Miss Ames and know she is well. What little Effect she has suffered will quickly fade. I took the liberty of dimming her memory. She will not remember me.

I trust, Elder Brother, that you will regard this Act in the light in which it was intended. We are of one Blood. Two centuries cannot change that. Let there be no more war between us. Let the Past remain dead, and Enmity forgotten.

Perhaps one day we shall meet again. Until then, I have my own Pilgrimage to make, following in your footsteps. By the time you receive this letter I will be gone from your City and the New World.

Pax.
Your Most Affectionate,
Adrian

Nicholas's hand convulsed, and the letter drifted silently to the floor.

Adrian. He could not form the name with his lips, but it echoed in his heart like the cry of a child lost in the dark.

Like an automaton, Nicholas walked into the library off the main hall and dropped into a wing chair. He stared at the heavy velvet drapes that blocked all the light from the windows, seeing only the laughing mirror image of his own face.

Laughing. He saw Adrian laughing, though his last memory of his brother was a visage contorted in hatred and despair. Cursing Nicholas uselessly, because human curses meant nothing to their kind.

But now he remembered other times. Earlier times, when they had been children in their mortal stepfather's home in the north of England. When Elizabeth, their mother, had been alive and able to guide them. Before they had chosen different paths.

Adrian had loved life, taken all it had to give. If their immortal mother had lived, his recklessness might have been channeled into something benign, even extraordinary.

But Elizabeth had not lived. She had gone mad, driven to it in her tragic efforts to become mortal, and had taken their stepfather's life in the last throes of that madness. Two boys had been left alone, with a few human retainers, to struggle with their sorrow—and with what they must become.

Two boys who had gone out into the world and been driven apart by philosophies and beliefs that would never be compatible. After their first separation, the night of Nicholas's terrible "initiation" in London, they had rarely met over the next eighty years.

Until Adrian had come to take Sarah.

Nicholas let his head drop back against the chair, weary in every bone and muscle.

I had no choice. What he had done to his brother was not merely revenge.

"A hundred years of solitude gives one a great deal of time to think." Solitude—Nicholas laughed bitterly. Torture was a more accurate word. But Adrian had broken out of his prison in the end, in spite of his brother's sentence of eternal damnation.

Adrian.

How long had he been free? How long had he watched Nicholas, unperceived, waiting for the proper moment to reveal himself? How much harm could he have done if he had chosen?

And Adrian had let Keely go. He had taken her deliberately, knowing her for Nicholas's friend, and then he had let her go unharmed. There could be no surer way of proving his sincerity.

"Let there be no more war between us."

Nicholas closed his eyes. Could he still feel hope after so much time? Could things truly change—could *they* change, being what they were? Could he put Sarah and the past behind him, and forget?

He is my brother.

Nicholas got up and paced across the room and back again, clenching his hands into knots at his back. To hunt down his brother, try to imprison him once more—

Nicholas had no wish to do it. Not again. Never again.

"Let the Past remain dead, and Enmity forgotten."

Spinning on his heel, Nicholas left the library and returned to the foyer. He stared at the note that lay abandoned on the Axminster carpet.

Slowly he bent to retrieve it. Like a man robbed of senses and reason he walked into the small parlor where he kept his only telephone and spread the note out on the table beside it.

He was dialing before he realized the number that had come unbidden into his mind. The phone rang once, and again, and then Diana's voice came softly over the line.

"Hello?"

Very gently he placed the receiver back in its cradle. With his other hand he reached for the note and crushed it until his nails dug into his palms.

SEVEN

How silver-sweet sound lovers' tongues by
  night,
Like softest music to attending ears!
      —William Shakespeare, *Romeo and Juliet*

The night of the Dreamseekers Foundation Halloween
Ball arrived cold and crisp, complete with eerie wisps of
clouds drifting over an atmospheric gibbous moon.

Diana glanced out the half-open blinds as she finished
the paperwork on her final session with José Sanchez.
They had terminated therapy by mutual agreement that
afternoon; she'd gone as far as she could in helping José,
and he was capable now of handling the rest on his own.
He was on his way to a new and better life, and there was
nothing more a therapist could ask for than that.

She stretched luxuriantly, allowing herself a satisfied smile. She was ready to celebrate. And a Halloween masquerade fit the bill exactly.

Diana rose from her desk, automatically smoothing the fabric of her costume gown. "Empress Joséphine," the clerk at the rental store had assured her, though Diana doubted that an empress would have been satisfied with the slightly threadbare costume. There hadn't been much left at such short notice.

Diana wondered if it wouldn't have been better to go in something a little less revealing. The white fabric was thin, almost transparent, high-waisted like a sixties granny dress and with a deep, square-cut décolletage. But something in this costume had caught her interest—perhaps the element of the romantic in it, a flashback to the dream of the mysterious horseman on the beach.

Remembering the dream of the gray rider—a dream she had been unable to forget—Diana thought that heroic figure would have been the ideal escort. . . .

Her vision of the gray rider melted into a memory of someone unmistakably real. Nicholas would be at the ball. When Judith had sent the invitation, she'd casually admitted that the reclusive Nicholas Gale was one of the trustees of the Dreamseekers Foundation, an organization that provided aid and scholarships in the arts to underprivileged youth—of which Keely had been a beneficiary. Judith herself was one of the Foundation's administrators. Keely didn't know of Nicholas's involvement, but it gave Diana another reason to be grateful to the man she had tried so unsuccessfully to forget.

Gratitude was much safer than the other unwelcome emotions she'd felt toward Nicholas Gale. To believe she could dismiss him from her mind and memory was the worst kind of self-deception.

Tugging her incongruous plain wool coat closer about

the thin gown, Diana waited in the hallway for Tim to arrive. He'd been eager to offer his escort when he'd learned Keely would be at the ball—and even on his modest teacher's salary he was more than happy to pay the substantial cost of his ticket. "All in a good cause," he'd said. *More than one good cause,* Diana thought wryly. *Getting in good with Keely's cousin.*

But Tim surprised her when he arrived at the door in a dashing Zorro costume, complete with black mask. He swept her a bow and offered his arm.

"Shall we go, my lady? The carriage awaits."

Diana suppressed a giggle, already feeling the magic of this night. In this gown and mask she was not herself, serious and practical Diana Ransom, but a regal empress who would draw all eyes without a trace of embarrassment. Even Tim had thrown off his usual guilelessness and had acquired a faint air of mystery.

Taking Tim's arm, she walked down the steps and past the last of the trick-or-treaters carrying their booty home, trailed by vigilant parents. Tim's '85 Tercel was hardly a conveyance for an empress, but he whisked them expertly through the congested streets and downtown to the old but still elegant Barbary Towers Hotel in record time. The streets around Market were busier than they usually were on a Sunday night, and even the city lights seemed brighter.

Masked men and women in costumes of every era and description entered the spotless glass doors of the lobby, following a series of playful, artistic signs to the grand ballroom. The moment Diana entered she stopped and stared; the vast room was a throwback to an earlier mode of decoration, with every wall and pillar covered in mirrored panels. And yet it seemed appropriate; it reflected the colorful costumes like a prism, lending magic that intensified the pleasant air of unreality.

Tim took her coat and, with a mumbled apology, disappeared. Diana hardly noticed his defection. She looked around, telling herself she was searching for Keely or Judith. But her heart mocked her as it urged her eyes to seek a certain mane of blond hair and a tall, elegant, unmistakable figure.

A small chamber ensemble on a platform to the rear of the ballroom played a transcription of Strauss's "Music of the Spheres" waltz, nearly drowned out by the bursts of laughter and conversation. Diana smiled at several passing gentleman, declining offers to dance. She had to resist the impulse to cross her arms in front of her half-exposed chest.

Before she had a chance to locate Keely among the knots of people, a tall and commanding figure in a wide-skirted Elizabethan gown, high ruff, and curly red wig swept toward her.

"Diana?" Judith's voice emerged from a face whitened by makeup, her eyes concealed by a red mask. "I hardly recognized you. Welcome." She extended a hand, and Diana took it. Judith's eyes swept over Diana appreciatively. "You couldn't have chosen a more flattering costume."

Forcing herself to keep from turning aside the compliment, Diana smiled warmly. "Thanks." She regarded Judith's far more elaborate outfit. "Queen Elizabeth?"

The older woman tilted up her chin. "But of course. And now I shall have at least one equal in this assemblage. Come and meet the others."

"The others" consisted of a mixture of wealthy society matrons delighted to dress up in support of a good cause; several trustees of the Foundation, ranging from a Harlequin to a robot; local celebrities, ill-concealed by their masks, surrounded by admirers; and the youthful beneficiaries of the Foundation's numerous grants. The young people's costumes tended toward the fantastic, many handmade. "Most of them are artists, musicians—original thinkers," Judith whispered as she completed another introduction. "Like Keely."

Automatically Diana stood on the toes of her slippered feet to look for her cousin.

"She's here somewhere," Judith said at her elbow. "Why don't you get some punch and mingle a little. I'll see if I can find her."

Diana sighed, rubbing her arms. She patted at her hair nervously. The Harlequin she'd met earlier came up to engage her in conversation, liberally peppered with rather weak jokes and earnest compliments. A flurry of motion caught Diana's distracted gaze, and all at once Keely emerged from the crowd, a green-clad sprite with a feathered cap, tunic, and tights, her face glowing with color and health.

"Diana!" Keely's eyes were bright as she put out her arms for a hug. Diana returned it briefly and studied her cousin from ankle boots to felt cap.

"I'm glad you came," Keely said breathlessly. "That's a great costume." She put her hands on her hips and threw back her head, *tsk*ing softly. "I know that look." With a dramatic flourish she pivoted in a slow circle. "Well? Are you ready to stop worrying yet, *Lady* Di?"

Diana gave Keely a self-conscious smile. "You look fine, Keely." It was true—Keely looked one hundred percent better than she had any time since her return from Las Playas. All traces of weariness and disorientation were gone.

"I feel great," Keely said.

Diana felt an upwelling of warmth, more than mere relief that Keely was back on her feet. How long had it been since *she'd* been at a social event just for the fun of it, spent time with friends? Not colleagues who shared her work, but interesting new acquaintances and people she genuinely cared about? The magic she'd felt earlier that evening washed through her again, making her shiver.

"Let me guess. A female Robin Hood?"

Tim swept dramatically up to them, flourishing his black cape. Beneath his mask he was grinning ear to ear, and his gray eyes were fixed on Keely.

For the first time in Tim's presence Keely's smile was quite genuine. "Why not?" she said, tilting up her chin. "And you're Zorro—"

"Which makes us two of a kind. Want to go find some rich to rob? There seem to be plenty here. Or would you rather dance?" His smile wavered as he glanced at Diana. "That is, if you don't mind, Diana," he added.

Diana made a regal gesture of dismissal, and Keely giggled. The sound was so light, so unforced, that Diana almost laughed aloud with her. "Who'll lead?" Keely said. But she was already taking Tim's extended arm and letting him whirl her into a slow waltz.

Way to go, Tim, Diana thought, watching them dance. Tim managed to trip twice over his cape, but Keely only laughed. Maybe this last episode with her "mystery man" had cured Keely of her attraction for bad boys. If she'd thought she'd been in love with Nicholas once, as he'd claimed, she had shown no signs of such feelings since her return from Las Playas.

Maybe now Keely would be willing to look at someone who'd be good for her—a stable, supportive, caring man like Tim.

And as for you, Diana . . . She found herself looking around for the one man she didn't see. *Maybe you ought to follow your own advice.*

Two weeks. She hadn't seen or spoken to Nicholas in two weeks, except for one brief phone call to update him on Keely's condition. Several times since she had thought of calling him, but there had never been a good enough excuse. They had been brought together by mutual concern for Keely; Keely—or a public event such as this one —would be the only reason to see him again. The only reason . . .

And then she saw him. Across the room, passing among the other dancers like a stalking leopard. His mirror image reflected from every pillar, every wall, until the room seemed filled with a hundred Nicholases. He turned at last and looked directly at her.

He smiled, and she felt her mouth go dry. She couldn't forget that smile in a million years, let alone two weeks. Everything she still didn't know about Nicholas Gale hovered in that smile, layers of mystery and enigma she hadn't come close to unraveling. . . .

And then, as quickly as he'd appeared, he vanished in the crowd. Too late Diana lifted her hand, and let it fall back to her side, fingers clenched. Resolutely she turned with a vivid smile to the pirate who solicited her hand for the next dance.

Allhallows' Eve.

A night when dreams walked freely, released from the dark abyss of Man's unconscious mind. Ghouls loped alongside ethereal maidens, and demons held truce with priests.

Nicholas always went out on Halloween night. He could don the fashions of his youth and not look out of place, returning to the one time of innocence he had known.

And there was a heady freedom, a wildness in the cool San Francisco air. On this night all rules were set aside, and he felt the beat of human life force almost thick enough to touch.

Tonight he was no different than the rest.

Sometimes he hunted on such nights, reading auras of women who passed, seeking new dreamers to ease his hunger. But he had no taste for that now. When he let his mind wander, he could think of only one dreamer. He always forced his thoughts away from her, because as the need grew stronger and the time came when he must feed, he faced a danger he had foreseen and ignored.

He had all but starved himself the past two weeks. Twice he had failed in his attempts to skim dreamers; it was as if he touched something repellent, something his system refused to accept, like too much rich food and drink he could not digest. He had sensed the risk in Las Playas when he had given in to temptation and entered Diana's dreaming mind. Now he knew he had been right. Having tasted Diana, his body wanted no other.

He wanted no other.

He tried to turn his thoughts away from her as he arrived at the Barbary Towers and made his way to the crowded ballroom. From all appearances the ball would be an unqualified success. The money generated from the tickets would supplement his own regular contributions, and—

He froze as he caught sight of Diana dancing in a rotund pirate's arms.

All thought, all reason fled. Hunger raced through him, driving rationality from his mind. He fixed his eyes on his goal and began to weave his way among the couples and knots of people, losing sight of her only to find her again in a reflection or a flash of white amid vivid color.

The dance ended just as he reached her. She turned to glance his way, a smile for her erstwhile partner still on her lips, and as her gaze caught his the smile faded.

She was lovely tonight, lovelier than he had remembered. Her aura was brilliant and potent, calling to him like a siren's song. His eyes dropped from Diana's face to her delicate neck and the creamy expanse of her bosom above the low bodice of her high-waisted gown. The gown was hardly of the finest quality, but it looked magnificent on her—the classic, gentle drape of the white fabric from just beneath her breasts to the floor, the small puffed sleeves, the tiny slippers just visible under the hem.

A pocket Venus, he thought, drawing from the memories of his youth. She had done something to her hair so that it curled around her face, in the fashion of one of the ladies of the *ton.*

He swallowed to wet his dry mouth. That she should choose such a costume was ironic. He saw her return his scrutiny, taking in his snug-fitting bottle green tailcoat, elaborately tied cravat, embroidered waistcoat, snug buff breeches, and polished Hessians. Proper lord to her lady.

Diana cleared her throat and smoothed the fabric of her gown over her thighs. Nicholas noted the gesture and felt a tightening in his body that had recently become familiar again.

"I hadn't known you'd be here tonight, Diana," he said softly.

She arched one brow in a show of nonchalance. "No? Judith sent me an invitation. It's only right that I help support the foundation that did so much for Keely."

The way she looked at him made him realize that Judith had revealed his true position behind the Foundation. He clenched his fists to hide the shaking of his hands.

"So it was—Keely who brought you here tonight, Diana?"

Faint color stained her cheeks, and he knew. He knew she had expected him to be here. And hadn't he, in his heart, expected to see her again?

Her clear blue eyes, framed by the white silk mask

she wore, still clung to innocence. He knew he could make her feel his hunger if he loosed it for only an instant; she was that sensitive, that perfect a dreamer.

He forced himself to look away from her eyes. From the moment he had read his brother's letter, he had stayed away from Diana. His conversation with Judith had changed nothing. Supreme irony: Adrian had unwittingly brought the two of them together, Nicholas and the one dreamer who could match, even transcend, the woman Adrian had taken from him. But Adrian had come to stand between them, his mocking image ever in Nicholas's mind.

"Because we are the same, brother," Adrian had said long ago. *"Fight it as you will: we are the same."* Nicholas had spent his life denying that avowal. And Diana had been put before him as the supreme test.

A test he might fail.

So he had stayed away, although she never left his thoughts. He and Diana had both been safe.

Until now. Now Diana's life force pulsed like a visible thing in the air around her, her aura flaring like a glowing mantle, driving him to the edge of endurance. He had waited too long. Now he could no more tear himself away from her than he could sever his own arm.

He looked at Diana until the color rose in her cheeks again and she tilted up her chin in unconscious defiance.

"That's a very impressive costume, Nicholas," she said. "Where did you find it?"

"I have a particular interest in the costume of the nineteenth century, and a tailor who has great skill at re-creating it." He let his eyes drop to the soft skin above the edge of her bodice. "Allow me to return the compliment. That style suits you very well, Diana."

She showed her teeth. "I'm afraid this came from a rack of theatrical leftovers."

"I assure you that no one would notice," he said, "given the woman wearing it."

Her fingers curled into the fabric draped over her thighs. "You do your costume justice, Nicholas. You play the role of gallant gentleman very effectively with the right props."

He was spared an appropriate retort as the music began again: Sibelius's "Valse triste," played at a slow dance tempo.

"Do you waltz, Diana?"

She blinked up at him. "I don't—"

But he grasped her hand, pulling her up gently before she could complete the protest. The first touch stunned him; by the time he had her in his arms, he had damped his senses so that he could hold her without being overwhelmed by his need.

And then he began to guide her in the dance. The waltz was slow; Diana held herself rigid for the first bars, her fingers barely touching his shoulder. He respected her reserve and held her away from his body, as carefully as if she were a debutante just given permission to waltz.

By the middle of the piece, Diana had lost her stiffness. Her body eased against his. Her fingers curved to fit his shoulder, and he drew her close with his hand at her slim waist. He could feel her heartbeat through her skin; through her clothing and his own; her eyes were closed, as if she were afraid to see how near he was.

Nicholas breathed in the smell of her hair. "At the time your gown was in fashion," he murmured, "the waltz was still a somewhat scandalous dance."

She made a small sound, muffled into his waistcoat. "Was it? I can't imagine why."

"A gentleman had to hold his partner at a correct and specific distance," he said.

"Which I notice," she said, "you aren't doing." Suddenly she laughed, flinging back her head to look up at him. "I should be resisting you like a proper lady."

"Shall we be daring, Diana, and fly in the face of convention?"

He caught a glimpse of wildness in her eyes before she pressed her face to his chest. She trembled, and as the music ended he stroked her hair and let himself savor the exquisite torment of her nearness.

"May I?"

A tap on Nicholas's shoulder shattered the spell. A tall, thin gentleman with whitened face and vampire accoutrements eased himself between them, swinging Diana away. Nicholas caught a glimpse of her oddly pale, almost frightened face before he spun on his heel and strode to the edge of the room, searching for Judith.

He found her almost immediately, but his efforts to get her onto the dance floor ended in defeat. "Not me," she said, that perpetual trace of sadness in her husky voice. "I'm busy entertaining the old folks." She laughed, a little hoarsely. "What happened to Diana? You made a lovely couple."

The melancholy in her brown eyes made it impossible for him to berate her for her misplaced efforts at match-making. "Carried away by a vampire," he said, focusing on Judith to keep from searching out Diana again.

Judith caught her breath, trying not to let Nicholas see the way her heart twisted inside her. He was unbelievably handsome in his exquisite costume, his eyes like fire-struck emeralds behind the gold of his mask. Here, in this magic place, it was all too easy to slip back in time to her sixteenth year when she'd first fallen in love with the man who had saved her life in war-torn France.

When he lifted elegant fingers to brush back a lock of his golden hair, she stared down at her own aged and wrinkled hand, turning it over and over.

If I can give you what I can't have, Nicholas, she swore silently, *I'll die happy.*

She blinked and looked up, prepared to crack a joke and send him on his way. But he was already gone. In spite of herself she searched the room for him, caught his reflection in a distant mirror very near the exit. Was he running away again? She closed her eyes, and when she opened them she glimpsed him at the opposite end of the room, approaching Diana as she accepted a drink from a man dressed as King Henry VIII.

My eyes are finally giving out on me, she thought wryly, adjusting her wig as she watched Nicholas take the drink from Diana's hand and lead her into the next dance. Rising in a rustle of skirts, Judith walked regally to the refreshment table and helped herself to a glass of champagne. She lifted the glass toward the swaying couple.

"To you, Diana. May you be the woman I never could."

She downed the champagne in one hearty swallow.

It was a most delightful farce.

Diana was most appropriately dressed tonight. Her aura was everything he had sensed at the gallery, and when he'd seen her with his brother on the beach at Las Playas—a promise fulfilled a hundredfold now that he touched her, felt her life force humming under the pale softness of her skin, beating in time to her pulse.

She was Sarah's true heir—not her elder sister, and not the young cousin who danced in a caped mortal's arms halfway across the ballroom.

No. *This* one was kin, not in appearance, but in spirit to the girl Nicholas had pursued and lost a century ago.

Diana Ransom was the object of desire, the danger,

the enemy. The one who could change his brother forever.

Who might win an immortal's love.

Adrian smiled, and the woman in his arms gazed up into his eyes, all unsuspecting. Still—innocent. Lovely Diana had no idea her partner was not the man she'd danced with earlier, her would-be lover. Adrian had taken special care to duplicate his brother's costume in every particular. He maintained his silence, and the woman was content to keep it.

He stroked her skin between her puffed sleeve and the upper edge of her glove, savoring the sensation. Nicholas had not initiated her fully. His mark was very faint in her life force.

But she shuddered at Adrian's touch, and her desire was manifest to Adrian's heightened senses.

Nicholas had not yet possessed her body. Understanding his brother, Adrian knew the reason. Nicholas was still afraid, even after a hundred years. Would he overcome his fear and take this lovely, unsuspecting mortal in truth as well as in dreams? Would he attempt to attain what he'd always coveted?

It would be so simple to lure Diana away now, secure in her belief that Nicholas held her in his arms.

Swinging Diana in a graceful arc across the floor, Adrian searched the room for his brother. *No. Not yet.* The game would continue. He closed his eyes and flung back his head as the music swelled.

When he won, his brother would never desert him again for the paltry dream of mortality.

The dance ended, and Adrian bowed deeply to his partner, noting the banked flame of repressed passion in her blue eyes.

"Nicholas—"

Diana reached out for Adrian as he drew away, her

dark brows pulled into a frown. But he could risk no more; he bent briefly over her hand to kiss her gloved fingers, and then melted away into the crowd.

Never fear, lovely Diana. We shall meet again.

The ball ended a scant hour before dawn.

The three of them had gathered by the chaos that remained of the refreshment table. Everyone but the caterers and cleanup crew had left—including, Diana noted with satisfaction, Keely and Tim. Together. Tim had forgotten entirely how Diana had arrived at the ball, but she hardly minded the minor inconvenience of his desertion.

Judith stretched, smiling at Diana. "These old bones weren't, made for costumes like this—I can't wait to get home and into my bed." She shifted her eyes to the man who stood staring out across the empty room. "I'd say it was a grand success, wouldn't you, Nicholas?"

He turned toward the women, his uncovered face more unreadable than it had been with the gold mask in place. "Oh, yes, Judith. A great—success."

Diana stared at Nicholas, knowing he wasn't even aware of her scrutiny. Since that last, surprisingly erotic waltz, when he had been so silent—when he had seemed so different in ways she couldn't define—he'd hardly spoken to her at all. And yet the charged tension between them had not abated. On the contrary, it had grown almost unbearable.

Judith stood up from the chair beside the refreshment table and winced, rubbing her back.

"I'm off to bed now. What about you two?"

Diana's gaze snapped back to Judith just as Nicholas's did.

"Your ride deserted you, Diana," Judith reminded her, "and I know that Nicholas took a cab here tonight."

She met Nicholas's unreadable stare. "It won't be light for an hour or two, but—"

"I'll find a taxi," Nicholas interrupted.

"Then you might as well share," Judith said reasonably.

Diana knew she ought to come up with a sensible excuse for going home alone, but there was none. Nicholas seemed to have reached the same conclusion; he bowed to both women with mocking, military precision, clicking his boot heels together.

"I'll find a cab," he said, and left the room with long, almost angry strides.

Diana shivered. She sat down at one of the chairs by the refreshment table, tugging off her long gloves. Judith took the nearest chair and rubbed off white makeup under her eyes.

"You haven't gotten Nicholas figured out yet, have you?"

Startled out of her incessant smoothing of the gloves over her hand, Diana glanced up. She composed her face into its coolest professional lines. "I don't know what—you mean."

"Any woman would—want to understand a man like Nicholas," Judith continued. She dropped her eyes and tugged at her full skirts. "I know he hasn't told you much about himself. That's his way."

Diana leaned forward, twisting the gloves into knots between her fingers. "You've already told me about the Foundation. He's hinted about his wealth, told me what you do for him. . . ."

"Believe me," Judith said, "even something that minor is a revelation for Nicholas." She regarded Diana from under her painted brows. "We haven't had much chance to talk, you and I. But I think you've realized he's something of a loner. He has few friends, and none of them knows more than one aspect of his personality."

Half-afraid of the direction the conversation was leading but driven by the need to know more, Diana nodded. "Keely doesn't know he's behind the foundation that helped her. She thinks he's an artist—"

"Exactly. Keely doesn't know, and never will. But Nicholas is more than merely a trustee—he founded Dreamseekers, and he still contributes most of the money. In Keely's case, the grant she received helped get her back on her feet, into art school, and funded her first showing last month. And she isn't the only one, not by a long shot. Nicholas is many things, Diana, but there aren't many people in this world who know even half of them."

Judith shook her head, a faint, sad smile on her face. "I'll be frank with you, Diana. I think you're interested in Nicholas for more reasons than simple curiosity. And I think the feeling is mutual."

Diana swallowed, her mouth too dry to form words.

"I've been Nick's friend for a very long time, and I know this much. He isn't a man who falls easily into any relationship. He has his reasons, and I have no right to reveal them. But, in spite of his lady-killer looks, he's alone. Has been for years. And he doesn't deserve it."

Alone. Diana closed her eyes. Alone in that big house by the ocean, confined by daylight. Alone at the table in Mama Soma's. She'd seen women fall all over him, but Judith said he was alone. . . .

"It would take someone very special to get under his skin," Judith continued softly. "And it probably wouldn't be easy." She sighed. "Nicholas has his reasons for doing what he does, living as he does—his 'ghosts,' if you will. And he—" Judith bit her lip in an uncharacteristic show of nerves. "He's not like ordinary men, Diana—"

That was an understatement. A man who couldn't

stand sunlight, who didn't seem to sleep or dream, who lived like a recluse, and had a bizarre, magnetic pull on her she didn't understand . . .

Diana lost the thread of all the questions she'd meant to ask. She'd become a therapist to help others, because of what had happened to Clare. Nicholas helped others because of something that haunted him. She had only recently begun to truly dream again, and Nicholas claimed not to remember his at all.

Coincidence and parallel. Layer upon layer. She penetrated one only to find more, endlessly wound like a mummy's wrappings.

"Are you ready to go, Diana?"

Nicholas stood behind her, her coat folded over his arm. He held it for her as she put it on, not quite touching her. He showed no sign that he'd heard any part of their conversation, but Diana felt strangely exposed under his gaze. She buttoned the coat to the neck and watched Nicholas help Judith up. Together they left the ballroom, passing the sleepy cleanup crew, and walked out onto the street where two taxis were waiting at the curb.

"Thanks, Judith," Diana said, taking the older woman's hand. "I had a wonderful time."

Judith's grip was surprisingly firm, and her eyes searched Diana's intently for a long moment before her smile reappeared. "Be careful going home," she said softly. "You never know what you'll run into on a night like this."

The streets were nearly empty as the cabbie left downtown San Francisco and headed north toward Seacliff.

Between Nicholas and Diana the silence had a life of its own, throbbing with repressed passion and unspoken desire. Heat gathered in the cab like molten metal in a crucible. Diana glanced aside at him and wet her lips.

"How did you meet Judith?"

Nicholas started. He looked down at his hands, clenched into fists on his thighs.

"It's a long story," he said tonelessly.

"She thinks very highly of you."

"Even Judith is not without her blind spots."

The revealing harshness in his own voice appalled him, and he uncurled his fingers with deliberate concentration. He felt Diana's eyes on him: weighing, analyzing, judging. . . .

"We met in Europe." he said at last.

She shook her head. "Is that where you were born, Nicholas?"

"England," he said. "Also a very long time ago."

Her laugh was a little nervous and unexpectedly sweet. "We've discussed your advanced age before. You're going to make me feel as though I'm on my last legs."

Sorrow caught hold of him like a hound shaking a rat, closing his throat with the grip of memory. She was young, so young, and her life would be as brief as a candle flame.

He turned his shoulder to her deliberately. "Forgive me my gaucherie, Diana," he said softly, "but I—"

The cab came to a sudden stop, and there was no more time for banter. His house loomed above them, vast and bleak and empty of life.

Instinctively, like a blind man seeking light, he turned back to Diana.

She was life. She was all mortality and fragile faith, piercing his defenses and stealing his will, not knowing what she did. She carried the essence, the vital spirit denied his kind for eternity.

He was weary unto death of eternity. He hungered. And he wanted her.

"Where to next?" the cabbie snapped.

Nicholas ignored him. He was speaking before he realized his own intentions. "Will you come in, Diana?" he asked softly.

Her body gave him her answer before it reached her lips, swaying toward him, wanting without understanding. Her eyes were as dark as the night-kissed bay, shadowed by desire. But she hesitated, some small sensible voice undoubtedly warning her that the next step she took would be irrevocable.

"For a little while," she said at last.

Nicholas held open the cab door, handed the cabbie a generous fare, and escorted Diana through the iron gate, guiding where she would have stumbled in the darkness. He stepped in ahead of her and flicked on the foyer lights. The small chandelier overhead glittered, drawing Diana's gaze and luring her through the door.

Without a word he led her to the library. He'd known he would bring her here; there was nothing threatening about this room with its warm paneling and tall shelves of books, nothing suggestive of seduction. He saw Diana relax as he brought up the lights to a dim glow and offered her the wing chair nearest the door.

"This is a beautiful room," she whispered.

At the sideboard he turned to watch her face. It was lifted, her eyes scanning the top row of books across the room. A soft brown curl had fallen across her forehead, and her lips were parted.

For a moment he forgot where he was—the year, the place, the circumstances. He was home in Yorkshire, in the library at Coverdale Hall, and Diana was a young woman of good breeding come across the lonely moors with her family for a fortnight's visit. His stepfather and her father were talking in the hall, leaving the young people discreetly alone for a few precious moments.

It would have been arranged, of course, but they did not object. They were both young, attractive, drawn to each other by spirit and health and preference as well as duty. Nicholas thought of bedding the girl, and of laughing children. Diana's eyes rose to meet his. . . .

The chime of the grandfather clock in the hall shattered his pleasant daydream. He snatched up the decanter and poured a generous measure of brandy into one of the snifters. He welcomed the false comfort it offered, though his inhuman metabolism would suffer for it later. Hiding the movement from Diana, he downed the brandy and turned back to her with an empty glass.

If she noticed his long silence she gave no sign of it. "I'm glad you like my library, Diana," he said softly. "I find it comfortable here. Would you care for some brandy?"

He expected her to refuse. In spite of her inner fire, he doubted she ever indulged in anything that might cause her to lose control. But she rose, smoothing her skirts with a nervous gesture, and nodded. When he handed her the glass, she took a quick swallow, made a face, and took another.

She trapped a discreet hiccough behind her hand. "Thank you." Holding the half-empty snifter, she walked across the library to the window and drew back the heavy curtains.

Nicholas downed a second glass, watching her movements. Diana was graceful and slender in her pale gown, vivid against the deep red velvet draperies. She seemed— more aware of her femininity dressed as she was, more vulnerable. A surge of unfamiliar emotion coursed through Nicholas. He let it pass without examining it too closely.

Emotion was an obstacle for him. It was Diana's emotions he must cultivate now.

She turned as he joined her by the window. He knew she was aware of him every moment, as he was aware of her.

"I've told you something of myself, Diana," he began. "And I suspect that Judith told you more."

Her dark lashes swept down to veil her eyes. "She's very loyal to you, Nicholas."

"Oh, yes." Nicholas eased the drapes from Diana's hand and let them fall. "She probably told you I don't often reveal the details of my life."

Turning with her back pressed to the drapes, Diana glanced up. "Yes, she did. You're quite a man of mystery."

"And you, Diana," he murmured. Under his gaze she took another sip of brandy and licked the moisture from her lips, provoking his body to greater hunger. "You remain a mystery as well."

She laughed. He thought he heard a trace of recklessness in the sound. "There's nothing mysterious about me."

"You underestimate yourself, Diana." Lifting her unresisting fingers to his elbow, he led her back to the chairs arranged near the hearth. "There are a great many things I'd like to know about you."

She sat down and let him take the empty snifter. The corner of her mouth lifted in a wry smile. "I would have thought you were the type of man who'd know everything about a woman in a glance—everything you needed to know."

It was defiance of a kind—defiance of him, and more: of feelings within herself she was not yet prepared to acknowledge. "Now you underestimate me," he said softly.

She looked down at her hands. "I'm—sorry. A psychologist should be the last person to make hasty judgments."

Returning to the sideboard, Nicholas refilled her glass. "You're not a psychologist here, Diana."

The clock ticked like a heartbeat in the stillness. Diana took the second glass from him without demur. "No. I'm not."

Nicholas turned on the stereo system set into the bookcase and sat down in the chair opposite hers, leaning back. Diana lifted her head at the sound of the melody: a Beethoven sonata. She sighed and settled into her own chair.

"You wanted to know something about me?" she said. Her voice had softened, the edges worn away by brandy and music. "Fire away."

Nicholas smiled at the image of his demure Regency miss raising her brandy glass and spouting slang. The brandy was having its effect on him as well; Diana's aura was visible to him now without any effort at all, surrounding her with a hazy glow.

"You haven't told me where you were born," he said. "About your family, how you came to be a psychologist."

Diana leaned her head back and closed her eyes. "I've lived in San Francisco all my life. Most of it, anyway. My parents died when I was eight years old. I had an elder sister—" Her fingers tightened on her glass. "Clare. She took care of me after our parents died."

"But you lost Clare as well."

Her eyes opened and fixed on his. "Yes. She—died when I was fourteen."

Nicholas knew that far more lay beneath her quiet words, but now was not the time to unearth old anguish. He leaned forward, clasping his hands loosely between his knees.

"It's difficult to be a child growing up alone," he said.

"Why do I get the feeling that you speak from personal experience?" she said softly.

"Perhaps I do, Diana."

"But you don't want to talk about it." She smiled sadly. "Fair enough. I'd rather not talk about my childhood either."

The blue of her eyes was very bright, suspiciously close to tears. Nicholas clenched his fingers together to keep from reaching across the space between them.

"I understand. It was Clare who inspired you to become a psychologist."

"I think," Diana said, setting her empty glass down on the end table with exaggerated care, "that you should have been the shrink."

He let out his breath very slowly. "Oh, no, Diana. Not me."

They looked at each other, and even in the absence of words there was an understanding, a sharing independent of dreams. The music had changed: now it was a slow, haunting melody, rich with the timbre of cellos.

Nicholas stood, the tempo of his heartbeat far outpacing the music. Without a word he held out his hand to Diana, and she took it. He drew her into his arms, and they began to dance.

There was no time then. No hours or minutes or seconds, only slow steps and warm skin and Diana's soft breathing. Her head grew heavy on his shoulder. She smiled up at him sleepily as he guided her back to the chair and eased her into it.

"I should be going, Nicholas," she muttered.

Nicholas walked to the antique armoire in the corner of the library and pulled out a folded blanket. He draped it over Diana, smoothing it around her shoulders.

"Stay, Diana," he said. "Stay a little longer."

She tugged the edge of the blanket under her chin. "All right. A little longer . . ."

He knelt beside her, patient as he had learned to be long ago. There was no need for compulsion. Diana curled into the chair and let her mortal nature take its course.

He didn't have long to wait.

EIGHT

Was it a vision, or a waking dream?
Fled is that music:—Do I wake or sleep?
—John Keats, *Ode to a Nightingale*

There was music. Beautiful music swirling around her, and color, and light.

And there were people: elegant women in high-waisted gowns that swept the floor, men in snug tailcoats and knee breeches. They were dancing, tracing out patterns on the mirror-bright floor, a stylized ritual of coming together and parting again.

Diana looked down at herself. She wore white: Her breasts were nearly bared by the sweeping décolletage of her bodice. Without thinking she snapped open the fan in her hand and held it strategically just below her chin.

"A shocking squeeze, isn't it?"

She turned sharply to the woman beside her.

"Judith?"

"Of course, my dear; and who else?" The older woman, dressed in a purple gown and turban with a sweeping feather, opened her own fan with a practiced turn of her wrist and waved it before her face. "Why are you not dancing?"

Diana stared around the room. She had never been here before, and yet it was familiar to her. The walls were decorated with moldings and painted in pastel colors; across the room, beyond the dancers, a great marble fireplace dominated the room. Chandeliers hung from the ornate ceiling. At both ends of the room were doors leading into adjoining chambers. Couples strolled through them, their voices a low hum under the music.

"There is Keely, the dear child. She has quite recovered."

Turning to look in the direction Judith pointed with her fan, she caught sight of the young woman. Keely's head was tilted up, the pale sweep of her throat adorned by a simple necklace of pearls. The man who engaged her attention had his back turned to Diana, but she noted the breadth of his shoulders, his elegant height, and the gold of his hair with a catch of her breath.

She glanced aside to question Judith, but the older woman was gone. In her place was a giggling knot of girls, every one of them shapely and empty-headed.

"Here he comes!" one of them whispered loudly.

The music died away all at once. As if making way for a king, the dancing couples broke apart and scattered to the edges of the room. One man waited in the center, oblivious to the stares. Pale eyes, hidden behind a gold mask, locked on Diana's. Keely, who stood beside him, waved gaily to Diana, taking the arm of a young man dressed in brilliantly mismatched trousers, waistcoat, and jacket. Diana recognized Tim with a start as the young couple disappeared into the crowd.

And then the gold-masked man was walking toward Diana, long unhurried strides that should have carried him to her within seconds. But the chamber seemed to elongate; he came on with agonizing slowness, and Diana knew that all eyes in the room were on her.

"May I have this dance, Miss Ransom?" he said, his voice deep, his smile mocking.

A buxom woman with bleached hair and a shocking chartreuse gown pushed her way between them. She smirked up at the masked gentleman and tapped his arm with her fan. "This is not a masquerade ball, sir," she cooed.

As if she had not spoken, the masked gentleman pushed past the affronted woman until he stood scant inches from Diana.

"Your card, Miss Ransom." He pointed, and Diana found the small card dangling from her wrist by a delicate cord. She opened it slowly. Every line was filled in with the same handwritten name. A name she could not read.

She looked up, suddenly angry. "Is this a joke?"

The masked gentleman's smile vanished. "No joke, Diana."

She forgot her anger as she gazed at him. She didn't need to see under the mask to know that he was handsome. His rich brown tailcoat enhanced his broad shoulders, and the fawn breeches he wore left little to the imagination. Her heart began to pound.

"Perhaps, then," she said, "you can tell me where we are."

The mask shifted as he arched an eyebrow. "You don't know, Diana?"

She jerked her fan in front of her face, aware that she

had revealed far too much. The temperature in the room had suddenly become stifling, and the man before her seemed to pulse with his own heat.

"The music is beginning, Diana."

He held out his hand, strong and aristocratic. She recognized that hand. A feeling of disorientation came over her, so powerful that she swayed with it. The gentleman caught her elbow, and the sensual thrill of his touch made her gasp.

The empty-headed girls behind her giggled in unison. "Don't you know what he is, Miss Ransom?" one of them shrieked.

"Come, Diana," the gentleman said. "All the dances are mine."

She went with him, struggling to make sense of the thoughts racing through her mind. The gentleman guided her into a gentle waltz, keeping the proper distance between them.

"Shall we be daring, Diana, and fly in the face of convention?"

Staring up into his face, Diana felt the floor tremble under her feet. "What did you say?"

He frowned. "I said nothing, Diana."

But she had heard him, as if he spoke directly into her mind. And that was impossible. Quite impossible.

The ballroom seemed to waver around her. It became darker, panelled in rich wood, shelved with rows of books. From somewhere, over the music, she heard the roar of the ocean and the thunder of horses' hooves.

All at once the man with whom she danced was the only solid thing in the universe. She tightened her grip on his coat and felt his hand anchor her as they whirled amid chaos.

And then, as she looked up into his face, she remembered.

"I know you," she whispered.

His graceful step faltered for the barest instant. The strong line of his jaw hardened, and the glitter of his eyes through the slits in the mask grew preternaturally bright. His fingers crushed hers, but she hardly noticed at all.

"We have met before," she said with growing wonder. And the memories returned: the beach, the horses, the wild lovemaking. This time it was she who faltered, enervated by shock and chagrin.

The man who danced with her was the gray rider. He had laid her down in the sand and taken everything he wanted of her—everything but her virginity. And she had given it willingly.

"Who are you?" she cried. Her voice carried in the hall; rows of pale faces turned to her in silent condemnation.

The masked gentleman—the gray rider—stared down at her as if at some terrible vision. "You can't," he whispered. "Impossible . . ."

Impossible. *Impossible.*

She did not belong here. The certainty washed over her like a tidal wave. But her partner did. This was his world, and he had drawn her into it somehow. It was all like some kind of wonderful, terrible dream. . . .

I'm dreaming.

She heard the small voice within herself, and she knew the words were true.

I'm dreaming.

The universe righted itself again. The ground was solid and real, the music unwavering, the couples in their elegant costume back in place.

I'm dreaming. This is my *dream. I control it. . . .*

Just as she had dreamed as a child. She was Diana Ransom, lucid dreamer, and she was asleep, creating her own fantasies. The old abilities had returned.

It was a kind of miracle; in waking life, she might have analyzed and puzzled over it for hours. Here, acceptance was a matter of moments.

She looked, unafraid, into the eyes of the man who held her. She was prepared this time for the shock of recognition.

Nicholas. Nicholas was here in her dream. He had not drawn her into his world; she had conjured him in *hers.*

As she had done, unaware, in her dream of the horses. Then she had not known the dream for what it was. Now she did. And she had recreated in her dreams what she would never dare seek in waking life.

Nicholas Gale, a masked lover who swept her away on the beach and made love to her in silence. Who danced with her now, still masked, hidden from that part of herself that could not accept so bold a desire.

I imagined you here, Nicholas.

He was as solid and warm and real as she had ever seen him: strong, elegant, handsome. Here, in this realm of fantasy, he could not unsettle her or threaten the balance of her existence. Here there were no questions she could not answer.

In my dreams, I can have whatever I want, and there can be no harm in it. Whatever I'm not afraid to take. All this is mine.

Somewhere the real Nicholas Gale went about his mysterious business in perfect ignorance of the part he played in her world of dreams. That Nicholas would never know, but this one—*this* one was hers.

Diana laughed.

Nicholas tightened his grip on her hand, and she flexed her fingers. "I'm in no danger of falling," she told him softly.

He looked startled, and she wondered at how perfect was her image of him. "You looked—distraught," he said.

"Not at all." The music swelled, and Diana closed her eyes, savoring the exhilaration of the dance. They seemed almost to be floating on air. Here, that was entirely possible. If she wished they could fly up into the sky.

In answer to her thoughts, Nicholas swung her about almost wildly, sweeping her skirts into the air. No debutante had ever danced like this. Out of the corner of her eye she could see bejewelled women ranged along the wall, whispering behind their fans; she looked right at them as she and Nicholas passed, and they dropped their eyes and melted away.

This was *her* world. She smiled up at Nicholas triumphantly. "How long is the dance?" she asked.

His strong hand pressed her against him. His shoulder bunched under her palm, and his powerful thighs moved intimately on hers. "How long do you want it to be, Diana?"

Her smile faded. He played along very well, her Nicholas-of-the-dreams, but she didn't want a puppet. She could reach up and remove his mask, but that would destroy what he was. She wanted the gray rider to sweep her off her feet. She wanted . . .

She wanted to lie naked in his arms, feel his caresses, shudder to completion once again. She wanted the ecstasy of surrender.

Her thoughts were swept away as Nicholas lifted her up and pressed his mouth to her bare shoulder. "The dance is over, Diana," he said against her skin. His tongue stroked her once, and a quivering began deep in her body. Through the gauzy fabric of her gown she felt his response, the heavy arousal his tight breeches could not conceal.

They stood alone in the center of the room, the last

strains of music dying around them. The other couples were watching, whispering of scandal, and Diana shivered with the excitement of the forbidden.

"I know a place," Nicholas murmured. His warm breath caressed her ear, stirred the tendrils of hair that brushed her neck. "Come with me."

She flirted with the idea of refusal, just to see what would happen. But she was given no chance. Nicholas clamped his hand around her wrist and pulled her with him, inexorable as a force of nature. Men and women scurried out of his path. He reached a pair of great mahogany doors at the side of the room and pushed one of them open, drawing her through behind him.

And then they were alone, in a vast gloomy hall that echoed with sourceless voices. Before Diana could speak, Nicholas pressed her up against the nearest wall, pinned her there with his body, and crushed her mouth with his own.

Her resistance was instinctive and brief. Within a moment she gave herself to him, as she had done on the beach; welcomed his invasion and the thrust of his hips that told her so clearly what he wanted.

What *she* wanted.

She freed her arms, tangling her fingers in his tousled hair. He made a soft sound, like a groan; she echoed it without shame. When he released her and took her by the hand, she followed where he led.

The room was utterly silent. There were paintings on the walls, stern men and women who looked down from their height with fixed, disapproving eyes. Fine carpet sighed beneath Diana's feet. The only light came from a fire in the hearth, warm enough to ease a chill on bare skin.

Nicholas closed the door behind them and turned the key in the lock. He leaned against the door, and Diana knew they were truly alone. Her heart began to race as she met Nicholas's veiled eyes.

My dream, she reminded herself. *I control it.* But her certainty deserted her as she looked at her lover: at the power barely hidden under his formal clothing, the carnal curl of his lips, the bold outline of his arousal trapped by a thin layer of cloth.

As he crossed the room, lazily intent as a cat, she backed away until her legs came up against something immovable. She reached out behind herself, touching carved wood and rich upholstery.

Nicholas smiled. "Surely you aren't afraid, Diana?" he mocked softly.

She wet her lips. "Why should I be afraid?"

He stopped inches away from her. "You have no reason to be."

No reason, Diana thought, shivering.

"You came here willingly," he reminded her.

Because I want this.

He moved closer, only a sliver of air between them. "I'll give you great pleasure, Diana." Lifting his hand, he curved his fingers to cup her breast.

Diana arched back with an involuntary cry. Nicholas's thumb grazed the nipple that peaked beneath the cloth of her bodice.

"You won't regret it," he whispered. He caught her about the waist with his free arm and kissed her again. His tongue took burning possession of her mouth. There was no gentleness in it, nothing but feral hunger; Diana gasped and wedged her hands against his chest.

"No, Diana," he breathed. "You aren't so innocent." He released her lips and rained kisses on her jaw, her neck, the hollow of her throat. Even as she struggled in his powerful hold, erotic excitement gathered like a storm in her body.

Warm fingers stroked from her shoulder to the skin above the low neckline of her bodice. With a swift gesture Nicholas tugged down the flimsy cloth, freeing her breasts into his hands.

She wanted to cry out his name, but no coherent sound reached her lips. His mouth followed his hands, closing over one nipple hungrily. He drew on her as if he would devour her, suckling and nipping. Diana could hear her own breath coming in short, hard pants. She could not have dislodged him if she tried.

He took her other breast in his mouth, lifting her up against him. His hair brushed her jaw as his tongue traced every contour within his reach. And then he eased her down again, along his body, so that she felt every hard line and curve and angle.

She looked up at his face. It was as taut as the rest of him, harsh with blatant desire.

"Lie down," he commanded. She felt the give of upholstery behind her thighs, the carved frame of a chaise longue at her back. Nicholas bent forward and she melted under him, her limbs heavy and unresisting.

For a moment he stood looking at her, limned by the fire behind him. His gaze caressed her bared breasts; she almost lifted her hands to tug up the bodice, but something in his expression stayed her.

He found her beautiful. Under his eyes her gown became transparent, clinging to her body like a second skin. Here—in her dreams—she could let him see her this way, vulnerable and utterly exposed. She could be a wanton, unashamed and glorying in her womanhood.

"I want to taste you, Diana."

Her body responded to his words before she remembered what it had been like before. She closed her eyes, feeling his weight settle on the end of the couch.

"Look at me."

She obeyed him. He leaned over her, his knee already wedging her legs apart. The gown was as light as a sigh, no barrier at all to his hands. The slide of soft cloth on her thighs and belly was familiar, so familiar; Nicholas caressed her bare hips and smiled.

"Your body is already eager to appease my hunger, Diana."

His smile was the last thing she saw before he bent his head to fulfill the promise of his words. The pressure of his mouth, the stroke of his tongue wrung small, desperate sounds of pleasure from her. She bent her head back on the curved end of the couch, reaching blindly to lace her fingers in Nicholas's hair.

He obliged her silent demands. His explorations were intimate beyond anything she could have imagined in reality; he dipped into her and teased the entrance to her body, returning always to the center of ecstasy. Again and again he brought her close to completion, only to withdraw. When it seemed she would go mad with it, he drew back, pulling free of her flexing fingers.

"I can't wait—much longer, Diana," he whispered.

She could not understand him. She was all blind wanting; it took several long moments for his words and movements to penetrate her senses.

He knelt between her parted thighs, unbuttoning his breeches.

"You're ready for me now," he said, his voice deep and coaxing. "I've wanted you for a very long time."

At last it was clear. She raised her head, watched in a daze as he freed himself and eased down over her body. The rigid length of him pushed at the soft skin of her thighs.

But something was wrong. Something she could not define hummed like an electric current from Nicholas, something threatening. Something—inhuman. . . .

The first stirrings of panic banished desire. *This isn't how I wanted it.* Diana tried to rise, but his weight trapped her.

He wanted. He wanted to be inside her. He wanted to take her, possess her, steal her away.

Somehow, he wanted her mind. Her very soul . . .

But this is my dream. My dream. This isn't what I wanted. . . .

The mere thought should have been enough; her will alone should have leashed the dream-Nicholas, turned him into an obedient lover. But he covered her like a cloak, whispering hot, erotic promises against her ear. She felt her thighs loosening to admit him in defiance of her own elemental fear.

You do want me, Diana.

She arched under him as he began to enter, sliding into her. His muscles were taut, arms supporting him and thighs settled between her own; he was a predator barely in control, held in check only by a thin veneer of humanity.

Then she understood her fatal weakness. Her dream would not obey her will, because her will was divided, wanting his possession and fighting it at the same time. An old quote came back to her, the mocking voice of reason: *"We are not hypocrites in our sleep."*

Nicholas slid deeper, stretching, pressing the final barrier her body held against him. His mouth closed over hers. He laid siege, setting fire to her fragile resistance. The heat grew beyond bearing; she surrendered to the inferno, and Nicholas made a low sound of triumph.

Fire. Nicholas had become a living flame, and Diana cast herself into it. As she had done another time, another place, in a dream only half remembered. No human took her now, but a god.

Now. Let it be now. . . .

But he did not complete what he had begun. She felt him drawing something out of her with his kiss and his body just within hers—something nameless that ran through her body like blood. Lassitude came over her, an aching emptiness in the center of her being.

The emptiness grew to an unbearable ache. "Please," she whispered. She lifted her arms to draw him in.

And he was gone. Gone from her body, from her sight; she cried out, and her eyes found his dim, smouldering shape wavering in the air like a mirage.

"No." His voice was distant, thinning to a sigh. "I cannot."

Like smoke his image broke apart, drifted away, slipped through her reaching fingers. She lay in the silent chamber, shivering in the sudden cold. The fire in the hearth had waned to embers.

Gone. He was gone, abandoning her to the void he had created within her. And though she understood that somehow she had been spared, she wept.

The bed she lay in was not her own.

Diana stared up at the brocade canopy over her head. Not her bed, and not her neat, understated apartment.

I fell asleep, she thought slowly. *In Nicholas's library.*

The implications of that circled in her mind for several uneasy moments. How late had it been—or how early? After five A.M., and she'd had at least two glasses of brandy. She wasn't used to drinking. There'd been music, and a slow dance, and Nicholas's voice. . . .

She sat bolt upright. The dream. Her first truly lucid dream since Clare had died. Music, and dancing, and Nicholas. Nicholas, making love to her, and leaving her.

Oh God. She pressed her palms to her hot face. She could remember every moment of it, as if it had just happened, here in this very bed. She still felt the hollowness of frustration, the dull ache of thwarted desire. Her nipples were painfully taut. There was moisture between her legs, and a dull throb where Nicholas had been just inside her. . . .

But it had been another room, a room built of her own fantasies, on a carved chaise longue. None of it had happened. It was no more real than the wanton Diana Ransom let loose by her reckless imagination.

Shivering, Diana rolled across the bed and put her feet on the carpeted floor. A wave of dizziness caught her by surprise, and she clutched at the carved mahogany bedpost.

Not enough sleep, she thought, *and too much to drink.* She searched the room for a clock; there was none, but the light filtering in along the edges of the drapes was bright.

She got up, testing her balance. Her coat and purse lay draped across the back of an antique chair. A valuable antique, like the bed and other furnishings. The room was warm enough, but she was acutely aware of the flimsy gown she wore, so like the one in the dream. *Obvious,* she thought, struggling for detachment. *Very obvious where I got the elements of the dream.*

But she wasn't comfortable until she snatched up her coat and pulled it on over the gown, buttoning it up to the collar. She walked to the window and drew back the drapes. The view was stunning, looking north over the wide channel where the bay fed into the ocean, with the Marin headlands shadowy in the morning light. Diana opened the window and breathed in the salt air, listening to the hiss of surf from the base of the cliff.

Somewhere a car horn blared. *Monday morning,* she thought; *I should be in the office.* But no—the angle of the sun told her it was early yet. Last night had been the

Foundation Halloween party. Last night seemed as far away as the outlandish world of her dream.

She let the drapes fall and moved quietly to the bedroom door. Nicholas must be here, somewhere; he didn't go out in daylight. She wondered if it would be possible to sneak by him. To see him now . . .

Biting her lip, Diana glanced at herself in the ornate mirror over the dresser opposite the bed. Her hair was matted, the curls all flat against her head like a cap. What little makeup she'd worn had rubbed away. Nothing there of the elegant creature who had danced with the dream-Nicholas in a crowded ballroom.

That wasn't really me, she reminded herself, her hand on the doorknob. *And that wasn't Nicholas, either.* But she opened the door; some compulsion she didn't quite understand tossed caution aside and sent her creeping down the hall. She paused, listening, and heard nothing but the distant ticking of a clock. The hall itself was hung with paintings that looked like perfect replicas of eighteenth- and nineteenth-century masterworks.

One by one she tested the doors of the rooms off the hallway. Each door was unlocked; each room was either empty or filled with furniture draped in dust covers, blinds or curtains closed. Not one room showed a hint of regular occupation. Only the room at the end of the hall had a few pieces of usable furniture on a bare hardwood floor. There was no bed in any of the rooms except the one she'd occupied. And no sign of Nicholas.

Where does he sleep, when he does sleep? she thought.

Frowning at a half-formed thought, Diana made her way down the stairs. The house was uniformly dark. She found her way into the kitchen, blinking in the gloom. It was neat and nearly bare except for a coffee maker on the spotless counter. She opened the small refrigerator and found it completely empty. Without understanding why she did so, she checked all the cupboards. Nothing.

What does he eat? Does he send out for food during the day and go out every night?

She wandered out of the kitchen and glanced at the double doors that led to the library. He might be there now, waiting for her to wake up.

Almost against her will, her feet carried her slowly toward the library. She walked in to find the room unoccupied, last night's strange magic dissipated and the music silent. The heavy drapes were closed against the morning sunlight. Her relief was so great that she fell back into the nearest chair, trying to recapture everything that had led up to the dream.

Nicholas had danced with her. Nothing more. No seduction. He had asked her about her life, and she had even mentioned Clare.

Clare. Clare was so much a part of what had shaped Diana. Not once in her dream had she thought of Clare and the price her sister had paid for surrendering herself, body and soul, to a man. She remembered clearly thinking it was safe, her erotic fantasy, because it was only a dream. She could do whatever she pleased, and control everything that happened.

Only she hadn't been in control. The dream had been lucid because she'd known she was dreaming, but her ability to shape the dream had failed somehow.

Diana stood and paced restlessly. How many books had she read on the subject? Lucid dreaming was rare, but hardly unknown. And when she was a child, she had always dreamed that way. There were some experts on lucid dreaming who believed you should never control your dreams but let them unfold as they would, and learn from what they had to teach.

What did last night's dream teach me?

The answer that came to her was too frightening to examine. And all her psychological knowledge of human nature, all her professional skill, could not untangle the Gordian knot in her own heart. . . .

Soft music broke the uncanny silence. A piano—not a recording, but someone playing in another room.

Diana followed the sound back through the hall and into a living area off the main entryway. The room was furnished elegantly with antique furniture, and in one corner, seated at a magnificent grand piano, Nicholas played with his eyes closed and his head tilted back in an attitude of rapture.

Feeling behind herself for a chair, Diana sat down. Nicholas played like an expert, like a man who should perform in a concert hall. His fingers danced over the keys effortlessly. And in the music—eighteenth-century, Diana thought distantly—there was enough emotion to make a stone weep.

She closed her eyes. With the slightest effort she would find herself back in the dream, transported to another time and place. The music held all the elegance and passion of the Nicholas in her fantasies. . . .

"Mozart," Nicholas said softly.

She started, sitting up in the chair. The music had ended, and Nicholas watched her from behind the piano, some profound emotion fading from his eyes.

"I—thought it might be," she managed at last.

"I thought you'd still be asleep."

Nicholas rose from the bench and walked toward her. She stared up at him, unable to move.

"Are you cold?" He glanced down, and she realized her fingers were clutching the collar of her coat around her face. She dropped her hands to her sides.

"Sorry about the gown," he said. "I thought it was best to—leave you in it."

Diana forced herself to meet his eyes exactly as if nothing had ever happened between them.

Nothing has. He doesn't know. He'll never know. . . .

"You fell asleep right after we danced. Out like a light. I didn't have the heart to wake you."

If he noticed her awkward silence, he had the courtesy not to show it. He moved to a richly upholstered chair and leaned on it casually.

"How are you feeling?"

The obstruction in her mind suddenly cleared. "I feel fine," she stammered. "Fine. Thanks for letting me borrow a bed."

"My pleasure," he said softly. The corner of his mouth lifted. "You haven't much of a head for brandy, Diana."

"I seldom drink." She composed herself and pretended interest in the chair she sat in. "The bedroom was very beautiful."

He shrugged. "A guest room. It doesn't see much use."

For the first time it occurred to her that other women might have slept in that bed. *"Doesn't see much use,"* he'd said. And Judith had told her last night: *"He's alone. Has been for years."*

Why should it matter? she asked herself. But it did, like so many other things about him that shouldn't affect her at all.

She let her eyes drop, remembering the way he had looked the night before. His clothing was something any ordinary man might wear at home: gray T-shirt, snug blue jeans faded almost to white, pristine sneakers.

Last night he had looked elegant, almost otherworldly. The elegance was still there, as much a part of him as his golden hair, but the artificial barrier of his costume was gone. He was still only a man, and she was a woman who was about to fall into a pair of viridian eyes.

"I should probably be going," she muttered.

"So early?" he said. "Surely you don't intend to sleep and run."

"I wouldn't want to impose—"

"No imposition, Diana. I seldom have the pleasure of company in the morning."

Morning. A time he would be trapped here, imprisoned by his sensitivity to sunlight.

She fixed her eyes on the base of his throat, unable to meet his gaze. The throb of his pulse was visible under the skin. She could imagine his touch as she had felt it in the dream, intimate and demanding.

"I'd make you breakfast," she joked weakly, distancing herself with words, "But I'm afraid I snooped and noticed you don't exactly have an overflowing larder. I suppose you don't eat any more than you sleep or go out in sunlight—"

Her joke fell flat. Nicholas's face took on an odd expression and then relaxed into a cool smile.

"But I do have coffee." Abruptly he moved toward her, reaching for her arm. "Indulge me, Diana. I—"

It was entirely irrational to try to avoid him. She let him touch her, and with that one touch he toppled her resistance.

"Nicholas," she whispered.

He put his arms around her—lightly, gently. Diana leaned against him, savoring his warmth and the strength of his body. So different from the dream-Nicholas, and yet the same—all tenderness, his hand smoothing her hair, his heart beating against her ear. Her blood sang as it had done in the dream, but now it was a quiet singing, blazing desire transformed to embers of contentment.

"Oh, yes," she said. Pulling back, she looked up into his eyes. "It must have been that brandy."

He smiled, slow and deep. "Remind me not to ply you with drink next time."

Next time. Diana shivered, and he tightened his hold. "Coffee, Diana," he commanded, steering her from the library.

He settled her in his kitchen, in a chair facing the window overlooking a small garden. The blinds were partly open to let in the sun; he walked through the bands of light twice before he remembered that she might think it peculiar.

Sunlight held little threat to him this morning. He was strong; Diana's life force filled him to overflowing. Even more potent than the other times, when he had thought he had reached the limit of what he could take without bringing harm to her.

He watched her as she sipped her coffee. Her eyes were heavy-lidded, almost dreamy, like a well-fed kitten's. His fears had been laid to rest; she had suffered no harm. She was a miracle, Diana Ransom—one in ten thousand.

And he had found her.

"What are you thinking, Nicholas?"

She was smiling. He traced the gentle curve of her lips with his eyes.

"About you, Diana."

Her soft skin took on a tint of roses. He could not see her now and not remember every moment of the dream. How she had looked in firelight, wanting him. And how she had startled him when she seemed to recognize his face.

"I know you," she had said. He thought then that he would lose his hold on her dream, that she might pull the

strands of it from his fingers. But in the end he had shaped it as he chose, playing on her fantasies and his own memories of a time long past.

Only at the end had he held himself back. The temptation had been very great. To sheathe himself in her warmth, to feel her around him as he skimmed the sensual overflow of her body's energy—it would have been pleasure beyond mortal understanding. But not once in nearly two centuries had he broken his most stringent rule, taken the risk that he might suck all the life force from a dreamer's body in the ecstasy of his own completion.

Even if he had consummated the act only within the dream, he might have lost control. . . .

Nicholas stared at Diana's bent head and forced his breathing to slow. He was not like Adrian. He never would be.

What are you thinking, Diana? Are you convincing yourself that there is no harm in dreams of pleasure? That what you experienced will never escape the boundaries of your own mind?

Suddenly she looked up. Thoughts moved behind her eyes like deep currents. "I—I think I should be going. It must be getting close to nine, and my first client's in at nine-thirty this morning—" She began to rise.

With a swift movement he stopped her, trapping her against the table. He smelled her skin, the soft woman-scent that permeated the gown and her hair.

"Don't go."

She would not meet his eyes. "I have my obligations."

Leaning on his arms, he bent over her. "There is more to life than your—obligations, Diana."

"I—"

He ended her protest with a kiss that just brushed her parted lips. Her body went rigid—as it had in the dream —and then melted into his arms. Her small hands came up to clutch his shoulders. Diana was the one who deepened the kiss, opened herself to him, whimpered soft breaths that mingled with his.

But he was the one to break away. There was a roar in his ears, a throbbing in his loins that nearly robbed him of reason. He had never touched Diana like this except in dreams. The reality was like the full blaze of the sun set against the flicker of a candle flame.

The effect must have shown in his eyes. Diana gasped, her hands sliding down his arms. He caught them before she could pull them away.

"I want to see you again, Diana," he said, cradling her fingers with utmost gentleness.

Her throat worked. "You—" She stopped herself, fixing her eyes on his chin. "I'm not very good at this kind of thing."

"Let me be the judge of that." He lifted her hands, one by one, and kissed her delicate knuckles.

She dared to look at him then. "I have to go slowly," she whispered.

"Oh, Diana." He cupped his hand to cradle the curve of her cheek. "There's all the time in the world."

NINE

In the burrows of the Nightmare
    Where Justice naked is,
Time watches from the shadow
    And coughs when you would kiss.
    —W.H. Auden, *As I Walked Out One Evening*

On a brittle Wednesday morning in early November, three days after the Halloween ball, Diana stood in the doorway of her storage closet and knew it was time to face the old ghosts.

She shivered, buttoning her woolen cardigan against the chill. The closet was filled with old client files, odds and ends—and Clare's things. The boxes had remained almost untouched since Clare's death, each one neatly labeled in black felt-tip pen and sealed shut.

Clare's things. Clare's sketches, unfinished paintings, experimental sculptures. Photos of Diana's sister in happier times. Diana took a deep breath and knelt beside the first of the boxes, removing the old, brittle tape carefully.

Strange. Diana smiled sadly, lifting a paint-stained T-shirt and holding it against her cheek. There had been times when Diana had felt like the elder sister, though she had been too young to take on that role when their parents had died. Clare had been a genius in so many ways; like many geniuses, she had been desperately vulnerable. The jobs she'd held to supplement the little money their parents had left had worn her down, robbed her of the time she would have spent developing her talent. Left her defenseless against the man who would manipulate and consume her.

She did it for me.

With shaking fingers, Diana pulled a cloth-muffled object from the box and unwrapped it. The photo of Clare and Diana had been taken in happier times; Clare's unconventional beauty was alight with a joy she'd seldom shown in the final days.

It must have been far more difficult than Diana had realized then. Though distant relatives had offered to take Diana in after their parents' deaths, Clare had abandoned a scholarship at one of the nation's top art schools in order to care for Diana herself.

Diana pressed her face into her sleeve. That had been the beginning. *If only I'd been older, able to see. . . .*

Able to see that Clare needed nurturing herself. Able to understand her silent pleas for help, answer them before Clare threw herself into the arms of the man who had drained her of the will to live.

A man who had promised what Clare could find nowhere else.

Diana set down the photograph and found another of

Clare alone—solemn here, with her long hair coiled atop her head. *You needed so much, and yet you tried to give me everything. When you thought you'd found someone to fill your own emptiness, he destroyed you.*

Adrian, a man Diana had never met and had seen only from a distance, who became the symbol for everything Diana hated. Loss of control, desperation, dependency, loss—need.

Diana's first nightmares had come weeks before the deaths of Eric and Jane Ransom, formless images of destruction that she hadn't understood—that had proved horribly prophetic.

But years later, at the time Clare had died, the nightmares had changed, become crystal-clear and sharply defined. Always Clare's destroyer had taken the form of something inhuman, rising from Clare's dead body. Apt symbolism for what *he'd* done to Clare—draining her dry, stealing her vitality. Looking back at Diana with mocking accusation, as if to say: *You couldn't stop me. You were just as much to blame. . . .*

And Diana's other dreams had ended. All the wonderful dreams that fed her as Clare's art had sustained her older sister. Clare's death had left Diana with only the nightmare, until that too had vanished. And Diana, placed in the care of well-meaning and unsentimental relatives, had left dreaming behind her and gone on to follow a career that would enable her to do what she'd never done for Clare.

And you have. She knew that was true, not merely wishful thinking or a convenient salve for old guilt. *You've helped people become stronger. And* you've *become stronger.*

Strong enough to welcome the return of dreams. Strong enough to accept her own weaknesses, to face the past without flinching, to envision a future for herself that could include a man. A man who was nothing like Adrian.

I hardly know Nicholas, she thought, putting Clare's photo aside. But a small voice whispered: *You know all you need to know. In your dreams. . . .*

She shook her head. It was broad daylight, and no time for night fantasies.

She unpacked the rest of Clare's things one by one. Time to let Clare into the sunlight again, out of the dark red haze of the nightmare. Time to let go and heal and forgive.

Gathering up several sketchbooks and photos, Diana set them down on the living room coffee table and glanced at the clock on the mantel. Already four, and she was supposed to meet Nicholas at the de Young Museum in less than two hours. *My first real date in years,* she thought wryly. And a safe date at that—Keely and Tim were coming along. Nicholas hadn't objected to that suggestion.

"There's all the time in the world," he'd told her. . . .

She grimaced and ran her hands through her hair. Time enough to shower, in any case—and overcome this ridiculous bout of nerves at the thought of seeing Nicholas again. After three long days in the office dealing with her clients' problems, this night was hers.

And, for the first time in years, she wasn't sure how it would end.

Standing on the open cement veranda of the de Young Museum, Diana hugged the small portfolio to her chest. Just below her, on the other side of the thick columned balustrade, moonlight danced on the water of the ornamental pond with its sculptures of a young piper and attentive leopards. Across the open space of the music concourse, with its hedges and neatly pruned grove of trees, Diana could see the long, pale shape of the Academy of Science, backed by the darker silhouettes of Golden Gate Park's towering pines and eucalypti.

A small party of young people walked passed her, bound for the museum. It was Nicholas who had suggested a visit to this special exhibit of early nineteenth-century European paintings. Diana hadn't visited an art museum in years. She'd never wanted the reminder of Clare.

But this was exactly the kind of thing Keely—and apparently Nicholas as well—enjoyed. On Wednesday nights the museum was open after dark, when Nicholas could safely venture out.

Diana glanced at the portfolio. It seemed appropriate that something of Clare's spirit was here with Diana tonight. Another step in letting go of the past. . . .

Some undefinable awareness broke into Diana's thoughts. She looked up, knowing who she would see. Nicholas was walking up the curved ramp from the sidewalk, Keely and Tim rapt in conversation right behind him.

He was as handsome as she remembered—as she had dreamed—dressed with impeccable simplicity in an oatmeal sweater, brown tweed jacket, and corduroy trousers. For a moment he stood in silence, looking at her as if he'd never seen anything quite so beautiful.

"Diana," he said softly.

She held out her hands, and he lifted them to his lips. A long, deep shiver coursed through her, as if something more than physical passed between them with his touch. His green eyes caressed her face and settled on her lips. The kiss was warm, undemanding, and over too quickly.

Keely came up beside them. She looked unreservedly

pleased at seeing Diana and Nicholas together; not the slightest sign of jealousy or regret flickered in her eyes. Her feelings for Nicholas were warm, but they extended no farther than friendship.

"I'd love to let you two have more time to yourselves," she said, arching her brows roguishly under the ever-present black beret, "but we've only got two hours to see all this." She grabbed Tim's elbow, pulling him forward. "Tim says he's ready for a few lectures on art—aren't you, Tim?"

Tim made an expressive gesture, lacking any of the awkwardness he'd shown in Keely's presence a scant few weeks ago. "A teacher should always be learning," he said with mock seriousness. "Especially when one has such a—lovely instructor." He grinned suddenly. "Shall we go in?"

Strange, Nicholas thought, *that brush strokes on canvas can take me back so easily.*

He looked over Diana's head at a large canvas by Jacques Louis David, depicting an angst-ridden yet oddly restrained classical scene. *The Death of Socrates.* He had never seen this one when it was first painted, but there were others here he'd viewed when the artists were still very much alive.

He'd been to the Royal Academy many times in his first century of life, and to the Louvre and most of the other great museums of Europe. The creative spark that drove men to paint had always fascinated him. It was very much akin to the life force his kind could tap. Perhaps even an essential part of it.

Diana, who stood poring over the almost invisible brush strokes, was not an artist except in the world of dreams, and yet her life force hummed around and through him every moment they were together.

"Quite a variety of styles," she remarked, moving on to the next painting. "I didn't realize—" She broke off as she stopped to examine the canvas. The woman David had painted was draped languorously over a carved Grecian-style chair, dressed in a flimsy sleeveless and high-waisted gown. The model bore no resemblance to Diana, but Nicholas thought he knew what was going through her mind in that moment.

"David was very much a product of his time," he remarked, ignoring her blushes. "But his brand of romanticism was balanced by a devotion to the classical ideal. Whereas this gentleman . . ."

He took her arm and steered her to the next group of paintings. "Johann Heinrich Fuseli," she read softly.

"This gentleman was driven in a different direction."

Keely, leaning forward between them, gave a brief laugh. "I see what you mean."

The painting was dark, almost muddy, with a grotesque giant crouched over a ram and a prone figure. "He was a contemporary of Blake," Nicholas said, moving close to Diana. "Each artist reflected a different aspect of his age."

"A darker aspect in this case, I think," Diana murmured. Nicholas followed her gaze to the next canvas. For a moment he had an overwhelming desire to guide her past it with a dismissive comment, but she was already staring in unmistakable fascination.

"I recognize this," she said. "I've seen it before."

Nicholas breathed out softly. "I'm sure you have, especially given your field of interest."

"The Nightmare." She glanced back at him, brow furrowed. He wanted to reach out and smooth the creases

away. Instead, he stood as close as he could without
touching her, forcing his own heart to slow.

The image of the painting was archetypal and unfor-
gettable. In the center of the canvas lay a woman draped
in pale colors, her arms and head bent back over the bed
as if in a faint. Crouched on her belly was a sinister
dwarfish figure, scowling at the viewer, and behind dark
draperies a wild-eyed horse looked on.

Diana shivered. "There's nothing clean and classical
about this."

" 'His domain was in air and hell, the clouds and the
grave,' " Nicholas quoted softly. "That's what they said of
Fuseli in his day. This one painting had considerable impact. It was parodied and copied countless times."

"I think I can see why," Diana whispered. "He understood the power of dreams and the subconscious
mind."

"The great ones do." Nicholas curled his fingers
around her arm, and she shuddered. "There are quite a
few more to see—"

"I wonder what inspired him to paint this?" Keely
remarked. "It even gives *me* the creeps." She shivered,
and Nicholas studied her grimly. Was Keely seeing Adrian
in that painting, snatching at some vague mental image of
what had befallen her before Adrian had taken her memory?

"Perhaps," Nicholas said, drawing Keely's eyes back
to him, "Fuseli was thinking only of something all human
beings experience. He used myth to mold reality."

"The way dreams do," Diana put in. "At one time
people believed that dreams were the work of otherworldly forces."

"And nightmares," Nicholas added softly, "the work
of creatures such as this—"

Keely shook her head and moved on. Diana stared at

the hunched and evil figure in the painting. When she looked at Nicholas again, her mouth was curved in a wry smile. "But we're much more enlightened these days, aren't we?"

Nicholas found it strangely difficult to meet her eyes. "Oh, yes, Diana. Much more enlightened."

This time Diana allowed herself to be steered on to the next set of paintings, though Nicholas felt by the lingering tension in her body that Fuseli's work had touched something deep inside her.

Keely and Tim wandered on, lost in themselves, Tim listening earnestly to every comment Keely offered. Nicholas's grim thoughts eased. Keely was clearly thriving on Tim's attention. She seemed to have forgotten she'd ever thought herself in love with Nicholas. If Adrian had done Keely a single good turn, it was in freeing her to find someone—a mortal man—worthy of her. Perhaps he truly *had* changed. . . .

Nicholas took Diana's hand in a sudden fierce grip, and she looked up at him with clear blue eyes that remained blind to his true nature. *Are* you *worthy of Diana, Nicholas?* he asked himself bitterly. Caught in a powerful desire to seek the freedom of the night, Nicholas led Diana through the wide halls and the high arched entrance doors until they stood alone under the light of a quarter moon.

"It's a beautiful evening," Diana said softly. "Not a trace of fog."

Nicholas looked down at her, aware of a formless ache in his body that had nothing to do with his need for her mortal life force. The three days since he'd seen Diana had passed with agonizing slowness. He'd had no need to visit his other dreamers at all; the thought seemed obscene now.

No, this was not the need to satisfy his will to survive.

Sexual desire, he told himself. He ached for her with a physical hunger nothing else could assuage. A hunger she had awakened in him after nearly two centuries.

Diana. So ready to be loved, so passionate. He could already see the changes in her, the birth of the woman she was meant to be. He envisioned the day when Diana would want what he could not give her. . . .

Nicholas stared up into the safe, reflected light of the moon. He could not afford to think beyond the present. She was his now, with her bright eyes and stubborn beauty and soaring dreams—filling him with strength, letting him catch a glimpse of what it was like to be mortal.

He could never risk more than a glimpse.

If the price he must pay was thwarted lust, it was little enough. For his brief span with her he'd allow himself the luxury of human vulnerability.

Her warm weight settled against him, fingers sliding between his. "You're very quiet tonight."

Nicholas rested his chin against her soft hair. Such a small gesture, to touch a woman this way, to hold her to himself as if they were simply lovers.

"I'm afraid my usual eloquence has deserted me in the presence of such beauty," he murmured.

She chuckled. "You're an eloquent liar," she accused. But she pressed her cheek to his chest and sighed.

"I'm happy, Nicholas," she said. A simple statement, words laced with quiet wonder that pierced him to the center of his being. "Does that sound foolish?"

He closed his eyes. "No." *Cherish this happiness while you can,* he thought, not knowing whether he spoke to himself or to her. *It's as fragile and brief as any mortal existence.*

Pulling free of his light hold, Diana gazed up at him. If she had wanted him to offer reassurances, protestations of emotion to match her own, she gave no sign of disappointment. "I forgot I'd brought something to show Keely —and you, if you're interested." She lifted the small black portfolio. From it she extracted a black-matted photograph of a pretty, solemn young woman, deep brown hair coiled atop her head. "This is my sister, Clare," she murmured. "She was lovely, wasn't she?"

Nicholas went absolutely still, staring at the photograph. Diana had already told him some part of the tragic story of her sister, but until now he had never seen Clare's face.

It was the mirror image of Sarah's.

He knew he had been silent too long, that Diana was staring at him, a faint frown between her brows. "Very," he muttered belatedly.

Diana rubbed at a fingerprint on the photograph with the sleeve of her sweater. "I did a little housecleaning today—a little rediscovering of things I'd put away too long."

He couldn't meet her eyes, couldn't bear to look down again until she'd tucked the photograph back in the portfolio, safely out of sight. Even then he felt himself lost in the very past Diana had courageously dared to confront —his *own* past, his own ancient fears.

It was a relief when Tim and Keely emerged from the museum, hand in hand, Keely still chattering while Tim's gaze hung on her face. There was something almost possessive in the way Tim held Keely's fingers in his own that belied the young man's good-natured gentleness.

"Keely's promised to come to the school and give a talk to the kids about art and how she got started," Tim said, his voice laced with pride. "They'll love it. Keely's a great speaker."

Keely blushed with unexpected diffidence, looking suddenly as shy as a young girl with her first beau. She glanced at Diana and Nicholas with a lopsided grin. "I'll know what to tell 'em *not* to do, anyway."

Diana's smile was warm as she watched Keely and Tim walk away, Keely's laugh trailing behind them. "He's good for her," she murmured. "I'm so glad—" She trailed off into silence. The moon silvered the curls of her hair, lingered in her eyes as they turned up to his.

Only minutes ago Nicholas had been thinking only of Diana, of entering her dreams once again and tasting the sweetness of her life force. To seduce her into sleep would have been the work of moments, either in his own home or in hers. She would fall so easily into his arms. But now—

"What now?" she asked softly, as if she had read his thoughts.

His straining senses perceived surrender in her voice, in the pliancy of her body where it curved into his and the aura that flared around her. But Sarah's face hovered between them, warning and reminder. Diana had confronted her own past only to trap Nicholas in his. . . .

He jerked away. Diana quickly concealed her surprise, but he knew she sensed his rejection. All at once her expression became shielded, that distant professional look that kept her safe.

"I'm sorry, Diana," he said hoarsely. "I have business matters to attend to this evening. Judith expects me. If you'll let me escort you home—"

Clasping her hands in front of her, Diana gave him a cool smile. "That won't be necessary. I have a client undergoing testing at the hospital sleep lab tonight. I think I'll run by on my way home and see how things are going."

It was the perfect escape. Nicholas let out his breath carefully and gave her his most charming smile. Her mask slipped under his onslaught, vanishing entirely as he bent to kiss her.

"Then I'll call you tomorrow, Diana," he said. "Pleasant dreams."

She blushed and dropped her eyes, but Nicholas knew her dreams tonight would be her own.

Diana lay in bed with the night-light on and wished desperately that she were not alone.

The feeling was entirely irrational. During daylight the task of confronting the past had seemed attainable, something she was prepared to deal with unflinchingly. But now the stack of Clare's sketchbooks lay on her bedtable untouched, and Diana found herself sitting in silence with Clare's melancholy photograph.

A few hours earlier she'd been blissfully happy with Nicholas and her friends around her. Until she'd shown Nicholas the photo of Clare—and he'd gone strange and distant for no apparent reason. She knew by now that he guarded his heart at least as closely as she did her own. He was still very much an enigma. But he had been the pursuer the morning after Halloween, and she had been the one who wanted to go slowly. . . .

She rubbed her aching eyes and gave a brief laugh. Before she'd met Nicholas she'd been frightened of her own sexuality, the part of herself that could lose control. The new dreams had changed all that. Remembering her dream, in which she and Nicholas had shared so much, she knew she would not be content with kisses for long. . . .

She had wanted him tonight. Wanted him as a woman wants a man, as she had never wanted a man before. But he had left her, and she was not eager to face the images her mind might invoke as she slept.

Images like the painting they had seen at the museum, that sinister "Nightmare" she couldn't seem to forget. The wizened visage of the creature in Fuseli's painting came back to her in vivid detail, leering atop a young woman's prone body. Reminding her too much of the vampire in her own nightmare.

Look at it as experience for your practice, she thought grimly, leaning back into the pillows. *Now you'll really know what your clients go through when they face up to their dreams.*

Diana closed her eyes, trying to focus her mind on tomorrow's roster of clients and the work to be done. The last thing she needed now was that painting on her mind when she fell asleep. She didn't even want Nicholas in her dreams tonight.

She didn't want to dream at all.

"Kiss me again."

He did, more lingeringly this time, and Diana leaned into his embrace with desperate urgency. He laced his fingers in her hair, the length of his hard body pressed to hers.

Need consumed her, need that seemed to come from within and without, licking along her nerves and gathering at the center of desire. Nicholas alone could give her what she must have; she whimpered against his mouth as he withdrew again.

"No, Diana."

Through glazed eyes she stared at his face: hard, stern, cruel with denial of her hunger. There was nothing in his eyes to reveal that he felt what she did—only a fathomless void, green gone the dead gray of the ocean before a storm.

Inhuman.

She reached for him, tried to hold him, but he slipped through her fingers. Like a righteous angel passing judgment he stood over her, golden hair haloed in an unearthly glow.

Fear and chagrin and anger warred within her. It was not enough. Not enough. She needed, she needed . . .

"More, Nicholas," she whispered. "I need more."

His mouth curved up into a smile of utter contempt. "More, Diana?"

She closed her eyes, but the look on his face was imprinted in her memory. There was no point in fighting a battle already lost. If he wanted her to beg, she would do it. She would prostrate herself at his feet.

"Please," she said, her voice as hoarse as if she'd been shouting. "Let me have it. Everything. Please—"

"You're just like your sister."

The pain she felt at his words was so intense that she flung up her arms before her face and cried aloud.

"Admit it, Diana." Suddenly her wrists were locked in an iron grip. Nicholas pushed them apart, his face inches from hers. His breath was furnace-hot. "Admit it. You have the same weakness, the same needs, the same desires. . . ."

"No."

"Yes." Forcing her arms behind her, Nicholas trapped both her hands in one powerful fist. "Clare was flawed, Diana," he rasped. "She was never meant to live in this world. You've tried to survive by denying what you are. But you still run away, don't you?" He brought his lips close to hers. "If you could, you'd escape into your dreams and never wake up. Isn't that true, Diana? Isn't it?"

His kiss held nothing of gentleness. His mouth crushed hers, sawing delicate skin against teeth until she tasted blood. The plunging of his tongue was a brutal possession.

"Isn't this what you want, what you need?"

She tried to gasp out denial, but she was afraid—afraid everything he said was true.

Who am I? she cried silently as Nicholas released her. *What am I?*

No one answered. She opened her eyes to find darkness, the vast silence of some cavernous space. She got slowly to her feet, raising one hand to her mouth. Her fingers found only the familiar curve of her lips, free of pain or evidence of Nicholas's assault.

She knew vaguely that she was dreaming, but it was not her will that drew her across the icy floor. A point of light pierced the endless shadows. As she drew closer it became a nebulous glow, illuminating a room backed by bloodred curtains.

The tableau was one she recognized: a young woman lying prone on a bed, arms and head bent back, helpless in the grip of some terrible vision. There was something crouched on her chest, something grotesque bending over the girl's arched neck. The hideous sounds the creature made came from no human throat.

Diana's first impulse was to turn and run. She knew that the creature would look up at any moment, focus its baleful eyes on her. Raw terror robbed her legs of strength and threatened to topple her like a patchwork doll.

But you can't always run away.

If this was a dream, she must face what it was trying to tell her. Face it, understand it, conquer it once and for all. . . .

The creature's misshapen head lifted. With agonizing slowness it swiveled toward her, its breath like a death rattle.

Diana stared, refusing to close her eyes. Just as the

creature's gaze sought hers, there was a scream and the drum of hooves on stone; from behind the red curtains a black horse appeared, rearing and leaping over the girl and her nightmare. It charged directly at Diana, its eyes nearly white with terror.

She flung up her arms. The horse brushed by her, a warm streak of life in the void, and disappeared. Hoofbeats echoed and died into utter silence. As Diana looked again at the scene before her it began to change, the red of the curtains spreading and flowing to tint everything in a bloody haze.

Where the creature had been stood a man, bent over the girl on the bed. He was dressed in black, hidden under a cloak that spread about him like folded wings.

I know him.

Diana forced her feet to move, one step and another toward the scene she had dreamt of so many times. The face of the spellbound girl was no longer unfamiliar. Clare's long hair tumbled to the floor, her lips parted in a parody of pleasure.

And as Clare's destroyer straightened up from her lifeless body, Diana knew what she would see. Pale hair, illuminated by some sourceless radiance. A face without features save for a monster's grin and predator's fangs, awash in blood. Colorless eyes that would turn at last to her own. . . .

"Don't you know me, Diana?"

The voice was a sibilant whisper, ageless and seductive. The face lifted, a pale blur seen through fog. Diana drove herself on until she stood only a few feet from the bed, refusing to look away from her enemy's veiled features.

"Who are you?" she demanded hoarsely.

He laughed, Clare's killer, with a musical lilt angels

would envy. Fangs flashed white and red. "Come closer and look, Diana. Or are you afraid?"

Afraid. Diana had never felt such terror. Another step and she would know at last. Another step and it would all be clear.

She took that step. The face resolved into flawless clarity.

"No," she breathed.

Clare's killer held her imprisoned with green eyes fashioned of sorcerous crystal. He flipped back his cloak with easy grace, revealing the elegant clothing he had worn the night of the ball, and afterwards in her dreams.

Stepping casually around Clare's body, he clucked softly and shook his head. "You were rather slow to grasp it, Diana. Considering your skill at dreaming, I would have expected to be unmasked long ago."

Unable to move, forcing the air in and out of her lungs, Diana watched him approach. He was still so beautiful, so compelling; her body betrayed her even as the bile rose in her throat.

"But it doesn't really make any difference, does it?" he asked. "Even though I'm not human—you've guessed that as well, haven't you?—you still want me, Diana. You're just like Clare, no matter how hard you fight it."

She shook her head violently, struggling to break her paralysis.

"And I—I want you." He lifted his hand, fingers poised to stroke her face.

His touch, that should have burned, was bitter cold. Her blood turned to ice under the skin of her cheek.

This is a dream. A dream. . . .

"I have waited so long. So long," he murmured. "Diana—"

Strength came back to her from some hidden source, setting her free. She struck out blindly, knocking his hand away. The bland triumph on his face dissolved into shock.

This is a dream, and I will wake up.

He reached for her, fingers curled into claws. Diana closed her eyes and willed herself away. For an instant he grasped her, and then she was fading, slipping from one reality into another, leaving her enemy behind.

"You can't run forever, Diana."

His voice pursued her, snapping like a fiendish hound at her heels.

Diana leaned against the wall, her pulse pounding in her ears. On the floor behind her the sheets and blankets lay tangled where she had thrown them from the bed. Every light in the room was blazing, but the red-laced darkness of that other world could not be so easily vanquished.

It was only a dream.

She whispered the words to herself over and over again until she began to believe them, and pushed herself away from the wall. With elaborate care she walked across the room and pulled her thick terry-cloth robe from the closet. Her fingers fumbled on the sash as if they were frozen.

Only a dream.

She knew she wasn't thinking clearly as she sat on the edge of the bed and picked up Clare's photograph and sketchbook. Slow shivers racked her body; she stared at Clare's sad eyes until it was the photograph that filled her mind, and not that lifeless body. Or the man—the *creature* —standing over it . . .

Now she understood why she'd stopped dreaming so

many years ago. The price she paid for the good dreams
was far too high.

Not as high as the price Clare paid.

Slowly she set down the photograph and opened the
sketchbook, the only one she hadn't looked through since
unpacking Clare's things. Many of the drawings in Clare's
other sketchbooks had captured reality with breathtaking
perfection. A grove of trees in Golden Gate Park; a street
scene in North Beach, thronged with people; an elderly
homeless woman with ancient, tragic eyes.

But other sketches came only from Clare's vivid imagination, windows on worlds only she could see or understand. This sketchbook had been Clare's last. Swallowing
around the thickness in her throat, Diana began to thumb
through the pages.

The images were disturbing, heavy with dark emotion, drawn from the chaos of a young woman's suffering.
Diana's hands began to tremble as she turned the pages.
Clare, she mourned silently. *Oh, Clare.* Grimly she forced
herself to work through to the end, until only the final
page remained.

The last sketch was unlike any of the others, utterly
distinct and without a hint of ambiguity. The face had
been made for an artist's hand: classically handsome,
framed by wavy golden hair, strong-jawed, and high of
cheekbone. The lips were curved in a faint smile, and the
eyes that gazed out of the picture held the intensity of a
panther's stare.

No. Impossible. . . .

Diana dropped the sketchbook into her lap with
nerveless fingers. *I'm not going crazy. I'm not.*

Just because the dreams had returned, because she
had seen the vampire's face and had believed—*known*—
he was not merely a symbol at all.

And saw that same face again in Clare's sketchbook. The face of Clare's destroyer.

Not human. The creature's taunting voice still rang in her ears. *"Even though I'm not human . . ."*

It was Nicholas's face.

TEN

—◦—

Sleep not, dream not; this bright day
Will not, cannot last for aye;
Bliss like thine is bought by years
Dark with torment and with tears.
                    —Emily Brontë, *Sleep Not*

His door was unlocked, as if he had nothing at all to fear in the world.

Diana flung it open, letting it rebound against the doorstop. Fear was the last thing she felt now. Grief and confusion and rage had driven it away, emotions as red as the color of the nightmare from which she'd escaped brief hours before.

I'm not crazy. This is real. . . .

Nothing so rational as thought drove her through the

quiet, darkened rooms. He was not in the library or the living room or the downstairs parlor. Sunlight streaked through the window blinds in the empty kitchen, mocking her with its gentle purity.

Her breath sawed in her throat as she bounded up the marble staircase. God. She'd slept here, under his roof. A wave of sickness washed over her, freezing her in place in the second-story hallway. She'd kissed him, dreamed of him, never guessing, never imagining . . .

It's insane, she cried silently. With a soft curse she drove the weakness away and started down the hall, her eyes fixed on the open door at the opposite end.

Nicholas was there, in the middle of a sparsely furnished room, sitting cross-legged on the hardwood floor. Diana caught at the door frame and gripped it as if the world might spin away from under her feet.

He was inhumanly beautiful, seated like some indifferent Eastern god in a full lotus position, clothed only in skin and muscle and diffuse light. His eyes were closed in utter relaxation, his chest rising and falling with deep, measured breaths.

Diana squeezed her eyes shut, pressing her face to the cool wood. Even now she could look at him and feel herself wavering. Not natural, this attraction, this need—no more natural than Clare's had been—

"Diana."

His voice was the same, the same as in the nightmare, caressing her name with a demon's skill. It pulled her away from the door and across the room until she stood over him, shaking and blind with hatred.

"It was you," she rasped.

His face, that face that Clare had captured so perfectly, reflected nothing but surprise. Unchanged in fifteen years, too perfect to be human. . . .

She wanted to launch herself at him, claw away the

calm façade he wore so easily. But she could not move—could only watch as he rose in a single lithe movement to his feet, an exquisitely formed sculpture brought to life by some ancient magic. He stood before her unashamed, naked to her eyes in soul as well as body, and her will was transfixed by his seductive power.

"He's not an ordinary man," Judith had said. . . .

"What are you?" she whispered.

"Diana—" He reached for her; the threat of his touch broke the spell. She flung up her hand, fist clenched. The puzzlement in his eyes altered to something unreadable.

"You killed her," she said hoarsely. "You aren't human."

The change in his expression was very subtle. His jaw tightened, and the curve of his lips flattened into a thin line. The part of her that could still analyze recognized it as wariness, an unconscious preparation for battle. His was a cold, emotionless readiness; her own fury felt like a helpless child's by comparison.

But while she was angry she couldn't be afraid. "I know what you did," she managed at last. "You've been playing some sick game from the very beginning." The sting of tears blurred her vision; she shook her head violently. Nicholas was a vague, sinister figure in her sight. "I've been dreaming, Nicholas. Dreaming the old nightmare. All these years since Clare died, and I never saw the face of the—creature who killed her."

Distantly she heard her name on his lips. "Your sister? I don't understand you, Diana. Please—"

She laughed. The sound held an hysterical edge. "You don't understand? Am I not being clear enough, Nicholas—or should I call you Adrian, whatever you are?"

The name hung between them, and its effect was immediate. The green of Nicholas's eyes narrowed to a thin corona around black. He moved for the first time since he'd risen, all the muscles of his body going rigid, his chin jerking up as if he'd been struck.

"Adrian?" he whispered.

"Isn't that the name you used with Clare?" she said. "The name by which she learned to trust you and love you, until you could drain the life out of her?"

Some foolish corner of herself had hoped, until this moment, that she might be wrong. That this insane notion was as impossible as it seemed. But the look in his eyes killed the last of her hope. He *knew* the name.

Losing her childhood ability to dream lucidly, after Clare's death, had made the line between fantasy and reality clear-cut when she most needed that barrier. The line had begun to blur with the return of the nightmare, and the dreams of Nicholas.

Now it had disappeared entirely.

Her dreams were *true*, as they had been so many years ago.

"You," she said softly. "You destroyed my sister."

He lifted his hand. It was shaking, deep tremors that coursed through his body. "No," he said. The gesture he made warded her away, tried to shield him from a truth he feared.

Afraid. Nicholas—Adrian, whoever, whatever he was —was afraid.

The depth of her weakness was apparent then. If she could look at him and still feel anything but horror and hatred, she could be destroyed by empathy—an inexplicable wanting—she wanted no part of.

Closing her eyes, she shut him out. A strange calmness came over her, a deep wellspring of power and righteousness that settled like a shield around her heart.

"It wasn't me, Diana."

She opened her eyes. All the visible emotion was gone

from Nicholas's face and body, but his gaze locked on hers with almost ferocious intensity.

Now she could look into his crystalline eyes and see that they were too bright, too intense to be—human.

"Wasn't you?" she echoed. Shrugging her purse from her shoulder, she unsnapped the clasp with surprisingly steady hands. The sketch she had crushed and smoothed out again crackled in her fingers. She thrust it at him.

"Look in the mirror. Look at the face of Clare's killer."

He snatched the sketch from her hand. The color drained from his skin, leaving it lifeless as the classical sculpture he resembled.

"I never saw this sketch until last night," she continued bitterly. "But Clare left it for me to find—all the evidence I need to know that my nightmare was true. I hadn't had the nightmare in fifteen years. Just before Keely disappeared I had it again. Last night, for the first time, I understood."

She swallowed, ignoring the sheer craziness of her words in the wake of her inexplicable conviction. "All those times you hinted that you were older than you looked—it was the truth, wasn't it? You haven't aged. And the vampire imagery was not only symbolism." She stared into his eyes, remembering how they had glowed in darkness—how he fled from the light. How he had fascinated her from the first moment they'd met. "You must have known who I was from the beginning. Did you intend to do to me what you did to Clare? What kind of thing are—"

He silenced her with ridiculous ease, simply by taking two short steps toward her. His face loomed over her, grim and ruthless. With a harsh exhalation of breath, Nicholas let the sketch fall from his fingers. It settled gently to the floor, whispering against the bare wood.

"I never knew your sister," he rasped. He spun away, stalking across the room and turning back again like a pacing tiger. His presence was fire given human shape, radiating heat and danger. "The—man—who drained your sister's life was my brother."

"Your brother," she echoed. Her face was utterly expressionless.

"My twin. Adrian."

In the silence that followed Nicholas held her gaze, knowing it was too late for the safety of comfortable lies. His heart felt frozen—not the familiar stasis of detachment, but something very like despair.

He had no need to look at the sketch again. The sheer cruel irony of it made him curse the Fates he had long ago rejected. If he had thought himself beyond shock, the events of the past two months had proved him wrong.

First he had met Diana Ransom, unlike any woman he had known since Sarah. Then he had discovered Adrian's escape, and that he'd taken Keely. Last night he had seen a photograph that had shaken him to the core. Now he learned that Adrian had been responsible for the death of Diana's sister fifteen years ago.

And Diana *knew* what he was, what Adrian was. Not consciously, not completely, but she knew. And she trusted her own intuition in defiance of logic and sanity.

She was as remarkable as he had believed.

Bitterness rose in him, resurrected like a long-forgotten enemy. Only mortals believed in Destiny. Only mortals had that luxury. . . .

"A twin," Diana echoed tonelessly. "A twin—like the man who took Keely."

He could almost see the pieces of the puzzle coming together behind her blind gaze—as he could see the abyss that lay ahead of them both. He had never looked into the future of his relationship with Diana, knowing well it must end before it went too far—as all his dealings with mortals must inevitably end.

Judith's voice rang in his memory. *"Did it ever occur to you that you might possibly underestimate humankind? That there might be a few other people out there who can accept what you are?"*

Adrian had touched Diana's life long before Nicholas had met her that day in Mama Soma's. Adrian, who had been his responsibility. Adrian—his reckless, half-mad brother—had unwittingly shaped what she was.

And she dreamed true. She had come into his life by some ironic twist of events, had suffered because of his kind. If she could be told the truth. . . .

The truth of what his brother had done to Clare and how Keely had unwittingly become Adrian's bargaining chip. And the truth of what *he* was—and what he had done to Diana herself.

Nicholas turned his head, squinting at the narrow edge of morning light seeping in around the blinds pulled down over the window. It had gone too far, now—too far to make her forget all that had passed between them, as he'd made her forget the mine. To reach so deeply into her mind could destroy her—as surely as if he drained her of life force. And she would always have her dreams to remind her, dreams that could drive her to madness unless she understood. . . .

He closed his eyes. When she knew, she would surely run from him and be safe again. Safe from his hunger, his growing desire to see in her what Sarah had promised so many years ago. He would make her understand all of it.

"Yes, Diana," he said at last. He walked slowly toward her, clenching his fists to keep from touching her.

"My twin, who I thought was—gone. A brother I haven't seen in over a hundred years."

Diana's face was waxen as a doll's. There was no sudden protest, no denial, no accusation of madness. He knew she heard his words clearly; her mouth formed the last three in silence. *A hundred years.*

Suddenly she looked lost, fragile, eyes huge in her pale face. She met his gaze and he saw her struggle to regain the safe rationality that had guided her life for so many years. Her vulnerability pierced him to the heart.

"No, Diana. You aren't insane," he said gently.

What he revealed to her now would forever alter her life.

And his.

"Your greatest weakness is that you care too much for these mortals, brother," Adrian mocked him in memory.

Nicholas blocked the voice, reaching out to Diana and letting his hand fall again. "I have—something to show you," he whispered.

He knew exactly where to look. The photograph had been perfectly preserved in a lower drawer of the armoire that was one of the few pieces of furniture in his meditation room. He had never been able to discard the photograph. Not even after he'd received Adrian's letter.

The letter was here as well. He left it where it lay. Retrieving his jeans from the room's single chair, he pulled them on with rough jerks. Carefully he removed the photograph from its envelope and walked back to Diana without once glancing at the image.

"You showed me Clare's sketch as proof. Now I have another piece of—evidence."

Diana's breasts rose and fell rapidly with the force of her breathing. Color seeped slowly back into her skin. She took the photograph from him slowly. Her face revealed everything she saw. Two men, standing side by side, nearly identical save for the style of suits they wore and the cut of their hair. Two brothers who had been photographed in their last moments as friends.

"I never knew about Clare, Diana, or what happened to her. This photograph was taken shortly before I last saw Adrian," he said. "In Nevada City, California, in the year 1890."

"Dear God."

" 'Did He Who made the lamb make thee?' " Nicholas quoted softly. "You asked what I was—what Adrian was. We are not ordinary men, Diana. That you knew already in your deepest heart, and in your dreams."

Once again she looked at him, searching his eyes, studying his face as if his nature could be read so easily. She shook her head with an exaggerated movement, searching for escape from the impossible.

He touched her then, knowing the time had come to make her understand. His fingers closed gently but firmly around her arm; the erratic flare of her life force washed over him in waves of heat. He touched her life force and drew on it, ever so slightly. She flinched back and then grew very still, the rhythm of her heartbeat rocking her body.

"Do you feel it, Diana? You've felt it from the beginning, haven't you, this thing that passes between us when we touch?" Carefully he released her arm. "I've never hurt you, Diana. I'm only bitterly sorry that you have suffered because of my brother." He looked away. "Do you fear me as the creature in your nightmares?"

His question cut through her withdrawal; her attention snapped back to him, courage unquenched.

"Everything within your rational mind denies what your dreams—and your body—tell you," he continued. "And yet you can't reject the truth, can you, Diana? Your dreams sense a deeper truth. They've prepared you for the things that human belief denies. The things I'm about to show you."

Gently he pried the photograph from her hand. Her fingers closed into a fist on empty air.

"I'm not crazy," she said in a flat, even voice. "I know that." Her breath caught, and all at once her eyes were blazing. "But I'm going to understand everything before I leave here, no matter what it takes. What you are, and what your—brother did to Clare." She braced herself like a warrior goddess ready to do battle. "You're going to tell me."

He almost laughed, but it would have been a cruelty to Diana now. "Yes, I will. I'll give you every explanation you could wish." He caught her other arm and drew her toward him. "If you are prepared to hear them."

She went utterly motionless in his grasp, like a small animal caught in the talons of a predator. She was unaware of her own life force, her burning aura, yet she felt what lay between them, what awakened when they touched. Her gaze never left his. "How can this—be happening?" she breathed.

Nicholas closed his eyes. "You chose your profession because you weren't afraid to look below the surface of human nature. Now you must look even beyond the human." He let his fingers brush her pale cheek. "I'm not a monster who will destroy you as Adrian destroyed Clare" —*liar*, his mind screamed—"but you'll have to trust me, Diana—as you've never trusted anyone before."

It was her decision. She had no reason to believe him, none at all to put herself in his hands. If she chose to trust him now, when her world, the rational foundation of her convictions, was crumbling beneath her—then he would step off into the abyss.

A long, deep shudder racked Diana from her toes to the top of her head. She breathed out a sound that might have been a laugh. "I've come this far," she whispered. "All my life I've tried to understand what happened to my sister. To my dreams." She tilted up her chin. "I've tried to figure out who *you* are, Nicholas Gale. I can't turn back now."

Turning away from her steady gaze, Nicholas hid the emotion he must at all costs suppress.

Neither of us can turn back, Diana. May your God help us both.

He took her down to the library, propping open the doors so that she would not feel trapped. Her walk was steady, her eyes clear, but she always stayed just out of his reach. He couldn't blame her. After he had told her everything, she would never suffer his touch again.

She stood by the chair closest to the door, declining to sit. Nicholas walked to the sideboard, giving her the safety of the room's length between them.

You care too much, Nicholas. Too much. . . .

"Tell me about your sister's death, Diana," he said.

Once again her face lost its color. "Is there a purpose to this?" she said hoarsely.

Nicholas poured himself a full glass of brandy and swirled it dangerously close to the edge. "To help you— understand. To help me explain—"

"All right." She stared at nothing, twisting her fingers together until the tendons stood out on the back of her small hands. "I have nothing to lose, do I? Not even my mind."

He let her take her own time to begin. Her voice was low and flat, devoid of emotion, filtered through a therapist's detachment.

She told him about the death of her parents, and Clare's determination to care for her younger sister. She spoke of Clare's fragility and genius; the sacrifices she had made to become a guardian to her sibling; the lonely sorrow that Clare had always tried to hide.

"She was vulnerable to—Adrian," Diana said, bracing her hands against the back of the chair. "He seemed to give her everything she had lost. For a while."

Oh yes, Nicholas thought bitterly. *He would.* "But you never met him."

"No. I only saw him from a distance. He never came to the house—she always went to him. But Clare told me about him a thousand times. How handsome he was, how bright, how exciting. How he made her feel that she could do anything, *be* anything." Suddenly she looked up, and Nicholas knew she was not speaking only of Adrian.

He took a long sip of the brandy. "Yes."

"He was like a—drug to her. A drug she couldn't get enough of." Diana's breath quickened. "Nothing was important but Adrian. She gave up everything else little by little. I could see her change, but I still didn't understand. Not even when the nightmares came."

The nightmares. Nicholas drained his glass. "Did Clare dream as well?"

"She did, once. We used to talk about our dreams when our parents were alive—the three of us, me and Clare and Keely. But after Clare met Adrian, she never spoke of them again—"

What kind of dreams did you give her, Adrian? Nicholas thought grimly. *Or didn't you bother with dreams at all?*

Diana threw back her head and closed her eyes. "It wasn't until she stopped sleeping that I realized how much Clare had changed."

Nicholas set down the empty glass. "Chronic insomnia," he said softly.

She looked at him without surprise. "Yes. After she

came home at night from seeing Adrian, she spent all her time pacing the floor in her bedroom, unable to sleep. It was as if she wasn't really there at all. And during the day, she couldn't function."

He recognized the symptoms she described. He had seen them, or hints of them, in his brother's early victims and in his own dreamers, before he had learned to be cautious. Chronic loss of sleep was one of the first warnings that a dreamer must be set free.

Or suffer the fate of Diana's sister.

Adrian. Adrian . . .

"Clare couldn't live a normal life," Diana said tonelessly. "The knowledge that she was failing in everything, in caring for me, devastated her. But Adrian was always there somewhere behind her, like an evil shadow. One night she disappeared—gone for over a week. I'd already begun to have the nightmares weeks before. I knew somehow that Adrian was the source of Clare's suffering. And then, only days after she returned without any explanation, she—"

Fighting the urge to go to her, Nicholas leaned back against the sideboard and clenched his fingers on the edge. "She took her own life," he said.

Diana moved away from the chair and took several agitated steps across the middle of the room. "After that day my nightmares grew more vivid. The vampire, bending over Clare. I think I saw his face the first time, but when I woke up—" She stopped only feet away from Nicholas and studied him with cold thoroughness. "I couldn't remember. For six months I had the nightmare. And then I stopped dreaming entirely.

"The nightmares came back only weeks before Keely disappeared. It was only when I finally tried to let go that I saw his face."

"Adrian," Nicholas whispered.

Her stare gave him no quarter. "I never found Adrian after Clare died. He didn't come to her funeral. Much later, when I was going through her things, I found diary entries she'd written before she died. They were nearly incomprehensible, but one thing was clear. He'd abandoned her just before she lost her will to live—took away the only thing she'd been hanging on to after everything else was gone.

"In every way that mattered, he killed her."

Nicholas closed his eyes. *As he killed Sarah.* "I'm sorry, Diana," he said. The words were desperately inadequate, and would be so much ludicrous babble when he had told her everything.

"Are you, Nicholas?"

He met her bleak gaze. "You said you'd let me explain, Diana—about my brother and about myself."

Feeling behind her for the chair, Diana backed up and sat down heavily, as if only the recital of her sister's fate had kept her standing. Nicholas walked softly across the carpet and took the chair opposite hers. "What I'm going to tell you will be—difficult for you to accept."

She breathed a laugh. "Do you have a coffin hidden in your closet, Nicholas? Do you sprout fangs and drink blood?" Her voice rose, taking on an almost hysterical edge. "Is *that* what really killed my sister?"

He would have given anything to go to her, hold her in his arms, hold her together when it seemed she might shatter like a porcelain doll. But he leaned back in his chair, assuming all the control she had finally let go. He turned his own voice into a soothing, caressing instrument of persuasion—the same voice he had used in the mine—and in this very room—when he had seduced her into sleep.

"When I told you I knew nothing of Clare or my brother's presence in San Francisco," he began, "I was speaking the truth. Fifteen years ago I was living in New York City and London, dividing my time between them. I hadn't been to the West Coast in nearly thirty years.

"The last time I saw Adrian was in Nevada City nearly a century ago. You see, Diana, Adrian and I are—immortal."

Immortal.

Diana didn't know what she had expected. If he had confirmed her wild supposition that he was literally the vampire of her nightmare, she would not have so much as blinked. Because she had gone well past the point of rationality.

She already knew he was no ordinary man. And she had, at last, abandoned herself to the relentless logic of her dreams.

Nevertheless, she had to fight down an hysterical urge to laugh until she cried.

"I was born over two hundred years ago in Yorkshire, England," he said quietly. He studied her face like a doctor expecting an imminent breakdown, and his mouth slowly curved into a humorless smile. "Do you believe me, Doctor?"

"Of course," she said flatly.

Nicholas rose to his feet, paced several strides and turned back again. "No. This is not the way." He stood over her, locking his arms behind his back. "Let us begin, instead, with dreams. *Your* dreams, Diana."

Something in his voice made her throw off the strange, fey mood that had gripped her. "My dreams?"

"Your dreams, and your nightmare. The nightmare that warned you about Clare's peril, that reappeared just when Keely seemed to be facing a similar danger—at least in your own mind. And the nightmare that brought you to me today. None of them were ordinary dreams, were they, Diana? They were true warnings, and you listened."

The gentle rhythm of his voice drained the tension from Diana's body, made her eyelids heavy. She gripped the arms of the chair more tightly.

"You hinted once that you had been a remarkable dreamer in your youth, Diana, and that you'd lost the ability after Clare died. But in these past weeks you've dreamed of more than the creature who took Clare's life, haven't you?" He dropped to his knees before her chair, clutching the arms inches from her fingers. All she could see was his eyes.

"Do you remember the horses?"

The image that leaped into her mind was vivid. Horses, running wild on an unknown beach. The feel of flexing muscle between her thighs. The gray rider . . .

Nicholas's fingers brushed hers, the lightest of caresses that sent a bolt of sensation through her body. "Do you remember the masked rider, Diana? How you felt when he took you in his arms and made love to you?"

She shivered, unable to pull free of his touch. "No."

"Yes. And then you danced with your mysterious lover at the ball. You wore white. He took you to a deserted chamber, and the firelight bathed your lovely curves—"

She tried to shut out his words, but everything inside her had become frozen and powerless.

"Now you wonder if you're truly going mad after all," he whispered, sliding his hands up her arms to cup her shoulders. "You thought your dreams were private, even if they did expose a deeper truth. When you dreamed of that phantom lover, you created a world for yourself alone."

Uncontrollable tremors racked her body. Nicholas began to stroke her arms, soothing her as he would a child. "You didn't know the identity of your phantom lover. You didn't know I was there with you, sharing your dreams. Sharing everything—"

Adrenaline surged through her, providing the strength she needed to wrench free of his arms. She stood up, forcing him to rock back on his heels.

Nicholas let his arms fall to his sides, holding her only with his impenetrable gaze. "We've established that I'm not entirely human, Diana, just as your nightmare told you. This is how I can begin to explain—what I am."

She believed him. God help her, but she did. Why balk at this amid all the rest? Heat surged into her cheeks, and it took all her will to keep from covering her face with her hands.

When her heart no longer slammed against her ribs and the haze had cleared from her mind, she found her voice again. "You—were in my mind."

"Yes." For the first time he looked away. "Entering your dreams to—take what I needed from you."

Diana sucked in a deep breath and concentrated on remaining utterly calm. "What you—needed," she whispered. The Halloween Ball dream came back in all its intensity, resurrecting the fear she had felt when she'd known the dream-Nicholas wanted more than just her body. . . .

The dream had not been a dream at all.

"Diana—I never sought you out. I did you no harm when I entered your dreams—"

"No harm—"

"I may not be human, Diana, but I've spent most of my life fighting not to become a monster. Like my brother."

The vampire. God, the vampire, draining Clare dry. . . .

"You dreamed of a vampire," Nicholas said, as if he'd

read her thoughts. "You may call us vampires, Diana. It's the closest human word for what we are. We live as— parasites—on something only humans can give us—something even more vital and powerful than blood."

Stumbling away from Nicholas, Diana rounded the chair until it stood as a shield between them. "Dreams?" she said faintly.

His words were matter-of-fact and totally devoid of emotion. "Not dreams. Life force. The formless, invisible mortal energy unique to living things—*qi, prana, élan vital* —there are names for it in a hundred cultures around the world, though most humans live their lives completely unaware of it." He raised his hand and flexed the fingers. "Our bodies do not produce what you take for granted. Without your vitality, we cannot live."

She stared blindly over his golden head. "Clare—"

"You told me that Clare died because she was— drained of her creativity, her vitality, the will to live. Your sister was my brother's victim, Diana, in the literal sense of the word." Nicholas rose to his feet slowly. "He hunted her down, seduced her, drained her of her life force, and left her with nothing to keep her alive."

No protest, no sound of any kind could pass the knot in Diana's throat. She pressed her face to the chair back and concentrated on her breathing, the beat of her heart, the muscles that kept her on her feet. If she looked up—if she dared to look at Nicholas's body, his face—she knew she would shatter into a million fragments.

"Adrian and I are alike in one sense, Diana," Nicholas continued softly. "We read the auras of mortals to find those who can give us what we need, whose life force is strong enough. Fifteen years ago your sister's aura—must have attracted Adrian, and he pursued her." His breath shuddered out in a betrayal of emotion. "But my brother and I chose different paths long ago. Adrian became a predator. His way was to take too much too quickly, too directly. I found another way to survive. When mortals dream, the life force we need is very close to the surface. We can skim away what we must have without bringing harm to the dreamer. The more powerful the dreams or the dreamer, the more we can take."

Through the hum in her ears she heard him move, but still she would not look up. "I learned—long ago how to choose my dreamers carefully, and give something in return for what I consumed. I learned how to give pleasure in mortal dreams, weave the strands of the dreamer's imagination into a pattern of sensual fulfillment."

She felt his heat, his power as he came to stand at her side, and her breath froze in her lungs.

"As I did in your dreams, Diana," he murmured.

His fingers stirred her hair, caressed the curve of her ear. Nicholas touched her, as he had done on a lonely beach, in an elegant firelit chamber, in other impossible times and places.

Something gave way in her then, all the tension expanding outward in a maelstrom of chaotic light and color and sensation. She staggered and Nicholas caught her, drew her close to his body, hard and solid and real.

"Diana," he said. "I could give you a thousand facts, and they wouldn't do any good. But there is another way."

Leaning against him, wrapped in his arms, Diana ceased to think. Life became sensation: the firmness of Nicholas's chest under her cheek; the steady beat of his heart; the smell of him; the way he moved; a thousand things that spoke more clearly than words.

"There is another way," he said. And her eyelids grew heavy as he murmured her name, took her hand and led her into infinity.

ELEVEN

There is a time for many words, and there is
also a time for sleep.

— Homer, *The Odyssey*

He hadn't been home in nearly two centuries, but his
memory had preserved Coverdale Hall as if he had never
left.

Diana stood beside him, wearing a high-waisted
morning gown that had also come down unchanged from
the time of his youth. He had given her the demure white
of a young girl, with a high neckline to preserve her mod-
esty—as if he could keep her innocent and ignorant.

As if he could keep her at all when this was finished. . . .

At first glance the library looked almost the same as

his room in San Francisco. He had copied his memories very faithfully when he'd had the house built on Seacliff several decades ago. The library at Coverdale Hall had always been his sanctuary, until the day he had been driven out into the world.

"What happened?" Diana whispered.

He looked down at himself, seeing what she saw: a man dressed impeccably in the clothing of 1805. The year he had abandoned the Hall. Diana's eyes raked over him and turned to herself. Her hands brushed down over the gown, molding it to her figure.

Nicholas averted his eyes. "What do you think has happened, Diana?" he asked softly.

She took a series of brief, shallow breaths. "My clothes—"

Leaving her to reach the obvious conclusion, Nicholas walked across the room to the heavy red velvet drapes that covered the window. For a moment he hesitated, less certain of what he would find than he should have been. But as he drew back the drapes light swept into the room, patterned across the carpet through the mullioned window.

And the view was the same. The green of the park swept down toward the beck, half-wild from the indifferent care of the viscount's gardeners. Trees planted a century before gave the park a more civilized air, but beyond them—beyond the beck and the borders of the estate— rose the fells, bare and stark against the wide sky.

Muslin rustled as Diana came to join him.

"Dear God," she breathed.

"Welcome to Coverdale Hall," Nicholas said, setting one hand against the glass. It was cold and smooth, every sensation perfectly defined.

Diana lifted her own hand as if to touch the scene

beyond the window. Her fingers spread and settled inches from his on the pane.

"This isn't San Francisco," she murmured.

"No. Those are the north Yorkshire Dales, Diana. As they appeared in the year 1805."

Her hand curled into a fist. "I'm dreaming," she said at last.

Nicholas struggled briefly with the desire to cover her hand with his own. "Yes. This is a dream. Your dream, Diana." He pushed away from the window and stared at the rows of books shelved on the walls. "Your dream, but my design, my—additions. The best way I can find to explain the impossible."

He heard her move, circling the room and touching the objects their minds had created. "This is my dream," she repeated.

"As were all the others," he said, pulling a book from the nearest shelf. It was heavy in his hand, smelling of leather and dust. "My kind don't dream, Diana. Just as we don't sleep. What we know of dreams comes from mortal kind. We are—craftsmen, if you will, who can shape the raw material of dreams but never create." He opened the book and found the pages covered with print he could not read. "We can only borrow. Or steal."

The book was lifted abruptly from his hand. Diana braced it against her midriff and stared at the rows of letters.

"If this is my dream," she said, "then I can control it."

In her hands the book began to change, blurring and shrinking. Leather bindings became modern cloth, the paper crisp and new.

Nicholas looked at her face, taut with concentration, and sighed. "You are a strong dreamer, Diana." He closed his eyes, gathering up the warp and woof of the dream.

Diana gasped, and he caught the book just as she dropped it.

Across a blank page, in bold letters, lay the words he had envisioned:

*All that we see or seem
is but a dream within a dream.*

"You see, Diana. Are you beginning to understand?"

She looked up, staring at him with her jaw set and her eyes ablaze. The fear and uncertainty of her final waking moments had vanished, replaced with the fierce determination he had come to admire.

"Shall we try it again, Nicholas?" she said tightly.

This time she was the one to close her eyes, brow furrowed with effort. The letters on the page shifted again.

So I awoke, and behold it was a dream.

Nicholas grasped what she intended when it was almost too late. Dropping the book, he caught her shoulders and dragged her against him. She remained rigid in his arms.

"No, Diana. You wanted to understand. This is the only way. Let me guide you—"

With a sharp breath she wrenched free of him. "You can't control me here," she gasped. The white muslin gown blurred at the edges, taking on new lines and color. Within a few seconds she stood before him in navy trousers, silk blouse, and blazer, armored in defiance.

Caught off guard by her focused power, Nicholas made no attempt to counteract her effort. He smiled mockingly at his own conceit. In spite of the shocks that had repeatedly beset her, she grasped what control she could and hung onto it as tenaciously as she did her sanity.

He bowed with all the grace at his command. "I concede this victory," he murmured. "But we have no time for sparring." His smile faded as he held her gaze. "I have much to show you, Diana." Looking at her flushed face and sapphire eyes, he found it strangely difficult to make the necessary promise. "When this is over, you'll be free, Diana. Free to dream as you choose for the rest of your life."

He averted his eyes before she could see too much. When his thoughts were still and cold as the waters of a frozen beck, he held out his hand.

"Come, Diana. Come with me."

After a long moment she put her hand in his.

Her sanity hung by a thread of resolution as Diana followed Nicholas into the wide, dark hallway.

I will see this through to the end, she told herself, chanting it like a litany. *I know this is only a dream.*

But Nicholas's hand was hot in hers, utterly real, burning with an internal fire. Inhuman fire—life force drawn from humankind. He was here, with her, within a world she'd had no part in shaping. Within her mind itself.

She realized she'd stopped when her arm pulled taut in Nicholas's grasp. He turned to look back at her, the clean lines of his features softened in the sourceless light.

"Come," he told her. There was no emotion in his voice. She lifted her chin and began to walk again, into a spacious entry hall with a tiled floor and a broad marble staircase sweeping up into darkness.

Their footsteps bounced and echoed in the unearthly stillness. Diana tried to conjure music—any music, from any era—and failed. She knew she was dreaming, and yet she was virtually helpless.

"Where are you taking me?" she said at last, defying the silence. Nicholas walked ahead of her up the stairs, pausing on the gallery above.

"Into my past," he said.

He turned to the left without looking back, and she followed. The open gallery became a wood-paneled hall, chill and sinister with lurking shadows. It seemed to stretch ahead of them into infinity, punctuated only by heavy closed doors.

Diana heard the cries even before Nicholas came to a halt. They swelled and receded, the wailing of a woman subjected to some unspeakable torment.

The door nearest to Nicholas swung open before he touched the tarnished brass knob. "Here, Diana," he said.

A blast of furnace heat swept outward from the room into which he led her. The cries rose again, almost deafening.

"My mother," Nicholas said. Diana stared at the great canopied bed that dominated the room. Amid tangled sheets lay a woman, writhing in pain, her sweat-darkened hair plastered to her waxen face. By the bedside, hunched in a chair drawn flush to the carved wooden bedframe, sat a black-haired man.

"Her name was Elizabeth," Nicholas said tonelessly, as if the woman's suffering meant nothing to him at all. "My stepfather, Viscount Coverdale, found her wandering the Dales when she was three months pregnant. The year was 1784."

The woman—Nicholas's mother—heaved convulsively on the bed, and from behind the concealment of bed hangings a woman in drab gray and white moved to her side and pressed a cloth to Elizabeth's flushed face.

"Years later," Nicholas continued, "when Adrian and

I were older, Elizabeth told us about our birth. It nearly killed her. Procreation among our kind is—was—often fatal. The drain on the mother's life force was considerable. That Elizabeth chose to risk it at all was remarkable in itself."

Unable to look away from the scene before them, Diana heard her breath catch and release in time to Elizabeth's struggles. She forced her eyes to the man at her side.

"Your father?"

Nicholas walked calmly into the center of the room, nearly to the bed itself. The three dream phantoms never looked up. "I never learned the name of my real father. Perhaps Elizabeth herself never knew. He was one of our kind, one of the last, as Elizabeth was. When she came to the Dales, she wanted only one thing. A safe place to bear her children."

His voice was drowned out by a sudden, violent shriek. The man by the bed surged to his feet, and the older woman rushed to the foot of the bed. For a long moment Diana's view was blocked, and she stared at Nicholas's cold, expressionless profile.

"She found it in Coverdale Hall," he said when the shrieks had faded to whimpers. "Elizabeth had all the appearance of youth and excellent breeding, in spite of her expectant condition. The viscount had lived in virtual exile here before she came. She exerted little effort to make him fall in love with her. He so forgot his place that he married Elizabeth, and claimed her bastard children as his own."

A new, different cry filled the space between his words.

"I was firstborn," Nicholas said as the older woman turned to reveal the red, wrinkled face of a newborn infant in her arms. "Adrian came an hour later. The viscount made me his heir—even after he learned what Elizabeth was."

"What she was," Diana echoed, watching the midwife rock the infant as his mother lay insensible and exhausted.

Nicholas reached out as if he would touch the child and dropped his hand an instant later. "A—vampire. Inhuman, born of a race older than mankind and almost vanished."

He looked back at the woman lying exhausted on the bed. "Elizabeth found in the viscount not only a protector but also a dreamer who could satisfy the bulk of her need," Nicholas said, leaning heavily against the bedpost. "She was able to survive with his life force and that of only a few other dreamers she found in the district. But one day she chose to reveal the truth to her mortal husband—as I'm telling you, Diana—and instead of recoiling in horror, he accepted everything she was. He told her nothing would change. We would be a family."

The dark-haired man at the bedside looked up as Nicholas fell silent again. His homely face was white with strain above the tangled ends of a loosened neckcloth. For an instant it seemed he looked right at Diana; he raised his hand as if to plead for help. Before Diana could be sure Nicholas's dream-phantom was aware of her presence, the woman on the bed gave a wailing cry that captured the viscount's full attention.

Diana had taken two steps toward the bed when Nicholas intercepted her.

"Come, Diana. I have more to show you."

He gripped her arm and ushered her away from the drama of birth and suffering. Only the knowledge that this was a dream—a dream of something long past—convinced Diana to go with him. She turned in the doorway at the sound of a second infant's cry.

"My brother," Nicholas said. But he gave her no chance to witness his twin's arrival. The door shut noiselessly behind them as they passed into the dark hallway once again. The cries that had drawn them to the room faded into silence.

Diana pulled her arm free of Nicholas's loose grasp. "What now?" she asked.

He looked at her intently, dropping back to match her pace. "Are you beginning to understand, Diana?"

She got no further than a shake of her head. A new sound echoed in the endless hallway—the music of a child's carefree laughter, incongruous in this forbidding place.

"Ah," Nicholas said, lifting his head. "The nursery."

The door at which he paused was like the others, but it opened on a scene far different from the one before. The room was small and low-ceilinged, and the faint glow of candles lent an atmosphere of cozy warmth. Two children sat on the floor opposite each other with a deck of cards between them. They were nearly identical—blond, angelic, handsome boys—but while one of them frowned over the cards in his hand, the other flashed his brother a wicked grin.

There was no mistaking the resemblance. One of these boys was Nicholas, and Diana looked from one to the other, fascinated in spite of herself.

"Adrian." A soft woman's voice called. "Surely you are not cheating?"

The grinning boy's head jerked up, and his smile transformed into something cherubic. "I, Mother?"

Clutching his handful of cards, the other boy sighed. "You've won, Adrian." He dropped his cards and took Adrian's from his hand, jumbling them together.

The rustle of cloth preceded the appearance of the owner of the woman's voice. Diana recognized her at once as the woman in the previous scene, restored to health and beauty. And she was beautiful: her hair was golden, drawn up in a simple style atop her head; her figure was slender and graceful in a wide-sashed muslin morning gown; and her face was as fine and aristocratic as an exquisite porcelain figurine.

As she knelt beside Adrian, the similarity in their features was immediately apparent. Diana glanced up at Nicholas beside her and drew in her breath. Nicholas embodied the masculine side of his mother's flawlessness. They were the same—the same breed, inhumanly perfect.

"It would grieve me to learn you've been cheating, Adrian," Elizabeth said, putting her arm around the boy's shoulder. "Have you?"

Adrian pouted, looking up at his mother under long golden lashes. "Ask Nicholas, Mother. He'll tell you."

The other boy never glanced up from his task of straightening the deck of cards. "I have no complaints, Mother," he murmured.

Behind the youthful pitch of the boy's words Diana could hear the deep, persuasive voice she had come to know so well. The boy Nicholas glanced up quickly under his brows just in time to see Adrian's unabashed grin of triumph.

Elizabeth smiled and shook her head. "Ah, Nicholas. Your loyalty to your brother does you credit, but you will not always be able to protect him." She moved between the boys, drawing them close against her.

"She was right," Nicholas said. Diana snapped her gaze back to the man beside her. "We didn't know then that the nature of our kind would force us to go our separate ways, that we would change so much." He smiled, belying the pain visible in his eyes. "We were happy then. I could never stay angry with Adrian for long when we were children. He always got his way in the end. I would have forgiven him anything. Anything."

Diana looked from Nicholas's face to the gentle domestic scene, two boys utterly safe in the arms of their loving mother. Elizabeth ruffled young Nicholas's pale hair.

"You must understand, my sons. There are rules and laws all living things must obey. Even our kind. To survive, to keep our sanity, we must learn these rules and play by them. If we cheat—if we always look for the easy way—we must pay the price in the end."

The boy Nicholas studied his mother's face, solemn and intent, while Adrian squirmed and rolled his eyes. "Mother," Adrian said, "Father said he would take me riding at sunset. May I go?"

Elizabeth laughed under her breath and pushed the boy away. "Go. But Adrian—we will talk of this later."

Adrian was on his feet like a shot, heading for the door. But Nicholas lingered, holding his mother's hand in his.

"We will be together, Mother," he said firmly. "We'll always be together."

Elizabeth pressed a kiss to her son's forehead. "Yes, Nicholas. As long as we live."

Diana came back to herself just in time to step out of the way as Adrian barreled through the door, oblivious to the dreamers. Young Nicholas followed more slowly, glancing back before following his brother down the hall. The darkness swallowed him up, leaving Nicholas and Diana to stare after him.

"I didn't understand then," Nicholas said. "When we were children, the rules seemed more flexible. We still didn't know the price that would be demanded of us." He turned back to the woman who stood alone in the nursery, looking out the window with her body carefully placed in shadow. "The young of our kind are almost like human children. We could survive as mortals survive, possessing our own life force. Our mother wouldn't take that innocence away from us."

Elizabeth drew away from the window, moving quietly about the small room, touching the plain wooden furniture with elegant white hands. Nicholas raised his own hand, spreading his long fingers as if to block out the sight of his mother's quiet sadness.

"Inevitably," he said, "we did lose our innocence. Elizabeth believed in rules and natural laws, but she hoped to circumvent them." Lowering his hand, he examined it intently. "She believed it was possible for one of our kind to become mortal."

Without another word he turned and started down the hall, letting Diana follow as she would. As she glanced back into the nursery it began to blur and fade before her eyes. Elizabeth vanished. Nicholas was only a silhouette at the end of a tunnel of darkness.

Heart racing with a mounting sense of dread, Diana jogged to catch up with him. Nicholas's face was set and pale as he stood in an open doorway. The sounds of unbearable grief came from the room just beyond.

The scene within was a nightmare in itself. The room was utterly bare except for a single large object. It took a moment for Diana to recognize it for what it was.

A guillotine.

The scratched wooden floor was blotched with old bloodstains. Sobs echoed in the room, sourceless and heartwrenching.

"Elizabeth died," Nicholas whispered. "She was an immortal, but she died in this room, after months of madness and despair. Because she wanted to be human." His breaths came in harsh gusts. "When my mother came to Coverdale Hall she knew she was one of the last of her kind. She could never tell us what had become of the others, those few she had met in her lifetime. She knew there was no future for us. She knew she would have to send us out into the world to make our own way, to survive by taking the life force from mortal humans. But she wanted more, for us and for herself."

Diana felt the vibrating tension in Nicholas's body, the leashed power in him that betrayed the intensity of his suppressed emotion. "Elizabeth knew that her husband was not strong enough to provide all she needed forever, that he would die as all mortals do. But she believed she had the strength, the ability to make a great change in herself. She believed that by refusing sustenance entirely, she could force her body to transform into the mortal state.

"On the day Adrian and I turned fourteen, she began the course that would lead her to madness and death. She refused to take life force from our stepfather or anyone else."

Pulling her back with him, Nicholas flattened himself against the door frame. Two boys—handsome young men now, dressed in men's clothing—appeared out of the hallway and walked slowly through the door to disappear into the shadows.

"We saw it happen, Adrian and I. Saw her refuse to take the very thing that would keep her alive. She had taught us what we needed to know when we reached adulthood, but then she gave herself to her dreams of mortality. Dreams she had formed sometime during her long life, legends she clung to and intellectualized. She became a recluse, slowly starving herself of life. Nothing the viscount did would convince her to abandon her hope of becoming human. Even when she began to go mad. At the end, our stepfather would not allow us near her at all. The last time we saw him was the day he entered our mother's room alone. He never emerged alive."

Tears stung Diana's eyes. "Your mother—killed him—"

"Yes. And when, after draining our stepfather of his life force, she realized what she had done, she used *this* to end her life in the only way she believed it could be done. By severing the spine beyond any hope of healing."

Diana dropped her forehead to Nicholas's chest and clutched at the lapels of his coat. "Oh, Nicholas—"

His muscles were rigid against her. "I'll spare you the unpleasant details of what followed. That was the end of our time of innocence in Coverdale Hall. The few retainers who had remained fled from this accursed place. But Adrian and I had come of age, and by the nature of our kind we had no choice but to seek sustenance among mortals. Our mother's death had taught us that we were not human. That we had only each other."

The room began to fade before Diana's eyes. Nicholas pivoted around to face the hall and released her slowly. Where there had been only a wood-paneled wall was now a wide mullioned window, looking out into twilight. Diana moved to the window and gazed out at the faint light that lingered on the grass and trees and distant fells.

There were two young men on the lane that led up to the door of the Hall. One of them was mounted on a sturdy bay gelding; the other was on foot, gripping his brother's gloved hand.

"Adrian was the first to leave," Nicholas said from behind her. "He was always the restless one. We could not live together at Coverdale Hall in any case, because our needs would have overwhelmed the local population. Adrian knew that London would provide everything he could ever require."

As Nicholas finished speaking, the mounted man

threw up his hand in salute, wheeled his mount, and started off at a gallop down the lane until he disappeared over a curve and into a stand of trees. The man left behind watched long after his brother had vanished. He turned very slowly, looking up at the Hall, a living portrait of loneliness.

"I was content to stay here for a time. Coverdale Hall and the title had been left to me. But, in time, even I felt the need to learn what the world held for an immortal. That was when I learned that human society was not for our kind. And that my brother—"

He broke off sharply. With a sudden jerk he closed the drapes over the window.

"That tale will come in time. I have one thing left to show you."

The spell that had held Diana mute and accepting throughout Nicholas's fantastic tour began to fall away as she focused on his face. The emotion she had sensed in him earlier had vanished, replaced by implacable coldness. She took an involuntary step backward, glancing behind her at the darkness through which they had come.

When she turned back to Nicholas he was gone. Diana found herself suddenly alone, understanding that she had the choice of which direction to go: advance or retreat, follow Nicholas to the end of the dream or retrace their steps back down the lightless corridor.

But she was here in this uncanny place because she had wanted the truth.

See this through to the end, she repeated to herself, and took one step and another deeper into the dream.

She found Nicholas waiting for her at a door unlike all the others in this endless hall. Behind him was a wall, utterly blank; the door to his left was incongruously modern, beige-painted wood with a shiny brass knob.

Nicholas nodded to her, clasping his hands behind his back. "This is your door, Diana," he said softly.

She studied his face, searching for some hint of what she would find. Nicholas offered nothing, revealed nothing; Diana clenched her fists and walked past him. The doorknob turned easily in her hand.

Again there was sound, filling her ears before her eyes adjusted to the darkness in the room. The cries were not of pain or grief. Diana listened for several moments before she realized what she was hearing.

Passion. The gasps and moans were cries of sensual gratification. Gradually her vision sharpened, and she looked into a room that was familiar as nothing else in the dream had been.

It was *her* room. Her room, at home, in the sane world of reality. On her bed lay a woman, nude, her head arched back and her lips parted on gasps of pleasure. Above her knelt a fully-clothed man, touching her, stroking her body, kissing her breasts and belly and thighs.

Diana knew the man was Nicholas. The woman on the bed jerked her head to the side, and her face was clearly visible.

"I have come to you," Nicholas said—her dream-guide, the man who stood beside her—"in your dreams, to take what I must have to survive. I have been your lover, Diana, your masked cavalier. You have fed me as no other woman has done in a century."

The only reply came from the dream-twin writhing on the bed, responding mindlessly to her lover's caresses. Diana flinched as Nicholas touched her, drawing his warm hand down her arm.

"Look, Diana. See how I live."

She looked, unable to move or think or feel. As if she had gained a new level of awareness, she began to see a faint glow about the dream-Diana's body, a nimbus of colored light. It wavered and pulsed like a heartbeat. As the dream-Nicholas touched her, something changed: The aura began to flux and flow from Diana to Nicholas, drawn like mist in a grade B horror film.

"I saw the brilliance of your aura the first time we met," Nicholas said, his fingers flexing on Diana's arm in a sensuous rhythm. "Though I never sought you out, I knew you could safely provide me with more than I had ever been able to take from a dreamer in this century. But you didn't suffer for it, Diana."

Even as he spoke, the dream-Diana gave a low cry and shuddered in unmistakeable climax. Above her, the dream-Nicholas flung back his head as a great wave of light rose up from the woman to surround him. He gave a wordless cry, suspended in a glow that turned him into something otherworldly.

"You had the pleasure of your dreams, Diana. And I survived, flourished with the strength of your life force."

The dream-Nicholas rose slowly from the bed. Something undefinable in his stance revealed newfound power; he bent over the dream-Diana to stroke her forehead and draw the sheets up over her sleeping form. Then he turned and looked directly at the watchers—directly into Diana's eyes.

Reeling with the effort to understand what she had seen, Diana took an involuntary step backward. But Nicholas's solid warmth was no longer there. She turned to find a blank wall behind her, the door vanished.

"I am here, Diana," the dream-Nicholas said. "Here, in your mind, in your dreams."

He advanced toward her, alight with inhuman energy. She watched in paralyzed fascination as he reached for her, touched her, began to pull something from deep inside her as he had done to her dream-twin. She could feel the pulse of life essence within herself being drawn outward, feeding the nimbus that enveloped Nicholas, making her sway with growing dizziness.

"Now do you understand?" he said, the resonance of his voice more real than her own phantom body.

She fought back because her instincts demanded it—because no man, no creature would control her. She formed a dream-shield around herself that repelled Nicholas, cast off his touch, obliterated his influence. His smooth, triumphant expression changed, altering to shock.

There was power in her, a power Nicholas could not touch or tap. Until this moment she hadn't realized it existed. Nicholas had taught her. She drew on the very life force he had tried to take from her, and turned it to her will.

I will wake up, Diana told him, told herself and the dream-world around them. *I will wake up.*

The room was the first to fade, walls dissolving around her, the bed with its mirror-image of herself melting into mist. She stood alone in the void with Nicholas, staring into his astonished eyes. And then he, too, began to vanish—like the Cheshire-Cat in *Alice's Adventures in Wonderland,* his body losing substance until only the glow of his eyes remained.

"Diana!"

She jerked violently awake, casting off the hands that held her to the chair. Nicholas knelt before her, his face frozen and pale. With a sharp breath Diana looked around the room. Nicholas's library—his real library, with a hundred tiny differences the dream world hadn't reproduced. Nicholas wore the jeans he'd had on when he'd begun his fantastic story. And she—she herself felt too nauseated and rattled to be anything but wide awake.

"Diana," Nicholas whispered. His fingers clenched hard on the arms of the chair, as if he too might fall without their support. He blinked slowly. "The dream—"

She was on her feet before his hand could shift to hold her. For a moment she stood over him, sucking in deep breaths of incipient panic.

His eyes were brilliant as they looked up at her, celestially beautiful in a fallen angel's face. The face of a vampire, an immortal who lived by stealing the very essence of life from human beings.

Diana fought to control the deep shudders that pulsed through her body. She could still see the images of the dream as if she had lived through them a hundred times, feel the substance of life itself flow from her own body into his.

She believed. God help her, she believed. And everything she had known about herself, her past, her very life was being sucked into a vortex of madness.

Nicholas disappeared, and Diana dropped back into the chair. She lost track of time, concentrating on drawing in one slow breath after another. When he returned it was to thrust a glass of brandy into her shaking hands.

"Drink it," he commanded roughly.

She drank automatically, and the burning liquid nearly choked her before she felt its effects. As Nicholas took the glass away their hands touched; something as potent as the brandy, as hot as blood, flowed invisibly from her flesh to his.

"No," Diana whispered. "No." Jerking free, she jumped up, swayed with sudden dizziness, and lurched away from the chair.

"Diana—"

She fled from his voice, from his reaching hand. She fled the library, the house, emerging into the blessed sunlight that would kill the shadows in her mind. She spun about when she had put the iron gate between herself and the man who had turned her world upside down.

He stood inside the doorway out of the reach of the morning sun. The eight feet of walkway between them might have been a thousand miles. Or the span of a mortal life.

Nicholas said nothing more. He watched her, leaning his head against the open door. There was nothing but unutterable weariness in his pose—a vulnerability that was wholly human—and a sadness so profound that Diana felt it in her bones.

In another moment she might go back to him. She could give herself up to dreams and leave reality behind forever. Nicholas had that power over her. He had only to look into her eyes. . . .

Diana gasped and turned away. She walked blindly to the curb, struggling to remember where she'd parked her car. *Can't drive,* she thought with sudden panic. *The brandy—*

But another car was waiting for her. Diana caught one glimpse of Judith's face through the passenger window of the ancient BMW and moved for the open door.

"I thought you—didn't drive," Diana said dazedly.

"Only on special occasions," Judith murmured. "And I suspect this qualifies."

Without another word Diana slid into the passenger seat. When she turned to look back at the house, Nicholas was already gone.

"I think we need to talk," Judith said.

Diana leaned her head back against the car seat and laughed until sobs closed her throat and the tears ran down her cheeks.

Judith offered no meaningless words of comfort; she simply drove, away from Nicholas's house and through the city until the sting of a stiff bay breeze dried Diana's tears.

"Here. You'll need this."

Diana took the tissue Judith offered, staring out the window at the crisp blue waters of the bay. Judith had brought her to the Marina Green, a stretch of grass and open space on the bay with an unobstructed view of the Marin headlands. The day was impossibly lovely and utterly unreal.

"You're not crazy, you know."

Diana felt her thoughts begin to reassemble like scattered puzzle pieces. "So I've been told," she said hoarsely. She balled the tissue in her fist and looked at Judith. "How did you happen to turn up when you did?"

Judith sighed. "He called me about a half hour ago. I think he had an idea you'd need someone—human to talk to."

Diana shook her head. "You've—always known, haven't you?"

Judith's gaze slid away, and she reached across the seat to open the glove compartment. She nearly dropped the package of cigarettes in Diana's lap before she got a grip on it and tossed it onto the dashboard. Pulling out a long brown cigarette, she put it between her lips.

"What he is? Oh, yes. For a very long time. And you can blame me for all this, if you like." Judith fumbled in the pocket of her loose silk jacket and withdrew a matchbook. She stared at it for a moment and threw it into the back seat. *"Merde."* A wry smile curved her mouth. "He made me give up smoking, you see. But he couldn't make me stop interfering in his life. Or yours."

Something in Judith's matter-of-fact tone did more to restore Diana's composure than any simple reassurances, but the protective numbness remained. "I don't think I quite understand—"

"No? Hardly remarkable that you don't." She laughed dryly around the unlit cigarette. "Let's take a walk."

They stepped out onto the sidewalk overlooking the small craft harbor where sailboats bobbed on the choppy water. Joggers and dog-walkers dodged around them. Diana breathed in the salty air as if its faint abrasiveness could scour the confusion from her mind.

"Begin at the beginning," Judith said, tugging her jacket closed against the wind. "He told you what he is, how he survives. What did he call himself? A vampire? Close, but we don't have a label for his species."

"His—species."

"I did a little research when I was younger, trying to figure out what he is." She breathed in an imaginary lungful of smoke. "I've known Nicholas all my life—all but the first eight years when I was a child growing up in Europe. It was 1942 when Nicholas saved my life." Her sharp brown eyes fixed intently on Diana's. "Only two human beings in the world know what he is, Diana. You and I. Perhaps because I was a child, learning the truth was easier for me to accept. But I can't think of anyone else in this world more capable of cherishing the trust he's given you."

Diana brushed at loose curls that had blown over her eyes. "Trust?" she whispered.

Judith touched Diana's hand. "Why don't you tell me how Nicholas came to confide in you?"

It was remarkably easy to spill it all out to Judith—the story of Clare's suicide and the childhood nightmare, the face that had come clear at last, the drawing, Diana's confrontation with Nicholas. And what Nicholas had told her about himself—and Adrian. Everything but the dreams she and Nicholas had shared. . . .

"I knew little about his brother," Judith said when

Diana paused. "Only that he had a twin that he hadn't seen in a very long time. But this . . . I'm so sorry, Diana."

Diana shook her head slowly. "All my life I've been looking for a resolution to Clare's death. I couldn't have guessed the answers would make me question my own sanity."

"Clare, the nightmare, your meeting Nicholas and learning what he is—anyone would see this as unbelievable," Judith said. "And you are a psychologist, trained to view the human mind as something rational."

Coming to a sudden stop at the edge of the Green, Diana turned to meet Judith's sympathetic gaze. "But dreams aren't always rational. It was only after—Clare died that I learned to define and label and box them up."

"And dreams are Nicholas's stock-in-trade," Judith said.

Sudden heat flared in Diana's skin, fire fed by erotic memories that even the past hours' revelations couldn't extinguish.

"He told me—he came to you in your dreams," Judith said softly. "He doesn't ordinarily make a habit of confiding the details of his—personal life to me. But when he met you it was different. I saw that from the beginning. He's never truly known any of his dreamers before you, Diana." She pulled the cigarette from her mouth and regarded it grimly before tossing it into a nearby trash can.

"I wish I could offer better advice. Only you can decide how to deal with what's been thrown at you. But I do have something to show you that may help."

Diana laughed. "That was what Nicholas said—"

Judith gave her a wry, understanding smile and started back for the car. "I promise this won't be—quite so traumatic." She opened the trunk and pulled out two leather-bound photo albums, handing one to Diana.

The photos were brown with age. Diana studied the first image with a shiver of recognition. In the midst of rubble stood a solemn-faced little girl in a patched dress. Beside her was a man who seemed the only beautiful thing in the ruins of war. His hand rested on the girl's shoulder.

"France, 1942," Judith said. "My family was part of the French Résistance, working to get Jewish refugees out of occupied France and across the channel into England. *Collaborateurs* found our little group, and killed all of them—except for me. Nicholas was also involved in the Résistance, though I never learned the details until much later. He found me hiding in the ruins of a French village after my parents died." She touched Nicholas's image gently. "He hasn't changed, has he?"

"No," Diana whispered. She forced herself to look away from the photograph and up at Judith. "How did you—find out what he was?"

"Quite by accident. Before we left Europe for England, I caught him—skimming from a dreamer, a woman he'd found in a Belgian hotel. At that point he was quite desperate for life force—he'd been too busy looking after me to hunt for dreamers, afraid I'd see what he was. But after I did, he explained it all."

"And you believed him."

"I was a child. Children can still see through the bars that close around us when we become adults. And I loved him from the moment he picked me up and carried me away from death and sorrow. He gave me a home in England, an education, the means to become whatever I chose."

Diana turned the stiff pages slowly. One by one the pictures were revealed: scenes of young Judith growing up; her graduation from high school, the attainment of her first college degree. Nicholas was always there in the background. A little different in each photograph—gray added to his temples here, a mustache there—alter egos for a man who never aged.

"You were beautiful," Diana murmured. A shiver raced through her. "Did he ever—" She choked on the question, but Judith read her unspoken thoughts.

"Enter my dreams? No." Judith looked toward the bay, gusts of wind tugging at her wiry gray hair. "Nicholas has a very powerful code, Diana. Those he takes under his wing—such as Keely, or the child I was—are never part of his hidden world." Her smile was distant and sad. "I tried to tempt him into—sharing my dreams. My life force. But he refused categorically. He only takes from those who can afford the loss of excess life force, who have enough to give without suffering. Women who never know him except as a figure in a dream."

For a moment Diana forgot her own confusion, suddenly aware of the emotional currents behind Judith's words.

She loves him, Diana thought. *She loves him—*

"That's why what's happened with you is different," Judith said. Her thin face had taken on a stubborn pride that rejected any misplaced offer of sympathy. "You are the exception, Diana. Not only for the strength of your life force, your ability to give Nicholas more than he's ever found with another woman."

Diana squeezed her eyes shut. "A—woman who can —feed him—"

"No. Don't you see? Nicholas would never have told you what he did unless he felt for you what he hasn't allowed himself to feel for any woman in all the years I've known him. He has the power to take what he needs without revealing himself. But he chose to tell you, Diana. He chose to risk everything to tell you the truth."

Opening her eyes, Diana stared into Judith's as if she

could strip away every possibility of deception. "What are you saying?" she breathed.

"I can't be any clearer," Judith said softly. "Maybe it isn't my place to be. I won't pretend there aren't risks, Diana. There always are when the heart is involved. And with Nicholas there will be still more. I know."

Gently she took the forgotten album out of Diana's hands and returned it to the trunk.

"Nicholas is a good man," she said at last. "And he *is* a man—as capable of all the finer facets of humanity as any of us. There are many things I don't know of his past. But I do know this. Whatever made him what he is—he wasn't intended to be a monster. His nature has robbed him of the comforts we humans take for granted." She sighed. "I'll be honest with you, Diana. Nicholas wanted me to warn you—to tell you to stay away from him. He all but begged me to. I think—" She hesitated and tossed discretion aside with a wave of her hand. "He's more terrified of you—of the way you've affected him—than anything else in his life."

The crazy urge to laugh came over Diana again, but she bit her lip and turned away until she had imposed control over herself.

"Thank you, Judith. You've helped me understand—a great many things."

"I'm glad."

Diana looked at her watch. It was almost nine in the morning, she had an appointment at nine-thirty—a new client, at that—she'd hardly slept, and she had absolutely no desire to go back to Nicholas's to get her car. It seemed—completely insane that life could go on exactly as it had before she'd met Nicholas Gale.

But it *had* to.

She smiled wearily at Judith. "Do you mind giving me

a lift home? I—don't think I should be behind the wheel at the moment."

Judith asked no questions on the drive home. Somehow Diana managed to be at her office doors only minutes after her new client arrived.

Mrs. Sahir had a haunted look, and eyes shadowed by many sleepless nights. Diana settled her in the most comfortable chair by the window and focused all her concentration on the young woman, gently urging her to talk.

"My husband wanted me to come," Mrs. Sahir said in a thready whisper, twisting her hands in her lap. "Because I'm afraid to go to sleep."

Diana kept her expression carefully neutral. "What happens when you try to sleep?"

The young woman closed her eyes. "I see—things standing over me—wanting to—hurt me—waiting for me to fall asleep—"

Diana had never needed her professional detachment more than she did then, reassuring her client and providing a neutral, sympathetic ear when her own thoughts were in turmoil. Even her safe, comfortable office seemed alien, distorted out of all recognition by the previous night's revelations.

"Am I crazy?"

Meeting Mrs. Sahir's frightened gaze, Diana shook her head. "No. Not at all. You have a sleep disorder, and by working together we'll find out what causes it and how to overcome it. You've taken the first step by coming here today, and that isn't always easy."

The young woman sighed. "How I would love to be able to sleep—"

Dear God. "That's what we're going to work for, Mrs. Sahir. Step by step. We'll go at the pace you're comfortable with. Making the decision to confront your fears is often the hardest part."

"I don't know if I'm—brave enough. But my husband says I can't just run away." Mrs. Sahir stared down at her hands. "He's right. It won't go away unless I make myself face those things that are waiting for me. . . ."

Mrs. Sahir's soft words haunted Diana long after the young woman had left. There were things waiting for Diana she couldn't turn her back on, questions left unanswered, and no matter what she did her life would never be the same. For fifteen years she had struggled to make her world stable and safe. Nicholas Gale had turned it upside down again.

He'd already done far more than invade her dreams, and it was too late to run—from him, or from herself.

"There are always risks when the heart is involved," Judith had said. And she'd said Nicholas was terrified of small, mortal Diana Ransom. . . .

That makes two of us, Diana thought as she stood at the window and watched her next client come up the walkway toward the house. But in the midst of her fear was something far more powerful, an emotion that reached across the miles and years to bridge the abyss that lay between an ordinary woman and the immortal who had changed her forever.

She opened the door to Mr. Bradley with a smile.

This isn't over, Nicholas Gale. Not by a long shot.

Leaning back in the hard wooden chair behind Tim's battered desk, Keely rubbed her aching head.

"Something wrong, Keely? The kids too much for you? You seemed to be handling them just fine—"

She looked up. Tim leaned over her, something comfortingly protective in the arc of his body above hers. His breath warmed her cheek.

"No. Not at all—the kids are great. It's just a headache." Keely pushed back from the desk, scooting sideways. Tim glanced across the classroom and out the windows to the cement playground where recess was in full swing and, with a sly grin, caught Keely's mouth in a swift kiss.

"Any better?" he whispered.

Keely smiled up at him, but even Tim's concern couldn't make the weird feelings go away. Or the name that persisted in crowding her thoughts into a painful ball at the center of her skull.

Adrian.

The name released powerful images: someone kissing her, lying beside her, speaking in a mad, melodic voice. . . .

"Adrian," she whispered.

"What?"

Tim's clear gray eyes and black hair swam in her vision and came gradually back into focus.

"Who's Adrian?"

Even Tim's soft voice couldn't quite mask the slight edge he gave the name. Keely stood up and walked into his arms.

"It's—not important," she said.

His hold on her tightened. "Someone from your past, I guess."

Her heart constricted painfully. Tim could affect her this way, when she'd never let anyone make her feel guilty for anything she'd done in her life. She pulled back to look into his eyes. "Hey. I've been honest with you about —the mistakes I've made—"

Tim stroked her hair back from her face. "Sorry. I'm

not exactly your macho type, but I guess I'm typical enough to wince at the names of your past boyfriends."

"But it's not—" The denial died on Keely's lips. Passion. She remembered passion, and pure unadulterated lust. All associated with that name. The memory made her feel slightly ill, used somehow.

She'd never felt this way in the past. She'd always enjoyed her flings with men, the reckless life-style she'd embraced. She'd even accused Diana of frigidness and wondered if her cousin would ever lose her virginity.

Now it was hard to imagine how she'd once lived— on the edge, with no regard for the consequences or the future. Dreamseekers had changed that—and Judith, and Nicholas, and Diana. And now Tim.

Tim, who was everything she'd avoided in men. Gentle, considerate, respecting her for what she was. Winning a little more of her heart day by day. Promising stability— and love—she'd never believed she could have.

With Tim, she didn't want to rush. The relationship between them was unfolding without any hint of impatience on either side. For the first time in her life, Keely wanted it that way.

"Like I said, it's not important," Keely muttered. She had no intention of letting Tim realize how troubled she was. Adrian—a name without a face, without a concrete memory to go with it—and a vague hint of danger—

Tossing up her head, Keely pulled gently at Tim's tie. "This tie is a little better than the ones you used to wear, but I think you still need a little loosening up, Timmy Boy."

Tim studied her a moment longer, a faint frown between his brows, and then shrugged. "Goes both ways. Consorting with me might turn you into a geek—horror of horrors."

"And you might end up not wearing ties at all by the time I'm through with you—"

Tim stole a surprisingly daring kiss just as the voices of his eighth-graders announced their imminent return from the playground. Keely pulled away and moved to the large easel she'd set up at the front of the classroom, thinking ahead to the next demonstration. But when she saw the idle sketch she'd drawn on the newsprint, she shivered and tore it off the pad.

She couldn't remember drawing the vampire at all.

TWELVE

Thus have I had thee, as a dream doth flatter,
In sleep a king, but, waking, no such matter.
—William Shakespeare, *Sonnet 87*

The night sky, at least, remained unchanged.

Nicholas made a small adjustment to the focus of his telescope, training it on the distant stars of Andromeda. For a long, unbroken moment he looked up at the constellation, imagining, as he had done in his youth, that his kind had come from another world.

It was a somewhat comforting thought. There might be others like him somewhere, still living, able to take mates and reproduce and live normal lives.

If there were no others like himself in that vast universe, then he was alone. Except for his brother, whom he prayed he would never meet again.

Cursing bitterly, Nicholas jerked back from the telescope and leaned against the railing of the balcony.

Diana was gone. Whether it was fear or denial or disgust that had driven her away didn't matter. The results were the same. She was gone.

Lifting his head to breathe in the cold city air, Nicholas took inventory of his body. The dream-tour he had given Diana had drained him far more than he'd anticipated; a visit to one of his neglected dreamers would be in order. Tomorrow night was soon enough. When he thought of going now, his stomach twisted into a knot that threatened to expel the brandy he'd consumed throughout the evening.

What never should have begun was finished. Diana had been poison to him. She had given him what no other dreamer could match—had even possessed the power to match his mind and influence dreams he alone should control. She was truly remarkable, incomparable. He would live the rest of his endless life unsatisfied.

And alone. As he must be. Sarah and Clare were proof enough of that. He could never be certain that he was truly better than Adrian.

Nicholas gathered up the telescope's weatherproof cover and froze in the act of fixing it in place. It was nothing so obvious as sound or scent that made his hackles rise and his heart stop in his chest.

She could not have come back.

He listened until he heard the unmistakable rhythm of her footsteps. She could not have come back. . . .

"You forgot to lock the doors again," Diana said softly. "Don't you know this is San Francisco?"

Turning slowly to face her, he let her see nothing of the turmoil in his mind. "I've never been afraid of common ruffians," he said.

Her brilliant eyes, clear and resolute, fixed unwaveringly on his face. "Of course not. You're immortal."

Nicholas finished covering the telescope and placed himself as far from her as he could. In spite of himself he searched her face, let his gaze wander over her body to note the stance of her legs and the way her clenched fists gave her away. His pulse quickened. "You believe, don't you, Diana?"

"Yes. I believe." She walked closer, detouring to the balustrade at the corner of the balcony. Her fingers curled around the railing. "Judith spoke to me, as you asked her to. And I did a great deal of thinking."

"Did you find comfort in the hallowed halls of rationality?" he said, deliberately mocking.

She looked up sharply, eyes narrowed. Her aura flared. "Don't you think it's a little too late for games, Nicholas?" she asked.

He pushed himself away from the railing. "Did you think this was a game?" he whispered.

Diana released her breath slowly. "No. But you didn't answer all my questions yesterday, Nicholas. And I've come to get the answers."

"About Keely, perhaps?"

She started, but her composure remained intact. "Your brother took Keely, didn't he?"

"Yes." He looked up at the stars. "It was after you came to me that I first realized my brother must be—in town. As I told you last night, I had not seen in him over a century."

"And you—tried to go after him and Keely when you realized what had happened. To stop him."

He felt the force of Diana's stare and turned to meet it. "Yes. Perhaps now you understand why I could not confide in you earlier, Diana. My concern for Keely was real, even though I knew nothing of your sister's fate. But, unlike your sister, Adrian let Keely go before he'd taken—too much."

Diana was silent a long while. "Fifteen years ago he took Clare, and now Keely."

Her unspoken question hung between them. The contents of Adrian's letter were burned in Nicholas's brain, but Diana need never know of it, or the part Keely had played in the bargain Adrian had struck. The lie he gave Diana now might as easily have been the truth.

"Keely's aura is powerful, as Clare's must have been," Nicholas said harshly. "We our kind—must constantly search for such signs of strong life force if we are to survive. I, too, was drawn to Keely by the strength of her life force. But Adrian wouldn't have bothered to resist it."

Before Diana could formulate another question, Nicholas began to walk toward her. He saw the change in her expression as she became more deeply aware of him, as his nearness broke through her protective wall of reserve. Her aura pulsed in time to her quickening heartbeat.

He understood clearly what had to be done—what last night's revelations had failed to do.

"And when you came to me that night in Mama Soma's," he continued relentlessly, "I didn't succeed in resisting *you*."

He crossed the balcony until he stood only a few feet from her. She tilted her head back to hold his gaze, but her stillness was that of a creature striving for invisibility.

"I didn't hunt you as Adrian hunted your sister. You came to me, Diana." He lifted his hand, skimming his palm along her rigid jaw. Energy arced between them, almost painful in its intensity. Diana trembled, her struggle for control a visible thing. "And now you come to me again after I set you free. After what my twin brother did to Clare—after what I did to you in your dreams. Why?"

Her eyes blazed, though she made no attempt to evade his touch. "I told you I—wanted answers—"

"You have as many as I'll ever give you, Diana." His fingers closed around her chin. "But you aren't being honest with yourself. A poor attribute in a therapist." He sighed with mock regret. "No, Diana. You want more. Much more."

Without another word he covered her mouth with his. Through hands and lips he drew on her life force, just enough to let her feel what he did. She fought for only an instant and then surrendered, her lips pliant, her body yielding its energy so sweetly—

He jerked free, gasping. *Drive her away,* he thought dazedly, *before it's too late.*

But she reached for him like a child fascinated by fire. "Nicholas—"

He stepped back. "Do you still have questions, Diana? Did Judith mention my other dreamers? How I take from them as I've taken from you?"

Her gaze held his, "Judith didn't have to explain. I understand—"

"Of course. Very noble of you. Very—broad-minded."

For the first time she looked away, color flooding her skin. He dared to touch her again, and her skin seared his. "You were privileged, Diana. Most of my dreamers never know what I do to them, though they enjoy it. You enjoyed it, Diana. You writhed and cried out and begged for more."

She gasped and closed her eyes. "Yes, Diana. You were a wanton in your dreams. A beautiful wanton who wanted only one thing." He bent close to her ear. "But your dreams were real. I played your body like an instrument. I invaded your mind and your most private fantasies to take what I needed."

Her breathing grew labored, and his own formed a harsh counterpoint. His mind was filled with the images his own words evoked. Images of Diana yearning for all he could give. Giving him all he could take. Creating wholeness such as he had never known.

"I stole your life-essence, Diana. I plundered the very heart of your dreams, knowing you could feed me like no other." He closed his eyes, breathing in her scent. "Your life force is as strong as any I've seen in a century. The temptation was too great. And in the end, I am the same breed, the same blood as Adrian." His cruel laughter puffed against the tendrils of hair at her temple. "You must be a very forgiving woman. Have you forgiven Adrian, Diana? Have you forgiven yourself for wanting the same kind of creature who destroyed your sister?"

He heard the sharp crack of her palm against his cheek before he sensed the blow. But it was not pain he felt, nor the sting of her anger. It was the sweet rush of her life force, transferred from her being to his. He shuddered with the potency of it.

Diana glared at him, her breasts rising and falling rapidly under layers of sweater and jacket. "Damn you," she cried. She was beautiful, so beautiful with her face flushed and the aura surrounding her pulsing with light and heat and color. Nicholas almost lost his resolve in the wonder of watching the azure fire spark in her eyes.

"Damn you," she repeated in a whisper. She drew in a ragged breath. "Do you think I can't recognize when someone is trying to protect himself with a wall of words?"

This time he felt as if she had struck him with a cudgel. He braced his legs under him and narrowed his eyes to slits.

"It's not I who need the protection, Diana—"

"But you *do,* Nicholas. You're trying to drive me

away. Why did you tell me what you were in the first place? Did you think I'd run because I couldn't handle it?" Her lips formed a humorless smile. "You knew just where to hit me, didn't you? You were in my mind. Two hundred years must give a man considerable insight into human nature. But even you don't know everything. Even an ordinary human being is too complex for you to take apart so easily."

She advanced on him step by step, stopping just before her breasts grazed his ribs. "I don't pretend to know what you are or how you came to exist. I don't even pretend to understand the way your mind works." She swallowed heavily, lifting her chin. "But if your intent was to scare me into disappearing, it backfired. I've been running away for a long time, but I'm through running. I have the courage to face myself, Nicholas. To face all of myself, even the parts I never wanted to see. There is nothing in the world more terrifying than that. Not even you."

Slowly, deliberately, she raised her hands, held them poised like weapons above his chest. His heart thundered. "But what about you, Nicholas? The past you showed me in our shared dream revealed more than you know. I can recognize pain when I see it. What has two hundred years of existence taught you? That you have to be alone? That you can't trust anyone with your deepest self? That you're somehow unnatural?"

Her soft-spoken words seared him to the bone. "Reasonable, incisive Diana," he said with utter coldness. "Ever the psychologist."

She didn't so much as flinch. "Maybe you need one, Nicholas. Maybe you're human enough for that. But maybe there's something you need more than therapy."

Without warning she pressed her palms to his chest. Through the wool of his sweater he felt her, closed his eyes as her hands slipped down around his waist.

"Maybe what you fear is something people have been afraid of from the beginning of time." Her arms tightened around his waist as her cheek grazed his chest, stroking up and down in a devastating caress.

"Diana," he groaned. Of their own volition his hands came up to grip her shoulders, pull her closer, hold her prisoner. The flow of her life force sang under her skin like music, penetrated his senses without effort. His body responded with arousal. Aching, impossible arousal . . .

He thrust her back so suddenly that she gasped.

"No," he snarled. "You mortal fool—do you want to suffer the same fate as your sister?"

Diana stared at him, trembling convulsively. "Nicholas—"

Spinning away, he strode the length of the widow's walk and back again. "I've shown you the smallest part of my nature, Diana. The safest part, the part of myself you saw in your dreams. And that is where it ends, Diana—in your dreams."

"I don't—"

"Of course you don't understand." He altered course and walked right at her, driving her back against the railing. "But your sister did. Adrian didn't visit her only in dreams." He sucked in breath as if the air itself carried the life force he craved. "He entered her body as well as her mind, as any mortal lover would. And the consequences were deadly."

He leaned close, catching a loose tendril of her hair and winding it around his finger. "Even we are subject to the temptations of the flesh. And there is no more direct way to gain what we must have than through sex."

Diana shuddered. "In my dreams—"

"Our—lovemaking was never entirely real," he said coldly. "Oh, your pleasure was real, Diana. But it was only your life force I took of your body. The rest was only the mating of minds—telepathic sex, if you will—and my expert touch." He feathered the lock of her hair against her flushed cheek. "It isn't that I don't want you. You are a beautiful, desirable woman, however much you've tried to hide it. And you are a passionate lover." His voice dropped to a purr. "Again and again I've imagined taking you in truth, Diana. Burying myself deep inside you, flesh to flesh. Hearing your cries of pleasure."

She swayed against him, and her soft gasps fueled his imagination. Painfully aware of the pounding tightness in his groin, he pushed her away. "But you see, Diana, if I were to become your lover in truth, the price you pay could be your life. I can guess how Clare came to lose so much of her life force that she could no longer go on living."

"Adrian—raped her—" Diana whispered.

"Not rape, Diana. Adrian was always—persuasive. Clare was not his—first victim." He swallowed. "As far as I know, there are no females left of our breed. If we wish to experience the sexual pleasures mortals take for granted, we must take them from human women. I learned long ago how deadly the act of love could be between one of our kind and one of yours."

Memories slashed through him. "In joining with a mortal woman—in reaching climax—we can easily take too much, drain every last vestige of life force that keeps your kind alive. It can happen over the course of a year— or in a single moment."

In spite of all his resolve, the last words dropped into a trembling whisper. Smothering silence descended over them both. He waited for Diana to ask him how he had learned that terrible lesson, but she only gazed up at him with a strange calm that shook him more deeply than shock or horror or accusation would have done.

"I," he said at last, "could kill you just as Adrian

killed Clare. You tempt me too much. And unless you leave me—"

Pivoting on his heel, he strode across the balcony to stare out over the ocean. *Leave me, Diana. Leave while you still can.*

But she did not leave. He heard her breathing, the way it changed as she reached a decision and acted on it. His body went rigid as she approached, paused, pressed her hand lightly to his back. She might as well have struck a fatal blow.

"No," she murmured. "I may never fully understand what you are, Nicholas. But you aren't Adrian. And you would never do to me what he did to Clare."

His intended roar came out as a whisper. "I am not mortal," he said. *"I am not human."*

"But you are a man," she said, spreading her fingers against his spine. "And you weren't meant to be alone."

His muscles jumped under her hand. "You're wrong, Dr. Ransom." She drew breath to speak, and he turned on her again, catching her by the arms and lifting her off her feet.

"This is real life, Diana, and not your private fantasy." Ignoring the plea in her eyes, he shook her. "All I ever wanted of you was your life force. As strong as you are, even your psychic energy can't regenerate quickly enough to keep up with my demands. I would have kept you until I could take no more, and then you would never have seen me again."

The flash of hurt in her eyes made him think he had finally won. Her lower lip trembled, and she bit down on it, hard, as if to punish it for revealing her vulnerability. Nicholas forced his gaze to beat at her, showing her only ruthless contempt for her weakness.

But his victory was short-lived. She blinked slowly, and though her lashes were wet her eyes glowed with an unshakable resolve. "Is that truly all there is between us, Nicholas?" she asked. "Is that truly all you need?"

Lifting her arms, she worked them around his neck and tightened with surprising strength. He could do nothing to stop her lips as they reached for his, parted under his mouth, and demanded a response.

He responded. A red blaze of desire overwhelmed him. He raised her higher, crushed her against him, sliding his hands down her body until he cupped her buttocks in his hands. She moaned under his kiss and moved her hips on his as he thrust his tongue into her wet warmth.

Even the touch of their lips was enough to loose his instinctive hunger. But now the hunger was intensified a thousandfold, made up of lust and nameless emotion as well as the physical need for sustenance. He began to draw on her, tugging at her life force, caught up in a maelstrom he could barely control.

Her fingers laced in his hair. "Nicholas," she sobbed. "Nicholas." There was no fear in her voice, no sign of weakness in her body. She gave willingly—her kiss, her life force—poured it into him as if she truly understood what she did. In the distant, sane part of his mind he almost thought she took pleasure in that giving even without the crutch of erotic dreams.

That had never happened before. Not with Sarah, never with his other dreamers. But none of them had known. And none of them had been Diana Ransom. . . .

She writhed against him. "Yes, Nicholas. I'm not afraid." Her breath filled his mouth as her life force filled his being. "I want you."

And he wanted her. He could drain her of life force and still never have enough, not until he was sheathed deep within her body. Everything would never be enough—

No. It was the greatest act of will in his life to push her away, release her lips, drop her to the solid ground. He felt as though he were tearing away some vital part of himself.

"No," he said aloud, clenching his fists. "No, Diana."

Her dazed eyes watched him without comprehension. Her lips were swollen, her skin flushed.

"It's not enough, Nicholas," she told him.

Not enough. Never enough. "I won't risk it," he said through his teeth.

Diana rested her forehead on his chest. "Then you plan to leave me in this state?"

Nicholas groaned. He had forgotten what it was like to be aroused to the point of madness. There was no price too great to escape this torment. And if Diana suffered as he did . . .

"There are dreams, Diana," he said hoarsely.

In dreams he could take her now. He could feed lightly, devote himself to pleasuring her without risk. Her dreams were more complete than any he had known. It would be almost like reality.

"Dreams, Nicholas?" she repeated softly. "I don't think I could sleep now."

He nearly laughed. "I can make you sleep, Diana. Don't you remember?"

Her smile faded. "This morning—"

"Yes. When I took you into my past." He turned away from her, crushing his fingers together behind his back. "Do you wish it, Diana?"

There was still time for escape, if only she would take it. But she sighed, long and deep, and he could almost hear her shiver.

"Yes."

Without meeting her eyes he reached for her hand, drew her through the French doors that looked out on the balcony. Her fingers, burning hot, laced between his. He took her into the guest room she had used before, with its antique furniture and great four-poster bed. Diana stopped and stared at it, casting him an uncertain glance like a virgin on her wedding night.

"Second thoughts, Diana?" he asked.

"No." She shivered, hugged herself, and deliberately dropped her arms. "What do you want me to do?"

He gentled her with the lightest of touches and guided her to the bed. "Lie down, Diana. Be comfortable. Relax."

She did as he commanded, though her body remained stiff on the covers. "Do you want me to undress?"

The picture she evoked drew an animal sound from his belly that he trapped behind his teeth. "That isn't necessary. It will be as before. Nothing has changed."

And he clung to that lie. He held it like a lifeline while he soothed her into sleep, took her deeper still, into the realm of dreams.

She was waiting for him there. In the dream they shared, she was gloriously naked, her petite form mortally perfect. As always, he was fully clothed, and he found himself in the costume of his youth. He knelt on the bed amid surroundings brighter and more vivid than any in real life, enveloped in the sound of celestial music. His boots seemed heavy and awkward, so he imagined them gone and stretched over her in stockinged feet.

She held out her arms. He kissed her with all the passion he had held in check before, bent on giving her everything she could desire. Hooking her graceful arms around his shoulders, she drew him down until it seemed he must crush her with his weight.

But this was a dream. He could do her no harm. She was powerful in the dream world, almost a match for him in spite of her size and mortality. With unexpected strength she arched under him and rolled so that he lay on the down mattress and she sprawled atop him.

"Is this my dream, or yours?" she whispered into his shoulder.

The answer locked in his throat as she brushed her lips across the pulse that beat under his skin.

"I think," she said at last, "that it's *mine.*"

As if he were human and she the immortal, he felt the will drain from his body. Her fingers, soft as butterfly wings, fluttered against his cheekbones, his jaw, his lips. They came at last to his neckcloth and began to work at the knot, loosening it with ease. Pushing the soft linen away, she kissed the base of his throat.

"Diana," he whispered. This was to be for her. For her, and not for himself. Once before he had come close to consummation in their mutual dream, realizing only at the last moment that even a phantom coupling would be too dangerous, that he might lose control and make the act real. The thought of their naked bodies against each other was too potent an image when he wanted so much.

He tried to push her away, but she had become a goddess in truth. Her fingers worked at the small buttons of his shirt, spreading the edges of it apart inch by inch. Her breasts, nipples taut, brushed the fine hair of his chest. She opened his shirt to the waistband of his breeches and pressed her cool cheek to his bare skin.

"No," he said. She didn't hear him. Her hand slid with agonizing slowness down over his hip, his thigh, back up again to rest with feather-lightness on his aching arousal. The thin layer of clinging fabric was no barrier at all to her caress. With a thought he could dispel that barrier, lie naked beneath her. He forced himself to block the image.

The only sound he heard was the harsh grating of his breath as Diana moved her lips on the ridge of his collarbone. She combed his hair with her fingers, let her mouth dip wantonly to his nipples. He brought his teeth together with a snap, knowing it had finally gone too far.

It could no longer be her dream. He must take control, guide it as he had before. In the end, she would have her pleasure. And he—he would have a chance to regain his sanity.

"Diana," he rasped, raising his hands to grip her arms. His muscles felt weighted with lead. "Let me go."

She rose up above him on her elbows, her nipples teasing his belly. "This is *my* dream, Nicholas. I control it. This is what I want."

Desperation, an emotion he was beginning to remember all too well, began to shadow his mind. "Not this way, Diana. Let me touch you." She dropped a kiss on his mouth, and he jerked his head so that it grazed his jaw. Something violent gathered like a storm in his chest. "Not this way."

With all the concentration and experience at his command, Nicholas summoned the dream to himself, grazed the edges of Diana's mind to take what she held of it. Her resistance startled him. Even as he regained his focus, he knew he had made a major miscalculation.

He had known from the beginning that Diana was a powerful dreamer. But he had always been in control. Now she challenged him for mastery of the dream-world, her will set against his. She lay flat against him like a living net holding him in place; brilliant color, reds and purples, flared outward from her body.

Don't fight me, she said into his mind, his soul. *You want this too. I'm not afraid. Take what I offer. . . .*

Somehow, in the midst of their struggle, his breeches had come undone. Her hand came between their bodies to cup his manhood. Two centuries of wisdom and discipline deserted him in a rush that left him gasping.

It was the man in him that surrendered—the weak part of him that heaved up and tumbled her over onto her back. Her clear blue eyes met his fearlessly.

"Yes, Nicholas. Now."

His fingers found her wet and ready. In the last instant he used what control remained to leash his inhuman hungers, giving himself entirely to the physical realm.

"Diana," he groaned, and thrust into her. Her body stiffened, and as he penetrated the fragile barrier in her body and took her virginity, the entire world turned upside down.

As the first waves of pleasure washed over him, he knew with utter certainty that the dream was over.

THIRTEEN

—

I arise from dreams of thee
In the first sweet sleep of night,
When the winds are breathing low,
And the stars are shining bright.
　　—Percy Bysshe Shelley, *The Indian Serenade*

Holding him within her body, Diana felt Nicholas with all the warm weight of reality.

Above them hung the tapestried fabric of the bed hangings, and from somewhere beyond the window came the honk of some late-night driver's horn.

She was awake. She had pulled them both out of the dream, stunned at her own strength, even as Nicholas plunged deep inside her. She had wrenched everything out of an immortal's hands and turned it to her own will.

There was no going back now.

Diana shifted to accommodate the fullness that pressed into her, and Nicholas breathed harshly against her ear.

"I'm still alive, Nicholas," she said gently, laying her palm on the iron-hard muscles of his back.

As if he were afraid to move, Nicholas held very still above her, most of his weight on his rigid arms. "God," he swore under his breath.

"You don't have to—stop, Nicholas," she said. She pushed gently down on his hips, and he shifted within her. That first penetration hadn't hurt at all. *I'm no sixteen-year-old virgin,* she thought absurdly.

"You were—untouched," he rasped, as if he had heard her thoughts.

"In a manner of speaking," she managed dryly. "It's only a matter of semantics."

Lifting himself carefully to meet her eyes, he gave her a look of outrage—thinned lips, drawn brows, clenched muscles. "Damn you," he breathed.

She almost laughed. "This isn't the eighteenth century, Nicholas. I'm not ruined forever."

"No. You might only have been—" Nicholas jerked up, and breathed out explosively as he moved inside her.

"But I wasn't," she said, stroking his back. "You didn't hurt me. I didn't feel anything but what I should feel. What I wanted to feel." She closed her eyes, savoring his body. "It isn't over, Nicholas. I don't want you to stop."

She had no need to look at him to know how much he wanted to continue. It almost seemed as though their very minds touched—not as they had in dreams, but directly. Nicholas was on the edge of explosion, and only the slightest provocation would set him off.

A thrill of purely feminine power coursed through

her—the knowledge that, mortal though she was, she could handle this being who was so different from herself and yet the same in the ways that mattered. She arched her hips, straining to take him deeper.

But he thwarted her. In one single motion he pulled free, rolled away, and came to his knees on the bed beside her. He pressed his forehead to the bedpost. Diana felt the emptiness of his desertion and could have wept.

Instead, she drew her legs up and reached for the tangled covers, pulling them up over her body.

"Do you think," he said hoarsely, his back to her, "that you are safe, Diana?"

She stared at the powerful contours of his torso. "I think you are more afraid of yourself than you need to be," she answered quietly.

His fist swept down toward the mattress and stopped a scant inch above it, quivering. "I held myself back, Diana. At the last moment, I found a way to cut off my natural hunger. The moment I was inside you I stopped. Do you know why?"

She shook her head, though he couldn't see. "I told you that it was during the act of love that mortal life force can be—siphoned most directly," he continued. "The point of danger for a mortal woman—for *you*—is in climax. I could drain your life force in a few moments of pleasure. If we had gone on, Diana—"

"Nothing would have happened." Hardly able to understand her own certainty, Diana reached for him without quite touching. "You said I was a powerful dreamer, with more life force than most. Did it ever occur to you that I might be strong enough to take whatever you dish out?"

He laughed, a harsh, weary sound. "Because you took over the dream? Made us come out of it?"

She frowned. "That's part of it. But when we kissed, on the balcony—you drew on me then, didn't you?"

"You felt it."

"Yes." Closing her eyes, she tried to reconstruct the tangled feelings. "I've felt it before in my—in our dreams, but didn't know what it was. This time, I knew." When she reached for him this time, she covered his hand with hers. "It was—remarkable. Even pleasurable. And now that I know what it's like, truly like to make love—"

With the slightest effort he could have jerked his hand away, but he left it where it was, fingers sunk into the sheets. "Is that—" He cleared his throat. "Is that how it felt to you?"

The soft uncertainty in his voice made her want to draw him down, cradle his head to her breast, comfort him in every way she knew. But she only smiled. "I felt that I was giving you myself, but not *losing* myself. I felt closer to you than I'd ever felt to anyone in my life." Swallowing, she added, "I was always afraid of loving a man, Nicholas, after Clare. Afraid a lover would steal my soul as Adrian did hers. But now I know I was wrong."

He would not look at her, but she felt his emotion as though it were her own. She almost imagined she could read his aura as he'd read hers—a jumble of colors and confusion, thoughts and feelings she couldn't name.

"I'm not a man, Diana," he said.

"But you are my—" At the last moment she closed her lips on the words she wanted to say. It was too soon. "You are my lover, Nicholas. I want you to make love to me."

He shook his head, but the gesture lacked conviction. "How many times must I explain, Diana? If we come to completion, together—"

"How long has it been, Nicholas?"

He went utterly still.

"How long since you made love to a woman?"

The grinding of his teeth was audible. "That is none of your concern—"

"You weren't a virgin, Nicholas?"

He gave a startled crack of laughter, and Diana found herself grinning in return. There was nothing humorous in this, nothing at all, and yet the release of tension was profound.

Very slowly he rolled toward her, bracing himself on his elbows. Golden hair tumbled over his forehead. "Was I that inept, Diana?"

Controlling her desire to pursue her advantage, Diana kept her hands to herself. "You, inept? It defies imagination." She met his gaze firmly. "Have you had two hundred years of practice, Nicholas?"

His lashes veiled his eyes. "In dreams, yes. But in reality—" Lifting his hand, he covered his eyes, and Diana was almost startled to see a rush of color under the skin of his cheekbones. "I am no virgin, Diana. But it has been a very long time."

She let out her breath slowly, and caution with it. "Can you tell me?"

"It isn't something I'd share with a lady."

She laughed aloud. He looked up, stone sober. "It is no laughing matter, Diana. Did you think I wanted to protect your virtue, or mine, by exaggerating the risk to you?"

This time she reached for him, gripping the clenched muscles of his upper arm. "Then help me understand. Don't you think I deserve that much?"

Her words struck him just as she had undoubtedly intended. He looked into her eyes until the blue of them faded to gray mist, an image of thick fog on a London night.

He began to speak, hardly knowing he did so. The

memories were very close to the surface—the safer memories, the older ones, those he could bring forth without flinching.

"I was twenty in 1805. I had inherited my stepfather's title, and Adrian had left Coverdale Hall some time before."

"The dream—" Diana's voice came to him distantly.

"Yes. I told you that Adrian went to London. I followed him two years later. Though I was not human, I had learned to pass for a mortal—and the *ton* was prepared to accept me with open arms." He smiled. "My stepfather had preferred to remain a recluse in Yorkshire for nearly all his life, and there was a considerable fortune. Adrian had been quick to take advantage of everything money could buy, including all the vices available to young men of that age.

"He was the younger, but he set himself to be my tutor in the ways of the world. London teemed with dreamers, far more than could ever be found in the north. He had his pick of them. But that was never enough for Adrian."

For a moment he relived his joy at being reunited with his twin, his excitement at the exotic life around him, his satiety at the wealth of dreamers. And Adrian's voice: *"Elizabeth died trying to become mortal. We are what we are, brother—we have the right to be what we were born to be. I shall live by that code as long as I exist on this earth."*

And so Adrian had done. He had led Nicholas into the gaming hells and dark corners of London's underworld. He had brought them both to the brink of scandal time after time.

"And then Adrian determined that it was time for me to know the joys of physical union," Nicholas said. "He took me to a bordello known for accommodating the most exotic tastes. He found me a woman more than willing to relieve me of my inexperience. And when she began to teach me, I understood immediately what the act of love meant to my kind."

Dropping back onto the mattress, Nicholas rested his forearm across his eyes. "I began to skim the woman's life essence, hardly knowing what I did. As she brought me to the edge, I—lost control. By the time it was over, I had drawn almost all the life from her body."

Diana was very quiet, very still.

"The woman never completely recovered. I heard she became an invalid, and—I did what I could to see that she was cared for. When I told Adrian what I had done, he laughed." Nicholas gritted his teeth. "He laughed. He said it didn't matter, one whore more or less. That was when I learned he had done the same thing scores of times. One out of three or four of his partners didn't survive his lovemaking—"

Abruptly he slapped his arm against the bed. No more. He would not speak of the ancient past, not when Adrian was out of his life, the scores balanced. "That was when I learned that it was no light matter to take a mortal woman, Diana," he finished tonelessly.

"I'm sorry, Nicholas," she whispered.

"Do you understand now?"

"You were a boy, Nicholas," she said. "You didn't understand what you were doing, and no one was there to explain." Her hand whispered across the sheets. "But I'm not that woman. Was she a powerful dreamer?"

"I don't know," he rasped.

"I think I can guess." The soft tips of her fingers grazed his arm. "You said once that you choose your dreamers carefully. You wouldn't take from anyone who could be harmed by it. And I wasn't harmed, Nicholas."

The stroking of her hand was almost hypnotic. Nicholas released the air trapped in his lungs.

"You stopped yourself in time even then, and now you're almost two centuries older." Her soft voice and the slight touch of her hand did more to reawaken his desire than the most erotic dreams of any other woman. "A person can live without sex, but not without the need for closeness—"

Almost violently, he trapped her hand under his and held it still. "That was one of the *first* things I learned to live without," he snarled.

But in spite of all his efforts, his mind leaped to the last time he had tried to find that closeness with a mortal woman.

Sarah. Sarah, with her sad eyes and tainted past. Sarah, powerful dreamer, who had seemed capable of giving him what no other woman could. In time, she might have accepted the truth. In time, he might have had the full relationship he had never dared with a mortal woman.

The kind Diana wanted of him now.

But he and Sarah had never had the chance. Adrian had taken that away from them, and all the choices Nicholas had planned to give her. All the hopes he had begun to harbor in his heart. All the dreams of an ordinary life.

And of mortality. . . .

"No," he growled. Sarah was gone. The woman beside him could never be what Sarah might have been. He would never take that risk again.

Her hand curled over his shoulder. "Your life," she said at last, "hasn't been easy, has it?"

"Easy? How many humans would give everything they possess for a chance at immortality?" He rolled his head away from hers on the pillow, trying to shut out the play of her fingers on the strands of hair that brushed his shoulder.

"But the price for what you are is high," she said

softly. "And I think—I think you would give up all your years, all your psychic powers, to be human."

Nicholas was grateful that she could not see his face, could not realize how completely she saw through him. He refused to betray himself by even so much as the clenching of a muscle.

"Yes," he said lightly. "It can be inconvenient to conduct all one's business at night."

"Because you can't walk in the sun," she mused. "Isn't it part of the vampire legend—that they die if sunlight touches them?"

Nicholas found himself smiling. "We are not undead, Diana. There is nothing supernatural about our—my—aversion to sunlight. The energy we take from mortals must be carefully nurtured. Sunlight saps that energy. If I had a dreamer every night, I could afford to indulge myself."

Diana's fingertips slid along the contour of his ear. "But you don't," she whispered.

His smile vanished. "Don't overestimate my nobility, Diana. Such dreamers are not easy to find, and there are always complications. I have long preferred a much simpler life."

The sheets hissed as she shifted among them. "Simple," she echoed, a wealth of skepticism in the word. "What else do you envy us mortals, Nicholas?"

He bit off a laugh. "There were times when I would have traded the uncounted generations ahead for one night of sleep. Or a true mortal dream."

"But when you—share my dreams—"

"They are yours, Diana. I only—weave them from the strands your own mind provides." Nicholas grasped at the chance to engage her intellect, draw them both away from the abyss of emotion. "In the mind of a powerful dreamer, dreams can become almost real. Artists, writers, poets, great thinkers, and philosophers—they are among the most potent dreamers."

"Like Fuseli?" A sudden tremor in her touch made him turn back to her. Her brows were drawn down, but it was a look more of concentration than unease.

"Like Fuseli, Blake, Mary Shelley, Beethoven—to name a few creators of my youth. But sometimes powerful life force can be found in ordinary people."

"Like me, Nicholas?"

His heartbeat picked up speed as her palm came to rest on his chest. The brocade pattern of the bed hangings suddenly absorbed all his concentration.

"You are far from ordinary, Diana."

He could not regret the words, even when Diana rolled toward him and lifted herself on her elbows, grazing his arm with her breasts. Her hair tickled his jaw.

"*Your* words, Nicholas." She pressed a kiss to the hollow below his cheekbone as her hand slid over his taut belly to the arousal he had fought to ignore.

The next logical action should have come easily to him. He should have reached down, gripped her delicate wrist, and ended her torment. He should have risen from the bed and escorted her to the door, sending her on her way.

But he did none of those things. He closed his eyes and let her touch him, lost to the persuasion of her caresses. When she straddled him, her thighs to either side of his, her tongue stroking the hollow of his throat, his protest dissolved into a groan.

"Make love to me, Nicholas," she whispered.

She moved on him, trapping his manhood between her thighs. She was exquisitely wet. Her hardened nipples teased his chest again and again.

"I'm not afraid." With instinctive expertise she closed

her fingers on his shaft and pressed it into her feminine heat.

"I want you to be part of me. Inside me." Her lips opened over his mouth. Something in him seemed to give way. Spearing his hands in her hair, he thrust his tongue deep. Her body went pliable as his arms came up around her.

"Yes," she breathed. Her body fitted perfectly to his as he carried her over onto her back, raising himself above her. "Nicholas—"

A thousand warning voices could not overwhelm the music of his name on her lips.

He cupped her face in his hands. For the first time, he did nothing but feel her skin beneath his palms, savoring the contact. Every tiny variation in texture, in heat, in shape was discovered by his stroking fingers.

Dark lashes swept down like a veil over her eyes. Her small, strong hands cupped his shoulder blades. He dropped a kiss on her mouth—gentle, undemanding— and then another on her chin, her cheeks, her forehead, her brows. The taste of her was indescribable.

"You are beautiful, Diana," he said.

Heavy-lidded, her eyes opened. "I feel beautiful," she said, wonder in her voice. "Because of you."

Nicholas was dazed by the sight and feel of her. He hadn't been with a woman in a century, but the need inside him—the need for *her*—went far beyond the hungers of the body.

He drove those thoughts away, all knowledge of anything but the silken heat of skin on skin, body on body. *Her* body: curves made to fit his hands, the drum of her heartbeat beneath the swell of her breasts, the welcoming cradle of her thighs.

Slowly. This must go slowly. He no longer questioned the inevitable, but he could never forget his control.

This would be for her.

He continued where he had begun, with her face. It was a miracle, that face: so gentle and yet so stubborn. He explored the shells of her ears with his fingers and then with his tongue. He kissed the tip of her nose so that she laughed, and then silenced the laugh with the pressure of his lips on hers.

Now he would only give. She was not afraid, and he would never give her reason to fear.

The pulse under her skin jumped as he opened his mouth over the tender skin between neck and shoulder. He bit gently, mimicking the act of the mythical vampire of human folklore.

But he tasted only her skin, the salt of perspiration and subtler things he could not name. Her fingers swept up into his hair, flexing rhythmically. They tightened almost painfully as he found her breasts and began to caress them with lips and tongue.

Her breasts were perfect, creamy and shaped as if by a master sculptor. The hard buds of her nipples had been made for the touch of his mouth. She arched under him, crying aloud softly, while he licked and kissed each breast in turn. His own arousal had gone beyond discomfort, and he reveled in the torment her sweet cries inflicted on him.

Down he moved, tracing the underside of her breasts with his tongue. Her ribs rose and fell sharply. He savored the feminine contours of her torso, the slight concavity of her belly, the arch of her hips. Her skin had a life of its own, quivering as he worked his way over every part of her.

He had done all of this before, in dreams. But this was different. This was unlike anything he had ever known, or believed could exist. No matter how powerful a dreamer Diana was, what they had shared in dreams paled against the reality. He understood now why she had not been satisfied.

Until he was inside her. And he wanted desperately to be inside her.

She urged him on, bucking against him. He drew his hands down her thighs, gentling her as he parted them. Her fragrance made his muscles go rigid with simple, instinctive lust. With utmost care he lowered his head, burying himself in the soft curls.

Wetness and heat and erotic scent invaded his senses. The first time his mouth touched her, she whimpered. Then his tongue parted the delicate petals, and the sounds she uttered made him tremble.

He grew drunk on the taste of her. He sipped what her body gave him so willingly, something as exhilarating as the life force of any woman he had met in his long life. He entered her with his tongue, and her cries told him he could go no further.

Sliding back up her body, he kissed her long and deep. Her nails scored his back. She sobbed his name again and again.

His control was nearly perfect when he slipped inside her. For a moment she went utterly still, and then she brought her legs up to wrap around his waist with all the ferocity of a mating lioness.

Her strength undid him. The second stroke went deep and true to the very core of her. She flung back her head, and met his thrust.

There was a fever in him. It began in his manhood buried within her body, streaked up through his veins and arteries and threatened to burst his heart. It robbed him of intellect, of will, of everything but the drive to make Diana his.

He took her utterly and completely, forgetting there were nearly two centuries of life between them and other barriers too powerful to breach. The fever grew to a raging fire. Without a single thought, he reached out to bind Diana to him in every way that existed. His mind touched hers, and he sensed the overwhelming rush of her life force gathering like a storm.

As she began to shudder beneath him, poised on the edge of climax, Nicholas became a creature of mindless hunger. Everything she possessed he must have; her body, her soul, her life force. Her life itself. He drew on her with all the power of his kind.

He never knew what stopped him. She made no sound, gave no sign that he hurt her, or that she had any desire to resist. But on the very brink, when he poised on the edge of completion, when he would have siphoned away the very essence that kept her alive, he went utterly still.

At that very instant she reached fulfillment. As her body tightened rhythmically around him, he felt nothing —nothing but numb despair. His body had become unfeeling, heavy and lifeless as metal.

"Nicholas?" she whispered.

He raised himself slowly, easing his weight from her. Her eyes were wide, tears trembling at the ends of her lashes. "Nicholas? Are you all right?"

He smiled for her. It was a simple thing, after all the rest. With his thumb he stroked away a tear and raised it to his lips.

"Tears, Diana?"

She smiled, dispelling any trace of sadness. "Because it was—unbelievable." She gave a watery chuckle, shaking her head against the pillow. "I've never felt so—" Suddenly her candid gaze faltered, and color flushed her cheeks. "So—"

Nicholas stared at his hand where it lay close to her tumbled hair. "I'm glad, Diana," he managed.

Lifting herself up, she kissed his chin. "You see?" she said gruffly. "You had nothing to be afraid of. It was wonderful. Wonderful." Catlike, she stretched beneath him. "I'm afraid you—wore me out."

Careful not to move too swiftly, Nicholas rolled away from her. His manhood was as heavy and full as before, but there would be no easing it. "You aren't—too tired, Diana?" he asked.

She chuckled. "There's an old cliché about people falling asleep after lovemaking. That's all it is, Nicholas." In response to her words, her eyelids drifted shut. "I hate to be rude—"

Stroking back her hair, Nicholas drew the sheets up between their bodies and lay on his side, watching her face. " 'Some must watch while some must sleep,' " he quoted softly. "I'll watch, Diana."

Her hand lifted and felt for him blindly. It came to rest just over his heart. "I wish you could sleep too, Nicholas," she murmured. "If only—"

If only. He closed his eyes and enfolded her hand in his, bringing it to rest by her side. "Sleep, Diana."

He lay beside her, unmoving, long after she vanished into that realm he could never truly enter. Gradually the unquenched ache in his body subsided, though that was little comfort.

Not when he knew how close he had come to what he most feared—and most desired.

If he had given himself over to ecstasy, he might have killed Diana. But she was a powerful dreamer. There was a chance, an agonizing chance, that he might have gained what he'd sought from Sarah.

Mortality.

No. Nicholas stared blindly up at the canopy. Diana would never know that such an option existed for him.

She would believe the risk was worth it, and it never could be.

Diana's breathing was deep and steady. She curled beside him, trusting as a child. The need to touch her was a constant torment, but he did not so much as brush her shoulder. When he closed his eyes, it was to recapture what could never come again.

But it was not only memory that claimed him. When he realized what was happening, the shock almost drove him out of it.

He was *sleeping*. For a few brief moments, he slept. And as he slept, he dreamed. For the first time in his long life, he dreamed.

But the miracle betrayed him. In the dream, there was a woman. He was making love to the woman, and when at last he saw her face he could hardly speak her name.

"Sarah," he croaked.

She turned her head, and Sarah smiled at him, trusting and unafraid. Even as he plunged deep into her body, her face changed. Diana's blue eyes were on his, brilliant enough to blind him.

As in life, he lost control. But this time he did not stop. He did not stop until Diana's eyes grew glazed and blank, until her smile became a corpse's grin. Her glowing skin shriveled under his caress. Her gasps of pleasure became death rattles.

He was killing Diana. Killing her. *Killing her*. . . .

He found himself on his knees beside the bed, heaving as if he could expel the imaginary life force he had stolen in his dream. Turning his head, he saw the room and Diana asleep on the bed, all as it should be, nothing changed.

Except himself.

FOURTEEN

—

I had a dream which was not all a dream.
　　—George Gordon, Lord Byron, *Darkness*

He was gone.

Diana stretched wide on the bed, flinging her arm across the place where he had been. The sheets were still warm with his body. Languidly she rolled over onto her belly, pressing her face to his pillow. It was permeated with the scent of him, as the very air seemed to hold the fragrance of their loving.

There was nothing but utter contentment in her heart at that moment, and she savored it as the miracle it was. She knew she had crossed over a threshold that had changed her life forever.

The realization was too new, too strange to dwell on.

Instead, Diana gave herself to memory, to the pleasant aches in her body and the unmistakable sense of womanly power.

This was what it was to make love, to give one's self utterly and receive in return.

Nicholas wasn't human, but he was a man. In one night he'd shattered the walls she'd been building around herself ever since Clare's death. He'd completed a part of herself she hadn't even realized was missing.

Swinging her legs over the bed, Diana blinked at the bright sunlight peaking through the open blinds. *Open,* she thought vaguely. That was strange. Perhaps Nicholas had done it for her.

She smiled. He'd called her a child of sunlight. But to become a part of his life, she would learn to become a part of his world as well.

Her clothes were neatly folded over the back of the dresser chair. Humming under her breath, Diana paused at the mirror to run fingers through her hair and grinned at herself. Her lack of makeup, worn away during the long night, troubled her not at all. Nicholas had seen into the very heart of her, and she had never felt more beautiful.

The smell of freshly brewed coffee drew her down the stairs and into the kitchen; she paused in the doorway and sucked in a deep breath, ready to greet him.

He wasn't there. The coffee was, hot and ready in a carafe kept warm by a timer in the coffee maker. Perhaps he was upstairs meditating, as he'd been when she'd come to him two days before. Or in the library.

But the library was empty. Like the rest of the house, it bore the unmistakable sense of his presence, but the quiet refuge with its books and antique furniture lay untouched. The upstairs meditation room was likewise unoccupied, as was every other she checked, some of which had obviously been unused for a very long time.

Diana frowned as she stood in the front doorway and looked out at the sun-washed street. Her car was parked at the curb, but Nicholas's van was gone. His light overcoat and fedora no longer hung on the antique brass coatrack in the entry hall. Had he actually ventured out in daylight? And without a word to her. . . .

Shrugging off her unease, Diana finished her coffee and rinsed out the mug in the sink. She had to get home anyway, to prepare for the weekend seminar on sleep disorders at Stanford University. She wouldn't see much of Nicholas for the next few days.

The thought didn't trouble her. Last night had bound them for eternity.

Eternity. Diana closed the front door behind her, frowned over the lack of any way to lock it, and walked down to her car. That was something she'd given no thought to at all: Nicholas's immortality. It hadn't seemed important after all that had passed between them in the past forty-eight hours. But now—now she'd have time to think about it in depth, consider what it would mean to them both.

Every relationship has its kinks, she told her reflection in the rearview mirror. *There's always a price.*

And she was willing to pay it—of her own free will and with eyes open, unlike Clare.

She had to concentrate to remember the way home. Her flat seemed almost strange to her. She dropped her purse just inside the door and surveyed the bland neutral colors with dissatisfaction. It no longer seemed soothing and peaceful. Diana felt a sudden urge to splash something red across the beige sofa and wheat-colored carpet.

Why not? She hadn't done any redecorating in a very long time.

Diana found Clare's sketchbook on the floor where she'd dropped it two nights before. She bent to pick it up, smoothing the wrinkled pages gently. Now she could look at Clare's sketches with new eyes. There would still be pain, and sadness, and loss, but for the first time she knew she could deal with it head-on.

I'm not afraid to remember you now, Clare, she told the melancholy face in the photograph that lay beside the sketchbooks.

Flicking on the stereo to a classical station, Diana ate a quick breakfast and began to pack. She'd planned to check in at a hotel near the university this evening; the seminar would last through Sunday afternoon. There would be a number of excellent speakers on the treatment and psychology of sleep disorders, and she'd have a chance to talk with colleagues she hadn't seen in far too long.

If only someone came up with a cure for Nicholas's condition, she thought. *He has the ultimate sleep disorder. . . .*

Grimacing, Diana closed the suitcase and set it next to the bedroom door. *If Nicholas could hear me now.* Immediately her thoughts turned back to the night before, and she completed her chores in a pleasant haze.

But by late afternoon, when she'd planned to leave for Palo Alto, Nicholas still hadn't called. Diana dropped by his house and found the door locked. Firm knocking brought no answer. No one at Mama Soma's had seen him that day. Her next step was to call Judith.

Diana found it almost easy to confide her concern to Judith. She knew immediately that Judith guessed what had happened between Diana and Nicholas, though the older woman admitted that Nicholas hadn't been to see her for several days.

But Judith was uncharacteristically silent on the phone when Diana asked her where Nicholas might have gone.

"I know I'm probably unnecessarily concerned, but I did want to see him before I leave for the seminar," Diana said. "If you have any ideas at all—"

"I do have an—idea, Diana," Judith said at last. "I think I'd better come over."

Judith appeared at Diana's door with a note in her hand, her face strained and pale.

"Nicholas left me this sometime last night," she said softly, handing Diana the note.

Diana read it, feeling strangely numb. The note, written in Nicholas's elegant hand, said only that he had left on an extended trip, and asked that Judith take care of his affairs as she always had. It gave no forwarding address, no number where he could be reached, no promised date of return.

Only the last line, read through a blur of unwanted tears, blunted the pain.

Take care of Diana.

Looking over Judith's head at the blue November sky, Diana carefully folded the note and returned it.

Take care of Diana.

"I don't understand," Judith muttered.

Diana smiled, blinking fiercely. "I think I do. He often commented on my—professional acumen. I think he expects me to understand his reasons for leaving."

"And do you?"

"I—" She dropped her frozen hand to her side, fingers still cramped from gripping the note.

Judith's expression was utterly grim. "I'd never have believed he'd turn coward."

Swallowing heavily, Diana forced out coherent words one by one. "Courage is relative. And—maybe it's my fault."

"Your fault—"

Meeting Judith's eyes, Diana nodded. "My fault because I knew what I wanted and I went for it, regardless of the consequences to either one of us. Because I had something to prove to myself, no matter what the cost. My fault because I didn't consider what sacrifices he might be making—or didn't want to believe I couldn't compensate for them."

Judith snorted. "I don't believe it. If Nicholas doesn't know what he's got in you—"

Diana cut off the older woman's declaration with a touch of her hand. "It's cold out here. Come in and have some coffee."

"No." Judith eased the gruffness of her reply with a stiff smile, jerking her head back at the waiting taxi. "I— have things I must take care of." Blinking rapidly, she took a backward step down the stairs. "I'm sorry, Diana. Later, when—" She broke off in confusion. "We'll talk."

"Wait." Diana went into the kitchen for a notepad and scribbled down the phone number of her hotel near the university in Palo Alto. "If he comes back—this is where I'll be."

Judith nodded stiffly and descended the stairs, moving almost like an old woman. At the curb Judith hesitated and looked back, her expression stern.

"He'll return, Diana," she declared. "And when he does—"

She didn't finish the sentence, but her meaning was manifest. Diana managed a smile until the taxi pulled away.

When he does, there will be a reckoning. But until then . . .

Until then. That phrase occupied Diana's thoughts as she drove south to Palo Alto and checked into her hotel, met colleagues for dinner, and looked over the seminar materials in the quiet of her room.

And when she lay down in the overlarge bed, she remembered what she and Nicholas had shared with aching intensity, and dreamed of him even though he was never truly with her.

He will come back. I know he will. . . .

The next day Diana blocked off every thought of Nicholas and concentrated almost fiercely on the speakers, taking copious notes and circulating among her colleagues between presentations. She smiled so brilliantly at one handsome professional acquaintance that she found him at her elbow throughout much of the day and asking her to dinner that evening. Diana accepted, and flirted with far more abandon than she'd ever believed possible.

But she gently declined her would-be suitor's more intimate suggestions and retired to her room alone, staring up at the ceiling until well after midnight. She cursed Nicholas, even called him a coward in her most private thoughts. But that same night, when sleep finally claimed her, she sensed his presence as she dreamed.

His appearance was vague, ghostly, as if he had projected his image from some great distance. Yet he was achingly real; he spoke gentle words she couldn't hear, reaching for her across the mists of her dreamworld.

"Come," he called out, his voice as deep and wonderful as she remembered. "Come to me, Diana. I need you."

But she crossed her arms and girded herself in dream-armor, frozen by righteous indignation.

"No, Nicholas," she answered softly. "*You* come to *me*. Come back to me."

He drifted toward her in a strange limbo, swirling mist and infinite space that Diana could not alter. When she tried to form the familiarity of her apartment, or Nicholas's library, the mist stubbornly refused to obey her thoughts.

But Nicholas was with her. His features were hazy; the mist seemed to form a mask over his eyes. The closer he came, the harder it was for her to concentrate on his face.

"Nicholas," she whispered, holding out her arms. "Where have you been? Where are you?"

He gave her no answer. His mouth stopped her words, capturing her lips with almost violent force. She felt the desperate possessiveness of his kiss, the almost mindless frenzy as he ground his mouth on hers and plunged his tongue inside.

After a few stunned moments she realized that something was terribly wrong. She began to struggle, pushing at his powerful shoulders. His arms might as well have been steel bands. His burning mouth fell to her neck and nipped it almost painfully; alarm bells went off in Diana's mind and began to echo in the mist.

Without thinking, she lifted her knee and caught him full in the groin.

He staggered back. His expression was blurred by the perpetual haze, but she felt his rage as if he had struck her a backhanded blow.

It was that sickening emotion that made her understand. Staring into the half-familiar face, she shouted into the rising wind.

"Who are you?"

Nicholas woke shouting.

He leaped from the narrow bed, flinging sweat from his eyes.

The shock of knowing he had slept again, had

dreamed again, was nothing to the horror of what he had seen.

Shaking with reaction, Nicholas stumbled across the small room in the predawn darkness and dragged on a shirt and jeans. He swallowed back the bile in his throat, reliving the images over and over.

He knew this dream—the second dream he'd had in all his long life—was true. In some way, it was real. The first dream had driven him away from Diana. But if the second one came to pass, and he was not there to prevent it . . .

Fool. Ignorant, trusting fool.

Cursing savagely, Nicholas left the cabin and raced out to his van. A hesitant birdcall sounded from among the pines that sheltered his isolated refuge in the Sierra foothills, but he heard nothing but his own frantic heartbeat.

Nicholas drove at breakneck speed on the narrow, twisting road to the nearest town, a collection of shacks and a single run-down gas station. The old pay phone was still in working order. He dialed a number and counted the rings one by one, grinding his teeth as they passed by unanswered.

After a full minute he hung up and dialed again.

"Hello?"

"Judith. Is Diana all right?"

The sleep-dazed voice on the other end of the line sharpened. "Nicholas?"

"Yes. Is Diana all right, Judith?"

There was a long pause on the other end of the line. "She's fine, no thanks to you."

Nicholas had no time for regret, and none at all for explanations.

"When did you last see her?"

"Last night. Why—"

"Listen carefully, Judith—I need you to go to Diana's house as soon as you can and make sure she's all right. If she—"

"Wait a minute. It's six A.M., and Diana's at a seminar at Stanford. Where are you?"

Hissing through his teeth, Nicholas fought for patience. "I'll explain later. I have reason to believe that Diana may be in danger. I'm coming back to San Francisco, but I won't be there until afternoon. I need you to be with her until I arrive."

"What kind of danger?"

"Damn it, Judith, don't cross-examine me now."

Judith's silent questions were almost audible, but Nicholas knew that his urgency had gotten through to her. After so many years, she knew better than anyone else how he thought. "All right, Nicholas. What exactly do you want me to do?"

"Get to this seminar and stay with her. If she's surrounded by people, she should be safe—"

"This sounds alarming, Nicholas. Should I call the police?"

"No!" Nicholas lowered his voice with an effort. "No. I'm—only taking precautions. Everything will be all right. I'll explain when I'm there." He felt all his usual eloquence deserting him. "I can't trust anyone but you with this, Judith."

"Why do I think your hidden past is about ready to jump up and bite me?" Judith said softly.

Resting his forehead against the scratched Plexiglas booth, Nicholas swallowed heavily.

"I'll explain everything, Judith. Just do as I ask. Take care of Diana."

"All right, Nicholas, all right. I'll be leaving in a few minutes." She gave Nicholas the address of the hotel in Palo Alto and cleared her throat. "I hope Diana doesn't think I've lost my mind when I show up at her hotel room at seven in the morning."

Nicholas dropped the receiver into its cradle and breathed deeply. If luck was with him, Diana would suffer no greater disturbance than being pulled out of bed at seven A.M. If his newborn dreams were no more than idle fantasies—nightmares—he would face nothing worse than telling Diana the full truth about his brother.

But if his dreams were true . . .

Nicholas got into the van and drove back to the cabin, blindly negotiating the narrow road with a steady stream of bitter curses.

The third time he pounded on the hotel room door, Nicholas thought he might be forced to break it down.

An occupant of the adjoining room stuck his head out and gave Nicholas a sour look. "What's your problem, mister?"

Nicholas didn't spare a glance for the irate man. He prepared to knock again, and the door swung open an instant later. Judith flinched back from his upraised fist.

"Oh, God. Nicholas. I—wasn't sure it was you," she said hoarsely, leaning heavily against the door frame.

"Judith, how is—"

He broke off as Judith stepped out into the hallway and he saw the ugly bruise spread across her left eye and cheekbone.

"Judith," he said sharply, catching her as she swayed. "Are you all right?"

She gasped, and under his grip the bones of her fingers felt desperately fragile.

"A little the worse for wear, but I'll survive. I'm a tough old bird. Diana—"

His throat closed on even the hope of words as he studied her face. She smiled lopsidedly.

"She's all right, Nicholas. Sleeping like a baby, in spite of all your racket."

For a moment Judith was the one to support him. "Sleeping," he echoed. "Now?"

Catching the edge of alarm in his voice, Judith met his eyes steadily. "Nothing so strange in that. When I came this morning, she woke up just long enough to let me in, said she hadn't slept last night, and went back to sleep. She's been asleep ever since."

"What else did she sleep through?" Nicholas asked quietly.

She touched her bruises and winced. "I think you know better than anyone, Nicholas."

Nicholas forced himself to study her dispassionately, searching for further injuries. "You *are* all right, Judith?" he said, despising himself.

"Oh, yes." She sighed. "Bruises and a sprain or two, nothing a few days won't cure. Diana wasn't touched." She gave him a wry smile that made his stomach knot. "*He's* long gone, though I was hoping you'd show up before nightfall."

He looked away. "Judith, I—"

"You could have told me what to expect, Nicholas. Seeing your duplicate came as a bit of a shock. I would have been prepared if I'd known."

Gathering her hands in his, Nicholas looked deep into her familiar, mortal-wise eyes. "Can you forgive me, old friend?"

She freed one hand to touch his cheek. "Forgive you? For what—not being perfect? For not being omniscient?"

"For being blind."

"We're all blind sometimes, even the best of us." Reaching into the pocket of her sweater, Judith pulled out a wrinkled sheet of paper. "He left this for you, Nicholas."

He took it without unfolding it. "Did you read it, Judith?"

"I was sorely tempted." She smiled wryly. "I was more than a little—curious as to what he intended. He threatened to break my arm when I didn't cooperate—oh, most charmingly, but he would have done it if I hadn't managed to faint. Faint—at my age." She snorted.

Nicholas felt chilled to the bone. "He tried to go after Diana, and you got in his way."

She arched one thin brow at him. "I knew I didn't stand much of a chance. He was too much like you."

The look on his face must have given him away, for Judith shook her head. "I thought it *was* you, at first, arriving earlier than expected. Even your voices are similar. But there was something that betrayed him, almost from the moment he entered the room. Something wrong —dark, twisted . . ."

It took every bit of discipline Nicholas possessed to keep him from exploding into violent, mindless action. The negligible weight of Judith's hand came to rest on his arm, heavy as the chains that had once bound his brother.

"Easy, Nick. We survived." Judith's fingers massaged the rigid muscles of his forearm. "The minute I regained consciousness I checked on Diana. She was still sleeping soundly, breathing normally—and *he* was gone. I made doubly sure of that." She glanced at the door. "See for yourself."

Nicholas took Judith's elbow gently and helped her back into the hotel room.

The king-size bed was empty, sheets draped half on the floor. Nicholas heard the sound of rushing water from the bathroom. He helped Judith to one of the chairs by the windows, stalked to the bathroom door, and listened to the sound of Diana's movements in the shower.

She was safe. Nicholas flung back his head and closed his eyes. He almost opened the door and went in, but the vivid image of what he would find stopped him cold.

Diana, her naked body glistening with water. Diana, blue eyes widening at the sight of him. Diana, in his arms, her lips opening to his.

"No." Nicholas calmed his breathing and stilled his immediate reaction. He walked slowly back to Judith and sat down on the edge of the bed.

"She must have woken up while we were in the hall." Judith said. She studied his face for a long, agonizing moment. "What about the note?"

He had almost forgotten about it. Unclenching his fingers, he began to pry the tight wrinkles apart, flattening the ball of paper into something readable.

His voice was hoarse and strange as he read the message aloud.

"There has been a slight change in plans, brother. The game isn't over after all. Take care that you do not forget the stakes. Mortals are notoriously fragile; the next one to get in my way may shatter."

Smashing the note in his fist, Nicholas was grateful for the numbness that came over him then. In this state he could feel nothing: not grief, nor betrayal, nor hatred. Nothing could interfere with the cold rationality of what he must do.

Judith groaned softly and settled back into the depths of the chair. "Notoriously fragile, are we?" She met Nicholas's gaze, her dark eyes snapping with a martial light. "I think we'd better begin from the beginning. Starting with

a few details about your prodigal brother—and how you
knew he was after Diana."

The shower had helped. It hadn't entirely taken away the
feeling of violation, but it had brought her firmly back to
reality.

Toweling her hair fiercely, Diana tried to drive the
dream-memories from her mind. She knew who he had to
be, the stranger who had come into her dreams, who had
looked so much like Nicholas. He had been as real—and
almost as compelling. So much like Nicholas, in fact, that
she had almost been fooled.

Adrian. The man who had taken Clare and Keely had
invaded her dreams.

*Damn you, Nicholas. How much more haven't you told
me?*

As Diana pulled on her robe and belted it tight, she
shuddered with far more than cold. When Nicholas had
come into her dreams, even to manipulate them, she had
welcomed him. Adrian had come as an invader, intent on
rape of more than her body.

You weren't helpless, she told herself as she opened
the bathroom door. *You fought him off. You won. . . .*

She closed her eyes with her hand on the doorknob.
God, she thought. *What next?*

That question had a logical answer. The one man
who might explain what had happened was gone. But
there was still Judith. That had surely been real, Judith's
turning up at her door at seven in the morning. Except for
the dream, Diana couldn't remember anything more. She
had fallen asleep—and when she'd awakened it was late
afternoon, she'd missed the entire Sunday program of the
seminar, and Judith was gone again. . . .

The sound of voices stopped her cold.

"You dreamed. That's something of a miracle in itself."

Diana leaned heavily against the doorframe. Judith's voice.

Judith was *here. . . .*

And then the second voice rose in the silence. Diana took a step into the room, and Nicholas lifted his golden head before he could possibly have heard her. When he turned his face toward her, she felt something inside her shatter into a thousand pieces.

"Nicholas," she said.

In one smooth, powerful motion he leaped to his feet. He stared at her, raking her with his eyes from head to toe, his chest rising and falling rapidly. He took one step toward her, stopped, and worked his fists into knots at his sides.

"Diana," he said hoarsely.

Neither one moved. The few feet between them yawned like a chasm.

"You came back," she said. In spite of her best efforts, the emotions she'd been fighting betrayed themselves in her voice. Nicholas flinched as though she'd struck him.

"Are you all right?" he asked.

Folding her arms across her chest, Diana struggled to match his calm tone. "Is there a reason I shouldn't be?"

Judith appeared suddenly at Nicholas's shoulder, moving stiffly to lean on his arm. "That's what we've been discussing, Diana."

With a single glance Diana took in Judith's bruises, breathing sharply in shock. "What happened, Judith?"

"Don't worry about me, at least not yet. Do you remember when I came by early this morning?"

Staring at the dark swelling around Judith's eye, Diana swallowed. "Until now I wasn't sure if that was part of the dream. I don't—"

"What dream, Diana?"

The harsh question came at Diana like a projectile. Nicholas's eyes, his glorious green eyes, had gone cold as chips of ice. He took a step forward, jaw clenched. "What dream?"

"The dream," she said slowly, "where someone who looked exactly like you attacked me."

Adrian's name hung unspoken between them, but Nicholas knew. A tic jumped in his cheek. "Did he hurt you, Diana?" he asked with deadly calm.

Judith groaned softly from behind Nicholas. "Would you mind if we all sat down and discussed this rationally?"

Immediately Nicholas moved to take Judith's weight and guided her back to the chair. Diana sat in the matching chair, her gaze shifting from Judith to Nicholas.

She wanted to touch him. She wanted to reach out and touch him, assure herself that he was here and real. She wanted to rail at him for leaving, demand explanations for everything she still didn't understand. She wanted to fling herself into his arms and give him a good solid left hook to that strong, noble jaw.

But she composed herself carefully and turned her attention back to Judith instead.

"You're hurt," she said. "That's part of all this business, isn't it?"

"Yes." Nicholas said between his teeth. "There are things I never told you about my brother, Diana."

A strange sense of calm came over her. "I'm no MD, but I think you ought to get that looked at, Judith," she said, nodding to the older woman's injuries. "There are a few doctors here at the seminar—"

Cupping one hand over her bruises, Judith eyed

Nicholas. "That's a very sensible suggestion. Maybe I should go look for one."

Nicholas stood, walking in a tight circle around the room with his hands locked behind his back. He glanced at Diana and breathed deeply.

"We'll all go, Judith. From this moment on, Diana won't be out of my sight."

Clearing her mind of everything but the necessities of the moment, Diana felt no inclination to argue.

"Now Adrian is after me."

Diana sat beside Nicholas in the passenger seat of his van. Behind them Judith slept soundly; her snores rose occasionally above the hum of the engine. Outside the tinted windows the night was eerily cloaked in a blanket of fog, through which the headlights of passing cars were little more than blurs of light.

Nicholas had already arranged for Diana's car to be driven back to San Francisco; he had emphatically refused to let her take it back herself.

But he had maintained a grim silence about the situation they faced.

"Perhaps I should have expected it," she said into the silence.

Only a portion of Nicholas's face was visible in the van's dim interior, and that part was hard and set.

"Should you have, Diana?" he said. "Until last night, I never suspected."

Diana examined her feelings, separating them out carefully and confining them to their own little compartments. "But you weren't shocked, were you?" she asked softly. "There are things you didn't tell me. About yourself, and Adrian—"

"You're right." Nicholas's expression was entirely

lost in darkness. "I tried to warn you, Diana. But now I'm going to answer all of your questions."

She sucked in a deep, fortifying breath. "You can start by telling me why you ran away."

He stiffened, his gaze fixed on the road ahead. "That is irrelevant now—"

"Not to me, it isn't."

The van surged forward as Nicholas's foot pressed on the gas pedal. "You were in great danger, Diana," he said in a hoarse rasp. "I sent Judith to look after you, and when she tried to protect you, she was hurt. Because of me. *Because of me.*"

She opened her mouth to protest, but he cut her off ferociously. "Listen to the unvarnished truth, Diana. I am the one who was ultimately responsible for your sister's death. It was my doing that Keely and Judith became involved in something that should never have touched them at all."

Responsible for your sister's death . . . Diana shook her head sharply. "It won't wash, Nicholas. No more word games." She stared at his set profile. "You never did say what became of your brother after he released Keely. I never even thought to question that at the time. But now—"

"Now," he interrupted, "now you have a right to know the full truth."

They drove in silence for several miles, passing the airport and the still waters of the bay on their way north to San Francisco. Nicholas's hands clenched and unclenched on the steering wheel.

"Everything I told you about Adrian was true, as far as it went," he said at last. "But the fact that he was able to harm your sister—to go after Keely, and you—was a result of my failure. My failure to see that Adrian would never harm one of your kind again."

Diana withdrew her emotions deep within herself, holding on tightly to the detachment she'd perfected in her years of therapy. "I think you'd better start at the beginning," she murmured.

He breathed a laugh. "Judith said the same thing." His strained humor faded quickly. "You already saw the beginnings of it, Diana. In the dream we shared."

"The dream—of your youth."

"Yes. I didn't see Adrian for many years after our parting in London. Just before I left England to travel the world, I learned he had been implicated in the death of a girl—a wealthy merchant's daughter—and had been forced to flee the country. At that time I had no more interest in society or the scandal that might reflect on me as Viscount Coverdale. I put my men of business in charge of conducting my affairs and left for the Orient."

"But you did see him again," she urged softly after the silence had stretched to several minutes.

"Ah, yes. It was inevitable. We met once or twice in Europe during the nineteenth century, and each time I hoped—" He broke off, turning his face into the shadows. "Each time it was apparent he hadn't changed. We could not bear one another's company for long."

The images of Adrian Diana had seen through Nicholas's memories and in her own dreams flooded her mind. "But he was your brother. Your twin."

"My dark half—" He spoke so quietly she thought she had imagined his words. "In the last quarter of the century I came to the United States. I intended to settle here, far from Adrian and our mutual past. There were dreamers in plenty, and a new life. I had made a place for myself here when Adrian caught up with me again." His voice had gone heavy and dark with emotion he refused to show.

"The last time you saw him—"

"Yes. Shortly after the photograph was taken. But our last meeting—was a tragic one, Diana. I told you before that Clare was not the only woman Adrian had hurt. There was a woman in Nevada City—a young, innocent girl—whom Adrian—seduced and drained of life. It ended any hope of reconciliation between us. We fought, and in the end I did what I thought would prevent him from ever hurting a mortal woman again."

Diana swallowed. "You—tried to kill him—"

"No. There is a—compulsion that prevents us from taking the life of another of our kind. A—trait that might once have been geared to aid our survival. I could not kill Adrian. What I did was far worse. I imprisoned him in a place from which he should never have been able to escape."

Diana closed her eyes in response to the harsh self-condemnation in his voice.

"In effect, I made it impossible for him to feed—condemned him to starvation and probable madness, believing he could not be let free to kill again."

Struggling to envision what he described, Diana felt her throat close and her chest tighten. "Your mother—"

"Yes. She gave herself to the same fate, though her motives were far different. In the end, her body drove her to sustain her life, and in her madness she broke free. She regained only enough sanity to kill herself. I denied Adrian even that escape."

"Then Adrian wouldn't have died of—starvation."

"No." He glanced at her, his face transformed into a demon's mask. "Without any hope of sustenance, his body should have gone into a catatonic state. I convinced myself that I might return one day and—" He made a bitter sound deep in his throat. "But I never did. And Adrian escaped his prison. I don't know when he freed himself, but he took at least one life to do it—some poor fool who stumbled across him. He gained enough strength from that to break his bonds. And then—"

"Then he found Clare," Diana whispered.

"And all these years I remained oblivious, didn't suspect so much as a chance existed that he might be free. Until you came to me about Keely."

Memories whirled in Diana's mind: that first confrontation with Nicholas, his veiled warnings—Adrian's invasion of her dreams . . .

"He—he didn't hurt Keely," she said slowly.

"It wasn't mere coincidence that Adrian chose Keely. He knew she was my friend. He left me a note after he let Keely go. He told me that he had escaped, but he wanted peace between us—that his time imprisoned had taught him the true value of life. He claimed he was leaving the continent for good. He offered Keely's release, unharmed, as proof of his good intentions." Nicholas laughed again, hoarse with pain. "Good intentions."

Without thinking Diana reached across the seat to touch his rigid arm. "He was your brother," she said. "You—wanted to believe him."

"Yes." His muscles jumped under her hand. "Until you told me about Clare, I had allowed myself to believe he might finally have changed. And because of my weakness, Diana, he's come after you."

Something undefinable passed from Nicholas's body to hers and back again, a sensation as real as emotion, as powerful as sexual ecstasy. Nicholas jerked and the van swerved sharply; the blare of a horn from the adjacent lane startled Diana into dropping her hand from his arm.

"Why?" she whispered.

Nicholas's voice was unsteady. "Revenge is the obvious motive. He has been watching me, Diana. He knows you and I had become"—his breath caught—"close."

She felt an absurd surge of joy. *Close.* Adrian believed

he could use her against Nicholas, hurt him, because of what they had shared—

The joy drained out of her almost as quickly as it had come. *Calm, Diana,* she admonished herself. *You can't afford to believe only what you wish to believe. . . .*

"It doesn't matter why he's come after you, Diana," Nicholas said quietly. "He won't get anywhere near you again."

Though he spoke without heat, without inflection, Nicholas's words vibrated with power. Diana studied his tense body, the slow flexing of his fingers on the wheel, all the signs of a man fighting for control. Of a man in the grip of emotions he dared not set free.

Silence fell between them again as Nicholas took the Mariposa Street off-ramp into San Francisco and drove toward Potrero Hill. They saw Judith home and into her bed; Nicholas tucked her in and stroked back her gray hair with a gesture of tenderness that made Diana's throat constrict.

By unspoken agreement they walked next door to Keely's apartment. She was out, so Diana used her key to get in and left a note asking her to call as soon as she returned.

"She'll be all right, won't she?" Diana asked, glancing around Keely's quiet apartment.

Nicholas stared down at a half-finished sketch left on Keely's worn couch. "Adrian won't have any further use for her now," he said bitterly.

Diana closed her eyes, praying he was right. "Why didn't Keely—remember who she'd been with when she saw your face after Adrian let her go?"

He took her arm and led her out of the apartment, his fingers almost painfully tight. "Adrian made her forget. We have that power. We can convince the mind of the dreamer that everything she experiences in reality is no more than a dream, so that certain memories become clouded, sliding away when the dreamer tries to grasp them."

"That would explain her memory loss—"

"And yours."

Before she could react he led her out to his van. "I'm taking you home now, Diana."

She came to a sudden halt at the curb. "What do you mean—my memory loss?"

Light from a street lamp caught in his eyes, carved deep valleys between his brows and around his grim-set mouth. "You were with me when I discovered that Adrian had escaped his prison, Diana. Do you remember the cave —and the skull?"

"A cave," she echoed, beginning to tremble. "The dream—"

"Not a dream, Diana. Reality. You followed me the night after we met into the Sierra foothills, into the mine tunnel where I'd imprisoned my brother."

All at once the half-forgotten dream came back to her, perfectly preserved, rich in every detail.

"The skull—"

"Yes. The unfortunate mortal who happened across Adrian and provided him with what he needed to break free. Just as you, Diana, unknowingly provided me with the means to free us both when the tunnel collapsed."

It seemed that the green of his eyes grew as transparent as glass, revealing the thoughts that moved like dark water beneath.

"You used my life force," she whispered.

"That was the first time," he said. "I helped you to sleep and dream, took enough of your life force to permit me to heal my injuries. And then I made you forget."

That, too, explained much—her disturbing feelings

for Nicholas after they'd met, the sense that they were far from strangers . . .

She met his gaze. "Do you expect me to feel betrayed this late in the game, Nicholas?" she said softly. "Do you think I would have begrudged you whatever help I could have given?"

In the wake of his grim silence, she was seized by a sudden desire to laugh. The thought of his trying to explain what he was then—in that place, with her distrust of him so powerful—was ludicrous.

Unable to stop herself, she smiled at him. "I completely understand your reasons for not telling me the whole story that day, Nicholas. And for what you had to do afterward."

His gaze snapped aside. "Diana—"

"You can't scare me away, Nicholas."

"No, Diana. I know it's—too late for that." He looked back at her, features sheathed in icy calm. "You'll see more of me now than you ever wished to. I don't intend to leave your side, until—"

He never completed the sentence. Instead, he reached for her, grasped her arms and pulled her close. Diana's senses leaped to life at his touch. What passed between them was electric—elemental and powerful.

"Adrian won't have you, Diana," he rasped. "He tried to defeat me once, and he failed. *He'll never have you.*"

And then he let her go. He opened the van's passenger door, staring into her eyes. "Home, Diana," he ordered.

Still shivering with the aftereffects of his touch, Diana never thought to disobey.

That evening Keely knew the dreams were real.

She sat very still at the table in Mama Soma's, a pencil clenched in her fingers, as the memories fell into place and formed an inexorable whole in her mind.

She dropped the pencil and reached for the *latte* she'd nearly forgotten, drinking deeply.

"I remember," she murmured, setting the glass down with shaking fingers. "I remember."

Adrian. She saw his face. In a single blinding moment, she knew the memories hadn't been dreams at all, and she had been robbed somehow of over a week of her life.

The face she saw was the mirror image of Nicholas. Adrian.

Keely looked anxiously around the dim coffeehouse, searching for Tim. He'd disappeared—in search of the bathroom, he'd said, but she'd suspected the loud music and smoke had been a little too much for him. He wanted so much to do the things she enjoyed. . . .

"I'm going to defeat him, Keely."

The beautiful, compelling voice that echoed in her mind was not Tim's.

"You proved to be an essential part of the game, my dear. And such a lovely part."

Keely squeezed her eyes shut as remembered sensations flooded back. Adrian's touch feathered over her bare skin, spinning her into a world of mindless pleasure.

"God." Keely reached for the half-empty glass and nearly knocked it over. Nausea coiled in her belly.

Adrian had wooed her and taken her away, drugged her with his voice and powers she could not understand, stolen her dreams, and used her again and again. Adrian, whom she had forgotten because he had somehow made her forget—forced her to dismiss her time with him as if it had been trivial, a young woman's casual affair.

Adrian wasn't human.

Keely doubled over, fighting waves of sickness. Adrian was Nicholas's brother. His twin brother. Keely had looked into Nicholas's face afterwards and not known it. She had not remembered then all the terrible things Adrian had told her, secure in his power over her.

"Shall I tell you, little mortal? You won't be burdened with the memory of it." His hands, his beautiful hands, caressed her hair. *"Now that you've served your purpose I'll set you free. All this will be a dream to you, an idle fantasy."*

His cool voice had poured his plans into her ears, and even then she'd been too deep in his spell to know what he was saying. She had never been meant to remember any of it.

But she did. Keely stumbled up from the table and ran for the bathroom, shuddering with dry heaves. Tim wasn't there. She leaned over the toilet until the spasms passed. When she lifted her head, her trembling mouth shaped a name.

"God. Nicholas—"

Nicholas was in danger. So much of it she still didn't understand—so much of it was just plain crazy—but that much she knew. Adrian was after Nicholas.

Keely splashed cold water on her face to clear her tangled thoughts. Grasping at a sudden vision, Keely pressed her hands over her eyes. Diana. Diana was tied up in this somehow. Keely could hear her name wrapped in the dulcet tones of Adrian's voice, dropping from Adrian's lips—

Adrian's lips. For a moment all Keely could see was a face bent close to hers, a fallen angel's face, green eyes filled with torment. All she could hear was a voice speaking of terrible suffering, anguish concealed in hatred.

Keely brushed water from her lips with the back of

her hand. Suddenly all she wanted was to find Tim, to be held in his arms, see an ordinary, loving face.

Turning away from the splotched mirror, Keely made her way back to the table. Tim still hadn't returned.

So I'll wait, she thought, hugging herself. *I need to talk to someone sane. . . .*

"Ah, Keely."

Her eyes focused slowly on the man who was sitting opposite the small table. "Nichola—"

But she knew. She stared into his eyes and went utterly still.

He reached across the table and ran the backs of his knuckles across her cheek gently. "I see you remember me, Keely. That will make matters so much simpler."

And he smiled.

FIFTEEN

> In dreaming,
> The clouds methought would open and show
>   riches
> Ready to drop upon me; that, when I wak'd
> I cried to dream again.
>   —William Shakespeare, *The Tempest*

Nicholas spent the night in a chair beside Diana's bed where she lay feigning sleep, until at last she surrendered to necessity.

He listened to the sound of her breathing as it grew soft and regular, heard with inhuman senses the steady beat of her heart. Once she gasped softly, but her body revealed nothing more than an ordinary mortal dream.

You fear her, he mocked himself. *You fear this little*

mortal's power. He feared Diana and her hold over him as much as he feared Adrian's desire for revenge.

As much as he feared himself.

He had intended to find a dreamer the night he had fled to the small cabin in the Sierra foothills—the very night Diana had lain in his arms. He had fully intended to leave Diana behind forever.

But the mere physical need for sustenance had been replaced by a far deeper hunger. Diana's life force had sung in his body, a constant reminder of her, of what he had abandoned. He had spent three agonizing nights alone in the cabin—until the dream had summoned him back.

Nicholas watched her now as she slept, so trusting in his presence. He looked at her and wanted her with a raging intensity that never waned. Every moment in her presence was torment. What he desperately wanted— what she believed *she* wanted—was only a gesture, a step, a kiss away.

But he had come too close to losing control when he had driven deep within her body.

She was fragile, this mortal woman. Those eyes, that looked at him with such foolish hope, would glaze and fade with the passage of time. That lovely body would lose its suppleness, betrayed by bone and flesh. The softness of her skin, that he had felt under his lips, would wither; the stubborn, giving heart beating under her breasts would grow still.

She was mortal, human, flawed.

She was everything he wanted and could never have.

"Diana," he sighed, turning his eyes away from the sight of her sleeping face, soft with an innocence he could never destroy. Time passed without meaning. He waited, heart frozen, for Adrian to appear. When dawn came, a strange lassitude washed over him, and he laid his head against the hard edge of the chair back and closed his eyes.

"Nicholas."

Her voice was slurred with drowsiness, sweet as bird song. Nicholas came back to himself with a strange, aching sense of sorrow.

"Who is Sarah?"

He jerked to his feet in one motion. Diana knelt on the bed, running slender fingers through her tousled curls.

"You—kept repeating her name," she said. Her gaze, still heavy-lidded with sleep, moved over his face, assessing, seeing far too much. "You were sleeping, weren't you?" She shook her head. "But I thought it was impossible."

Nicholas swallowed and reached for the chair behind him as if he might fall. *Impossible.* Until he had met Diana, it *had* been impossible. Until he had tasted her sweet life force, he had never known what it was to sleep or dream—dream his *own* dreams, drawn from his own mind.

He had refused to consider what it might mean, that he should begin to experience even so brief a taste of mortality.

Diana rose from the bed and walked toward him, her hand extended. "In the hotel room—I remember Judith saying something about a miracle—"

Nicholas silenced her with a single look. "Would you like to claim credit for it, Diana? Very well." Catching her chin in his hand, he examined her face coldly, as if he were cataloging some intriguing new species of life. "I've admitted before that you are unusual among dreamers. It appears that your life force is powerful enough to bestow a taste of what your kind has always taken for granted. To my knowledge, this is the third time I've slept since the night you gave yourself to me." He bowed to her. "See how profoundly you have transformed me, Diana."

The harsh mockery of his tone had its effect; he saw it in her eyes, felt it in the subtle flinching of her skin under his fingers. But she refused to look away.

"Who is Sarah, Nicholas?"

He let her go as if she'd burned him. "It isn't any of your concern."

"You were *dreaming* of her," she said softly. "Calling out her name."

All the old bitterness he had drawn on to quell her curiosity turned on him suddenly, draining him of the will to fight her gentle stubbornness. "I don't remember," he said tonelessly. "I don't remember."

She was silent a very long time. "It wasn't the first time you dreamed, was it?"

In a nauseating rush he remembered the first dream —the night he had taken Diana—in which he had become something unspeakable, done the unthinkable to the woman standing so calmly before him. The dream that had driven him away from her and left her open to Adrian's evil.

"No, Diana. Not the first time."

"But you never dreamed before we were—together," she said relentlessly.

"Never." Looking into her clear, honest eyes, he let her have a small victory. "Do you wonder how I knew that Adrian was after you, Diana—how I knew to return?"

She went very still. "You dreamed it," she murmured.

"Yes. My experience with mortal dreams served me well. I recognized my *own* dream for what it was—and I dreamed true, Diana."

She smiled. The expression was as deadly to him as sunlight. "Judith was right. This is a miracle." She moved forward a step. "You've slept—dreamed—things your kind aren't supposed to be able to do. Things only humans do—"

He backed away, nearly upsetting the chair. "I have no use for miracles," he said harshly, "unless you can summon one up that will guarantee Adrian's defeat."

For a long moment she only looked at him. Silently she turned away and began making the bed. She sat down on the white duvet and ran her palm over it gently.

"I also dreamed, Nicholas. Of Adrian."

The fear that came over him was so strong that his legs almost refused to carry him to the bed. "What?"

Her gaze lifted to his. "It was all *my* dream, Nicholas. He was never truly there."

He looked away before she could see his profound relief. "Perhaps you'd better explain, Diana."

"I will—but first I want to get a few things straight."

Her tone was so calm, so matter-of-fact, that he found himself marveling at her. After all she had endured and all he had told her, she could speak as if they faced an ordinary adversary. Yet she, more than anyone, knew what Adrian was capable of. . . .

"Do you intend to watch over my bed for the rest of my life?"

Her expression was deadly serious now, dark brows drawn down over eyes that refused to release his own.

The answer that should have come readily was not within his mind. He had spent the night turning the dilemma over and over, examining it from every angle. The only solutions that came to him were unacceptable or unbearable.

Diana read his thoughts with ridiculous ease. "Isn't that what this comes down to? If you believe you're the only one who can protect me from Adrian, you'll have to be with me every moment. Or did I misunderstand?"

He wanted to lash out with cruel mockery, irrational anger, anything to deflect her devastating insight. Instead, he offered her a crooked smile.

"You didn't misunderstand, Diana," he said.

Closing her eyes, she moved her lips in a silent invocation. "All right. Considering that you seem to be less than happy with the necessity of being my bodyguard, and I have responsibilities I can't just drop, this doesn't strike me as an ideal solution."

Nicholas stared at her in stunned silence. It had never occurred to him that she might reject his help, after all she had been through, after the threats she had faced. "I've never believed you were truly a fool, Diana," he said at last.

She tilted up her chin. "But I am. A stubborn, mortal fool."

His fingers itched to grasp her arms, pull her up from the bed, and hold her against him. He clasped his hands tightly behind his back.

"Do you have a better suggestion, Diana?" he said harshly. "You can't stand against Adrian."

He knew there was no need to invoke Clare's name. Diana remembered; the knowledge moved in her eyes like deep river current. "Not alone, Nicholas. But then, neither can you."

Something snapped in him, something he'd been holding in check for the all the long hours since his dream of Adrian. His body vibrated with unexpelled energy he could not afford to lose. Breathing deep and hard, he tried to focus his concentration on his careful disciplines of control.

"I defeated him before," he said tightly. "I will do it again, because there is no other choice—"

Without warning she reached for his hand, closing

her fingers around his fist. "The thing you're forgetting, Nicholas, is that this isn't just your fight. It's mine."

Cursing bitterly, he grasped her shoulders and lifted her to her feet. "No, Diana."

Again she smiled; brave, stubborn, and utterly relentless. "This is where my dream comes in. You see, Nicholas, the night Adrian came to me, he didn't win. I fought him off. When I realized he wasn't you, I took control of the dream and drove him away." One corner of her lip twitched at his silent disbelief. "It wasn't easy, but I did it."

He shook her. "If you think that proves—"

"Hear me out. You said yourself I'm a strong dreamer. And the last dream *we* shared—" Color rose into her cheeks. "If you remember, I took charge of that dream as well."

Devastating memory swept over Nicholas. Her sweet seduction would remain vivid in his mind when everything else was dust. His hands loosened, letting her slide down along his body. He felt himself grow hard, and no amount of will would dispel his instinctive reaction to the feel of her in his arms.

Feminine power flared in her eyes. "I've spent a lot of time listening to you, Nicholas. Now you listen to me. You're going to need my cooperation to protect me, but you're going to need my help even more. *Last* night I dreamed that Adrian was defeated—but only because you and I worked together." Her small hands came to rest on his shoulders. "Together, Nicholas. Side by side. I don't know how it will happen, but I know that this dream was giving me the only solution. We'll win—through our dreams, Nicholas. *Our* dreams."

"You'd risk your life because of something you dreamed, Diana?" he rasped.

"You were the one who made me remember the

power of dreams, Nicholas. You gave them back to me. And now you—even *you've* dreamed. I've never been more certain of anything in my life. I won't hide and cower until Adrian decides to show up again. It was my fight from the time Adrian drained Clare of her will to live. It's still mine, as much as it is yours. We fight together, or Adrian wins."

Nicholas struggled with insidious hope. "And where do you suggest we set the battleground, Diana?" he asked softly.

Her brows lowered. "I don't know. I wish I did. But that's something we'll do together, Nicholas. I only know we can't let Judith and Keely be any more involved than they already are—"

"My brother left me a note threatening harm to anyone who got in his way," Nicholas interrupted grimly.

"And they've already been hurt," Diana said, her fingers stroking him through the fabric of his shirt. "We can't let that happen again."

"No." He lifted her hands from his shoulders, very gently, and set her back from him. The subtle torment of her nearness eased only a fraction. "We should—send them away."

"And that's not going to be easy." Diana gave him a lopsided smile. "Judith already knows the situation, and Keely will have to be told something. . . ."

She drifted off into her own thoughts, frowning intently as she walked into the bathroom. Nicholas glanced at the bedside clock and considered how to guard Diana through her work day. She'd already made it clear she wouldn't abandon her responsibilities.

Just as he knew she'd never abandon her reckless determination to face Adrian at his side.

But I will make my own plans, Diana, he told her silently, listening to the quiet rhythm of her movements.

Because I don't know whether to believe your dream—or mine.

Whatever the cost, he would see Diana safe. For all her courage, only *he* could end his brother's persecution of humankind. He would keep Diana close and be her shield, and when the time came . . .

Diana had no need to know that when the time came, he would face Adrian alone.

When Nicholas answered Diana's door, Keely closed her eyes and muttered an uncharacteristic but fervent prayer.

"I found you," she said. But as she looked up into Nicholas's face, she shuddered. His was as cold, as hard as Adrian's had been.

But he didn't smile as Adrian had smiled. He stepped farther back into the shadows, out of the afternoon sunlight, and let her into the hallway.

"Diana's with a client," he said softly. Keely looked past him at the closed office door. Nicholas was here with Diana, in her house, in the middle of the day. Keely had no reason at all to be surprised.

"I came to see you, Nicholas," she said at last.

He arched an eyebrow. Outwardly his body relaxed, and Keely knew he was trying to make it appear as if nothing were wrong. But she knew better. She knew far too much.

"If you'll come upstairs—" he began.

"No." Keely swallowed the nausea that always came when she focused on Adrian's message. "This—won't take long."

Something in her voice must have given her away. Nicholas caught her arm as she swayed; his muscles tensed at the contact.

"What is it, Keely?" he demanded, his voice grating with fear she could almost feel.

She closed her eyes, welcoming the almost-pain of his grip. "I have a message—from Adrian."

His reaction was lost to her as she retreated into her mind and repeated the message, word for word, as Adrian had implanted it the night before in Mama Soma's. She had felt violated then; she hated the part she had played, the part she was forced to play now. The sound of her own voice was drowned out by Adrian's rich baritone.

It was when Nicholas let her go that she knew she had fulfilled the compulsion.

Nicholas's face was white, his eyes the only points of color.

"Are you all right, Keely?" he whispered.

"Yes." She swallowed thickly, folding her arms across her chest. "He was never really after me. I remember it all now. I'm—sorry, Nicholas."

"Sorry?" He laughed and shielded his eyes with his hand. "You humble me, Keely."

"Don't blame yourself, Nicholas." She touched him lightly, remembering the time she'd thought she was in love with him. It seemed a century ago, in another life. Now Nicholas, like Diana, was only someone she'd do anything to protect. "It was—one hell of a trip."

Her weak attempt at humor broke through. He lowered his hand and met her gaze. "He won't hurt you again, Keely. I'll see to that."

Tears came to her eyes and she shook her head angrily. "He wants to destroy you, Nicholas."

"I know." For a moment he looked lost—vulnerable, mortal, a man facing impossible odds. He smiled sadly. "If I don't come back—take care of Diana."

"Damn it," she swore, flinging herself into Nicholas's arms. They closed about her automatically, as if she were the one needing comfort. "Don't get yourself killed. Diana lost too many people she loved. Don't *you* dare leave her."

He shivered. "Keely," he murmured, touching her hair. "There's too much you still don't understand—"

She hit his shoulder with her fist. "I understand enough," she said in a choked whisper. "Even I know when two people love each other—"

Abruptly he set her back, his hands closing around her arms. His face had become utterly implacable, every trace of vulnerability gone. "Say nothing of this to Diana, Keely," he said harshly. "Swear it to me."

"But she has a right to—"

"No!" His fingers tightened and eased again only when she gasped in pain. "She must know nothing. This is between me and my brother."

Keely knew if she gave him any reason to doubt her now he would do as Adrian had done, force his way into her mind and compel her to obey. She was not afraid of Nicholas—not even now. *But I'll be damned if I'll be any man's puppet again—even an immortal vampire's.*

Jerking free, she stared at him grimly. "Nicholas, I—"

The office door opened behind them, and a young man walked out, glancing nervously at Nicholas. Diana followed; her expression transformed from detached professional to woman in love the moment her gaze found Nicholas. She said a last few reassuring words to her client, who edged past Keely and Nicholas and out the door.

"Keely," she said with a strained smile. All at once her eyes changed, took on the look of someone guarding fearful secrets. "I've been wanting to talk to you—"

But Keely was already moving beyond the reach of Diana's voice—and beyond the necessity of giving Nicholas a promise she had no intention of keeping.

"We'll go out tonight, Diana."

Nicholas's abrupt statement startled her as she locked the office door behind her last client and found him waiting in the hall. She knew he'd virtually stood guard at her door all day. For a few hours she'd almost managed to put thoughts of Adrian out of her mind; Nicholas's face revealed little, but she knew *he* had not. There was a subtle wildness in him, in the brilliance of his eyes, that brooked no denial—something infectious that took hold of Diana the moment he touched her.

"Adrian won't come after us if we're surrounded by people," he murmured. He hesitated only a moment and pulled her into the circle of his arms. "You said you didn't want to be locked away, Diana. I want to take you out of here."

Feeling the strength of his body, the fierce protectiveness in his embrace, Diana knew happiness that no threat of danger could dispel. The fact that they still had no real plan for confronting Adrian ceased to trouble her once she had left the silent prison of her house. Unassailable joy armored her as she'd once been armored by careful control and cool detachment.

It was a glorious evening, crisp and clear as late autumn nights could be. Wrapped in her warmest coat and Nicholas's arms, Diana never felt the cold. She had almost forgotten to be afraid.

This was far more powerful. Adrian could not stand against such happiness.

Nicholas took her first to the Magic Theater at Fort Mason Center. There was a new play by a local playwright —a comedy that Diana thoroughly enjoyed. Even Nicholas laughed several times.

But the intensity she had sensed in him earlier didn't

fade as the evening progressed. They walked along the Marina Green beside the bay, watching reflected lights dance on the dark water. Afterward Nicholas drove them downtown, where Diana laughed around a mouthful of sandwich from David's Deli while Nicholas sipped coffee and gazed at her as if he might never see her again.

They ended up at the Sir Francis Drake Hotel on Union Square. The famous Beefeater doorman ushered them into the lobby, and an express elevator took them to the Starlite Roof, into a lush room of giant brass pillars and burgundy carpet, tuxedoed waiters, and the elegant music of a jazz quartet.

At a small table lit by a flickering candle, Nicholas sipped brandy and Diana sampled an expensive wine she never would have tasted in the past. And then they danced to a mellow rendition of "Someone to Watch Over Me," Nicholas holding Diana very close. It seemed to her that they danced on air, with the high windows framing all the city below them.

It was after midnight when they headed for home. Diana hadn't wanted the evening to end. But Nicholas was not leaving; he was with her—truly with her—and no price was too high to pay for that miracle.

Diana fed another log into the fire and closed her eyes as the warmth bathed her face. Nicholas was playing a soft Beethoven sonata—the "Moonlight"—on the virtually un-used piano in the corner of the living room. The piano had been her mother's; she'd never learned to play it. Clare had been the pianist.

She felt a profound joy that its music had been set free at last. Clare would have approved.

The strains of the sonata died out into a faint vibra-tion that hummed along Diana's skin. She stretched and turned to look at Nicholas, as she had done countless times that evening.

Golden firelight gave him the look of some primitive god. He rose slowly from the bench, each movement cloaked in sensual promise. Suddenly he looked directly at her, and she almost caught her breath at the inhuman, compelling beauty of his eyes.

She'd known it would be tonight. Her vague plans of seduction wouldn't be necessary after all. In the course of one evening Nicholas's reticence had vanished. The reasons he had fled the last time no longer mattered at all.

Tonight Nicholas would come to her again; tonight he would truly understand that her dreams were true, that they were meant to be together. Not only in fighting Adrian, but for as long as her mortal life should last. . . .

He walked toward her, his feet noiseless on the carpet. His hunger was a tangible thing; within herself she felt the response, the warmth of arousal, and something deeper still—the upwelling of life force to answer his need.

She held her arms up to him as he knelt beside her, a god of fire whose slightest touch inflamed her senses. He pulled her against him, his breath feathering her neck and shoulder as he drew back the collar of her blouse.

"I need you, Diana," he whispered.

She knew not to expect the other words, the ones she had finally admitted to herself. Nicholas was not yet ready to say them. But his need was enough; she flung back her head and gasped as his tongue traced the angle of her jaw.

"I know what you need," she said, lacing her fingers through his hair. "You can have it, Nicholas. All of it."

He stiffened for an almost imperceptible moment before his caresses resumed. "You can—give me strength, Diana. Strength to meet Adrian when the time comes."

Though he spoke with seductive gentleness, she understood the cold practicality behind his words. He needed all the life force he could take to match his brother—and she was the one to provide that life force. Her dreams had told her she was the only dreamer he would ever need again.

As he unbuttoned her blouse and slid it away from her shoulders, she gathered her resolve. There was one way for him to take life force that was more effective than any other. A way that had crumbled the barriers between them before and could bind them anew.

And she wanted to feel him inside her again. She wanted to be one with him in every conceivable way. If she could only help him overcome his fear . . .

Nicholas's palms whispered over her aching nipples as he pushed the edges of the blouse apart. "Diana," he murmured, sliding his hands around her ribs, his thumbs teasing the undersides of her breasts. "I've taken much from you, and given you so little in return."

So little, Nicholas? She arched her back as he cupped her breasts almost reverently. *No. Never that. You've given me back my heart. . . .*

As if he'd read her thoughts he lowered his mouth to hers. His kiss was tender and fierce at once, and she felt the first gentle tug within her body as he tasted her life force. He pulled her to her knees against him, her breasts pressed to his shirt, and the evidence of his desire was boldly outlined through his trousers.

Deliberately she reached down between them and brushed his arousal with her fingertips.

This time he showed no reaction at all. He caught her wandering hand in his and lifted it, turning it over to kiss the palm, licking each finger with long, lingering strokes.

"Let me pleasure you, Diana," he whispered. Diana lost any hope of pressing her own advances as he began to caress her, kissing the hollow of her neck, teasing her hardened nipples with his thumbs and catching the lobe of her ear in his teeth. Liquid heat began to rush through her body, blood and nerves and life force combined, pooling between her thighs.

What little will to resist she possessed spilled like the blouse in a heap at her knees. Nicholas took her mouth in a gentle, persuasive kiss, running his tongue at the joining of her lips to coax them apart, massaging her breasts with his hands.

"Nicholas," she whispered, alight with joy, aflame with wanting him. When he bent her over his arm and covered her breasts with his mouth, she flung back her head, closed her eyes, and let the sensations overwhelm her.

He eased her to the floor before the fire. His breathing remained even while hers grew ragged and harsh; his expert embraces disposed of her rationality as swiftly as he removed her clothing.

No, she thought dazedly. *This isn't the way. I want you with me, Nicholas—inside me, joined with me. It's what has to be. I know it. . . .*

But she could not voice the words. She could only gasp and moan as he touched her wetness with his fingers. She felt herself spiraling down, down, far beyond the reach of thought or will.

It was only when she opened her eyes again and saw him kneeling naked between her thighs that she knew she was dreaming. She had let him carry her into sleep as he had done the first time, in the mine where it had all begun. Behind them, the fire blazed beyond the confines of the hearth, licking at her flesh as Nicholas did. She arched upward with a cry when his tongue tested her readiness.

His body covered hers, his solid weight no different from what it had been in reality. His caresses never ceased as he slid inside her, easing deep with exquisite care.

This is the only way, Diana, she heard his silent voice whisper somewhere in the vicinity of her heart. *The only way.*

She had no protest to raise against him. Nicholas had mastered her with his perfect control, leaving her with nothing to hold and shape and turn to her own will.

As he filled her aching body and moved in the ancient rhythm, a deep and unexpected pain rose in her soul. As he took the life force she willingly gave him, she felt bleak despair rush into the empty places left inside her. And when he brought her to inevitable fulfillment, the tears flowed freely.

She woke to find herself standing on the crest of a hill, with a sere brown landscape sweeping away on every side.

The Yorkshire Dales, she thought, remembering. *This is another dream.*

But there was something wrong about it, something *other* that made her realize she was an intruder in this place. She glanced down at her body and saw that she was naked, but she hardly felt the cold late autumn wind that ruffled her hair and stirred the heather at her feet. The icy kiss of a snowflake settled on her shoulder.

A moment ago she had been somewhere else, where there had been walls and fire and pleasure, and she had not been alone. *Nicholas,* she thought, stunned by the pain that came with the word. *Where are you?*

"He is not here, child."

The woman who stood before Diana was familiar, achingly familiar, celestially beautiful in her sashed, full-skirted gown. Her lips curved upward in a beatific smile.

"Elizabeth," Diana murmured.

"He has run away, has he not?" Elizabeth said, shaking her golden curls. "He was never as bold as my Adrian. Which do you suppose is the wiser, child?"

She lifted her head as if at some distant sound, and a moment later Diana heard the cry. Far across the dales something moved, a lone sign of life in this lonely land.

I am dreaming, Diana thought, and attempted to clear her sight. But the dream resisted her control, and it was only when the figure came closer that she could see what it was.

"Mother?" The child wandered toward them and stopped, oblivious to the women on the hill. "Mother, where are you?"

"Such a pity," Elizabeth said, making no attempt to attract the child's attention. "But he must learn to survive alone. It is the only way for us."

With a growing ache in her throat Diana watched the golden-haired little boy stumble in a wide circle, his breath coming in sobs, and fall abruptly to the ground. He sat there, unmoving, his face lifted to the gray sky.

"Nicholas," Diana said slowly.

Arching one eyebrow, Elizabeth lifted her aristocratic nose. "Waste no pity on him, child. You'll gain nothing in return."

Diana studied the perfect face. "What kind of mother are you?" she asked, racked with unbearable sorrow.

Elizabeth laughed gaily. "Why, I am quite mad. All I wanted in the world was to be mortal—to grasp the elusive thing that mortals call love—but that, as Nicholas learned, is quite impossible."

Driving her fingernails into her palms, Diana shook her head. "I don't believe you." She turned back to the poignant scene of the lost boy, and lifted her arm. "I'll take care of him—"

A violent blow nearly knocked her off her feet. Elizabeth, her face a mask of rage, clawed shrieking at Diana's hair and bore her back into the heather. "Stay away from him, you bitch!" Elizabeth screamed. "Stay away from him, or I'll kill you!"

Diana raised her arms to ward off the blows, but Elizabeth's strength was terrifying. Diana knew without a doubt that she was fighting for her life. The sound of the other woman's cries was like the wail of a lost soul in torment.

And then Elizabeth's weight eased, shifted, altered, the softness of her skin growing firm and taut, the lovely face metamorphosing before Diana's gaze.

Only the eyes remained the same: green, intent, trapping her where she lay. Nicholas's eyes—his face, fully as mad as Elizabeth's had been.

Inhuman.

She felt his bare skin rubbing on hers, the violence of his assault focused in one place. His huge, rigid arousal pushed into her like a battering ram. Powerful hands wrenched her thighs apart.

"Stay away, Diana," he grunted, heaving atop her.

Diana tried to wedge her hands between them, felt her helplessness as Nicholas reared over her, readying to drive deep. "No, Nicholas. Please—"

"Stay away," he snarled, red seething between his narrowed lids, "or I will kill you. . . ."

His shaft was a burning brand, and she knew the penetration would tear her apart. With all her strength she began to fight him, beating at his iron shoulders with her fists, bucking her body under his.

Nicholas smiled. His teeth came to needle-sharp points. "Too late, Diana," he said. "Too late." And he crushed her mouth under his lips, drawing blood, plunging into her and sucking, sucking. . . .

She could hear the sounds of her own harsh breaths, the mindless cries of a woman lost in the act of love. . . .

The place where she lay was close and dark, rank with the stench of cheap perfume and sheets that had been aired too seldom. There were other sounds, other cries in the distance, beyond the door, but they made no sense. She could think of nothing but the pleasure of the moment.

It was pleasure, exquisite pleasure, just as Adrian had told him. Diana opened her eyes and saw the face beneath hers, felt the contours of an unfamiliar body, and the shock released her. She burst upward to hover above the writhing figures on the narrow bed, feeling what they felt, knowing at once where she was.

London. The year was 1805, and the man below her —the man in whose body she had briefly resided—was Nicholas. The fine white shirt he wore clung to his back, and sweat slicked his golden hair. His hips moved, and the painted woman beneath him groaned.

Diana closed her eyes to shut out the sight, but all around her, in the very air, she could feel the heavy aura of sex and the vibrations of Nicholas's latent power. The woman's theatrical gasps were a travesty of passion. No effort, no will could free Diana of this place; at last she opened her eyes and forced herself to see it through.

All at once Nicholas reared up, and the woman's cries rose to a shriek. In horror Diana watched as the painted eyes went wide, grew blank with fear as her smudged lips worked soundlessly.

It was Nicholas who cried aloud, a deep groan of despair. He convulsed violently. Diana could *see* the life force of the woman, a mist of muted color that coiled outward from her body and flowed into him. And as the woman was drained of life, Nicholas seemed to grow, to expand, to fill the dingy room with his ravening hunger.

"No, Nicholas," Diana gasped, reaching for him,

stretching her arm until she thought her bones would snap. "You'll destroy yourself—"

"But that would only be justice."

The *fille de joie's* chamber vanished, and Diana found herself in a valley among wooded hills, bright with the new growth of spring. California, the Sierra foothills—perhaps very near the mine where Nicholas had first skimmed her dreaming mind.

And the woman who stood before her now, dark hair coiled atop her head in a loose chignon, was as fresh and lovely and alive as spring itself.

"Clare," Diana whispered.

The image of Clare smiled, but her hazel eyes looked right through Diana. "Justice," she repeated softly. "There must be an end."

Diana's heart labored in her chest. She took a step toward Clare, felt the rustle of skirts around her legs—long, sweeping skirts like Clare's, flaring out from a cinched waist. She extended her hand, afraid Clare would vanish as the other dream-images had vanished, before she could speak to her, before she could ask all the things she so desperately wanted to understand.

"Clare—"

"I am not Clare."

Diana stopped, clenching her fist. The woman's smile faded, and her eyes focused on Diana at last.

"I am not Clare, but she is here with me. *They* destroyed us both."

Dizzy with nausea, Diana braced her feet on earth that seemed to heave and shudder. "Who are you?"

"Don't you know, Diana? I am Sarah." Her soft lips lifted in a sneer. "The woman Nicholas—loved."

Sarah. Sarah, a name Nicholas had called out in his sleep, his face a mask of pain. Sarah, who could have been Clare's twin.

"I loved him," Sarah whispered, "and he destroyed me." Tears ran down her porcelain cheeks. "He must pay."

Unable to look away, Diana gazed at the young woman in her high-collared blouse and narrow-waisted skirt, a vision of stylish beauty from another time. A time before Diana's birth, when Nicholas had given his love to a mortal woman.

"Has he told you he loved you?" Sarah laughed through her tears. "Never believe him, Diana. They are incapable of loving. They have no souls. They only take, and take, and take. . . ."

"I don't believe you." Drawing on the hope that had sustained her through everything that had happened, Diana met Sarah's bitter gaze. "I can't believe you—"

"Then you are a fool." Suddenly Sarah lifted her skirts and took a swift step forward. "I am here to warn you. I am dead, and Clare is moldering in the grave. Because of *them.* But you—" She flung up her head. "He is coming." Her lovely, tragic face broke into a radiant smile. "Nicholas—"

He appeared on the crest of the hill, elegant in a dark jacket and pale trousers, hat in hand. He glided down the hillside without a false step, and his eyes were all for the woman who gazed up at him so adoringly. He took Sarah's hand, drew her close, kissed her deeply while his gaze passed over Diana as if she didn't exist.

"I have been waiting, Nicholas," Sarah sighed as he drew back. She turned to smile at Diana, and as she began to walk with Nicholas across the tender grass, Diana saw the object that had materialized before them.

A coffin. A dark, expertly constructed coffin, lined in velvet. The top of it was open; a butterfly alighted on the edge and fanned its wings.

Nicholas and Sarah paused, embracing and kissing,

Sarah's fingers wound in Nicholas's hair. "I love you, Nicholas," she murmured against his lips. "I love you."

Turning Sarah in his arms, Nicholas looked over her shoulder. For the first time Diana saw his eyes. They were icy, expressionless, as empty as a marble figure's. He seemed almost to see Diana then. But he swung Sarah around and set her on her feet in a swirl of skirts.

Sarah glanced back at Diana. "Remember, Diana. The price is too high. Too high." Beaming at Nicholas, she took his offered hand and stepped lightly into the coffin that lay among the spring wildflowers. He bent over her hand to kiss her soft knuckles, and eased her down on the red velvet lining.

Working legs as cold and dead as stone, Diana walked across the grass. When she could see into the coffin she lurched to a stop.

Sarah seemed to be sleeping, her hands folded across her chest, her rosy lips gently smiling. But even as Diana watched, her soft young face began to wither. Her delicate skin shriveled, her eyes receded into her skull, and the supple, graceful body began to fold in on itself. Cloth and flesh melted away from bone, and even the grinning skull began to crumble.

Nicholas plunged his hands into the coffin and held them out before him, letting the white dust sift between his fingers.

"Dust," he murmured in a voice devoid of emotion. "All dust." Bound by silent anguish, Diana watched Nicholas raise his head, turn slowly to face her. His eyes fixed unerringly on hers. Remorseless, inhuman eyes.

"Run, Diana," he said. He began to walk toward her, long unhurried strides like a predator sure of its prey. "Run."

But she stood where she was, paralyzed and numb. "No, Nicholas. I love you—"

"Run." His voice rose as the green world around them took on a bloodred haze. "Run, run, run. . . ."

A blast of furnace heat struck her, lifted her from her feet, burned her clothing from her body. A blazing maelstrom spun her into the air, up and up and up until the very earth was left behind. And then it let her go, and she was falling, falling, plunging to her death—

Diana woke with a violent jerk, her arm flung so close to the fire that her skin was burning hot. Breathing hard, she drew her arms against herself and rolled over onto her side.

She was alone. Dazed by the vivid memory of the dream, Diana struggled to her feet and leaned heavily against the nearest wall. No trace of Nicholas remained in the room.

Swallowing back the thick taste of fear, she knew that Nicholas had left her. Again.

"Damn you," she said, voice shaking. "No."

She slammed her fist against the wall until the pain reverberated through her bones.

"You can't win on your own, Nicholas," she sobbed. "And I love you. I love you—"

She ran to the front door, oblivious to her nakedness. But she knew it was already too late.

"Adrian!"

Nicholas heard the harsh challenge of his voice ring among the tall eucalypti and pines of Golden Gate Park. At midnight the vast park was eerily still. Homeless folk in their makeshift bedrolls hardly stirred as he passed; a stray dog barked challenge and was silenced.

But *her* voice beat in his mind, in his blood, through

his nerves and muscles as he strode across the wet grass toward the Arboretum.

"I love you, Nicholas."

His foot struck a fallen branch that almost sent him sprawling before he recovered. He could not think beyond this moment. Diana's declaration drove him on like a demon's lash at his heels.

Later there would pain. But for now there was only the nightmare that must be faced—and defeated.

He flung back his head, his breath whistling through clenched teeth. With every moment he lost life force, wasted in useless emotion. With every instant he felt himself coming closer to the edge of sanity.

Because of the dream.

The dream. He felt the dream like a sickness that would not abate—the fourth and longest dream of his life. He had been a child, lost and abandoned. He had been a beast bent on rape and destruction, glorying in Diana's helpless body under his. He had relived the incident in the London brothel that had set the course of his existence. And he had seen Sarah go to her death. . . .

"Adrian!" he shouted again, coming to stand before the high iron gates of the Arboretum. "Damn you, Adrian—"

Like an echo of the past, Adrian stepped out from the deeper shadows, his black clothing almost invisible in the night.

"I knew you would come, elder brother."

Sixteen

I am weary of days and hours,
Blown buds of barren flowers,
Desires and dreams and powers
And everything but sleep.
> —Algernon Charles Swinburne,
> *The Garden of Proserpine*

"Where are you going, Keely?"

Tim stood in the bedroom doorway of her apartment, running his hand through tousled dark hair. Keely looked up, cursing softly, and slid the small handgun into her purse. She let go of the front doorknob.

"I just couldn't sleep. Thought I'd take a little walk or something—"

"After midnight?" Tim smothered a yawn behind his hand. "Come back to bed. I'll make you sleepy."

Keely closed her eyes. At any other time . . . She tried not to look at the clock on the wall.

"You go back to bed, Tim. You've got school tomorrow."

Frowning, Tim walked toward her, scratching just above the waistband of his boxer shorts. "You aren't telling me you were going for a walk, alone, at this hour—"

"I've been taking care of myself for a long time," Keely said sharply. "I can take a walk any damn time I please—"

"Pax." Tim lifted his hand in a gesture of appeasement, but his eyes were fixed on hers. "What is it you're not telling me?"

Keely sighed. Tim saw too clearly with that strange, almost unsullied innocence of his. She turned away, gathering her hair in a rough ponytail and pulling it into a rubber band.

"No drug deals going down, if that's what you mean," she said grimly. "You're just going to have to trust me, Timmy Boy."

"Even though you don't trust me?"

They stared at each other. Keely imagined a pair of dice and gave them a mental toss.

"Okay." She smiled at him, showing all her teeth. "You want trust? I'll give you trust. But don't say I didn't warn you. Go get dressed."

"What?"

"Hurry up. I don't have much time. Someone I care about is in a lot of trouble, and I'm going to have to explain it to you on the run."

It was like looking into a distorted mirror, a flawed and sinister image reflected back to trap Nicholas in memory.

The only other of his kind in all the world as far as he could determine. His other half. His shadow . . .

"Adrian," he whispered.

His brother bowed, all unstudied grace. "You are punctual as always, brother. But then your noble sense of responsibility was ever your greatest weakness."

Nicholas took a step forward, staring into Adrian's eyes through the bars of the gate. "I got your message, Adrian," he rasped. "You swore to leave Diana alone—and the others—if I came to meet you here tonight."

Spreading his hands, Adrian smiled. "And I will, of course, abide by my promise—once we've had our little discussion."

Nicholas reached for the gate and pushed. It swung inward, unlocked. "Will you honor this promise as you honored the first, when you said you were leaving the city and the continent? That you'd learned from your mistakes?"

Adrian backed out of the way, smile undiminished. "Ah, Nicholas. You always held me to impossible standards. Actually, I *have* learned from my mistakes—and you have very little to lose by hearing my proposition."

Little to lose. Nicholas refused to let Adrian read any emotion on his face. "You can't win, Adrian—"

"Because you defeated me before? I admit that came as a surprise, brother. But I spoke the truth when I said I had changed." His gaze raked over Nicholas slowly. "You are looking fit, Nicky. The years have been kind to you. But I believe you will find they have been more generous to me."

His voice softened. "Did you ever wonder what had become of me in my prison? How it might have been if our situations had been reversed?"

The very gentleness of Adrian's voice flayed Nicholas

with bitter grief, the guilt he had never been able to forget. "If there had been—any other way—" he whispered.

"But there was, Nicholas. There still is." He extended his hand. "Come, brother. Let us talk."

Ignoring Adrian's hand, Nicholas fell in beside him, knowing he walked with a deadly enemy. They started down one of the paved paths that wound through the Arboretum. Adrian veered to the right, into the Australian garden. The sharp scents of exotic plants rode on the night breeze.

"What do you want, Adrian?" Nicholas said when the silence had stretched too long.

Adrian glanced at him with a parody of affectionate indulgence. "Patience, brother. That was what I learned in my prison. I had a very long time to contemplate my past sins. Have you?"

Nicholas came to a sudden stop. "No more games, Adrian," he said hoarsely. "What is your price for leaving Diana alone—for the remainder of her life?"

"As many brief years as that may be," Adrian murmured. He glanced at his perfectly manicured nails. "Your devotion to your dreamers is quite touching. But then again—Diana is hardly an ordinary dreamer, is she, brother?"

With an effort Nicholas kept himself from striking that calm, mocking face. *What do you want?*

Adrian looked up. "Very well. No more games. I know the power that flows in your Diana's body, brother. I know it matches and exceeds Sarah's. And I know that she, like Sarah, may have the ability to give you what you most want in all the universe." He sighed. "Don't deny it, brother. You have thought of it. Only your innate—nobility has prevented you from testing the theory again."

"You killed Sarah—"

"We were through that before, a hundred years ago,"

Adrian said. "The past is dead. Or haven't I paid sufficiently for that—"

"And Clare," Nicholas interrupted harshly.

Adrian shook his head. "That was regrettable, but also past. We speak of Diana now."

The very coldness of Adrian's voice as he spoke Diana's name made Nicholas tremble with suppressed rage. "So you know what Diana is," he said, struggling to match Adrian's dispassion. "But I have no intention of trying to—"

"Have you not, brother?" Adrian began to walk again, never looking back. "In the years since I escaped my prison I had ample time to explore the theories in which you once held so much hope. It might interest you to know that I found an old man in India who admitted to having once been immortal. One of us." He laughed softly. "Do you know what he told me, Nicholas? That the key to mortality lay not only in finding the right human partner, one strong enough to transfer the necessary life force into her immortal lover. No—" He stopped again, lacing his fingers behind his back. "There is another essential ingredient, Nicholas."

Nicholas caught up to his brother in a few long strides. "What is it, Adrian?" he demanded, forgetting the terrible barriers that lay between them.

Adrian turned his head. "Ah, no, brother. It's enough to know that I see a real possibility of your finding your mortality with little Diana—and I have no intention of letting you achieve it."

A darkness drew down over Nicholas's eyes. "Revenge, Adrian?" he whispered.

"Not so simple, brother. You see, I have tired of being alone all these years, with no companion worthy of me. These mortals are nothing. They are good for only one purpose." Suddenly he pivoted to face Nicholas, and his eyes were alight. "But you and I are alike, Nicholas. Once we were together—and once I tried to show you that we are the same."

Nicholas closed his eyes. "You failed—"

"Did I, brother?" Adrian's light touch came as a shock that reverberated through Nicholas's body. "I don't think so. I think you have always known the truth. And now I will offer you a chance to accept it."

Nicholas understood even before Adrian spoke the words.

"Come with me now, Nicholas." Adrian's words vibrated with power, with emotion he hadn't revealed until that moment. "Leave these mortals behind, and let us take what the world has to offer. Together, Nicholas. As we were meant to be."

Staring into his brother's eyes, Nicholas felt the pull of Adrian's offer, the unexpected vulnerability in his brother's eyes, the loneliness—the need. A need like the emptiness Nicholas had come so close to filling when he'd found Diana Ransom.

Adrian stepped closer, his fingers closing on Nicholas's arm. "Think of it, brother. How have you spent these past decades—living like a monk, hoarding your life force, denying yourself the pleasures of life—all because of your endless guilt. Now you are free to bury that guilt forever."

Closing his eyes, Nicholas clenched his fists and listened to the sound of his own heartbeat. "You called me here to strike a bargain, Adrian," he said tonelessly.

The rasp of Adrian's breathing was a bitter sound in the stillness. "Of course, brother. Our bargain. Isn't it clear? If you come with me now, I will swear never to touch your Diana again—or these other mortals you hold so dear. But in return you will swear, on your noble honor, never to seek your mortal lover until she is dust—

and that you will give up your search for mortality forever."

Nicholas laughed soundlessly. He had already abandoned that hope. The sacrifice was easily made.

But to give up Diana forever . . .

Hadn't that been what he planned all along, once he'd realized that he could no longer trust his own control with her? Adrian offered him a perfect escape—and ensured Diana's safety into the bargain. Safety from both of them. Because if Nicholas remained with his brother, he would know if Adrian ever broke his word.

And his own nightmare of killing Diana could never come true. . . .

"There is one other small concession I will require from you, brother," Adrian said softly. "A certain unresolved matter that still lies between us. Once you taught me a valuable lesson by leaving me in solitude that was somewhat—uncomfortable. Now I think the time has come to teach you that same lesson."

Looking up at the stars overhead, Nicholas smiled. "Then it's revenge after all."

"No. You wrong me, brother. I never hated you. I will not abandon you as you did me. At the proper time, I'll let you go—and then, I think, we will truly be the same."

Nicholas tried to memorize the patterns of the stars, knowing there was nothing but blackness where he would be going. "I'll never become like you, Adrian." He sought his brother's gaze. "If I'm imprisoned, how will I know you'll keep your word not to hurt my people?"

"Your lack of faith in me is truly—" Adrian broke off, his gaze raking the path along which they had come. "I see we are no longer alone, Nicholas. Friends of yours?"

Nicholas jerked his head up. The movements in the

brush close to the path were noisy and obvious. Adrian's smile chilled him to the heart.

"Come out, little mortals. It would be a shame if you were to miss our family reunion."

There was a moment of stunned silence, and then Keely emerged from the bush, leaves caught in her hair, aiming a small handgun at Adrian's heart.

"Don't move," she whispered, jerking up her chin. Tim burst out behind her and immediately took a half-crouched position between Keely and Adrian.

"How charming," Adrian murmured. "Is this your new lover, Keely?" He made a show of examining Tim, who stared from Adrian to Nicholas in dawning comprehension.

Nicholas was moving before Adrian had finished his question, coming to stand in Adrian's path. "Leave them alone," he said hoarsely.

"But of course, I—"

"Get out of the way, Tim. You, too, Nicholas." Keely's voice was almost steady. "I know how to use this." The gun quivered in her hands. "I'm here for only one reason. To make sure *you*"—her gaze fixed fiercely on Adrian—"don't hurt anyone. Not even your brother."

Adrian laughed, a sound of genuine amusement. "Did I neglect to tell you, my dear, that we immortals have little to fear from mortal weapons?" Pushing past Nicholas, he began to walk toward her. Tim straightened to his full lanky height and refused to move.

Keely set her jaw and stepped to the side, adjusting the aim of the gun. "Don't try me—"

Nicholas lunged after Adrian. In a movement too swift to follow, Adrian thrust his elbow into Nicholas's belly and sprinted toward the mortals. Sucking in air, Nicholas heard the sound of one shot and then another.

He flung himself up and grabbed his brother's arm as a third bullet hit Adrian.

Adrian glanced at Nicholas, only the narrowing of his eyes revealing pain. He touched his chest; his fingers came away bloody. "Your concern for me is indeed gratifying, brother. But I assure you I'll—recover within the hour."

Holding Adrian with all his strength, Nicholas looked at Keely. Her face and Tim's were colorless masks; the gun lay at Keely's feet.

"As I tried to make clear," Adrian said through his teeth, "your—gallant efforts have been wasted, my dear. But your courage is commendable, and I would hate to see it go unrewarded."

With another sudden lunge Adrian broke free of Nicholas, pushed Tim aside, and jerked Keely into his arms. He kissed her, hard and swift. Tim flung himself on Adrian; Adrian swatted him back with a negligent turn of his arm.

Nicholas's vision went red. He charged Adrian, skidding to a stop only when Adrian held Keely as a shield between them.

"Ah, brother. You have so little faith in me." Caressing Keely's face with a blood-streaked hand, Adrian released her. "Run, little mortal, and take your gallant knight with you. You will not see me again."

Keely's gaze was stricken as she looked to Nicholas. Tim grabbed her arm and pulled her back into the bushes, his expression blank with shock. The sound of their retreat haunted the silence long after they were gone.

Bending down with a wince to pick up the abandoned gun, Adrian turned it over in his hands. He emptied the chambers of their remaining bullets, let them fall, and tucked the gun into his belt.

"An amusing diversion, as I'm sure you'll agree," Adrian said. The flow of blood from his chest had already stopped. "The loyalty of your mortals is admirable. But I believe you were questioning my word not to harm them. . . ."

Nicholas stared at his brother, shaken by Adrian's unexpected mercy, heart and mind battered to numbness.

All traces of mockery were gone from Adrian's face. "You may trust my self-interest, brother. I never wanted your precious mortality. The world is full of dreamers, and Diana Ransom holds no attraction for me. She has served her purpose—as has Keely." His voice changed. "But rest assured that if you refuse me now, I will hunt Diana down and destroy her, and those others I let escape tonight. I was never bound by your mortal ethics—and I am free of the chains that bind *you*."

Chains. Chains of emotion that had entangled innocent mortals, that had brought Nicholas inevitably to this end.

"And before you resolve to attack me when my back is turned, brother," Adrian said softly, "remember this. If you raise a hand against me, Diana will die as Sarah died."

Nicholas forced his mouth into a parody of a smile, feeling nothing at all. He extended his wrists like a prisoner waiting to be bound.

"Shall we go, brother?" he said.

"This is the message," Keely said dully, slumped in a chair at Judith's kitchen table. "You—Diana—are to go in five days' time to Adrian's prison." She looked up, meeting Diana's eyes for the first time since Judith had called Diana to come over early that morning. "He said you'd know what that meant."

Closing her eyes, Diana struggled to practice the breathing exercises she'd taught her clients so many times in the past two years. "I know," she whispered.

Yes, now she knew. How Adrian had sent Nicholas a message through Keely, by invading her mind; how Nicholas had met Adrian in the park so soon after he had left Diana. How Keely had attempted to interfere, and had escaped with a second message imprinted in her mind.

Nicholas had given himself into Adrian's hands in order to save Diana.

"Adrian said to come alone, and no earlier, or Nicholas—" Keely straightened in her chair. For an instant the numbness of her expression gave way to defiance. "He wants to trap you both, Diana. He used you as the bait for Nicholas, and now—"

"Nicholas is the bait for me," Diana said. She felt surprisingly calm knowing what she must do. The knowing was better than the despair that had come over her last night when she'd found Nicholas gone. The purpose of Adrian's game was irrelevant. She would do exactly as he expected.

"You can't go alone, Diana," Judith said. Her eyes were hollow, circled by bruises gone yellow and gray. Deep shadows sculpted her thin face to gauntness. "You haven't got a chance."

Diana met Judith's troubled gaze. "I have more of a chance than you think—but only if Nicholas and I are together. I wish I had time to explain, but—"

"Don't you think this concerns Keely and me, Diana?" Judith touched her bruises gingerly. "Keely made the mistake of going in unprepared, but—"

"No. I'm not letting Keely get any more involved," Tim cut in.

Tim moved closer to Keely, looping his arm around her shoulder. He no longer wore the stunned look of a man whose reality had been yanked out from under his feet. There was a solid strength about him, a protectiveness Diana was profoundly grateful for. "I know the whole story now, crazy as it is. I also know Keely would throw herself into danger all over again if someone didn't stop her." He set his jaw, looking from Diana to Judith.

Diana nodded calmly. "Tim's right, Judith. The three of you can't help with this. You'll only get in the way. I acknowledge that you've all been deeply affected by— what's happened between Adrian and Nicholas, and I'm sorry for the pain you've suffered, more than I can say. But this fight can only be fought one way, and by two people."

"You and Nicholas." Keely looked up, her hazel eyes suddenly clear.

"Yes." Diana touched Keely's hair. "I think you understand. I'll always be grateful for what you tried to do. Thank God you're safe. But I'm with Tim on this. The three of you have to stay here."

Crossing her arms, Judith glared at Diana. "How are you going to stop me, Diana?"

Diana walked to Judith and took the thin hands in her own. "By appealing to your love for Nicholas. What would it do to him to know you'd been hurt because of him? You don't have the power, Judith. This battle will be fought—and won—through dreams." She squeezed Judith's fingers. "Trust me, Judith. Please. There is no other way."

Dropping her eyes, Judith pulled her hands free and turned her back, shoulders hunched. Diana swallowed painfully.

"I'll be—leaving in five days, as Adrian ordered. Until then I have to get my schedule rearranged and take care of a few minor matters."

Grim silence settled over the room, making a bitter mockery of the sunlight glazing the warm tiled kitchen. Diana bent down to hug Keely, who returned the embrace with fierce emotion. She took Tim's hand, and the young man nodded with perfect understanding.

Only Judith refused to turn.

"Promise me, Judith," Diana said at last. "Promise you won't follow."

Abruptly Judith strode to the kitchen counter, opened one of the lower cabinet drawers, and removed a matchbook and a half-empty pack of cigarettes. With slow, deliberate motions she removed one cigarette, lit it, and took a long, deep pull.

"All right," she said. She blinked, leaving a sheen of tears over her eyes. "But come back, Diana. Save him, and come back."

Tossing the smoldering cigarette in the sink, Judith left the room without another word.

On a gray Saturday afternoon Diana drove into the Sierra foothills and down the rutted, narrow dirt road to the abandoned mine. The chain link gate across the entrance to the ravine was open, and she drove through without hesitation.

She remembered the place from before, though it had been dark then; it was nearly as ominous now, hemmed in on all sides by steep hills, bare trees, and silence.

When she reached the gaping black mouth of the mine tunnel, she got out of the car and pulled on a raincoat over her thick wool shirt. Half-dried mud sucked at her boots, and her breath frosted in the air. Soon the November rains would be replaced by winter's snow, but she could not afford to look so far into the future.

She could only stare at the mine, waiting, until Adrian appeared. She was almost prepared when he did.

Adrian leaned carelessly against the support timbers,

heedless of the filtered daylight, and smiled a fallen angel's smile.

"Hello, Diana," he said softly. "We meet again."

Diana felt the difference more than she saw it, but she knew she would never confuse Nicholas and Adrian again.

Adrian was *power*—power that eclipsed Nicholas as the sun shadows the moon. He was beautiful, as Nicholas was beautiful, as he had been in her dream when he had first come for her.

He called to her with his eyes, with his smile, promising the sweetness of pleasures beyond imagining, as he had once promised Clare.

But inside, beneath the smile, under the power, Adrian was empty.

"I did not misjudge you, Diana," he said. "The game will be played through to the end." His voice was music, a blending of seduction and command honed into a perfect weapon.

"Where is Nicholas?" Diana asked stiffly, taking a step forward.

He caressed her with his gaze. "Well enough for the time being, thanks to your prompt obedience."

Sucking in a deep breath, Diana stiffened her muscles to keep from swaying. Nicholas was alive. He was safe. Unless Adrian was lying . . .

He shook his head. "Diana, Diana." Adrian glided forward. "You are as transparent as all mortals."

Moving as swiftly as a striking snake, Adrian grabbed her wrist. Until that moment Diana hadn't believed that any man but Nicholas could rouse her with only a touch. But Adrian's palm lay like a brand on her flesh, sending a shockwave of pure erotic energy into the very center of her being.

"Ah," Adrian sighed, closing his eyes. "Yes. The promise is there."

Tensing her muscles, Diana tried to jerk her hand away. He held it easily. "Let me go," she said with frigid calm.

His smile was flawless. "But of course, Diana, if that is what you wish." Countering her resistance effortlessly, he lifted her fingers to his lips and touched the end of her fingertips with his tongue, one by one. "If you are prepared to leave Nicholas in my tender keeping forever."

Shudders racked her body. "You bastard," she breathed. "What do you want?"

He pressed her palm flat and licked it slowly. "Nicholas asked the same question when he came to me five nights ago." Drawing her finger into his mouth, he laved it with his tongue. "It was remarkably easy to bring you both to me."

He released her hand and cupped her cheek. "Your devotion to each other is truly touching, whatever the motivation. In your case, I believe I understand. Nicholas—" Abruptly he let her go. The pleasant expression on his face never wavered. "But that is why you're here, Diana. To help me in a little experiment. To test a certain theory."

Strolling back toward the mine, Adrian picked up a loose rock from among the rubble fallen about the portal. He tossed it aside. "Nicholas was quite noble in offering to sacrifice himself for you, Diana. He believed I would leave you alone if he allowed himself to be willingly imprisoned—as once he imprisoned me."

Diana started toward the mine entrance, but Adrian blocked her path. "That was not enough to satisfy me, however. It was necessary to test you as well, Diana. To learn how much you would sacrifice to save the man you love."

She stared at him, hatred and hope freezing the air in her lungs. "Let him go, and I'll do whatever you require."

"Will you indeed." Adrian arched his brow. "Even if it means giving up those few years you have left to save the life of a being who has already lived two centuries and will live a hundred more?"

Numb acceptance washed over Diana. "Yes."

"You do love him, don't you?" He *tsk*ed softly. "As if my brother had a use for your love. Still, perhaps it may sustain you when you face the end of your mortal life."

Bracing her feet on the muddy ground, Diana balled her fists. "I want to know that Nicholas is alive and well before I—"

Adrian raised his hand. "Patience, little mortal. Would you sell your soul to the devil without reading the contract?" His expression changed; the mockery faded as he reached for Diana, letting his hand drop when she flinched back.

"There are a few things you should know before making your final decision," he said, his voice stripped of music. "And it *will* be final, once I set events in motion."

Turning his back on her, he paced a slow circle around the clearing. "Has Nicholas told you how our mother died? Ah, I see he has. Did you know I was there when she took her life by severing her head from her body, after she had killed our stepfather in her mad hunger?" He brushed at his chest, as if he were wiping away spatters of blood. "*He* was not with her at the end. But he surely told you what became of me when he chained me in this mine." He laughed. "He could not imagine it. The madness, the pain, the hunger. The endless isolation. There are no words for that suffering in any mortal language."

Diana's throat closed with unexpected pain. She remembered her last dream with Nicholas—and Elizabeth, the immortal mother who had abandoned her children.

Knowing what Adrian was, how he had driven Clare to her death, used Keely and tormented Nicholas, undoubtedly taken countless lives—even knowing that, Diana felt a profound and unwanted pity.

As if he felt her emotion, Adrian whirled to face her. His lip curled. "Five days ago I bought Nicholas here. I staked him out in the sun, and let the life force drain out of him. You know our needs, Diana. Feeding as seldom as he does, Nicholas cannot risk exposure to sunlight." Adrian turned his face upward as the sun slid out from behind a cloud. "You see that I have no such difficulties, because I don't allow mortal ethics to restrain my hunger."

He made another casual circuit of the clearing. "When Nicholas was properly weakened, I imprisoned him within the cavern where he once left me. There he has been, Diana, for the past four days. Empty of life force, starving. Desperate. At the edge of madness—as our mother was when she drained my stepfather, whom she believed she could love."

Diana closed her eyes. Adrian's intentions were suddenly crystal clear. She remembered the skull in the cavern, the unfortunate mortal who had found Adrian and provided the life force that set an immortal free. At the cost of his life.

"You see, Diana," Adrian murmured, "Nicholas has convinced himself that he is a highly moral creature. But even he, with his high ideals, has no recourse against the inexorable hunger to survive that drives our kind. If a mortal were to be put in with him now. . . ." He shrugged eloquently.

Opening her eyes, Diana met his gaze. "You think he'll kill me."

"That is the question, is it not? The very purpose of our little—experiment—"

"Do you hate him so much?"

Adrian sighed. "Such simple emotions are no part of our kind, Diana. Nicholas has almost convinced himself they are possible—and it is my duty to show him his error."

Diana was long past any possibility of shock. Unexpectedly, Adrian's cold words renewed her faltering hope. She took several strides toward him.

"If it's an experiment, you must have some doubt as to the outcome. Why?"

For the first time Adrian's face revealed surprise, quickly hidden under a smooth, cynical smile. "You can still surprise me, little mortal. Let me pose *you* a question: Did Nicholas ever confide to you his deepest desire—and his greatest fear?"

Staring past Adrian at the tunnel entrance, Diana set her jaw and refused to give him a single advantage he could use against Nicholas. *He'll talk without any prompting,* she thought, *because he must tell someone. . . .*

"I think you know, Diana," Adrian said. "You are perceptive enough to recognize his fear of involvement with mortals. Does the name Sarah mean anything to you?"

Sarah. With an effort Diana hid her reaction, fighting back a shudder of foreboding.

Sarah, whose name Nicholas had spoken in his sleep. Sarah, who had come to Diana in that last dream and warned her of a terrible price: *"I am the woman Nicholas loved. . . ."*

"I see you do know the name," Adrian said.

Diana closed her eyes, remembering. *"I loved him, and he destroyed me."*

"Did he tell you that he loved her, Diana?" Adrian's voice receded as he walked away. "Sarah Danvers, a young girl, a mine-owner's daughter from these very hills. Over a century ago, now. Oh, Nicholas played very hard at being human in those days. He even worked deep in the mines to hide away from the sun. But he wanted more than immortality, Diana. More—or less."

"He wanted to be mortal." Diana whispered. She opened her eyes and stared at Adrian without seeing him.

"Yes. An old legend among our kind, that such a thing is possible. When Nicholas found Sarah, he thought he'd found the way." Adrian turned and walked toward her. "But Nicholas didn't tell you much of those days, did he, Diana?" He caught her chin in his hand. "I doubt very much that he told you how he stole Sarah from me, and killed her."

Adrian's face blurred in Diana's sight as the dream played back in her mind: Nicholas's teeth bared in a snarl as he crouched like a mindless beast to tear out her heart —his empty, remorseless eyes when he guided Sarah into a coffin and watched her crumble to dust. . . .

It had been a dream. But Diana knew how terribly real dreams could be.

"In all fairness, I think he went a little mad," Adrian said, stroking her cheek with his fingers. "Insanity runs in our blood, Diana, just as does our need for what only mortals can provide. Nicholas saw what he wanted in Sarah—innocent young Sarah—a life force strong enough to grant him the one thing he would have at any price. And so he seduced her away from me, and raped her, and destroyed her."

The images rolled through Diana's memory in nauseating waves: Nicholas sprawled on top of her, preparing to thrust deep inside her and kill her in the act; his body heaving as he drained the prostitute of her life force. And Sarah's face, her eyes, trusting him as he led her to her death.

"But my brother reaped only weakness from his act, Diana," Adrian continued inexorably. "Like a monk fallen from grace, determined to drive out the sins of the flesh, he punished himself. When that wasn't sufficient recompense to ease his guilt, he turned on me."

Adrian's voice was so perfectly reasonable, so convincing. "Nicholas's fatal flaw is that he let his guilt eat away at him, until he lost himself in illusion. He hates me because I am the part of himself that he cannot acknowledge. The part I must *make* him accept."

The hypnotic rhythm of Adrian's voice, Adrian's touch sent Diana spiraling into a place where the line between reality and fantasy, truth and falsehood, vanished utterly. She jerked her head free of his light hold.

"You're lying," she rasped.

"Am I? It hardly matters if you believe me, Diana. But perhaps you'll understand more clearly why I sought out your sister fifteen years ago. All that endless time I spent in my dark prison, I thought of what Nicholas had taken from me. And when I was free again, I followed the trail that led me to Clare."

Comprehension lanced through Diana. Two faces, two women so nearly alike as to be identical—Clare, and Sarah, separated by a century and joined in death . . .

"Surely you've worked it out, Diana. Sarah was your ancestress. She bore a daughter before she died, an illegitimate child sired by a human mate who had abandoned her. I traced that child's offspring to your sister, and thought I had found Sarah reborn."

"And you killed her." Amid the shock, Diana clung to the one certainty that remained. Her gaze locked on Adrian's. "You were there when I was a girl," she said with icy loathing. "I saw you in the nightmare. . . ."

Adrian shook his head. "I do regret your sister's

death, Diana. It was never my intention to take so much. I didn't realize how—fragile she was."

The genuine regret in his voice almost pierced the armor of Diana's hatred. "And yet you're ready to kill me just as you killed Clare—torture, perhaps destroy your own brother as part of your game," she spat.

There was a strangeness in Adrian's eyes, and his smile had lost every hint of mockery.

"No, Diana. I'm prepared to give you a chance—the chance Sarah never had. You know the facts; your decision will be an informed one. I will let you go now, if you so choose—if you are willing to abandon Nicholas now and for all time and leave him to my—brotherly care."

Her heart protested before her mind could find the words. *Never. . . .*

"But if you choose to stay, Diana, I will put you in Nicholas's cell, and leave you there. If you are strong enough—if you are stronger than Sarah was, if you pass the test—you and Nicholas will be free of me forever. If not—"

Waves of sickness washed over Diana. She braced her feet apart to keep from falling.

If not, I'll be dead, drained of life—and Nicholas will survive to know what he did to me—

"You understand, Diana. Rest assured that I will take good care of Nicholas if you fail to emerge with him. He will be free in either case—*if* you choose to enter the cavern."

Diana stared at him blindly. "Keely and Judith—"

"Will be safe from me whatever you decide. Perhaps you would like a moment to think it over, Diana."

And he was gone. She stood alone in the clearing, caught in broken shafts of light cast through bare branches by a westering sun.

Soon it would be night. Nicholas's time. Night and darkness.

God help me, she prayed. *I'm afraid. But I love him. I love him. . . .*

Tears pushed past her eyelids. *"Nicholas was quite noble in offering to sacrifice himself for you, Diana."* Adrian had said. *"It was necessary to test you as well . . . to learn how much you would sacrifice to save the man you love."*

If she walked into that mine the man she found there would not be a man at all. If she walked into that cavern, she would face her ultimate fear: of losing herself, giving everything she was to a man who might literally drain her of life itself.

"It is time, Diana."

Adrian's voice was almost gentle, his expression almost tender. Diana looked directly into his eyes.

"You know what I choose," she said softly. She unhooked the small flashlight from her belt and began to walk toward the yawning mouth of the tunnel, knowing that Adrian followed. At the last moment, as the darkness closed around her, Adrian strode past and led her deep into the passage.

She knew the place at once. She had seen it last in a dream that hadn't been a dream at all. A great slab of rock lay across the entrance to Nicholas's prison.

I am not afraid of the dark, she said silently. Defiance sparked within her, pushing back the darkness like a flaring sphere of light.

"I am not afraid of the dark!"

"Brava, little mortal," Adrian said at her elbow. She turned her flashlight beam into his face; his smile chilled her soul. It was the look of a man who knew he had won everything.

"I will give you one last piece of advice. The key to

your survival may lie in your very mortal weakness—and in Nicholas's. That great weakness that mortals call strength." He gave a brief, bitter laugh and grasped the edges of the rock slab, pushing it aside. A moment later he took the flashlight from her unresisting fingers.

"After you, Diana."

She plunged into a deeper blackness than any the night could hold, Adrian at her back. After a few steps she felt her heart clench in recognition. Nicholas was here.

Waiting for her.

"Nicholas," Adrian called softly. "I have brought you a gift." Diana heard him turn, pause again. "It's all you will have, brother. Make the most of it." He laughed again, and the mocking echoes were followed by the scrape of the stone slab being lifted into place. "One last gift for you as well, Diana." Something rolled at Diana's feet. She bent to curl her fingers around the flashlight just as Adrian sealed her into deathly silence.

Diana pivoted slowly. "Nicholas," she whispered.

Something moved, an almost imperceptible shifting, a rattle of pebbles to her right. She turned to face the sound.

"Nicholas, where are you?"

His breath was the next thing she heard, a long, low exhalation like the gasps of a dying man. She flicked on the flashlight.

His eyes were wild as an animal's, reflecting the beam in a wash of bloody red.

"Nicholas," she gasped. "Thank God—"

"Stay—away from me, Diana," he said, his voice a raw whisper, "or I'll—kill you."

SEVENTEEN

Deep into that darkness peering, long I stood
   there, wondering, fearing,
Doubting, dreaming dreams no mortal ever
   dared
      to dream before.
                    —Edgar Allan Poe, *The Raven*

All the world was torment and pain and ravening hunger.

He had needed no sight in this darkness, no hearing where the only sounds were distant, meaningless echoes. His skin had long since turned to ice, his heart laboring to keep him alive as the rest of his body shut down.

He had clawed at the walls like a trapped animal, dragged himself to the sealed entrance and bruised his fists against it before the last of his strength had fled, screamed her name until his throat was raw and hoarse. *Diana, Diana, Diana. . . .*

But she was gone. She was safe, free of Adrian and himself. The price had been paid in full.

She could not have heard him. He had known that madness had come at last when her voice rose like music in the silence, speaking his name.

So he welcomed the madness, embraced it gladly as salvation. Until the light came, and he saw her face.

Lucidity lasted only an instant, and then he was lost in insensate desire, perceiving only that his deliverance lay within that fragile mortal form.

Emotion twisted inside him, freed from its icy prison, slashing great gaping wounds in his blighted soul. The shadow of her body was limned in light, and her aura flared around her, calling him to take and consume.

Diana was *here*. Here, with him—and in deadly danger.

He stopped himself from moving toward her, though instinct and need made the blood sing in his ears and readied him to take her. Her lips were parted, her eyes wide on his—not afraid, not afraid when she should know what he would do if she came too near.

His vision hazed. Soft words rose in his mind, shaped to lure her to him. *Come to me, Diana. Come. I need you—*

And she would come, trusting, into his arms while he possessed her completely, irrevocably, fatally. Just a few feet, a touch to end this agony . . .

Blind rage coiled in his belly. He found his voice, forced it to obey his shattered will.

"Stay—away from me, Diana, or I'll—kill you."

He knew only that she had stopped, her aura a seductive glow to his fading vision. Salvation and damnation,

Diana crouched and waited a few feet away, just beyond his reach.

"Nicholas," she said. Her voice trembled, almost imperceptibly—took on shape to his muddled senses, color that arced upward and ran like blood to pool on the cold ground.

"Stay—away," he managed again when she shifted. Adrian had done this. He cursed his brother slowly, methodically, focusing on each foul word. The pattern of syllables gave him an anchor in the maelstrom of hunger.

Adrian had broken his word yet again. He would have his revenge. . . .

"No," he rasped. Sanity. He must keep his sanity, his control. Words. Words and sentences to form a cage around the beast that clawed at his gut.

"What has he done to you, Nicholas?" Diana whispered.

She sensed it. The deepest part of herself understood, the primitive ape that cowered in the presence of the predator. But she would not heed that warning.

He listened, waiting for her to move closer, his slow, dull heartbeat rocking his body. But she remained where she was.

Words. Speak, focus on rational discourse. The predator had no such means of communication.

Nicholas heaved himself up on his elbows and focused on her aura with all the life left in him.

"Drained me, Diana," he rasped. "Adrian—" He tried to clarify his thoughts, but she took them from his mind.

"I know," she said. "He told me—he left you here—" Her aura snapped like fire in a wind, pulsing with reaction.

The sound he made might have been a laugh. "To go

mad," he said. *Mad. No, use words to keep control, sanity* —"As I left him."

Abruptly the light went out. Diana moved again, her feet scraping on gravel. As if she instinctively grasped the nature of his struggle, she kept her voice detached and level. "Nicholas—"

Self-loathing rose like bile in Nicholas's parched throat. "Did he—hurt you, Diana? Did he—"

"I'm all right. He didn't touch me."

The feeble strength went out of Nicholas's arms in a rush, and he let himself drop back to the ground. "No. He—brought you here instead." Coughing, he pressed his face into the dirt.

"I came here of my own free will," she said, almost too softly for him to hear. "I never would have let you go to Adrian alone if I'd known what you planned. And I'm not going to let you suffer, Nicholas." The unmistakable sound of movement came to him, and he tried to roll away from her even as his body yearned toward her.

"Diana!" he rasped urgently.

"I'm not coming any closer," she said softly. "I know what Adrian thinks will happen."

Light flared, faintly red, from the place where she sat. Anger, he thought. *Talk, Diana,* he urged. *Talk, make me listen—*

"When you left me that night, I knew it had something to do with Adrian," she continued. "And then he— sent me a message, through Keely. That I had to meet him here if I wanted to save you."

Nicholas rolled onto his back, every bone and nerve singing with pain and insatiable hunger. "Adrian's bargain —was to leave you alone if I came with him." A laugh scraped his raw throat. "He—planned this. He knew." All the air burst from Nicholas's lungs as if an invisible fist had slammed into his chest. "He brought you here—to die."

The silence in the cavern was absolute. Diana's breathing quickened and steadied again.

"No, Nicholas. He's wrong, and so are you."

Desperation gathered in the pit of his stomach, coalescing into sound that emerged as a ragged roar. "No!" His cry shocked her to silence. "I'll kill you, Diana. I'll drain your life force and—leave you nothing but an empty husk. Don't you understand? I'm like Adrian. There is— nothing left but hunger. I have nothing left to fight it. Nothing—"

His voice cracked and faded to a croak. With curled fingers he clawed at the cavern wall.

"I don't believe you," she said, cloaked in her stubborn mortal courage. "You've deceived me many times, Nicholas, because you thought you had to. But not in this. You aren't like Adrian. You weren't the one who killed Clare. Or Sarah."

Shock held Nicholas rigid. "Sarah," he echoed.

"Adrian told me about Sarah," Diana said. "But I had already heard you speak her name—and saw her in the dream the night you left—"

"The dream." Bracing himself against the cavern wall, Nicholas pushed himself over to face her again. The simple movement exhausted him. Diana's aura pulsed blue like cool water placed before a man dying of thirst. "I dreamed of Sarah that night, Diana. I dreamed."

She understood him. "And I was there. I didn't realize it was your dream, not at first. But it all made sense. I knew I was somehow an outsider. I met your—mother, while you were a lost child. I was there with you in the brothel. And Sarah spoke to me. . . ."

He remembered. Some part of himself had become

Sarah as she warned Diana, his guilt and fear speaking through the phantom image.

The coffin. Sarah looking at him with trust and love—

"You saw me kill her," he whispered.

"Did I?" Her aura flickered. "Adrian said *you* killed her when you tried to take her life force to become—mortal."

So she knew. "And you—didn't believe him, Diana?"

Her breath caught in a sound of pain. "There was a moment when I almost believed him."

"And he did—speak the truth." Nicholas concentrated on each harsh word as he forced it from his throat. "I was seeking mortality when I found Sarah over a century ago. She died because of my desire to be—human."

Diana was very quiet. "I'm long past the point of accepting simple explanations for anything, Nicholas," she said. "It's too late to drive me away."

Too late. Nicholas pressed his cheek to the cold earth. "I will—tell you about Sarah," he whispered. "So you understand."

Gravel rattled. "It isn't necessary. I trust you—"

"Trust? Save your trust until I'm—finished."

In the wake of her silence he pressed himself against the cavern wall and began to speak. "I came to the United States after years of wandering. Europe, Asia, Africa—searching—looking for answers."

As he slipped back in time he clutched gratefully at the distance it offered. "I learned ancient disciplines in Tibet and China, India and Japan, that I thought would enable me to—control my hunger. And in my travels, I found another of our kind."

Diana's aura betrayed her shock. "But I thought you and Adrian were the last—"

"We are now—to my knowledge. I—" His mind was suddenly filled with the memory of the man he had met in

India, the immortal who had told him the ancient legend. Adrian, too, claimed to have found such a man after his escape from the mine, a former immortal who had achieved mortality. . . .

"He was the only one I ever discovered," Nicholas said, breathing sharply. "They—thought him a holy man in his land, but he had spent a century searching for death."

"He wanted to die?"

Nicholas cracked out a laugh. "He wanted mortality. And he shared his—theory of how it might be obtained. How if one of our kind found a mortal strong enough, powerful beyond all others in life force, he might become —human."

"As you wanted to be," Diana murmured.

Nicholas hardly heard her. "There are no laws made for our kind, no science to explain our natures. The holy man's belief was as good as any other, but I—held no hope of proof."

"Until you met Sarah."

The name still struck like a whip, laying bare the old guilt and bitterness. "I came to America because it was the one place I—had not yet explored. In 1887 I arrived in California, and took work as a hard rock miner near Nevada City." Catching his breath, Nicholas shaped memories into halting words. "I had been—with the Danvers Mining Company for two years when I first met Sarah, the daughter of the owner. When he learned I was a—'civilized' Englishman, Danvers elevated me to shift boss and, in time, offered me a partnership.

"Danvers was a widower, and Sarah—was his greatest treasure. The first time I met her, I knew her life force was richer than that of any woman I had known. She was spirited, innocent, beautiful. I knew—she might fulfill the conditions the holy man had laid out, and I was tempted beyond reason. But I would not have touched her, even when my status as partner to her father brought us together. When—she said she loved me, I convinced Danvers to send her away to a finishing school in San Francisco."

"Is that where Adrian found her?" Diana whispered.

"No. I had not seen my brother—in many years, and I thought we would never meet again. I intended to leave California before Sarah returned. But within a year she had come back to Nevada City—pregnant by some itinerant confidence man she had met in San Francisco. Her father was devastated, and Sarah's spirit was shattered. Within a few months Danvers died in an accident while inspecting one of his mine shafts, and—I was there to hear him beg me to marry Sarah, look after her and the child."

"The child," Diana said slowly. "My ancestor. Adrian told me."

Nicholas shuddered. "I gave my word to Danvers," he continued doggedly. "Sarah still believed she loved me. I convinced myself I could not hurt her by taking what I needed.

"But I waited. A year after Sarah and I were wed, when her child was a few months old, Adrian appeared out of nowhere to offer his—congratulations. He was unchanged, charming, dangerous—but he was still my brother. I welcomed him in my profound naïveté. I wanted to forget the past, and I thought—I thought I had the world in that moment. One night I—left Sarah alone with Adrian. When I returned, Adrian was gone—and Sarah was lying naked on our marriage bed, dying."

Diana gasped, and Nicholas drowned his sorrow in the harsh satisfaction that she might finally understand. "Adrian seduced her, took her, drained her life force until too little remained to keep her alive. She—recognized me just before she faded into a coma from which she never awoke. The last thing I saw in her eyes was terror."

Diana's aura fluxed with emotion, but she did not speak. Nicholas took the story to its bitterly ironic conclusion. "I buried Sarah, sent her infant daughter to live with good people who could care for her, and hunted Adrian down. He had not run far. In spite of what he had taken from Sarah, I defeated him and—imprisoned him in a mine long abandoned by the company. I never saw Sarah's child again." He swallowed. "I never guessed who you were, Diana."

"Until you recognized Sarah in the photograph of Clare," Diana said. "But when Adrian escaped, he tracked down Sarah's descendants, and found my sister."

Nicholas gathered his legs beneath him and worked his way into a sitting position against the cavern wall, ignoring the renewed waves of sickness. Diana moved in turn and he went utterly still, following the flow of her aura with hungry eyes.

"Now you see that—I was as much to blame for Sarah's death as Adrian was," he whispered. "For your sister's death as well." He turned his head away, struggling to blunt his hunger. "I am no different—from my brother."

"You're wrong." Diana's aura leaped up like a flame, burning through his closed lids. "You must believe that, Nicholas. *You aren't your brother.*"

Helplessly he opened his eyes, mesmerized by her life force. If he had been his brother, he would have taken her long since. She would be an empty shell, and in ages to come some wanderer might find her staring skull as he and Diana had found dry bones in Adrian's empty tomb. . . .

"Did you love Sarah, Nicholas?"

Diana's question caught him hard and rocked him to his aching bones. "Love?" he repeated numbly.

"Did you love her?"

He wanted to crawl across the ground and shake her, drive that deadly word from her mind. His fists closed on empty air. The mere thought of touching her readied him instantly. The need in him redoubled, pounding with every heartbeat against the flimsy barriers that kept him from her.

"Listen to me, Diana," he rasped. "I have—tried to make you understand. In this darkness you believe we are the same. You—cling to your mortal faith because I can speak in words and sentences of things long past."

"Nicholas—"

"You cannot *see* me, Diana. You ignore the part of you that—recognizes the truth. You tell me I'm not my brother, but what remains of me now is—not a rational thing. It is that inhuman nature Adrian revels in, relentlessly hunting the—one thing that will keep my body alive."

Diana's breath came faster "I know what you are," she whispered. "Just as I know what will save us both."

Nicholas surged up and lunged toward her clumsily, willing her to run. "I could drain you with a touch, Diana," he snarled. "A single touch. But it wouldn't stop with that. There is a—thing within me that knows only mindless lust, and I have no more strength to fight it." He fell to his knees, knowing she had not moved, was deaf to his warnings. "I want you now," he said hoarsely. "I want to bury myself inside you and take, just as Adrian took Sarah."

He could smell her now, the human, woman's scent of her; feel her warmth, hear the pulse that beat under her skin. The shape of her body flowed like a shadow haloed by light.

"You want me, Nicholas," she echoed, "but you won't hurt me, because I will give you what you need in full knowledge. Unlike Sarah, and unlike Clare. Because *I* want *you.*"

"No—"

"And because I love you."

The truth was there in her aura. Nicholas fell forward onto his bruised palms. She did not deny that the danger existed. She believed her mortal love could conquer it.

"I tried to tell you, the night you went to Adrian," she said from some great distance, "that we had to be together to defeat him—fully *together* in every way. No barriers, no walls." Her breath caught. "Bound together by something Adrian can't understand and can't face."

Nicholas cursed her silently, trying to shut her out. A great roaring filled his ears, but even that was not enough.

"Love, Nicholas—"

The roaring became a torturous dissonance that filled his head. *No,* he cried silently. *No, no, no—*

In the grip of burgeoning madness, Nicholas leaped up and flung himself at Diana, his hands grasping and holding. He tossed back his head as the first waves of her life force broke against him.

The shock of it gave him clarity for a few precious moments. Diana lay under him, her breasts rising and falling rapidly. He snatched his hands away from her arms.

"Love," he gasped harshly. "Do you think love will save you?"

Even in the darkness he could see the contours of her face, her mouth, the dark frames of hair and lashes. He caught the brief flash of her teeth as she licked her lips.

"Yes," she answered simply. "You reminded me that dreams can be real, that some risks are worth taking—"

"Dreams," he spat. "The first time I left you, Diana—

that first night I tried to make love to you—I dreamed. Dreamed of killing you in a place like this—"

He tensed his muscles to pull free of her and felt ancient instincts take control of his body. The only movement he could make was toward her. Toward life—or death.

Incredibly, she smiled. Fearless, sensible, foolish Diana smiled at him, and her hand lifted to touch his face.

"I'm not afraid of your dreams, Nicholas." Her fingers grazed his stubbled jaw, and he jerked away. It was almost too late.

"Diana," he whispered brokenly. "I could not love Sarah. I tried, but—there is no love in my kind."

Her body trembled under his. Through the growing haze that shrouded his mind, Nicholas mustered his final assault.

"Lest you think yourself—an exception, Diana, understand this: If I had believed it was possible, I might have tried to—take mortality from you. But I could have given you nothing in return."

He thought at last he had made her understand. Her eyes closed tightly; sorrow and pain infused her life force. If she resisted him—if she hated him, he could find the strength to let her go. . . .

But her eyes opened once again, and the spectral light surrounding her flooded with the colors of determination and acceptance. A strange, irresistible peace reached out for Nicholas with gentle tenacity just as her fingers uncurled to cup his face.

"I'm no longer afraid of the dark," she whispered.

His will deserted him as her firm hands drew his lips to hers.

Diana had prepared herself for violence.

Lying beneath Nicholas, his breathing harsh against her mouth, she had known what she faced. He was wild; she had felt his struggle from the moment she had entered the cavern, his desperate and brittle grip on sanity. She had made her decision, and there was no going back.

Her body was ready to accept him, reacting instinctively to his need and his nearness.

"There is no love in my kind."

After one moment of wrenching pain she had driven his desperate warning from her mind and her heart. She'd believed love would save them both—but Nicholas's need for what only she could give might bind them strongly enough to win the battle.

It *had* to.

So she readied herself to match him, expecting a brutal animal coupling in which she must struggle to channel the life force he would rip from her body. He was little more than a shadow above her, beating with primitive ferocity, but she could imagine his face. His eyes would be mere slits, inhuman and merciless; his jaw would be rigid, his hair tangled wildly over his forehead.

But it would still be the face of the man she loved. She closed her eyes, waiting for his hands on her body.

They came, not harshly, but with gentleness. His fingers trembled as he framed her face and drew his thumb across her lips. She felt the savage control with which he held himself in check, and wanted to weep.

Drawing in a deep breath, Diana reached within herself to draw on the life force coiled and waiting. She envisioned it flowing freely, like blood, gathering beneath her skin where Nicholas's hands touched her.

And then she pushed outward. *Take it, Nicholas,* she urged silently. *Take it and grow strong. . . .*

He gasped harshly, arching upward. Her body lifted

to meet his, and when he descended again she drew him into the cradle of her thighs. His arousal pressed into her through their clothing.

"Diana," he said hoarsely.

"Stop," she whispered, concentrating on the growing heat where he pressed her hips. "Stop fighting it. Take me, Nicholas. Take all of me." She thrust upward again, suddenly blind with a need that matched his. "Take life."

He groaned, an animal sound, and with one hand he ripped her shirt down the middle. She hissed through her teeth as his mouth fell hungrily on her breasts, sucking deep and hard. The intense pleasure of his fierce caress sent the life force spinning wildly through her body; it seemed to flow through her breasts and into Nicholas's urgent mouth. He licked and kissed and devoured her while she caught his damp hair in her hands with tiny cries.

This was how it was meant to be, what was meant to be. . . .

Her nipples were taut and throbbing and wet with his kisses when he lifted his mouth again to hers. His tongue thrust inside and curled around hers, and his hand wedged between their bodies. His touch, that had been so cold at first, had grown warm with her heat. His fingers slid down her belly, unzipped her jeans and worked beneath the waistband to her aching womanhood.

He found the source of pleasure unerringly. Diana arched upward, and he stroked her until she was lost in pulsing, erotic heat. Effortlessly her life force began to pool where he touched, drawn to his fingers. He shuddered above her. She was hardly aware when he tugged her jeans down to her ankles; his fingers slipped into her wetness and plunged deep. He worked in a rhythm that threatened to take her into madness with him, and then suddenly he withdrew. He stretched over her, pressing his rough cheek to hers.

"Diana," he groaned. "I have to be inside you."

"Yes." She gave him the word as a gift, knowing all choices were long since past.

A moment later he was pressed to her, nothing between, his arousal burning hot as it pushed against her moist skin. He jerked spasmodically, still fighting one last battle with his desperate need.

His mouth moved on her throat. "I can't stop," he breathed harshly. "Too late."

"I won't let you," she gasped in answer. Before she had finished speaking, he drove deep inside her.

There was a moment when Diana was aware of only two things in this dark, silent world: Nicholas utterly still within her body, and her own life force shooting like liquid fire to the core of her womanhood. He shuddered and began to move, slowly at first, as if he still hoped to be gentle, and then with deep thrusts that wrung groans from his throat. He drove hard enough to rock her body almost violently, but all Diana felt was pleasure; pleasure such as she had never felt before in all the times they had been together. Pleasure that sang in her life force as she opened herself to him in every way she knew.

Even as he began to draw on her, sucking her life force rhythmically in time to his thrusts, she was not afraid. The more he demanded, the more perfectly she matched him. With every movement she felt him grow stronger, flush with life; in the giving and taking she knew the bond between them was forged anew—a bond that Nicholas might deny for the rest of eternity, but utterly real. He took from her, took her very being into his body as she took his into her own.

Diana cried aloud as light and life force crested to blinding intensity, lifting her from the hard ground. Nicholas roared a wordless, tormented sound, and for a split second he almost wrenched free of her. But then his muscles trembled violently, hip and belly and thighs, and he plunged full-length inside her.

Completion came as something indescribable, beyond the power of mere thought to grasp. Diana felt her life force explode outward in a sunburst that burned its way into Nicholas even as he spasmed and spilled his own seed within her body. A tide of energy flowed from some endless source, filling them both to the brim, linking them at the very root of existence.

Nicholas lay stretched over her body, the sharp tremors in his muscles easing slowly. Sweet lassitude drifted through Diana—not the weakness of depletion, but the deep contentment of victory. She held Nicholas to her, ignoring his weight and the tears that pooled in her eyes.

"Diana."

Her name came from very far away, and she was inclined to dismiss it. But it came again, this time accompanied by a dull pain in the vicinity of her face.

"Diana, wake up!"

She opened her eyes to the unexpected brightness of light and a glittering green gaze locked on her face. Nicholas crouched over her, pointing the flashlight's beam into her eyes.

She drank in the sight of him. His expression was no longer contorted in fear and rage; there was wonder in his eyes, wonder and something else she was afraid to identify.

"Are you all right?" he said, touching her cheek.

Stretching, she let herself feel all the aches and bruises in her body. There was a sharp rock grinding into her back, but until now she hadn't noticed it. With the slightest effort she could touch the life force within herself —dormant now, but there. Always there.

As Nicholas was there, still bound to her by life itself.

"Don't you know, Nicholas?" she said softly. "Can't you feel it?"

He gave a half-strangled laugh. "I didn't kill you, Diana."

"Because I was right."

His breath shuddered out. "You—aren't hurt? Weak?"

"No. Pleasantly sore, but—"

He scrambled to his feet—easily, with no trace of feebleness. She heard the crunch of his footfalls moving away.

"You're all right, Nicholas," she said, sitting up slowly. "You're—whole again."

His reply came from the far end of the cavern. "Whole?" he echoed hollowly. "You saved me, Diana."

Absently she pulled the edges of her torn shirt together, though she felt little of the cavern's chill.

"We saved each other," she said softly.

His shadow-shape flowed toward her again. "Diana," he said in a ragged voice. "Don't look for what doesn't exist."

Diana stared into the darkness, clasping her arms around her knees. Her irrational sense of well-being drained out of her in a rush, leaving her suddenly cold.

Nicholas was well again, no longer on the verge of madness. His body thrived on the life force that she had given him, and he was strong—strong enough to match his brother. But now that he had what he needed and found her undamaged, he withdrew.

As if he had felt nothing that she had felt—no binding, no mingling of spirits as well as bodies. Nothing to hold them together when this was over.

Diana turned her eyes to the ground and began to feel for her discarded jeans.

"What now, Nicholas?" she asked at last.

Nicholas moved past her, pointing the flashlight at the blocked cavern entrance. "Now I get us out of here."

She watched him run his hands along the stone slab. "What about Adrian?"

He stopped. Diana rose and tugged on her jeans. "When Adrian made his bargain with me, he said we'd be free of him forever if we walked out of this mine. But he didn't expect me to survive, Nicholas."

Nicholas put down the flashlight and set his weight against the slab, testing it. "Then we'll have the advantage of surprise."

"And if he's waiting outside?"

He hissed through clenched teeth. "You've given me the strength to fight him—"

Gravel rolled and scraped under his feet. Diana heard his breathing become labored as he pushed at the rock and shifted position to try again. She joined him on his third attempt and felt the unyielding weight of the slab that Adrian had lifted so effortlessly.

Nicholas broke away, striding blindly across the cavern. He slammed his fists on the opposite wall and leaned against it, dropping his head between his outstretched arms.

"I can't move the rock, Diana," he said.

"You may still need time to recover."

His only answer was a soft curse. She picked up the flashlight and joined him, touching his rigid shoulder. With an explosive breath Nicholas turned and caught her hand in his.

"Adrian will be back," he said harshly. "To—observe the results of his handiwork."

Resting her forehead against his chest, Diana listened to the strong rhythm of his heart. "Perhaps this time he'll keep his word—"

"Do you really believe that, Diana?"

No. Neither one of them could afford to take that risk. Nicholas's despair was her own, as tangible as the heat of his body. But a stronger emotion had brought her to this cavern, a certainty that refused defeat.

"Then we'd better be ready for him," she said. "I know how to defeat him, Nicholas. How we can do it together—"

Nicholas released her hand and turned against the cavern wall. "You've done enough," he whispered. "I almost lost—"

"Listen to me!" Diana pressed into him, pushing him against the wall as if she had the strength to keep him there. "Dreams are the answer. *Our* dreams."

He began to shake his head, and she caught his face in her hands. "You've told me that your kind doesn't dream—that you only ride on the dreams of mortals, shape what is already in human minds. But *you* have dreamed three times. And I am a powerful dreamer, Nicholas. Even when you've shaped my dreams, I've been able to take control. Do you remember? In the dream of Coverdale Hall, with the books? And when we first made love—"

He shuddered, and she knew he remembered every moment. "Diana—"

"When Adrian came to me at the seminar, tried to control me within my dream, I forced him out. *I* did it, Nicholas." She caught her breath. "Neither one of us can defeat Adrian alone. But with both of us, together, creating and shaping a dream . . ."

She spoke until the tension in his body changed and his gaze fixed on hers with fierce and sudden hope.

"It won't deceive Adrian long," Nicholas said when she had finished. "He'll feel your life force within moments."

"I trust you to do a very good job of distracting him." Diana cupped his cheek in her palm. "Trust *me*, Nicholas," she whispered.

His lip curled up in the familiar, half-mocking smile. " 'What fools these mortals be,' " he quoted softly.

To all appearances she was dead.

She lay close to the cavern wall, a few feet from Nicholas, her arms outflung in an attitude of arrested terror.

They had waited a timeless span for Adrian's coming; there was some source of outside air in the cavern, but Diana was beginning to feel the chill and the growing strain of their vigil. Nicholas had warmed her with his body as best he could before a scrape of stone warned them that Adrian had at last returned.

Diana felt the beat of her heart against the earth as she listened to the whisper of Adrian's approach.

"Are you well, brother?"

Adrian's voice was strangely free of sarcasm, touched with hesitation. Clenching her teeth, Diana concentrated on damping her life force as low as she could. Footsteps moved closer to her, paused.

"Ah. I see my experiment failed," Adrian said softly.

She heard Nicholas shift. "Damn you, Adrian," he rasped. "If I could kill you—"

"Fortunate for both of us that a biological imperative prevents our kind from killing our own." Diana held her breath as Adrian moved away, toward the sound of Nicholas's voice. "Poor little mortal. She had great courage. I —regret that this was necessary."

There was a sharp grating of movement, and Nicholas made an inarticulate sound of rage.

"Ah, brother. Now you know how I suffered all those years. And I think, perhaps, I understand your suffering.

But now—" He sighed. "Now you realize your mortal dreams were no more than a fool's ambition. Such limitations are not for us, Nicholas. To attempt to be other than we are leads only to this." Diana imagined the gesture he made toward her. "Now you and I can live as we were meant to live. . . ."

Adrian stopped suddenly, and Diana could sense the change in him. "But something is not—quite right. What is it, brother?" Slowly, inexorably, his footfalls returned to Diana. "The little mortal is—"

Diana braced herself and heard Adrian's soft grunt as Nicholas hurled himself at his brother. In the same instant Diana lunged up, flailing out blindly, slapping warm cloth as her fingers clutched Adrian's leg. With her other hand she reached for the final, essential contact.

Nicholas's palm slid across hers, and their fingers intertwined.

She had never been completely sure it would work. Adrian was powerful; Nicholas didn't know if he would be able to pull Adrian into their dream. But Diana flung all her strength behind him, willed herself into sleep, plunged through the intermediate stages and into the world of dreams.

And the others were there with her. Nicholas, his face suddenly visible and stunned at their success; Adrian a distorted mirror image of his brother, his eyes blank with shock.

"Where—" Adrian began. Nicholas released his brother abruptly and drew Diana away, holding her close. Adrian glanced at them and at the still-formless world on every side. He shook his head.

"A dream." He looked at Diana and bowed. "How severely I underestimated you, little goddess. And yet I find myself—pleased that you survived." His gaze swept to Nicholas. "But this"—he gestured at the mist surrounding them—"is not yet victory."

Diana lifted her chin. "We knew you wouldn't keep your word, Adrian."

Adrian looked away. "Ah, Diana—" He made a negligent gesture with one hand, and Diana felt dizziness surge through her. Nicholas shuddered. Wordlessly they moved closer, standing as one against Adrian, and Diana drew deeply on her life force and all her skill in dreaming.

The world around them took on solidity: grass under their feet, a night sky still wreathed in mist, the distant silhouettes of trees. Adrian blinked and dropped his hand.

"Yes, Adrian," Nicholas said softly, his hand holding Diana's in a bruising grip. "You did underestimate Diana. And me."

Adrian shook his head. "You were always weak, brother." The newly formed world flickered and darkened, taking on the aspect of the cavern in which their bodies still lay.

The battle began in earnest then. It was the test, the crucial trial that would prove whether or not Diana's deepest beliefs had been right.

As Adrian fought to draw them back to reality, Diana struggled to maintain the dream. Nicholas was her anchor, still and uninvolved—until suddenly she felt a wave of power flowing from him into herself, a return of the life force he had taken multiplied by a thousand. With a burst of confidence she solidified the ground and trees and sky, felt Nicholas join her imagining with his own.

All at once the traces of cavern walls vanished. Adrian staggered, his eyes widening. "This becomes interesting," he said. "Very well. I will play the game your way. The end will remain the same."

The two brothers stared at each other as if victory could be won in a duel of locked gazes. Diana sucked in a deep breath and gathered her life force for the next move, knowing it would come without warning.

Between one blink and the next the first changes began. As if by unspoken agreement, Nicholas and Adrian altered their clothing simultaneously. Adrian's dark trousers and turtleneck became polished boots and snug breeches and tight-fitting black jacket, while Nicholas donned the same costume formed out of mist in every shade of gray.

"Shall we begin with a duel, brother?" Adrian asked. He bowed to Diana, and she found herself naked—naked by Adrian's will, mocked with helplessness. Nicholas growled in his throat, but Diana stayed him with a touch.

To counter Adrian in this was surprisingly easy. Diana closed her eyes and clothed herself in a high-waisted gown, long-sleeved against the chill of the dream night. The gown was white, like the one she had worn in the ballroom dream so long ago. She knew instantly the color was wrong. The gown must be red—fire red, passion red, blazing with defiance.

"Ah," Adrian breathed. "Brava." His attention shifted back to Nicholas. "We are now equal, brother. Shall we be civilized?"

A flicker of emotion crossed Nicholas's face. He lifted his hand, and there was a pistol in it—an antique firearm that Diana knew would be deadly in the right hands. Or when wielded by a powerful dreamer.

Adrian produced his own pistol. "You have challenged me, Nicholas. The winner will take everything."

Diana's mind was suddenly filled with images. She understood the custom the brothers intended to follow, and stepped forward in a sweep of skirts to Nicholas's side.

"You can't do this alone, Nicholas—"

He glanced at her coldly. "Stand back, Diana."

Adrian saluted Nicholas with the muzzle of his pistol, and turned. Diana prepared to intervene, but the mist seemed to wrap itself about her ankles like invisible shackles.

"Nicholas!" she shouted, her voice shredding to nothing. He ignored her as if she didn't exist.

Measuring the distance with deliberate steps, the brothers acted out a farce of an honorable duel. They turned simultaneously, leveling their weapons. Nicholas hesitated, his face a blank mask, and fired.

The bullet that left Nicholas's pistol in a blur of speed stopped halfway between the two men and hung in midair. Unable to move, sick with fearful anger, Diana watched the brothers struggle silently for control.

And then the bullet fell harmlessly into the grass. Adrian aimed his weapon while Nicholas dropped his arm and stood waiting for his brother's shot.

"No!" Diana snapped the bonds that snared her feet and plunged into the path of Adrian's bullet. Focusing all the concentration at her command, Diana wove the ubiquitous mist into an invisible shield. She twisted to face Nicholas. "Together, Nicholas," she said urgently. "This is our fight!"

Her words finally got through. His gaze lost its strange, distant look, darkening with emotion.

"Will your little mortal fight your battles for you, brother?" Adrian taunted. The ground beneath his feet was seared and blackened. Even as Diana watched, the dream world wavered and grew hazed with red, mist turning to steam, fissures running through the earth to expose seething fire like blood.

Adrian changed. His body shrank in on itself, became a hunched figure, baleful and grotesque, mounted like a wizened ape on a huge black stallion. Green eyes peered out from the misshapen face. Adrian grinned, revealing pointed yellow teeth.

"We are already damned, Nicholas," the grating voice of the Adrian-nightmare cried. "Come embrace your destiny!"

Nicholas snarled and leaped forward, his body blurring into golden flame. A black lance appeared in Adrian's hand; it swung with deadly intent toward Nicholas.

"No!" Diana ran toward them, transforming her skirts to dry jeans and sweater with a single brief thought. Her feet sank deep into sand, and she saw stretched around them a beach she remembered from a dream, bordered on one side by ocean and endless gray sky.

Nicholas dodged the lance, but not quickly enough. A jagged dark wound ripped through his gray coat at the shoulder, searing the cloth. He fell back just as Diana reached him. With all her strength she tugged him out of the path of the stallion's striking hooves.

Rolling over her in the sand, Nicholas shielded Diana with his body. For a moment their gazes locked. There was no time for words. Diana spoke to him with her heart and mind.

Together . . .

Nicholas understood. He began to transform before her eyes, rising up out of the sand: a magnificent golden stallion, nostrils flared for battle. He swung his great head, and Nicholas's green eyes locked on hers. Without hesitation Diana leaped onto his back, grasping the mane in her hands. She shaped herself a lance of light just as Adrian's black brute came at them again.

With a harsh bugle of rage, Nicholas reared onto his hind legs and slashed at his enemy. They smashed together with an impact that would have unseated Diana in the real world. But this was her dream, and here she was a warrior fighting the last and most desperate battle. Her light lance shattered into sparks as it struck the black stallion's marble-slick hide.

"You will not have him, mortal!" Adrian shrieked. Diana barely had time to create a new lance as Adrian drove his mount toward them again. Nicholas's powerful muscles bunched between her legs as he sprang forward, spraying sand. This time she felt a blow strike Nicholas across his chest, staggering him. He lurched sideways and Diana fell, losing the lance. She hit the sand with an impact that knocked the air from her lungs.

Time itself went still. Nicholas lay before her, naked and in human form. As if his skin had gone transparent, Diana could see his heart beating in his chest—a heart wreathed in tiny chains, chains that snaked through his arteries and muscles, tying him to pain and isolation. His heart labored to break the chains until it seemed ready to burst, but they were stronger than his will.

Blind rage gripped her. She leaped to her feet, forming the lance once again and bracing the butt of it in the sand as Adrian charged at Nicholas's prone form.

A shriek rent the air. The tip of Diana's lance struck the stallion deep in the chest, and it reared and vanished in a column of smoke.

Adrian lay at her feet, unconscious. Diana stared down at him, her rage fading to numbness. Nicholas stirred; his fingers closed on fistfuls of sand and relaxed again.

Together, she'd told Nicholas. They must be together to win. And now Adrian was defeated and at her mercy. Nicholas was incapable of taking his life, but *she*—

Diana closed her eyes. She knew she could destroy Adrian. This dream was truly hers now. She could be certain Adrian never hurt another Sarah, another Clare— and spare Nicholas the agony of a decision that would haunt him forever.

Dropping to her knees, she clenched her fists over Adrian's prone form. *Dear God. What should I do?*

"Diana."

The soft voice—*voices,* speaking as one—answered her anguished prayer. Diana opened her eyes.

Two women stood behind Adrian, wreathed in mist, identical save in the clothes they wore.

Clare smiled at Diana, her face utterly at peace. And Sarah, beside her, looked from Adrian to Nicholas and met Diana's gaze at last.

Diana scrambled to her feet and reached out as the apparitions began to fade from her sight.

"Wait!"

But they were gone, and Adrian looked up at her with death in his eyes.

EIGHTEEN

Tell me not, in mournful numbers,
Life is but an empty dream!
For the soul is dead that slumbers,
And things are not what they seem.
— Henry Wadsworth Longfellow,
A Psalm of Life

Why don't you end it, Diana?"

She stared down at Adrian, her face white and her eyes haunted as they met his. Brown curls shivered in an ocean breeze; her lips parted as if she would speak.

Adrian made one last grasp at control of the dream, but he knew it was futile. Even the wind would not still at his command.

Diana had won. Diana, and Nicholas.

Adrian pushed himself up on his elbows, too weak to do more.

"Well, Diana? You have all the power now."

She shook her head. Her blue eyes cleared, and the mist that wreathed the beach began to recede. She turned and knelt beside Nicholas, stroking the tangled hair from his face with a gesture of such tenderness that Adrian looked away, despising his weakness.

"It didn't end as you expected it to, did it?"

Her soft voice drew Adrian's gaze back to her again. She cradled Nicholas's head in her lap, her love for him brilliant and strong in the aura that embraced them both.

"Your experiment," Diana prompted. "The test of your—theory."

Adrian attempted a cynical laugh, but the sound caught in his throat. "Did you guess the purpose of the game, Diana?" he asked. "From the moment I saw you and Nicholas together on the beach at Las Playas, I knew *you* were to be at the heart of the inevitable battle to come."

Diana touched Nicholas's face. "You were right."

"Yes. You earned something I have never given any mortal, Diana—my respect." He smiled grimly. "The apparent strength of your mortal passion for Nicholas intrigued me. I wished to learn if the bond between you—your love—was strong enough to save you from his hunger when nothing else could."

"But when it did, you couldn't keep your word to let us go," she said. Her eyes blazed. "Did you finally realize that we mortals have sources of strength you'll never understand?"

Adrian rolled onto his side, showing Diana a mask of utter indifference. "I underestimated you greatly, Diana. But you are stronger than any of the others." He shivered, caught in memories that suddenly had the power to move him. "Stronger than Sarah, whom Nicholas did not love—and stronger than Clare, who believed she loved me."

Diana made no effort to conceal her emotion. "Were *they* part of your experiment too?" she whispered. "Are you so different from your brother?"

Something in her anguished question struck Adrian to the core. For an instant he hovered on the edge of telling her the truth. Not *different. The same. I wanted to show him he was wrong in rejecting what we are, wrong to want what destroyed our mother—wrong to think he could turn away from me forever. . . .*

No. Adrian bared his teeth, smothering the pathetic voice into silence. He would never reveal his innermost heart to any mortal. Not even now.

"Ah, yes. My brother. You survived the test, Diana, but the results remain inconclusive. I understand your human emotion no better than I did before. You have defeated me—but have you truly won?"

Her hand curled into a fist on her thigh. "I don't—"

"You have proven your love for him, Diana, and the strength of that love. Does he return your devotion? Isn't that what you want of him, what you're afraid you'll never have of your immortal lover?"

He knew he had struck to the core of her vulnerability. She tried to hold his gaze, but her aura flinched with pain, and her eyelids fluttered to hold back tears.

Adrian felt no satisfaction in his minor victory. He felt nothing at all. He watched Diana regain control, wiping roughly at her face.

"We take the risks we have to, mortals that we are," she said at last. "We make our choices and we live with them, whatever the price."

"And now yet another choice falls to you." With a concerted effort Adrian gathered his strength and pushed up to his knees. He nodded at Nicholas, who breathed steadily but didn't stir. "The decision is yours. What will you do, Diana?"

The battle she fought within herself was transparent even to Adrian's battered senses. Everything had changed irrevocably because of this one mortal woman. Nicholas had changed, and *he* had changed. He had no will to fight death if Diana chose to be his executioner.

With blinding insight Adrian grasped what would become of Diana if she were forced to kill him. She would be destroyed, shattered by crippling remorse just as Nicholas had been from the day Sarah had died and he'd imprisoned his only brother.

But, even after all this, Adrian did not want Diana to be destroyed. The revelation stunned him.

He stared at Nicholas and looked slowly into Diana's eyes.

"Let me go, Diana," he said.

Her expression was frozen. "Let you go after all you've done?" Her voice broke. "How can I trust you? How many more will you hurt?"

Even as he struggled for an answer, Diana's gaze lifted and widened, focusing on something behind him. He turned and went utterly still.

The two young women who stood over him might have been avenging angels come to drive his damned soul to hell.

He sank back, crouching like some beaten thing, and found his voice trembling when he spoke. "Did you conjure them up to punish me, Diana? Is this your vengeance?"

But he knew she had not. Her mouth moved without sound; she settled Nicholas gently into the sand and rose.

"Clare," she whispered.

Clare smiled, and her entire body seemed to glow

with an inner aura. "Diana," she said. "Don't be afraid to follow your heart."

Sarah looked down at Adrian; he flinched violently as she reached for him, her delicate fingers extended to brush his arm. The touch sent heat and light exploding through his body, blinding him to everything but the truth.

"Don't you see?" Sarah said. "He, in his own way, has also changed."

Abruptly Sarah released him. Clare nodded, the compassion in her eyes as devastating as Sarah's touch.

Adrian forced himself to his feet, swaying with shock. "Go—and sin no more," he whispered. With an effort he focused on Diana's pale face. Nicholas stirred beside her, fixing on Adrian the moment his eyes opened.

"Adrian," he croaked.

Diana knew Nicholas saw nothing but his brother when he rose and stumbled toward Adrian with a broken cry.

She caught him in her arms and held on. "Nicholas. Nicholas, listen to me—"

He stopped, muscles going rigid. He broke away from Diana; his eyes were glazed with shock.

"Sarah," he whispered.

But it was Clare Diana saw walking toward them. Thick mist materialized out of nowhere, rising between Nicholas and Diana like a gray wall.

"Don't worry, Diana," Clare said. "Nicholas is where he needs to be."

Diana swallowed. "Is this my dream? Or are you—"

"Does it matter?" Clare grinned, and her arms were warm and solid as she embraced Diana. "It's time to move on, Diana. Let the old stuff go. Don't grieve for me any more."

Time stopped, and Diana caught a brief glimpse of something profound, something that shone in Clare's eyes and through her body like cleansing fire—a moment of perfect vision given to one bereft of sight.

And then Clare was gone. Diana found herself holding air.

"Diana."

She turned toward Nicholas. A wall of mist still lay between them, chest-high. He reached out to her and dropped his arms all in the same motion. His face was utterly without expression as he looked across a few feet of sand at his brother.

Adrian said nothing, but Diana knew he understood the judgment being passed behind Nicholas's emotionless stare. Just as she knew Nicholas had not been left untouched in those moments when he'd been separated from her by the mist; he had not been alone.

But now Nicholas faced the decision Diana had already made. She knew she could not interfere. Only Nicholas could choose to let his brother go.

Nicholas took a single step toward Adrian. Their gazes locked; the air shook with distant thunder. The cold perfection of Adrian's face cracked like ruined marble. He flung back his head, lips forming a wordless cry.

"Go," Nicholas whispered.

Adrian turned clumsily in the shifting sand and began to run. His body became a blurred shape in the mist and grew dim, dissolving just as the world, and the dream, shattered around them.

Reality returned slowly, like hesitant bird song after the hunter has passed.

Diana looked up from where she lay on the damp

earth. She could smell the cold freshness of the air. A ray of morning sunlight bathed her face.

Outside, she thought. *We're outside.*

She pushed up to her knees and looked for Nicholas. He knelt on the ground with his back to her, facing the dark mouth of the mine portal.

Adrian's gone. Diana rubbed her hands on her jeans, remembering the end of the dream. *It's over.*

She should have felt relief. When she thought of Clare, there was a sense of closure, of letting go. It didn't matter whether or not Clare had been only a creation of her dreaming mind. The emotions had been real, just as the change in Adrian had been real.

But as she looked at Nicholas and felt his wordless sorrow, she knew it wasn't finished. Just as Adrian had said near the end.

Have you truly won, Diana?

She got to her feet and walked slowly toward Nicholas. He could have been miles away. Kneeling beside him, she studied his stark profile.

"Nicholas."

Carefully she touched his arm, brushing his torn and dirty sleeve. A shudder raced through him, and his lips parted.

"He's gone," he whispered.

"Yes," she answered softly. "You made the—right decision, Nicholas."

He shook his head, the once-bright golden waves of his hair tangled and streaked with dirt. "Did I?"

Running her hand down his arm, Diana found his fingers and laced hers through them tightly. "You trusted your heart, Nicholas. Sometimes that's all we can do."

"My heart—" His voice cracked, and the muscles in his jaw worked spasmodically for control. "If my—heart —was wrong. . . ."

Diana folded his unresisting hand between both of hers. "He was—flawed, not evil. He had something of you in him, Nicholas. Enough to make him capable of changing for the good."

The first obvious cracks appeared in Nicholas's expressionless mask. "Flawed," he echoed. He barked a laugh. "So you—found it in *your* heart to forgive him, Diana?"

She understood what Nicholas asked on a level deeper than words, deeper than logic, deeper than the pain and bitterness—and need—he concealed from the world. Her heart twisted in her chest, caught between hope and despair.

It was not Adrian who wanted absolution now.

"Sarah—forgave me," he said. "In the dream, near the end—she came to me and forgave me. For not loving her. For letting her die."

I was right, Diana thought. Nicholas hadn't been alone when Clare had come to her, asking Diana to let go of old sorrow. Behind the wall of mist, Nicholas had been offered his own freedom from the past.

If he would take it.

"Can you forgive yourself, Nicholas?" she whispered.

For the first time he looked at her, his eyes revealing nothing.

"For not stopping him sooner, Diana? For involving Clare and Keely—and you—"

Diana met his gaze steadily. "For being flawed. For making mistakes and having weaknesses like we all do." She sucked in a deep breath. "For being—human."

He didn't deny it as she'd expected, didn't do anything but stare at her blindly. His hand in hers was still as death. Instinctively she felt for his life force, remembering how she had touched it while making love and in the final dream. It was like trying to capture fog. She could not seem to find the place where hers ended and his began.

"Adrian was your brother, Nicholas," she said, "and you loved him."

"Love is a human emotion," he rasped.

Diana closed her eyes. *So is pain,* she thought bleakly. *So is denial, and impossible hope.*

"And the price is too high."

She forced herself to look at him again, at his shadowed face and his lithe body, bowed as if he could draw life from the very earth.

"What about the price of immortality, Nicholas?" she asked numbly.

His head lifted. "They are the same. Loss, Diana. The inevitable death of everything you are fool enough to love."

The ache in her chest was so intense that Diana had to catch her breath. "At one time I would have agreed with you. After Clare died I—didn't think the risk was worth it. I had lost my parents and my sister and Keely, and I wasn't going to lose anyone again. Or risk losing myself."

"And yet you risked everything in the end."

She smiled a little. "Yes. And it *was* worth it, Nicholas."

Nicholas got to his feet, his back turned to her. "Do you know what time it is, Diana?"

She blinked, caught off guard by the prosaic question. She glanced automatically at her wrist. The narrow leather band was scuffed and the crystal was scratched, but it was still running.

"Seven-twelve," she said.

"In the morning," Nicholas added softly.

It took almost a minute of staring at the dial of her watch before she realized what he meant.

She looked up, gazing at Nicholas and the long shadow he cast over the ground.

"The sun," he said. "It's day, and I feel nothing. No weakness. No discomfort at all."

He spoke as if to himself, the words dry and clinical. Diana gathered her feet under her and rose. Nicholas's face was turned toward the sun, and the light formed a white halo about his hair.

In a dizzying rush she remembered the other clues: his inability to move the slab over the cavern entrance after they'd made love; Adrian's enigmatic talk of Nicholas's desire to be human, of his "experiment" and the parallels and relationship between herself and Sarah; Diana's own certainty that she and Nicholas must work together to defeat Adrian.

"You—are mortal," she whispered.

He turned just enough so that she could see his profile, blurred by the brilliance of the sun behind him. "Poetic justice, Diana. Adrian took Sarah from me—a woman who might have given me mortality—and he gave me you in her place."

Dazed, Diana shook her head. "When we made love—" She clenched her fists. "You knew."

"I guessed. I knew something had changed, but I couldn't be sure—and I didn't dare think of it. I was afraid if I had become mortal, I'd little hope of defeating Adrian."

But we defeated him, Nicholas, she cried silently. *Together, both of us human, with the power of our mortal dreams.*

"Then you have what you always wanted."

Nicholas pivoted slowly to face her, but the sun in Diana's eyes made his face a formless shadow. "Yes. Everything I've always wanted."

Diana swallowed, Adrian's voice echoing in her memory. *"Does he return your devotion? Isn't that what you want of him, what you're afraid you'll never have of your immortal lover?"*

"Do you regret it after all, Nicholas?"

He took a step toward her. "Do *you,* Diana—having given so much and received so little in return?"

The sun made her eyes water, so she closed them. "But I did receive something, Nicholas. I got back my dreams, and my heart, and my hope. I learned—not to be afraid of the dark."

"And is that all you wanted?"

Scraping the heel of her palm across her eyes, Diana shook her head. "Sometimes dreams aren't enough. But the fight—the struggle—is better than surrender. Without the fight, life has no meaning. Without the risks, we can't understand the joy." She wanted to laugh at her own pompous pronouncement. But it was true. She understood that now. What had been theory was something she knew in the depths of her soul.

"But I owe you more than my life," Nicholas murmured. His voice had changed, slipping effortlessly into the dulcet tones of the seducer. But there was no emotion underneath that deep music. "I have wealth, Diana—influence if I choose to make use of it. Two centuries of knowledge and experience that a psychologist might find very useful. There are many ways I can repay you for all you've suffered because of me."

Keeping her eyes firmly shut, Diana refused to surrender the shreds of her self-control. He knew what she wanted from him, and yet he mocked her with his quiet offer.

"There is no love in my kind, Diana—"

She would not say the words again, not even though they would be burned in her soul until the day of her death.

"I would make a fascinating case study, wouldn't I?" he continued lightly. "A man who has lived two hundred years, who has developed several human lifetimes' worth of psychoses. A man who survived without the need to sleep or dream. A man whose life has drastically altered."

She heard his approaching footfalls, but she could not seem to move.

"Think what you could learn, Diana," he whispered. "Think of the contributions you could make—"

Blinded by tears, Diana opened her eyes to the sight of his shadowed body inches from her own. She flailed out to drive him away, letting the grief and anger overwhelm her.

"You aren't some damned—case study," she gasped. Her hands slapped his chest, sending a shock wave through her nerves. "Damn you, I—I—"

Nicholas trapped her hand over his heart and held it there with mortal strength that was still far greater than hers. His fingers were trembling. Diana became gradually aware that his heartbeat was as rapid as her own.

And she felt his life force. Not raging like a fire that might consume everything around it, or faltering with weakness that only a mortal could restore. It was the twin of hers, flowing like deep water under a quiet surface.

"I feel your life force, Diana," he said, "but I no longer need it. That hunger is gone."

The first tears spilled over and ran onto her cheeks. She let them fall unheeded. Nicholas flexed his hand and caressed her fingers absently in a slow, hypnotic rhythm. She did not look up. She would not look up and meet his eyes.

"This mortality is very—new to me, Diana," he said slowly. "Perhaps you would give me some free advice."

Her throat was too full for answers. She squeezed her

eyes shut again, sending a fresh wave of tears coursing down her face.

"We have something in common, Diana," Nicholas said. His touch brushed feather-light across her face to catch the moisture and draw it away. "They left me alone —my mother, my stepfather, Sarah, even Adrian—" His voice caught. "They and every being in this world I—" He stopped, and the next words were forced from his throat as if they were made of broken glass.

"How do you deal with the pain?"

Diana swayed under the impact of his anguish and her own. "Don't you know?" she said, her voice cracking. "We cry."

"Diana," Nicholas groaned, pulling her into his arms. And then there was nothing else—no place, no time, only the two of them, and Nicholas's silent tears mingling with her own.

When the world returned and the storm had passed, Diana looked into his eyes and shivered. They were soft with vulnerability, no longer crystal but deep water and growing things, the color of life. He smiled crookedly and curled his fingers behind the nape of her neck.

"I'm—afraid I need yet more of your guidance, Diana," he said. "Humans, it seems, are not so unlike immortals after all. They require something intangible to survive."

She gazed at him wordlessly.

"I see I must be more explicit." His smile vanished as he cupped her cheeks in his hands. "I can live without life force, but, oddly enough, not without you. Can you still love me, Diana?"

She clutched the front of his torn shirt as if she might fall. " 'What—fools these mortals be,' " she quoted, grinning up at him like the mortal fool she was.

With a whispered oath he dragged her into his arms

again, his lips tracing her hairline and the arch of her eyebrows and the tip of her nose.

And when his mouth met hers it was like a circuit closing, love and life force pulsing through them both in waves of ecstasy. Heaven itself seemed to take them into its embrace, bearing them up into a dream of paradise.

The voice of an angel fallen to earth sounded in Diana's heart.

"I love you," Nicholas whispered.

NINETEEN

—

If we shadows have offended,
Think but this, and all is mended,
That you have but slumber'd here
While these visions did appear.
                    —William Shakespeare,
                    A Midsummer Night's Dream

The bouquet sailed over the heads of the young women crowded in front of Diana, bounced out of grasping fingers, and landed, as if by magic, in Diana's modestly raised hands.

Keely, beside her husband on the low dais at the head of the mirrored ballroom, grinned with wicked delight at Diana. Judith—who had wryly refused to stand with the single women and vie for the bouquet—gave an unrestrained whoop.

Watching from among the bachelors, Nicholas admired the attractive flush in Diana's cheeks. She fidgeted with the bouquet as if she didn't know what to do with it, shrugged, and returned Keely's grin. When her gaze met Nicholas's, her eyes hid nothing of her feelings.

She had never been able to hide them from him.

Keely and Tim dashed off to change into their going-away clothes, but Nicholas hardly noticed. The noise in the ballroom died as he made his way toward Diana and Judith. He no longer felt the life force of the women he passed, but his sense of Diana, of her vitality and warmth and love, never faltered.

Several young women were clustered around Diana, whispering and laughing. Judith watched it all with quiet indulgence. Barb, from Mama Soma's—looking almost conservative in a beige leather skirt and jacket—was cracking a joke that made Diana's blush deepen. Barb glanced up as Nicholas approached. Her eyes widened, and she whispered a comment behind her hand. By unspoken agreement the young women drifted away to find their own escorts, and Judith moved up to link her arm through Diana's.

"I knew you could do it," Judith said.

"Do what?" Diana asked, her gaze seeking Nicholas across the rapidly diminishing space between them. "Catch the bouquet?"

Judith assumed a mask of of profound wisdom. "This is a serious matter, Diana. I see I'll have to speak to Nicholas—"

"That isn't necess—" Diana broke off as Nicholas joined them. He glanced at Judith, arching an eyebrow.

"Speak to me about what?"

"Keely and Tim are about ready to leave," Diana said quickly. "Come on, you two."

Keely and Tim reappeared at the doorway to the ballroom, grinning giddily. The wedding guests rushed toward the couple and laughingly pursued them out through the lobby and onto the sidewalk where the limousine waited. Showers of birdseed bombarded the newlyweds; Keely looked at Diana, winked broadly, and blew Nicholas a kiss.

And then they were gone. Dabbing surreptitiously at her eyes, Diana leaned into Nicholas's arms. He held her very close and swallowed around the tightness in his throat.

"I like weddings," Judith commented beside them. "I hope it won't be too long before I'm invited to another one."

Diana slipped free of Nicholas's embrace. "Would you like to come back to our place for coffee, Judith?"

The older woman shook her head. "I promised Nicholas I'd finish looking into some new investments." She gave Nicholas a knowing look and Diana a brief hug. "Go take advantage of this beautiful evening."

Nicholas called a cab for Judith, and they said their good-byes. The June afternoon was flawless, with a light breeze coming off the ocean and a sprinkling of cottony clouds against a brilliant sky. Nicholas held Diana's small hand in his, lifting his face to the sun. It was still a miracle to him, walking in daylight with Diana by his side.

They strolled down a sidewalk crowded with San Franciscans enjoying the perfect Sunday weather. Nicholas noted the admiring male glances that followed Diana and felt a stab of purely human jealousy. He slipped his hand around her waist; she glanced up with a smile.

"You don't mind the walk to the car, Diana?" he asked again.

"I don't blame you for not wanting to park in that cold, dark underground garage," she said. "You've had enough darkness to last you a lifetime."

Nicholas swung her to a stop and kissed her, in full view of interested bystanders. Someone whistled. Diana grabbed the lapel of his tux and yanked him back into motion, ducking her head.

"Sorry, Diana," he said, unrepentant. "I find myself impatient to get home. Is this the usual consequence of weddings?"

They reached the alley where Nicholas had parked the new hunter green Saab convertible—his dark van had long since been donated to charity—and Diana gave him a sideways look, blowing a loose brown curl out of her eyes. "I still can't quite believe Keely and Tim are married. If you'd told me such a thing was possible six months ago . . ."

Nicholas unlocked the car door and held it open for her. "Stranger things have been known to happen, Diana," he said softly.

She looked up at him, and he bent to kiss her again, more lingeringly. This time she didn't break away until her breathing had quickened and her skin was flushed to the neckline of her blue silk dress.

"Strange how—hungry I am right now," she murmured, loosening his tie with teasing fingers. "I think we'd better hurry home."

Every minute of the short drive back to Nicholas's house on Seacliff, he daydreamed in vivid detail of assuaging Diana's hunger. He hurried her up the walk from the garage and through the iron gate, aching with his need for her.

"I'm glad Keely and Tim decided to rent my flat when they're back from the honeymoon," Diana said with studied nonchalance as Nicholas let them in the front door. "Keely's and Tim's apartments are much too small for two, and they won't be disturbed when I'm with clients downstairs. It'll be nice to get completely away from the office when the work day is do—"

The word ended in a gasp as Nicholas swept her off her feet and carried her up to the newly furnished master bedroom.

Some time later Nicholas yawned and glanced sleepily at the bedside clock. Moonlight streamed through the open blinds and painted patterns of shadow over Diana's graceful curves. She stretched sensually, as uninhibited as a goddess disporting in Elysium.

Diana. His need for her was more powerful than the hungers that had driven him in the two long centuries before he had known her. He could not have enough of her if they lived for an eternity—her beauty, her passion, her wisdom, her courage, her joy of living, her dreams. And her love.

Above all, her love.

They still shared dreams. When she had given him mortality through the unstinting gift of her life force, she had passed on her ability for lucid dreaming. Like Diana, Nicholas could dream his own dreams, shaping them to his will as once he had shaped the dreams of others.

The emotional and mental link between them was so strong that they could dream in tandem—create dreams beyond imagining that carried them into realms of wonder and safely back again.

But he could have lived without the dreams, miraculous though they were, as long as he had Diana. Even when sleep claimed them they were never truly apart.

Diana looked at him through heavy-lidded eyes. "I forgot to ask you earlier what Keely was discussing with you so intently during the reception."

Nicholas turned on his side and gathered her against him. "Not jealous of the bride, Diana?" he teased.

She grinned lazily, leaning forward to kiss his jaw. "There are some immortal traits you seem to have hung on to, Nicholas," she said. "Such as overweening arrogance and—" She giggled as he growled softly and pressed her back into the sheets, his teeth nipping gently at her shoulder.

"—and," she continued in a slightly muffled voice, "an incredible amount of stamina. No, don't distract me. What were you two talking about?"

Nicholas sighed and rolled onto his back. "It was about Adrian, Diana."

She went still. "What about Adrian? He hasn't come back or—"

"Nothing so terrible. Keely had recently—recalled a few more details about the time she spent with him last year. The memories have remained incomplete, but she felt I should know what she did remember."

"Can you tell me?" Diana asked in a small voice.

Pulling her on top of him, he framed her face in his hands. "I'll never keep anything from you again, Diana. Believe that." He closed his eyes. "Keely remembered part of a—conversation she'd had with Adrian. Or, more accurately, a monologue he'd indulged in while she was with him. Apparently even he needed someone to listen, however unwillingly."

If she heard the faint trace of bitterness in his voice she didn't show it. "He didn't hurt her, Nicholas."

"I know. In any case, he—told her something of his plans for you and me, Diana—and something of that theory he put to the test when he left you in the cavern with me."

Diana rested her cheek against his chest, tucking her

head under his chin. "He said he wanted to see if my love would save me from you—"

"There was more to it than that, Diana. He knew that you and Clare and Keely were descendants of Sarah—and he realized *you* had the same strength of life force that Sarah had. That you might be able to make me mortal."

"Yes. He told me that—"

"But he didn't tell you that the key to his 'theory' was a human emotion he didn't truly understand."

Nicholas ran his hands down the length of Diana's back, reminding himself that she was safe and real. "You see, Diana, after he'd escaped from the mine, he found a man who claimed to have once been immortal. Adrian knew I believed we could achieve mortality with the right mortal woman, but in this former immortal he discovered an element I had never considered."

"He hinted at something like that," Diana murmured.

"Adrian observed you and me that evening on the beach at Las Playas, when we were searching for Keely." Nicholas brushed a stray curl back from Diana's forehead. "For all the time he and I have spent apart, Adrian knew me well. He told Keely that he believed I could love you as I'd never been capable of loving a mortal woman."

Nicholas saw understanding spark in Diana's eyes. "Love—"

"The man Adrian met, who'd become human, claimed that the key to mortality for our kind was love. Not only the love a human partner gives to one of us—but the love we must learn to feel in return."

"Of course," Diana said, propping herself up against his chest. "It's so clear now."

"But Adrian only learned that after he escaped the mine. He told Keely he was afraid of being left alone, of being the last of our kind." He felt the sting of moisture in his eyes, still unfamiliar. "I believe he—killed Sarah because he was afraid she would give me mortality. Perhaps he didn't intend to kill her at all, but only wanted to disprove the hope I'd clung to for so many years. He followed her descendants—you and Clare and Keely—for the same reason. He pretended to despise humanity, yet he knew if I were to become mortal, he would lose me."

Diana worked her hands under his shoulders and hugged him. "Oh, Nicholas—"

"Don't pity him, Diana. He chose his course."

She pulled away and touched Nicholas's face. "But he gave us both a chance in the end, didn't he? He knew all along we might win." She smiled, a little sadly. "I knew when Adrian first came after me that you and I had to be together to defeat him. But I never guessed my dreams were trying to tell me our being together would bring all the answers we both were looking for. Maybe—maybe Adrian will find whatever he's looking for. Even love."

Nicholas was content with the silence that followed, thinking of Adrian, aware of his own life force—constant, undying, whole—flowing through his body.

"I was afraid to hope for mortality," he said at last, rousing Diana from half-sleep, "even after I realized you might have the strength to give it to me. But I'd already begun to wonder what was happening to me after that first night you and I made love. I slept, and dreamed, for the first time in my existence." He smiled, tracing Diana's mouth with a fingertip. "I realize now that I'd already begun to love you."

Diana pressed her lips to his eyelids and then to his mouth. "I know." She rested her cheek on his shoulder. "Did you ever—wonder what happened to the rest of your kind?"

His body stiffened by reflex, and he deliberately relaxed each muscle in turn before replying. "Every day of my life," he whispered. "Perhaps we were never meant to live on this earth. An affront against nature—"

"Your—people weren't evil, Nicholas," Diana said, lifting her head. "Knowing you, I know they couldn't all have been like Adrian. And even he was not completely dark." She flattened her hand over his heartbeat. "Did you ever consider that your people may have given man as much as they took? Dreams, inspiration, escape—things you can't begin to imagine? All those great artists and thinkers you showed me—so many of them were inspired by dreams. Do you truly believe I'm the only one who has benefited by an immortal's touch?"

Nicholas held up his hands in a gesture of surrender. "Diana," he said hoarsely, "you don't need to ease my guilt. It seems to be part of the—human condition."

"A part we need to learn to let go. But that wasn't my point." Her brows drew together as she searched for words. "It all comes back to Adrian's theory. Maybe each of your people found their other half, their human counterpart. Not only a perfect match in life force, but something more powerful."

Humility and something very like awe washed through Nicholas. "Love," he said simply.

She kissed him with all eternity in her eyes. "And maybe, just like us, they found it."

For some time afterward they were pleasantly engaged in leisurely kisses and caresses. When Diana briefly excused herself, Nicholas got up and walked to the dresser to examine the bouquet Diana had tossed there several hours before.

She stopped at the foot of the bed when she saw what he held in his hands.

Nicholas glanced at her. "How serious is this human custom of catching the bride's bouquet?" he said softly.

An attractive flush started in her cheeks and worked

its way down her body. Nicholas smiled with cool appreciation, turning the bouquet over in his hands.

"Your friends seemed to find it significant, as did Judith. I understand the woman who obtains it is supposed to be the next to wed."

She fidgeted and looked away. "It's just a superstition. It—doesn't mean anything—"

"No." Nicholas shook his head, frowning thoughtfully. "If I'm to be mortal, I wish to do these things in the proper way. No half measures."

Diana took a few hesitant steps toward him and bounced down on the bed, crossing her arms across her breasts.

"I suppose we'll need to order a new one," Nicholas mused. "I doubt this will be adequate for a second ceremony. Flowers are notoriously short-lived."

She jumped off the bed, clothed only in a blush and indignation. "Nicholas—"

"Didn't I tell you?" he said, pretending total obliviousness to Diana's exasperation. "Judith is impatient to be my—'best woman.'" He set the bouquet back down on the dresser, stroking the delicate, already withering petals. "She'll be very disappointed if you refuse me."

He heard Diana's breath catch. "Damn it, Nicholas. Is this supposed to be a proposal?"

Struggling to suppress a grin, Nicholas pivoted to face her. He walked toward her with solemn, measured steps and dropped gracefully to one knee.

"You see me humbled before you," he said gravely, catching her hand in his. "Will you be my bride, Diana?"

Her mouth opened and closed again as she stared down at him. "Yes, I—" She grinned suddenly, eyes glistening. "Yes!"

Nicholas rose and cupped her face in his hands, kissing her with utmost gentleness. When he released her, he tapped his lower lip with a show of thoughtfulness.

"As I said, I wish to do this properly." He looked from Diana to the rumpled bed. "It would be—difficult to forgo the pleasures of your bed until the wedding, but perhaps if we set the wedding date for next Sunday—"

"Next Sunday!" Diana planted her hands on her hips. "Here's another mortal secret for you—weddings take a great deal of planning. Invitations, booking a venue . . ." She shook her head, shaking her halo of brown curls. "Just because you're an independently wealthy dilettante, *I* can't just take off and leave my clients without carefully rearranging my schedule, and—"

He stopped her protests with his lips. When he carried her back to bed, she was flushed and dazed and no longer inclined to speak at all.

"Never fear, Diana," he said tenderly, coming down beside her. "I leave it in your hands. We have all the time in the world."

About the Author

Susan Krinard graduated from the California College of Arts and Crafts with a BfA, and worked as an artist and free-lance illustrator before turning to writing. An admirer of both Romance and Fantasy, Susan enjoys combining these elements in her books. She also loves to get out into nature as frequently as possible. A native Californian, Susan lives in the San Francisco Bay Area with her French-Canadian husband, Serge, two dogs and a cat.

Susan Krinard was "born to write romance,"
says *New York Times* bestselling author Amanda Quick.
If you loved PRINCE OF DREAMS, watch for
Susan Krinard's next exhilarating fantasy romance,
STAR-CROSSED,
on sale in late summer of 1995.

Here is an excerpt from this intoxicatingly passionate
novel . . .

In Susan Krinard's next fantasy romance, STAR-CROSSED, on sale in July 1995, the hero and heroine are from two different worlds. Literally. From the moment she saw him, sixteen-year-old Ariane Burke-Marchand loved Rook Galloway with all the passion and pain of unrequited love. It made no difference to her that the handsome Kalian was not deemed suitable for her. All she knew was that she could not resist this mysterious creature.

But love perishes quickly in the heat of battle. Eight years later, Rook is no longer the love of Ariane's life, but her sworn enemy. Sentenced to life imprisonment on a prison planet in the League following a murder conviction, it seemed that Rook would never see Ariane again. But in order for Ariane to begin a new life with her betrothed, she feels compelled to see Rook one last time. . . . Little does she know she is about to become an unwitting pawn in Rook's desperate game of revenge.

"I'd advise against it, Lady Ariane," the warden said, his hands clasped behind his back. "The work stations have minimal security. Out there we don't need it. But it's not set up for visitors. The men out there—"

Ariane smiled patiently as he shook his head, but her thoughts were far from this small, cluttered office so removed from the harshness of the Tantalan wilderness. *Out there,* he said. Out there where prisoners from all the worlds of the League labored to fill their sentences, and died if they were lucky.

Out there, where Rook Galloway was condemned to a life of endless misery. She'd read about the prison world before she'd come to drop off the shipment of drugs and electronic equipment from Espérance; Tantalus was a convenient place to dispose of criminals who were judged to be beyond rehabilitation.

Like the murderer of her brother.

Eight years ago. Ariane turned to look out the tinted window at the jungle. Eight years ago she had seen the Kalian condemned to death, only to have his sentence commuted to life imprisonment on Tantalus. The League had been responsible for that. Grand-père had wanted him dead. But the League did not approve of such barbaric practices, and the Patriarch had bowed to the pressure.

Ten Kalians had been sent to Tantalus. Only one was still alive, according to the records the *d'Artagnan's* computer had accessed.

Rook Galloway.

In eight years Ariane had come to terms with her grief. She thought the bitterness and hatred were finally behind her. It should have been possible to forget Galloway and let him rot on Tantalus.

In two Espérancian weeks she would be meeting Wynn on the League space station Agora. In two weeks she would be giving up her freedom, putting behind her the three glorious years in space piloting a swift courier ship between Espérance and her family's business interests throughout the League. And she would go home to become Wynn's bride, confined to a sedate life in Lumière, no longer a rebellious girl but a woman of the Elite, bred to bear heirs and hold her husband's honor as she'd once held her own.

There would be no room for dreams or regrets.

Once she had dreamed of exploring the stars. Finding new worlds, free to do as she chose. If Jacques hadn't died . . .

Ariane shook her head. She had come to terms with the loss of freedom, of everything she had become. But she had not been able to forget the Kalian who had made her understand the meaning of sorrow.

She could still remember the Kalian's face. Remember the way he had looked at her, pleading, begging her for something she couldn't give. And during the trial, when he'd testified—because Grand-père favored the League ways now—when he'd had a chance to defend himself. And had claimed innocence.

Innocence. Ariane closed her eyes. He could not be innocent. And yet when she had been sent with a shipment to Tantalus, she had found herself unable to leave.

Not until she'd seen him. One last time.

She turned to face the warden. "I understand the dangers, but I must speak to this man. It's of grave importance." Fixing him with her most commanding gaze, she played her family's rank and reputation for all it was worth. Even here the Marchand name was known, and long ago she'd learned how to use the beauty and poise and unconscious authority bestowed by her breeding to get what she wanted.

Pursing his lips, the warden regarded her for a moment longer before slapping the pad back on the desk. "Very well, Lady Marchand."

Rook paced his cell, three strides up and three back, using the mindless, familiar rhythm to bring his thoughts back under control.

He had never expected to see her again. He had never believed that it could all come back with such staggering force to reawaken emotions only the old Rook Galloway might have recognized.

One by one his companions had died, until only he remained. And he'd survived—survived because it was the nature of his kind, and because old Fox had asked it of him.

Even Fox was gone now. Rook had learned the old, almost forgotten secrets from Fox and concealed the knowledge he'd been given, believing then that he might use it one day. To escape.

Like a captive shadowcat he'd struggled, clung to the fragments of hope, driven by anger. Anger had kept him alive, fighting fate, refusing to surrender. But after eight years, despair had entered his soul at last and eaten at his resolve like some alien, insidious disease for which there was no cure. He had learned to accept, to cast off emotion. There had been a kind of peace in the acknowledgment of despair. Peace in his utter aloneness.

Until *she* had come to Tantalus and shattered that peace.

The guards had taken him to the interrogation room and he'd seen her face. High walls had crumbled in an instant, and the man hidden within them had lain exposed. Weak, cringing, thrust again into a holocaust of bitter memory.

He'd wanted to run, but it was too late. He had learned to feel again.

Rage. Sorrow. Yearning.

Hope.

And hatred. Hatred for the woman who had come to torment him, and for all she was. He tasted that hatred, turned it over in his mind, greeted it like an old friend. Hatred was an anchor in the maelstrom of emotion. He could find strength in it, a new means for survival. A new purpose.

Ariane Burke-Marchand. She had given him that purpose.

Rook closed his eyes and let the images play out in darkness. He thought of the woman, and of the child she had been—the one person who symbolized the tragedy that had befallen his people and condemned him to hell.

He remembered the smudged, anxious face of a girl just old enough to believe herself a woman; a tangle of dirty hair, wide dark eyes. He remembered her angry curses, her loyalty to a brother she loved.

He remembered the way she had looked at him in the end: accusation and horror, a gaze stripped of innocence.

He remembered her at the trial, when she had spoken softly of what she had seen when her brother died. She'd been only a tiny part of it, of the deliberate web of lies spun to trap his people. Conspiracy, they'd called it—a conspiracy of the educated Kalians to turn on their patrons, careful plans of revolt and blackmail and violence exposed just in time.

But he had never hated *her*, even when her carefully guided words had helped condemn him. He could not hate a child.

But she was no longer a child. She was Marchand. And she had come to Tantalus with her doubts and her questions eight years too late.

Rook worked his hands, still feeling the shackles. He had wanted to touch her. He had wanted it desperately, without comprehension, even as he'd hated her and everything she was.

And when she'd touched him— He shuddered, remembering light and sensation and denial. Something had happened between them, something inexplicable. In a single moment he'd relived the tragedy that linked them, Marchand and Kalian, and he'd wanted to make her feel it, force her to understand, to know the truth. He had wanted *her*. . . .

The clear shielding of his cell rang with a sudden blow, and Rook pivoted to face the guards who stood on the other side.

"Hey, Galloway!" the older one said, rapping his stinger against the shield a second time. "Missing your girlfriend? Hear she came all the way from Espérance just to see you!" He snickered. "Who'd have thought you were worth it, eh? Such a nice little armful she is. Too bad your hands were tied, eh?" Both guards laughed, and the younger one made suggestive movements with his hands.

Black rage shivered through Rook, more familiar this time, almost sweet. A day ago he would have been indifferent to their jibes. Now he held himself in control, silent and still, staring—until they dropped their eyes with scowls and curses.

"The warden wants to see you, Galloway," the younger guard said at last. He fingered his stinger. "You gonna give us any trouble?"

Rook looked away to conceal his sudden, fierce joy. *Trouble*. Let them believe he was still the broken savage, a dull creature good only for backbreaking labor, lost in his own world. Let them believe until it was too late.

The guards raised the shielding, and he let them push him into the corridor while he listened to the Tantalan night.

He could almost feel *her*, somewhere near, just out of reach. He went quietly with the guards and thought of Ariane Burke-Marchand.

She had resurrected him. She had made him feel again. Unwittingly, she had restored his purpose and given him the means to act.

She was his link to the past, and his key to the future.

Today Rook Galloway had been reborn.

———

The flight back to the main prison grounds and the world's single spaceport was accomplished in silence. Morning light, heavy with mist, pressed like something solid against the helijet canopy.

Hudson, in the seat beside her, seemed sobered by what he had seen. Ariane hardly noticed his uncharacteristic quiet; she concentrated on piloting the helijet and keeping her mind a perfect blank.

She couldn't seem to dislodge the hard knot in her throat.

The sleek, familiar shape of the *d'Artagnan*, poised for flight on the spaceport landing field, was a sight that Ariane could focus on with relief. The starship was still hers—at least for a few more days. Ariane refused to think beyond those few days of freedom as she flicked the switch that opened the docking bay in the *d'Artagnan's* stern. She guided the Dragonfly smoothly into place, and Hudson turned to look at her, his young face grim.

"There's a routine security check I'll have to run on your ship, Lady Ariane," he told her. His voice was low and gruff with strain.

Ariane closed her eyes. "I need to be on my way as quickly as possible," she said, securing the helijet. Lights came on in the bay as the outer doors sealed behind them. Hudson followed her as she hopped down on to the deck and paused to consult her wrist remote, initiating preflight procedures on the main computer.

"It won't take long, Lady Ariane," he said. "By the time you get clearance, I'll be finished." He gave her a strange, apologetic smile.

Sighing, Ariane started for the air lock that connected the docking bay to the small cargo hold. "What do you need?"

He ducked his head. "Permission to examine your hold and cabins, Lady Ariane. A formality."

A breath of wry laughter escaped her. "I'm not likely to be harboring fugitives on my ship, but I'll clear you."

She led him into the cargo hold and left him there, making her way through the final air lock and into the *d'Artagnan's* living quarters. There was something almost oppressive in the empty silence of the common room; even the cockpit seemed less a sanctuary than a cell.

Ariane shuddered and dropped into the padded pilot's seat. *Don't think about it,* she commanded herself. *At least this ship is something you can count on. Something certain.*

One by one she ran through the preflight routines: checking the stardrive's balance for sublight flight, priming the ship's life-support system, carrying out all the necessary tests. Again and again she forgot sequences that she knew by heart, remembering Rook's face.

Remembering how he had made her feel . . .

No. Her fingers trembled on the keypad as she made the final entries. *You won't have to think about it much longer. It's over. It's out of your hands.*

But the memories remained while the ready lights came up on the control panel. She leaned back in the pilot's seat and passed her hand over her face.

Honor. All her life she'd been raised by the codes of the Espérancian Elite. Like the *d'Artagnan,* honor was solid and real. It had been insanity to doubt, to question. Duty and honor would send her back to Espérance. Honor would give her the courage to face a life of confinement. To accept.

To forget Rook Galloway.

Letting out a shuddering breath, she rose and began to pace the tiny space of the cockpit restlessly. Hudson should have been done with his "routine" check by now. She flipped on the ship's intercom.

"Mr. Hudson? I'm ready for takeoff." She waited, tapping her fingers against the smooth console. "Mr. Hudson—"

"Here, Lady Ariane."

She whirled, reflexes honed through years of training as a duelist snapping into place. Hudson stood just inside the cockpit, a disruptor in his hand.

Aimed at her.

Her first impulse was to laugh. Hudson looked so deadly serious, his mouth set in a grim line that seemed so much at odds with his boyishly untouched face. But she clamped her lips together and balanced lightly on the balls of her feet, waiting.

"Did you find some—irregularity, Mr. Hudson?"

He moved another step closer. And another, until he was within touching distance. "Call for clearance to take off," he said, gesturing with the 'ruptor.

Ariane revised her first assumption. It wasn't what she had supposedly done; Hudson had simply gone crazy.

"I know—how it must be, Mr. Hudson. Alone here, far from home—you want to go back home, is that it? To Liberty?"

He stared at her, light blue eyes shadowed beneath his uniform cap. "Liberty," he repeated.

Considering the best way to move, Ariane tensed her muscles for action. "You must feel trapped here, so far from home. After what we saw . . . I understand. But—"

His smile vanished. "Trapped," he said softly. "What do you know about being trapped, Lady Ariane?" His voice had gone very deep and strange. "Call the tower for clearance. Now."

For the briefest instant Hudson's eyes flickered to the console behind her, and Ariane moved. She darted at Hudson, whirling like a dancer in the ancient way her family's old Weapons Master had taught her as a girl. She might as well have attacked a plasteel bulkhead. Powerful arms caught and held her; the 'ruptor's muzzle came up against her head.

Shock held her utterly still for one blinding instant. Hudson's hand burned on her arm like the bitter cold of space.

"I don't have much to lose, Lady Ariane," Hudson said softly. "You'll call for clearance. Everything is perfectly—normal."

She considered fighting again; honor demanded it. To put the *d'Artagnan* in a starjacker's hands was unthinkable.

But there was far more at stake. Marchand honor and Marchand interest demanded her safe return, to wed Wynn Slayton by inviolable contract that would bind their families forever. Her death now would gain nothing at all.

Clenching her teeth, Ariane hailed the prison port and made the final, in-person request for clearance. The bored officer's voice on the other end of the commlink never altered; her own was perfectly steady as she acknowledged her clearance to lift.

Abruptly Hudson let her go. "Very good," he murmured. "Take her up."

Ariane thought quickly as she dropped into the pilot's seat, Hudson breathing harshly over her shoulder. *He's only a boy. He can't know much about Caravel-class starships. . . .*

Her hand hovered just above the control stick. It shouldn't be too difficult to fool the young guard, make it seem as if they were leaving the system. And then—

Warm fingers feathered along her shoulder and slid under the thick hair at the base of her neck. "Oh no, Lady Ariane. It won't be so easy this time."

Her throat went dry as her hand fell from the console. Abruptly he let her go, stepping away. She turned in the seat to look up at the man who stood over her.

And he *changed.* As if he were made of something other than mere human flesh he began to change: slowly, so slowly that at first she didn't realize what she was seeing.

The young man's softness vanished, cheekbones and hollows and sharp angles drawn forth from Hudson's unremarkable face. Sandy hair darkened in a slow wave under the uniform cap. An old scar snaked over skin tanned by relentless heat.

The eyes were the last to change. Blue faded, warmed, melted into copper.

Rook's eyes.

They held hers as he swept off his cap, freed the dark hair that fell to his shoulders.

The man who stood before her wore the tailored uniform of a Tantalan guard as a hellhound might wear a collar. A wild beast crouched on the deck of the *d'Artagnan*.

A Kalian.

Reaction coursed through her, numbing her hands and stopping her breath.

"Mon dieu," she whispered. "You."

No table separated them now, no adamantium cables confined him. His hard gaze swept over her with contemptuous insolence.

"Yes," he said softly. One straight, dark brow arched, stretching the scar that slashed down across his cheekbone. "No words of welcome, Lady Ariane?"

She knew the voice now, deeper than Hudson's —a difference never questioned, as she had never questioned the young guard's grim silence on the return from camp.

Rook was here, and Hudson was gone. Hudson had never been here at all.

"How—" she began, but he spoke over her whispered question.

"Another gift of the Shapers, Lady Ariane," he said, "one your kind never knew about. The ability to reach into our bodies and alter our very cells as you would put on a mask. Uncommon even among my people." He held up his hand, and it blurred before her eyes. Strong, scarred fingers narrowed to Elite elegance. "I've waited a long time to use it."

By sheer force of will she stilled the clamor in her mind. "Where is Hudson? What did you do—"

"He's safe enough," Rook said. For a moment

his attention wavered, metallic eyes moving over her head to the control boards.

Ariane thought of his hand holding the disruptor. He was too fast, too strong. Disarming him would be next to impossible. Fear rose like bile, alien and unwelcome.

No, she thought, beating the emotion back fiercely. *You have to think. Your mind has to be clear. . . .*

The heat of his palm came to rest again on her shoulder, moved toward her neck to slip under the open collar of her shipsuit. His thumb made slow, intimate circles on the delicate skin over her collarbone. She focused on the steady motion of his breathing, the stolen uniform stretched taut across his chest.

"How—" She swallowed, counting her heartbeats until she could speak with the appearance of perfect calm. "How did you take his place?"

His harsh croak of laughter drew her eyes back to his face. "More questions, Lady Ariane?" He said her name the same way he had in the prison camp, as if it were a curse. "Haven't you learned the danger of asking questions?"

Pride forced her to meet his gaze unflinchingly, though she wanted nothing more than to look away, blot out his harsh features. Her skin shuddered and jumped under his touch.

"A pity there's no time to satisfy your curiosity, Lady Ariane," he said at last. "But as I said, I'm desperate. I have nothing to lose."

His hand closed lightly about her neck, turning her inexorably back to the console. He could have snapped her neck with no effort at all. He ordered her to lift—a casteless criminal, a murderer, commanding a woman of the Espérancian Elite.

And she found herself obeying him, taking the *d'Artagnan* up as if she had no will of her own, clearing atmosphere with Rook's hand always there, like a lover's.

The blackness of space closed around them at last. Ariane clenched her fingers on the arms of the pilot's seat and stared at the ready lights until they blurred in her sight.

With almost painful slowness his hand slid down her shoulder.

"You should never have come to Tantalus, Lady Ariane," he said in a tone devoid of any emotion at all.

Ariane jerked. "You won't get away with this," she said calmly.

Rough fingers lifted her hair away from her neck, let it fall slowly back to her shoulders.

"No, Lady Ariane?" he whispered. The cold muzzle of the 'ruptor caressed her cheek. "You'd better hope that I do."